Friday's CHILD

LINDA CHAIKIN

M

HARVEST HOUSE PUBLISHERS
Eugene, Oregon 97402

Scripture quotations are taken from the King James Version; and from the New King James Version, Copyright © 1982 by Thomas Nelson, Inc. Used by permission. All rights reserved.

Cover by Koechel Peterson & Associates, Minneapolis, Minnesota

While the author is aware that heather blooms in August and September in Scotland, she has chosen to allow it to bloom a little early in 1940 for the sake of her story. She hopes the fastidious gardeners among her readers will excuse the exercise of a little literary license in fiction.

FRIDAY'S CHILD
Copyright © 2001 by Linda Chaikin
Published by Harvest House Publishers
Eugene, Oregon 97402

Library of Congress Cataloging-in-Publication Data
Chaikin, L. L.
    Friday's child / Linda Chaikin.
        p. cm – (A day to remember series)
    ISBN 0-7369-0657-6
        1. World War, 1939-1945—England—Fiction. 2. Women—England—Fiction. 3.
     England—Fiction. I. Title.

PS3553.H2427 F7 2001
813'.54—dc21

                                       2001024282

LINDA CHAIKIN
is an award-winning writer
of more than 19 books.
Friday's Child is the fifth book in the
popular A Day to Remember series.
Linda and her husband, Steve, make their
home in California.

~

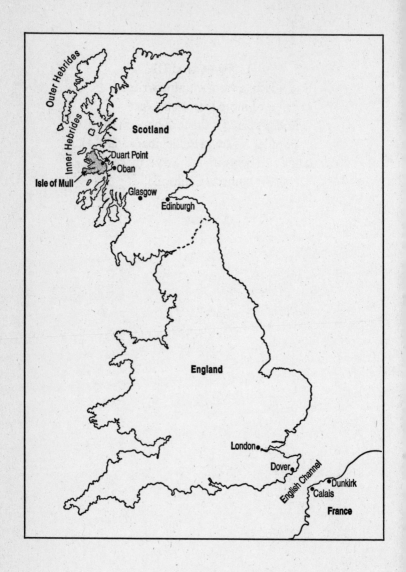

PART ONE

London
June, 1940

1

Though 1940 found the people of Europe fighting with all their might the threat and terror of Nazi Germany, for Vanessa Miles this June day in London was peaceful and calm, with no harbinger of personal storm or danger lying ahead...that is, until an unexpected telegram arrived from Scotland.

Summer afternoon shadows lengthened behind the chestnut tree that grew tall in front of a modest two-story rented house. A rectangular plot of minty green grass grew thickly, waiting for the mower's blade. Mauve roses were opening into blooms, anxious to replace their fading sisters' dropping petals. The afternoon breeze was laced with a potpourri of ripening flowers, herbs, and the hint of coming rain.

On so quiet an afternoon, promising so much to the young and hopeful in spirit, it was difficult for even the most pessimistic to believe that German bombers encircled the skies of Europe, raining down destruction and death, coming ever closer to London, where the bells of St. Paul's Cathedral still rang out with clarity each Sunday morning.

Vanessa stood beside an open window in the rented house on Grimmes Street. Its sparsely furnished rooms had recently been turned into a church-sponsored clinic and office headquarters for DPs (displaced persons) from all across Europe. Vanessa, for the last month of her three-month visit in London with the Warnstead family, had been helping Mrs. Warnstead with the reams of paperwork required to locate missing refugees in an attempt to rejoin them to their children. In the short time Vanessa had worked at the clinic as a volunteer, she'd learned that the slow and painful process seldom produced satisfying results. The church was presently sponsoring forty-three children who'd been recently smuggled safely out of Europe ahead of the rapidly advancing German front.

In the large converted parlor, Vanessa closed the window and irresolutely turned back to her desk, the softness of her smile melting away. The walk to the Warnsteads' home would afford her some uninterrupted time alone to think about returning to New York. She should have left weeks ago. With England threatened, one would naturally assume her to be anxious to return to the security of the States, but as the time to depart drew nearer, she found herself wavering. It would break her heart to leave her brother Kylie, now a pilot in the RAF, and it was just as difficult to say goodbye to Andy Warnstead...

Vanessa had first arrived in London in March after receiving Mrs. Warnstead's polite invitation. She had come with several intentions on her mind and heart, none of which were yet resolved. She felt as though she were adrift like a balloon upon fickle winds.

Thoughtfully, she folded the telegram that had arrived that afternoon and placed it inside her handbag for the walk home. She would need to discuss everything with her brother first. She massaged the tight muscles at the back of her neck. If only he hadn't become a pilot. He was prone to take such daring risks, and his resentment over their father's departure when they were small children added fuel to his sometimes reckless moods. His anger had always run more deeply than her own, like a raging river,

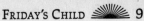

while hers had been more like a quiet stream. With war and death looming on the horizon, the possibility of reconciliation between Kylie and their father seemed still a desirable, if perhaps an unrealistic, goal. The hour seemed late. Lacking paternal guidance, Kylie's emotions had sometimes run rampant. She couldn't help but smile tolerantly. She had always been close to him, even protective, though they were a mere twelve months apart. Like their mother, Vanessa had perhaps made too many excuses for him while growing up. Kylie was going to be a handful for any girl willing to try to curtail him.

Her smile faded again as she picked up her handbag, slung its strap over her shoulder, and glanced at her wristwatch. The man who sent the telegram said four o'clock. He was late. Had he changed his mind?

She had promised Mrs. Warnstead she'd stop at the butcher shop on the way home to pick up a chicken. Tonight was a special gathering—Andy and Kylie would be home this evening. Andy was following in the steps of his father, Colonel Nelson W. Warnstead of the Royal Air Force. Andy Warnstead was one of the main reasons for Vanessa's visit to England.

She left the parlor, which had been turned into a large office with many desks, tables, and boxes filled with papers on refugees, and walked briskly across the worn carpet into the front hall. There was a long front desk in an alcove where Janet, busy at the telephone, lifted a hand goodbye, causing her new engagement ring to sparkle beneath the light. Vanessa smiled, thinking how she'd been the matchmaker who had brought Janet and her navy man together.

Vanessa pulled the clipboard toward her and signed her name in the off duty column before collecting her light summer jacket and matching clutch hat from the cloakroom. She stood a moment before the small mirror, absently tucking a few strands of her fine golden-brown hair into place, unmindful of the pretty face that looked back with smoky olive-gray eyes and naturally dark lashes and brows.

Wearing summery pumps, her confident footsteps quickened as she left the front door and went down the steps. An overcast sky was settling along the Thames. Bees buzzed, intent on finishing well for the day, and sassy sparrows chittered in the branches of the chestnut tree. It might have been any summer afternoon in England when romance was in the breeze and the promise of tomorrow sang its song bravely undisturbed.

A gardener at heart, Vanessa couldn't resist the lure of the flowers and paused long enough to pick some gardenias and blue larkspurs for her bedroom. After carefully placing the delicate petals in a paper bag, she proceeded happily, hurrying past familiar evergreen shrubs toward the walkway beneath the old chestnut trees.

The white front gate was ahead. Vanessa's feathery lashes squinted to look down the tree-lined sidewalk toward the busier streets by Pelham's Market. Then she noticed him.

The stranger was standing across the street leaning against his automobile, hands in the pockets of his comfortable tweed jacket, his hat pushed back from his forehead. Even so, she couldn't see his face clearly in the tree shadows. At first, Vanessa thought he was watching her, but then she decided he was surveying the house, and while his manner suggested that he had a certain curiosity about it, he didn't look like a refugee from Europe. He seemed too at ease for that.

When she closed the gate behind her, the click caught his attention. He straightened from his lounging position and came toward her in a slow but determined stride. She waited, eyeing him. One didn't see many young men out of uniform in England these days.

As he drew near and stopped, she said, "Hello. The office is still open. Go right on up. Janet will help you with any questions."

His thick hair was an unusual dark gold color; his eyes, milky brown. He was of medium stature, with straight shoulders and back, and his jacket was from a good store, with leather patches at the elbows. Though he seemed young, perhaps twenty-eight, Vanessa would have described him as the gentlemanly sort, whose demeanor suggested the comfort of hearth and fire. She could envision him in a leather chair with Irish setters on either side of his long legs, and a good thick book to read while wintry rains danced on the windowpane.

He seemed to be studying her with more than average interest. Then he said, "Fair hair, smoky green eyes, and a good height too."

She was accustomed to men's heads turning in her direction, but she generally paid little attention. Yet, to have a stranger walk across the street and speak of her looks in detail was unnerving, even though she had been silently measuring him as well.

"If you'll excuse me," and she was prepared to walk on about her business when his unexpected laughter delayed her.

"I'm terribly sorry, Miss Miles. I must sound entirely glib, if not downright fresh. It's just the surprise of seeing how much you resemble him. It's remarkable." He flashed a boyish smile that dampened any earlier notion of brashness.

She looked at him silently. Understanding began to dawn, and as it did, her tension increased.

"My name is Scott Morgan. Did you receive my telegram?"

She recovered. "Yes, but I expected—"

Her hand absently touched her handbag where she'd placed the telegram suggesting she meet her biological father in Scotland. She had expected his representative to be someone much older.

"I don't know what to say about the request, Mr. Morgan. As you can imagine, it came as something of a shock. I need to discuss the matter with my brother first, since any meeting affects him too."

"Of course," he said congenially. "I expected that would be the case. He's here in London, isn't he? The Royal Air Force?"

"Yes. He moved here a few years ago to finish his education, and he ended up formalizing his British citizenship. His best friend's father is Colonel Nelson Warnstead."

"Very commendable."

"Yes...and I can't promise anything where Kylie is concerned. He's resentful toward his father—as you would understand."

"Actually, no, I don't." And when her brows lifted, he added, "But maybe you can help me understand."

"It should be simple enough." He was moving too quickly as far as she was concerned. She didn't appreciate his attempt to shrug off the pain she and Kylie would naturally feel over abandonment. "I need a little more time."

"All right. May I call you in the morning for your answer?"

She clutched her handbag. "I'd like to know first whose idea this was. Did *he* send you?"

"Naturally, Miss Miles, when you say 'he,' you mean Robert Miles, your father."

She had expected her emotions, like a stick of dynamite, to explode at the mention of her father, but she hadn't expected the inevitable moment to bring such pain. *Robert Miles, your father—*

Scott must have realized the impact of his words, for he paused. "I'm sorry," he said more gently. "I didn't realize."

Realize what? That a child can feel real pain and loss over a parent they've never met? How *could* he know so little of such things!

He glanced into the front garden, where there was a stone bench near low-growing English daisies. Vanessa didn't care to sit down, but it was awkward standing by the gate.

"I'm all right, thank you," she said when he began to take her arm, and entering the front yard again, she walked to the bench on her own.

Seated by the white daisies, hearing the last of the insects droning, she made an effort to regather her poise. "This famous Shakespearean actor is not my father." And when he gave her a quick glance, she explained calmly: "Oh, I know he's my blood father, and Kylie's too." Her clear, lucid gaze swerved to his, and her shoulders straightened. "What I mean is—"

"I'm well aware of what you intended, Miss Miles," came his quiet but firm voice. "I don't think it would do either of us any good to sit as a judge of the past."

But his own attitude borders on being judgmental with me! thought Vanessa. *Why? Is he so loyal to my father that he will not accept criticism from his daughter? Then what is there left to say?*

"I was hoping," he went on, "that *you* at least would listen to what I have to say about your father before allowing resentment to keep the door bolted from the inside."

"If you are implying that my brother would be even less likely to listen to this than I am, then I think you're right."

"Yes. I gather he has no sentiment toward his father."

She bristled. "Kylie has genuine reasons for his lack of sentiment, Mr. Morgan, as do I. It appears to me that Mr. Robert Miles has not shown much fatherly sentiment toward a son and daughter that he brought into this world."

His square jaw tightened, but his voice remained controlled and polite. "Believe me, I'm not here to defend anything your father may have done. But the past *is* the past."

She stood, discovering in a very short time that her own emotions were more raw and throbbing with pain than she had imagined. Even her breath came rapidly. "I wish I could agree with you that the past is the past without there being serious consequences. But it's not as simple as you seem to want to make it. One doesn't wait until he's lived out his life, giving all of his care and attention to the daughter of his second marriage, and then suddenly decide to reach out across his deathbed to bestow his patriarchal blessing on children he abandoned!"

She stopped suddenly. She had been so sure she could handle this surprise telegram from Scotland and its invitation. She had always thought herself the steady one, the one who might be able to bring her father and brother together. Now she knew her ragged heart could be just as painful as Kylie's when touched.

Scott Morgan also stood up from the bench. "I've upset you."

"Is it so surprising, Mr. Morgan? Do you think you can just walk into my life and throw this at me and expect a response that contains no hurt feelings?"

"No. I suppose not. I really *am* sorry."

She sat down again, her restless fingers seeking relief in the feel of a daisy on the sage green bush beside her.

"How is it you're involved exactly? Your telegram said very little, except that he thought he had only a few more months left and wanted to talk."

"I'm a friend of your father's."

There was something in those words that made her glance at him. He was standing with his hands in his jacket pockets, and there was a slight frown between his brows. She felt that she was the object of the disapproval of his warm brown eyes, and she found she didn't like it. Why should it matter what he thought of her?

"I've been working for him during the past few years, the last year in Scotland at his estate. I also knew him here in London when he was on the stage."

"You look rather young to have appreciated his acting career."

He smiled. "I was a very young writer at the time. Your father encouraged me. I owe him a lot. He's retired now and living on an island off the coast of Scotland." He looked at her hopefully. "And he wants to see you."

Vanessa concentrated on the white petals of the daisy. "You also mentioned he wished to see Kylie."

"Both of you, of course. But if you can't come together, then one at a time, at your convenience. The Isle of Mull is not far from the mainland."

"There's a war going on, Mr. Morgan. My brother's recently finished flight training and will soon be assigned to a squadron.

Perhaps my father doesn't know England is fighting on several fronts."

His mouth turned at the corner. "He is aware, Miss Miles. As am I."

Vanessa realized she knew next to nothing about who he was or what he did, except that he was an American writer who worked for her father. Robert Miles had retired from the theater, so what manner of work was he doing now? Why did he need the services of Scott Morgan? She didn't think he had reached the age where he would need physical help, though he was ten years her mother's senior when he married her in New York and then brought her to London. Her mother, Mary Williams, had lived a lonely life. She had never fit in with her husband's flashy friends. They had been witty, beautiful, and talented. Vanessa's mother had been unassuming, even shy. She thought that was what Robert wanted when he fell in love with her, but things had changed soon after Vanessa was born. He might have left her then, except she was expecting Kylie. As Robert's career soared he'd become more and more absorbed in the adoring admiration of the theater-going world.

They were several years into their marriage when he'd met and starred with the beautiful Norah Benton. Not long after that he left Vanessa's mother and married Norah.

Vanessa snapped the daisy from the stem and looked up. She felt anything but sentimentally disposed toward the man who had left her mother for another woman. Yet, there was so much more to think about than herself. There was Kylie, and now, yes, even her father. Suddenly he wanted to see them. Why? Was a relationship possible after all these years?

But God, because of the death of His Son, Jesus Christ, is able to shower grace and mercy on those who deserve nothing but His righteous judgment. For a child who claimed the name Christian, there really was only one right response—to be merciful also.

Vanessa looked away from the bright gaze of Scott Morgan to the cool white flower with its golden center. Love was at the center of anything that truly mattered.

She heard herself saying: "I'll speak to Kylie tonight. It's all I can promise at the moment. You must understand your telegram was completely unexpected."

"Yes, I'm very aware. If I wasn't impressed with all I'd heard about you, Miss Miles, I'd never have taken the chance to send it."

"You've heard about me?"

"Your father, despite what you think, has kept up with what you've been doing through the years. Your brother as well."

How? she wanted to ask. *Our unspectacular lives aren't lived on the stage for other people to admire.* To think that her father knew anything about her and Kylie was hard to accept. Was Scott merely saying this, hoping to soften her heart?

He seemed to know her thoughts. "There is more to the story about why he left."

She cast him a quick, sharp look. "Are you saying there is some justification for his betrayal?"

"No, that's *not* what I'm saying, Miss Miles. Just that there is another side to this sad story. You had the benefit of hearing your mother's side. You witnessed her pain, her bitterness. As children you and Kylie might have thought there was no such pain for Robert."

"My mother did suffer," she said. "Far more so than he ever could or would allow himself. He was *selfish.* All he thought of was his career—and what made *him* happy and successful. That's why he walked away from us. It was easier to shed his responsibility and just take what he wanted from life. The rest of us could just muddle along in our own squalor and misery."

"Perhaps everything you say about him is true. I wouldn't know that dark side of him, but I do know a little of human nature. And it's easy to blame the other person, to shed responsibility by playing the victim and vindicating one's bitterness."

Her brows lifted. "Are you suggesting my mother played the victim? That she wanted to make her pain real to us, his children, so that we would never forgive him?"

"I'd be foolish to suggest such a thing. I didn't know your mother. I know only what Robert told me about her."

"And that was?" Vanessa, like a riled kitten, was ready to do battle for her mother's reputation, both as a loving and hard-working woman, and as one who'd faithfully taken her and Kylie to Sunday school.

Scott smiled and shook his head. "I'd never enter such high waters, Miss Miles. I'm sure I'd end up drowning in the praise you could heap upon her character. And, I hasten to add, I'd have no cause to doubt a word of it."

She wondered what her father *had* said about her mother, but Scott wasn't likely to betray him by telling her. Vanessa had no reason to doubt her mother's grief, or the hardship the three of them had gone through after Robert had left.

She stood, still holding the daisy.

"I didn't come here to upset you," he said. "I'm afraid my forthrightness has done just that. I didn't know of any way to explain things without being open about it."

His expression had softened. He wasn't condemning her feelings, and she was relieved. "I appreciate forthrightness, but I don't know why my father wants to see me. What does he want?"

He shook his head. "He didn't explain his reasons, and I didn't ask."

"Does he feel he can reach Kylie through me?"

"Perhaps that's part of it. I'm inclined to think he has more than one reason. I'm here because of what your father needs, Miss Miles, not what I want." He added gently, "It's not even what you want or need that concerns me now. Robert Miles is a tremendous man. He's gifted; he's given so much of himself to the theater, to people who have benefited from his gifts. I want to see him live out his last months in peace."

It would have been so easy to lash out. *Oh, yes,* she could have said bitterly, *he has given himself to his devoted audience, to his second wife, his daughter, but nothing to me. Nothing to Kylie. Yet you come asking me to go to him? To be the loving daughter to whom he denied everything? Because love is everything, and he gave me none of his love!*

Tears burned behind her eyes, and she turned away to make sure he didn't see her wet lashes. She had shed too many tears over her father, her mother, and even Kylie. "Robert is not a well man," Scott was pleading. "War is upon us. It's bound to grow more deadly with the coming months, perhaps the years. Who knows? If ever you would see him, Miss Miles, it is now. Won't you please consider going to Scotland, even for two weeks? Let him have his word with you. Try to arrange a meeting between him and his son. I know you won't be sorry."

She wondered how he could say that. She might end up being hurt.

Now is the time. Today is the hour of redemption. The ideas from Scripture fell like gentle rain upon her feverish soul. *Give, and it shall be given unto you.*

"Kylie has received his wings, and soon he will join a squadron of fighters," Scott went on. "Neither of us need comment on the risks involved, the long months ahead...I'm sorry even to remind you about the dangers of flying a Spitfire."

Yes. He didn't need to remind her of the risks the pilots were taking each time they climbed into the cockpit and flew off to meet the German Luftwaffe. She knew very well. Andy had already been in battle at Dunkirk.

She blinked back the tears the way she managed to do so often recently about so many things. *Trust in the Lord. Tomorrow is in His faithful hand. Fear not—fear not.*

When she turned to face him, her cheeks were dry and her gaze was calm.

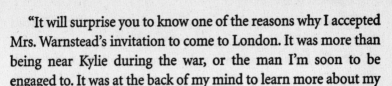

"It will surprise you to know one of the reasons why I accepted Mrs. Warnstead's invitation to come to London. It was more than being near Kylie during the war, or the man I'm soon to be engaged to. It was at the back of my mind to learn more about my father. To meet him, if I could."

He looked at her a long moment. "You don't need to tell me. I'd rather guessed that about you. Then you'll come?"

She delayed, fingering the daisy that was beginning to wilt so quickly. The moment slipped away, and before she could answer, she and Scott Morgan turned toward the house to an anxious voice.

"Vanessa?"

Vanessa moved toward the steps, the daisy between her fingers as she recognized Mrs. Warnstead's voice.

A woman in her late forties came toward them. The tone of her voice told Vanessa much about Julia Warnstead: The worry of the last few months and the uncertainty of the future were plain on her face. It was easy to worry when your husband's squadron was based here for the defense of London. Her son, Andy, had fought the Luftwaffe in France, and her daughter, Francis, was a nurse.

Mrs. Warnstead, who had given up nursing years earlier when she'd married the colonel, had returned as a volunteer and was now the director of the church-based clinic under Dr. Elsdon, a retired missionary from Hong Kong. Mrs. Warnstead remained an attractive woman, retaining a youthful figure through rigorous dedication to playing tennis with the colonel four times a week. Her auburn hair was sprinkled with silver and worn in a younger style that brushed the top of her shoulders, but it suited her well.

Watching Julia Warnstead hurrying toward her, Vanessa thought, *I hope I'm as selfless at her age with those I love best.*

It took a tested faith to be able to trust God with those you love. It was sometimes easier to risk one's self than a husband, son, or daughter. Today her hazel eyes were filled with worry.

"Vanessa, I'm so glad you're still here. I—" Then she saw Scott Morgan, who'd been standing beside the hedge.

At once Mrs. Warnstead's good manners took over and whatever was worrying her was put momentarily aside. She smiled. "You've a friend with you. I'm sorry to have interrupted." She held out a hand toward Scott, who took it immediately. Vanessa introduced him, saying nothing of his reason for being there. She would wait until alone with Mrs. Warnstead this evening to explain.

"Is anything wrong?" Vanessa asked her when the introductions were over.

"I'm afraid so. Francis just called me. She's down at the harbor, at the warehouse Dr. Elsdon rented last week. The doctor is there as well. He desperately needs medical supplies. There are wounded."

Vanessa had managed to bring several trunks of supplies with her from New York when she'd sailed to England, a gift to Dr. Elsdon from a missionary group in New York. Now, after seeing the medical needs, Vanessa wished she could have brought a whole ship full of supplies from friends in the States!

"Wounded? What happened?" Scott asked.

"A fishing vessel picked up a number of survivors from a boat crossing the Channel."

"They were attacked?"

"Yes. The boat was strafed by a German plane. It's a miracle anyone survived, but some did, including a small child who's apparently deaf. Francis says some are sick. They must have been so when they left France. And some are wounded, including women and children."

For Vanessa, the suffering was still new and tragic enough to bring a visible wince, though she was trying to adopt the calm dignity of Mrs. Warnstead and Francis.

"Francis says Dr. Elsdon needs supplies at the warehouse right away. Can you bring them?"

"Yes, of course," Vanessa said quickly.

"I would go, but I've an important meeting in an hour with Lord Jessup. It's about the church leasing the warehouse."

"Oh, but I don't have the key to the medical closet," Vanessa said.

"Dr. Elsdon gave me a key. The crate will be heavy. I suppose I'd better call a taxi since the colonel has the car this afternoon."

"No need to wait for a taxi, Mrs. Warnstead," Scott spoke up. "My car is across the street. I'll bring Miss Miles to the harbor."

"Oh, bless you! I was worried to send her alone. Come this way; we'll need a strong man to carry the crate." She hurried back across the garden walk to the front steps with Scott following. For a moment, Vanessa watched them go before joining them.

Beneath darkening clouds the late afternoon sky bore traces of crimson and gold that reflected over the Thames. The quiet of the summer twilight lingered, untouched by the serious news. The birds were nearly silent, the bees were gone, and the flowers were closing their delicate petals in the breeze. *Whatever trials lie ahead, faith must be an eternal optimist,* she thought. Not because faith was blind to reality, but because God was the object of true faith and sovereign over time and events. In the end, God's plans and purposes would triumph. To Vanessa, this was a soft pillow to rest her weary head upon at night.

Still clutching her daisy, she followed them toward the house.

2

Vanessa hurried across the street beside Scott toward the car parked under a chestnut tree. She glanced up at the twilight's increasing cloudiness. This was nothing like New York's hot summer nights. The evening air carried with it the feel of approaching rain upon the winds.

He set the precious box down on the curb to retrieve his keys and open the trunk. "I noticed that some supply crates inside Dr. Elsdon's office have your name on them." His look questioned her. "I was told you weren't a nurse."

She wondered who would have told him. Was it true that her father had kept up with her activities, or was Scott simply trying to soften her resistance toward going to Scotland? If she thought he were trying to engineer the right emotional responses from her...

"Francis is the nurse," she told him. "She graduated with a degree just last month."

"Just in time."

Both Francis and her mother had commented on the timing of her graduation. Francis had intended to work in a private physician's office around Bodum, but since the war began nurses were in such demand that she'd told Vanessa her conscience wouldn't permit her to live a peaceful life in the country, helping a rural doctor whose worst concerns might be a farmer's pulled ligament or a baby delivery.

"After the difficult retreat from Dunkirk, Francis shelved her plans and decided to work here at the charity clinic. Her mother is helping to run it with Dr. Elsdon's help. The children at the center are just a small fraction of the growing numbers swelling every orphanage and hospital throughout England."

Closing the trunk with the medical supplies safely stowed in it, he nodded soberly and opened the car door for her. As they drove toward the harbor, she told him how the need was so great that many wealthy aristocrats were opening up their estates to be used as hospitals.

"What did you do in New York?"

"I worked in theater costume design. I learned the craft from my mother. Sometimes after school when I didn't have homework, she'd bring me to the theater with her, and I'd watch and help. I began to love designing costumes. After I graduated from school, she got me my first job in her department. After two years I actually exceeded her and was promoted, but she was never jealous. My success was hers also since most of what I'd learned came from the many hours she spent with me."

He was thoughtful. "So that's how Robert met your mother."

She hesitated, not wishing to discuss it, though her mother had told her the story. Robert Miles had been a famous stage actor even before he'd come to New York to play the lead in *Hamlet*. He was able to sweep others along with his enthusiasm for the theater, and Mary had been awed by him. She was a young designer then, and Robert had taken a fancy to her and insisted she accompany him to lavish parties with his friends. Along with being singled out by Robert Miles came the blessings and the curses of being important in the theater world. Vanessa's mother had been furiously promoted into a certain stardom of her own.

Robert had insisted as only he could that, thereafter, her mother design his costumes for whatever part he played. His manager, producers, and writers all wanted to continue to work with him, and soon learned that pleasing Robert meant walking on eggshells. Eventually they were married, and their first child, Vanessa, was born in London on one of Robert's opening nights. Mary eventually left the theater to raise her family while pregnant with Kylie.

Years later, after Robert had left them, Mary returned to America, and after some difficult months got her first job on Broadway. Though she never regained the kind of success she'd known under Robert's backing, she had made them a comfortable living and had done well on her own. Vanessa was proud of her mother and all she had taught her.

Vanessa changed the subject. "Dr. Elsdon is the physician at the clinic run by the church Mrs. Warnstead attends."

"Yes, a veteran Hong Kong missionary, I understand."

"He has contacts with Christian friends in America who sent over those boxes of medical supplies with me on the ship."

He smiled. "Then the mystery of your name on the crates is solved."

"The clinic needs just about everything for the DPs," she told him. "Almost everything the British government has goes to the military. Private groups and charities must rely on the generosity of friends in America, Canada, and Australia. At Mrs. Warnstead's clinic, the DPs are mostly children who've been separated from parents or other family members trying to get out of the Low Countries and Poland."

"Too late for Poland," he said quietly.

She'd heard the ugly story of the devastation at Warsaw after she arrived in London. Poland was now under Nazi control, as were Denmark and Belgium. And Communist Russia had invaded Estonia, Latvia, and Lithuania. Finland had fought off hundreds of thousands of Russian soldiers but had eventually ended the fighting in March of that year. *They were very brave,* she thought proudly, a country of only four million against Stalin's Russia—about 200 million. The little country of Finland had shown the world a display of national courage rarely equaled in history.

And now—brave, bold Norway. Dreadful fighting between the stalwart Norwegians and the Germans had been raging since the German army invaded in April. For two months the Norwegians had stymied the Nazis. Now, with no more help coming from Britain and France, Norway was lost, as was Finland.

"Most of the refugee children will be orphans. Their families were killed trying to escape in the snows of Narvik and Helsinki," she said sadly.

Scott's pleasant features hardened. "The German planes fire upon any refugee caravans they see on the roads toward France. Like Warsaw," he said with a controlled anger in his voice. "Children, babies, the old—none of them mean anything to the Luftwaffe. They bomb soldiers protecting their land from invasion as well as civilian caravans trying to get out of the way."

That he understood, and shared her anger as well as her pity for the victims, brought comforting camaraderie, if only briefly.

"So you're a volunteer. Do you help Mrs. Warnstead and Francis?"

She smiled vaguely. "No again. I help Mrs. Warnstead's bridge club friends."

Scott's head turned to look at her across the seat. Someone honked. Vanessa smiled. "Better watch where we're going, Mr. Morgan."

"Bridge club friends? Somehow you impress me as being more committed than that." He drove more carefully through traffic toward the harbor.

"The bridge club ladies are involved in helping locate members of the children's families. Our goal is to bring about happy reunions. The search for a mother, big brother or sister, grandparent, or uncle is endless."

Vanessa didn't mention that there was seldom a father to be found to claim the child. They were either somewhere on the front lines fighting, dead in a ditch, or, just as sad, a prisoner of war in a German concentration camp.

"Nice work you do," he said quietly.

"I wish I were more successful."

"At least you try. So here you are, all the way from America, separated all these years from your father, not to mention a half sister, trying to bring *other* families together."

He looked across at her. To hide her true emotions from him, she remained silent and looked out the car window. Her fingers were interlaced tightly on her lap.

He went on. "Maybe it's my turn to bring about a reunion. If not a happy one, a meeting, at least."

It was difficult to handle his directness. She experienced a dart of anguish. She brushed her hair away from her cheek as the wind blew against her face. Scott wound up his window. The silence lingered. Unexpectedly he laughed, but it wasn't altogether relaxed. "All right, Miss Miles," he said. "I'll be patient and wait for your answer. You said you need to talk to Kylie, so I'll take you at your word."

Vanessa was watching for the warehouse as she leaned forward in the seat. "That's it, over to the right. You can park by those shipping barrels—that's Dr. Elsdon's car."

The harbor was veiled in gray mist, shrouding ghostly outlines of ships, great and small. She heard the babble of voices, foghorns, and the creaks and groans of briny old hulls smelling of the sea.

They left the car, and Scott carried the supplies while Vanessa hurried toward the large building located on the north end of the docks near an unloading zone for passengers and cargo.

Outside the warehouse there was a receiving area sheltered with a rough wooden roof and beams. Vanessa saw a group of beleaguered people huddled together on benches. Others congregated on the wooden floor, sitting on blankets dispensed earlier by charity groups and the International Red Cross.

Vanessa caught a glimpse of Dr. Elsdon attending the injured, and Francis appeared in the warehouse doorway, looking wind-blown and exhausted. Vanessa felt a tug at her heart. She had grown to love Andy's younger sister in the months she'd been living with the family and helping at the clinic. She was a generous girl and unashamedly patriotic.

Francis, her brown hair pulled back and pinned off her neck, saw Vanessa and waved anxiously, gesturing for them to bring the medical supplies inside.

"I was afraid you'd already left the clinic," she said when Vanessa ran up with Scott.

"I was just leaving when you called," Vanessa said. "Where's Dr. Elsdon?" She glanced about the area under the roof, feeling sympathy when she saw the Norwegian refugees, several old men, more women and children, even some babies. One of the infants was crying with a voice that sounded hoarse and exhausted while her mother gently rocked her in her arms, looking hollow-eyed and dazed. Vanessa noticed a bandage on the baby's head and her heart wrenched.

"Has the baby been looked at?" she asked Francis.

Francis's brown eyes smiled at her. "I knew that would be your first question." She looked toward the fair-haired mother and infant and sighed. "Yes, but—" She started to say something, then glancing at Vanessa, appeared to change her mind. "Here, I'll take the box to Dr. Elsdon."

"It's quite heavy," Scott told her. "Just show me where you want it, Miss Warnstead."

"This is Scott Morgan," Vanessa explained, seeing Francis' curious glance. "A friend," she added, perhaps optimistically.

Dr. Elsdon was moving quickly toward them, his silver hair windblown and a scowl on his forehead. "Thank God," he said reverently when he saw Vanessa and Scott holding the box with the big red cross stamped on the side. "I thought you'd never get here."

"We came as soon as we could," Vanessa hastened, feeling guilty. Perhaps she and Scott had taken a little too long.

"Bring it inside the warehouse, young man, will you?" He left them, calling quick orders to Francis.

"Yes, Dr. Elsdon," Francis answered, and she gave Vanessa a harried glance, losing her professional face. "Do you suppose you could stay a while?"

"Yes, of course," Vanessa said quickly, shivering as a gust of wind from the sea struck against her. "How can I help?"

"Lady Blanchard sent her chauffeur down with jugs of hot tea and sandwiches, but I haven't had time to hand them out. There's the captain of a Scottish fishing boat who needs help too. He's the one who picked up the refugees, and he has a cut on his hand. It's not serious, but it needs a dressing."

Nice man, Vanessa thought, glancing around for him, but she didn't see anyone who looked like a fisherman.

Inside some cots had been set up along with tables and benches. Even in June the warehouse was damp and chill. She could imagine how cold it must be in winter. She unpacked the baskets and set the sandwiches out on a long, low table. She was pouring lukewarm tea into cups when she sensed someone's unfriendly gaze. The feeling startled her. Vanessa raised her eyes and glanced around the dingy warehouse, but she detected no one watching her from the shadowy periphery. Dr. Elsdon and Scott were across the room with the injured. Francis was busy with a little girl who must have been about five years old. Vanessa's heart softened. Such a pretty child, with long tawny-colored hair, clutching what looked to be a small storybook. There was a shiny necklace around her little neck and a matching bracelet on her arm.

She chided herself. It must have been her imagination. There certainly wasn't any unfriendliness among the grateful Norwegians, who were managing to smile at their rescuers despite their personal tragedy and pain. There wasn't much for them to celebrate; some of their comrades had been lost at sea and were presumed drowned. She noticed a grandmother holding a two-year-old boy. These people would find temporary shelter here, but after that? The policy of the British government was not yet clear in the matter of all refugees seeking safety in England.

Then she glanced at a certain man who confirmed her suspicion. He was watching her, and it seemed there wasn't a spark of warmth or gratitude on his face. He sat on the floor with his back against the wall, one booted leg drawn up, resting his arm across his knee as though in a skeptical mood.

He wasn't Norwegian. He was as dark and earthy a man as she had ever laid eyes on. He wore a soiled black woolen peacoat frayed at the cuffs and a knitted cap that she believed smelled of codfish oil. His coal black hair curled at the ends and could have used a good washing and trimming. The slashing brows were as dark as his eyes, and his trousers were what she could only describe as shiny, like sharkskin leggings that might be worn by seamen in the wild Cornish coasts of England. She was sure there was a knife inside his sleeve or boot top, perhaps even a pistol under his coat.

Vanessa's first reaction was to recoil in surprise over the distrust in his eyes. Why would he dislike her? Then she realized that what she took for a sinister stare might not be personal at all, but caused by circumstances: the war and its hardships or the mishap at sea. This must be the Scottish captain who had been so heroic.

She turned her glance away as though she hadn't noticed him. She piled sandwiches and cups of tea on a large wooden tray and began making the rounds among the rescued Norwegians. They were still wet and huddled in blankets. Despite their hunger and cold, they were restrained and exceptionally polite, saying "thank you," in a thick Norwegian accent.

She came to the little girl being cared for by Francis. Vanessa smiled tenderly and handed the child one of the cookies that were always included with the sandwiches in case there were children among the refugees. The girl simply stared at her with large sad blue eyes.

"Poor darling," Vanessa whispered.

"Yes, I'm sure she's deaf," Francis said quietly.

"You don't mean it? Is she with anyone?" Vanessa noticed that none of the other women stayed near the girl as they naturally would have had she belonged to them.

Francis shook her head. "No one knows anything about her. Not even her name or how she got aboard the boat."

Vanessa looked at Francis. "Is that possible?"

"It's happened before. We had a boy come to us once, but he was older, eleven, and could tell us how he'd lost his mother and made his way into France by himself. But this one can't communicate."

"Could it be from shock?"

"Yes, I was about to mention that." She glanced across the warehouse toward Dr. Elsdon. "I'll see what the doctor says. He's caring for the worst of them first. We're waiting for an ambulance now."

Vanessa gently brushed a strand of tawny hair from the child's face. "Maybe she belongs to one of the seriously injured."

"That's what I'm hoping." Francis took the cookie and handed it to the little girl, smiling encouragingly.

Vanessa stooped to eye level. "Hello, sweetie, can you speak English?"

"That's the first thing I tried, and the other women spoke to her in Norwegian, but she doesn't bat a lash."

The child stared back at Vanessa with wide eyes and clung to the little book as though it were all the comfort she had in the world. Vanessa glanced at the storybook—it appeared to be new and in good condition.

"I don't think she'll eat for us now," Vanessa said, "but I'll leave this sandwich and cup of milk just the same."

She stood, glancing around to make sure she hadn't forgotten anyone. She didn't want to go near the dark stranger, but she knew she couldn't continue avoiding him longer without being rude. Such a husky-looking man must be quite hungry, and her sense of fairness and compassion won, as did her curiosity. He didn't like her. Had he mistaken her for someone else?

Vanessa walked carefully across the damp, warped floorboards and stopped in front of him. "Tea?"

The square jaw could easily have been carved from granite, and an otherwise pleasant mouth was hard and unsmiling. There was a scar alongside his temple that looked to have been there since boyhood. She had wanted to give his unfriendly behavior the benefit of the doubt, thinking she might be wrong, but facing him, her doubts crumbled. It was as though she were the source of his surly mood! Distressed, Vanessa nevertheless continued her task with dignity.

"Would you like a sandwich?" Her voice sounded normal. She waited for the expected curt refusal and was surprised when it didn't come. He pushed himself up from the floor, showing his towering stature and ironclad strength. He surprised her further by politely removing his knitted cap.

He looks like a gypsy, she thought. *Wild, unstable, and handsome as can be.*

"You must be hungry."

"Aye, I'm obliged."

"Take several, sir. There are more back at the table."

His eyes checked out her face with muted wariness. "You're very kind, Miss Miles."

He knew her name!

His mild tone took her off guard. The brogue was far from typically Scottish, and was tempered instead with an English farm-country accent that lent it a certain charm. She had expected a slurring voice, such as she was accustomed to hear on the wharf from the dockworkers. "You know my name?" she asked, brows lifting.

He gestured his head across the room without speaking, to gaze upon Scott Morgan.

"We both work for Mr. Miles at Gowrie House, Isle of Mull."

She couldn't have been more surprised. When she looked at him, wondering, his midnight eyes became unyielding. It was clear, however, that he didn't like Scott either.

"You work for my father, Robert Miles? On his estate?"

"Aye. Been working there most of my life, longer than his possessing the land, I dare say. I was born and raised at Gowrie House. I'm caretaker for Mr. Miles. Name's Kerc, not that my name matters much." He looked away from her steady gaze, putting his cap back on. "Thanks for the food. If you'll excuse me, miss, I'd best be getting to see about my fishing boat."

"Wait, please."

He stopped and turned to look down at her.

Vanessa nearly blurted out: *I want to know why you don't like me!* Just in time, she caught herself. At least she now knew there was some association for his dislike. Aside from her curiosity over his reasons, any thoughts that this stranger might ignorantly harbor against her probably didn't matter that much.

"Then you were the captain of the fishing boat that picked the refugees from the water?"

His dark eyes were nearly impossible to read.

"Aye. Selling fish and eels is tradition on Mull."

"What you did was most commendable. You saved many lives."

"Ruined my boat too. That Nazi plane tore it to pieces and enjoyed it like a fox in a henhouse."

Vanessa noticed a missing button on the front of his faded jacket and that his hand was injured and splotched with dried blood and starting to swell. His calloused palms were quite a contrast to those of a literary writer like Scott Morgan. She suddenly felt compassion for him. He must work exceedingly hard and have little to show for it. It was typical of the servant class in England, Scotland, and Ireland.

"I'm sorry you lost your boat, but—" she stopped, not wishing to sound indifferent about his loss.

He seemed to pick up on her train of thought.

"But it was worth saving the lives. Aye, so it was. All's not lost, though, even if she took enough bullet holes from that Nazi plane to near sinking. She can be repaired."

"It was a blessing for them that you happened to be fishing in the area. You were a long way from Scotland."

He gazed back at her silently. It was apparent she would get no more information. She glanced at his hand. "The nurse asked me to have a look at that. You could get an infection."

He shoved his hand into his coat pocket. "No need to trouble yourself, miss. It's nothing I can't handle myself. Been doing it all my life."

Her lips tightened. "Yes, I can see you have. Well, I wish you the best. I haven't decided to visit Gowrie House yet, but if I do, I suppose I'll see you working about the grounds."

She turned to leave. "Miss?" she heard him say.

She looked back as his gaze went across the warehouse to where Francis was helping a young pregnant woman who was trying not to cry.

"The little one on the blanket there—the one you gave the cookie to. Mind telling me if she's spoken yet?"

"No, I'm afraid she hasn't. Then she didn't speak aboard your boat when you rescued her?" Vanessa inquired.

"Not a word. Thought she might have by now. None of the others know who she is. Seems a bit odd, if you go asking me."

"Francis—that is, Miss Warnstead—is looking into the matter. We're hoping her parents might be among the injured." She looked toward those that Dr. Elsdon was helping with emergency care. "Or…" and she let her voice fade to the obvious outcome. She sighed.

He glanced thoughtfully about the warehouse at the refugees huddled in blankets gratefully drinking tea, then he focused on her again.

"Rightly speaking, it's none of my concern, but you ought to stay away from Gowrie House. I wouldn't be putting trust in Scott Morgan if I was you."

She looked at him, astounded by his effrontery. Before she could respond, or ask why he would speak so, he walked past her and out of the warehouse into the gray dusk of eventide.

As she carried the empty tray back to the long table, her troubled thoughts must have been showing. Scott was waiting, and he looked at her with unexpected sympathy. He took the tray from her, and then poured them both tea. He turned thoughtfully toward the exit where the Scotsman had vanished.

"I see you've had the misfortune of meeting our caretaker."

Compared to Kerc, Scott was pleasant and easy to be with. "Yes. He mentioned knowing you."

Scott seemed amused. "That may be, but I don't think anyone on Mull knows Kerc, or even wants to try. He carries around a chip on his shoulder. Cross him, and he wouldn't hesitate to crack your skull. That's my impression, anyway. After an absence he returned to Gowrie House a few years ago, and though he keeps long hours and earns his wage, he's a blight when it comes to his mood."

"Why is that? And why didn't he like me? I could see it in his face."

"Who knows? For one thing, he wants a girl who's far above his class. I suppose that's frustration enough for any man."

She felt uneasy, worried. She handed Scott a sandwich, but he refused politely.

"Why did he come back as caretaker if he isn't happy there?"

He shrugged. "He works for your father. And your father has some strange attachment to Kerc."

Vanessa, surprised, looked for an explanation but received none.

"He also fishes the waters thereabouts and sells the catch, mostly to eating houses, I think. He makes a lot of runs. I suppose that's how he happened to be in the right place when the Norwegians needed help." He looked at the refugees, shaking his head sadly. "Dr. Elsdon seems to think half the company was lost at sea."

"Yes, such a tragedy. Oh, Scott, when will it end?"

"End? My dear, I don't think the war's even begun in earnest yet. Only God knows the end from the beginning, or why our generation was chosen to face all this misery."

Vanessa, heartsick, lapsed into a painful silence.

"The little girl's parents must have been lost," he was saying. "It's unfortunate, but all too common."

She needed to speak of something else, if only for a moment, and reverted back to their previous topic of conversation. "Then the caretaker gets along with my—with Robert Miles?"

"He must," he said. "He stays. That's about all I know of him or want to know."

Vanessa read between the lines. The caretaker was a troublemaker.

"I've spoken to Robert about him, but he approves of his work on the grounds. Your father, I'm afraid, doesn't have a good command of things the way he did a few years ago. He tells me it's nearly impossible to get someone familiar with the island and growing season."

It was interesting how Scott, who was also an employee, thought it important to take it upon himself to speak to her father about the caretaker.

"Your half sister, Lucy, is a garden enthusiast. Some of the best roses in the area grow on the estate, thanks to Kerc, or so she insists. The roses have quite a history, I'm told, but I haven't delved into it. Anyway, Lucy attributes their blooming for the first time in thirty years to Kerc's 'magical' touch."

There was humor and tolerance in Scott's brown eyes that told her something new about him. He had no tolerance for the caretaker, but he did for Lucy Miles. Scott appeared to find her amusing.

Scott became aware of her gaze on his face, for he lifted his cup and drank his tea, turning toward Francis.

"Lucy approves of Kerc?" she pursued, wanting to understand as much about Gowrie House as she could before she went there...if she went.

"Lucy seems to think he has 'powers.'" Scott looked sheepish, as though the notion embarrassed him, a practical man. "You have to understand Lucy," he added quickly, as if afraid Vanessa would decide against her. "She is rather confused about what she wants in life right now. She's easily swayed by her aunt, Theo Gowrie. Your father is too busy to pay attention to Lucy. She needs him, but he's not there for her."

Vanessa withdrew again briefly into her own pained silence. If anyone knew what it was like to need a father and not have him there, it was herself and Kylie.

"Kerc reminds me of a gypsy," she mused.

"An apt description. A thieving, murderous gypsy is more like it. He's been without parents most of his growing years, I'm told. It made an undisciplined thief out of him."

"He appears to work very hard. What do you mean about a 'thief'?"

"Oh, he has grand notions about his ancestors descending from the great Trevalyans of Scotland. Truth is, he's born of servant class—from generations of the same. Look, you're scowling, my dear, and I don't mean to sound prejudiced, but he worries me. I don't like his hold on Lucy or—" he stopped abruptly, as though he'd said too much.

Unfortunately, he hadn't said enough. It began to dawn on her what might be behind Scott's dislike of the caretaker. Even if Lucy's friendship with Kerc were innocent, Scott might not see it that way if he were jealous. Maybe that explained what Kerc had meant. Perhaps Kerc suspected Scott of bringing her to Gowrie House to separate him from Lucy Miles.

"Did you come because you wanted me to reconcile with my father, or because you think I can somehow influence the outcome between Lucy and Kerc?"

Scott showed disapproval over her bluntness. It had upset him, but at least it had leveled the turf between them. She didn't mind being involved for a good purpose, but she did want honesty, and she wasn't inclined to become a dampener in a sticky, complicated romance between members of the upper class and a caretaker.

If Scott had been feeding her sentimental pabulum about her ailing father wanting to see her and Kylie before he died just to achieve his own desire toward Lucy Miles, she would bid him goodbye here and now, shutting the door to Scotland.

But he appeared to sense that, for he said quickly: "Really, Vanessa, it's not what you think. I came to you in good faith. It's important you see your father, for his sake, so forget Lucy."

"Will you?" she asked evenly.

"Will I what?" he frowned, as if confused.

"Forget Lucy Miles."

His light brown eyes flickered. "Look," he said restlessly, "let's get out of here, shall we? I need to talk to you plainly...away from this morbid environment. There's so much more that's important for you to understand. Your friends can handle the refugees now."

Vanessa looked toward Francis. Her emotions were torn over the circumstances Scott was bringing into her life. The more she learned about Gowrie House, the more involved it was becoming. She wasn't sure she wanted it this way. Yet all this seemed larger than her own private plans. Like a windstorm catching her up through no fault of her own, she was being carried along to some final destination. Even meeting the caretaker here tonight had only drawn her deeper into the bog. To what blessed or frightful end was all this leading her?

"Do hear me out, Vanessa," Scott urged quietly.

"I'll tell Francis I'm leaving, but I've got to get back to the Warnstead house. We're expecting company tonight."

"I'll take you home," he said quickly, his eyes pleading. "And on the way I promise to tell you the truth. All of it."

3

Rain clouds had blown in from the North Sea, dark and stormy. As Scott drove to the Warnstead house, he explained his reasons for coming to London. Vanessa listened in silence, growing more uneasy as the truth unfolded.

"Your father isn't a well man. He had a heart attack last year, and there's no guarantee he won't have another. His doctor has tried to get him to a London hospital for tests, but he won't leave his work. On top of that he's disappointed with Lucy—" He glanced toward her. "She's determined to marry a man your father disapproves of, but he won't do anything to stop her. It's as if he's given up since Norah died."

She looked at him.

His voice softened. "She was everything to him. She made his life worth living. When he lost her, he lost everything he cared about except his work."

Vanessa fought a tide of resentment. She didn't want to think kindly toward the woman who had taken her father away from her and Kylie. Vanessa knew how much her mother had suffered after he left the three of them.

"You're upset," Scott said quietly. "I can tell because your jaw-line turns square."

She glanced toward him, one brow lifted. "Not very flattering, Mr. Morgan."

He smiled but turned his eyes back to the road. "I understand your anger, Vanessa, but it doesn't do anything to help matters in Scotland, and that's what concerns me now."

"Fair enough," she managed tonelessly. "I'll need to know the truth before I can decide what to do. You say Robert is ill and isn't concerned about the error his daughter Lucy is about to make in marrying a certain man?"

"Yes, but it's not correct to say that Robert doesn't care about Lucy. He does. That's why she—well, never mind that now. Robert is a gifted man, if an emotional one. But you need to understand that while neither of us would condone everything he's doing or has done in the past, we must deal with him as he is."

"And just what is it that you seem to think I can do for him now, and where do you think that leaves me and Kylie?"

"Presently, I think your father is very aware of his mistakes."

Mistakes? She bit her lip and made no response, staring ahead. Drops of rain were plopping on the cold windshield and running slowly down toward the motionless wipers. Scott reached over and turned them on. The sound of the blades swishing away the water filled the car. Vanessa stuffed her chilly hands into her pockets.

"He wants to see you. He hasn't explained why, but I think he wants to unsettle Lucy a little. After all, though your father has lost a lot of things important to him these last twenty years, he still has money." He glanced at her. "Quite a bit of it, actually."

She stiffened and looked at him. "Are you suggesting he wants to use Kylie and me as pawns to *coerce* Lucy into behaving as he wishes? Because if that's the reason you're asking me to Scotland—"

"Slow down," he said, smiling tolerantly. "You're jumping to conclusions about Robert. I don't know his motives, Vanessa, but I can assure you his request has nothing to do with hurting you or Lucy. That would not be typical of him."

She felt that she had reason enough to disagree and said, "I won't be used to goad Lucy into anything."

"Of course not. If I thought that was his motive, I'd not ask you to go there. I'm fond of his daughter." He paused a moment, and then added, "And neither do I want to see you hurt any more than you have been."

She thought his including her was mere politeness. Did Scott care more about Lucy than he wanted to tell?

"This man Lucy intends to marry against Robert's will," Vanessa asked cautiously, "is he the caretaker?"

His brows shot up. "Kerc? No, the man's name is Jodrell. He's from Edinburgh." He stared ahead. "She doesn't seem to see she's making a mistake. She's all wrapped up in her own plans."

Vanessa wondered how involved Scott was in Lucy's escapades.

"You'll meet the man Lucy intends to marry soon enough if you come to Scotland."

From the way he lapsed into tense silence, Vanessa considered again the possibility that he cared for Lucy. But whatever the reason, Scott disliked the man, and he obviously didn't wish to discuss it now.

"You mentioned dangers a moment ago?" she said, uneasily.

"Oh, emotional dangers, to both your father and Lucy. Someone needs to alert them."

"I don't care to be the catalyst, if that's what you or Robert are thinking," she said.

"No, but your presence would help."

"I don't see how." Her main thought was for the chance of bringing a reunion of sorts between Kylie and his father. She had no illusions, nor did she expect her half sister to open her arms to her, especially if her father had some scheme to interject her in the middle of an inheritance struggle. She wanted none of it. And talk of financial support should have occurred when her mother was struggling to raise her and Kylie alone.

Vanessa recognized her bitterness for what it was and kept its tentacles from tightening about her. She would not be smothered by it. The question facing her now was, what did God want her to do? Involve herself in Scotland, or go home to New York before the war worsened?

"If only you would come to Scotland for a little while," he was saying. "Robert would be pleased even with a two-week visit."

Vanessa was thinking how those words would have brought such joy when she was a girl growing up. *Your father would be pleased if you'd come and see him.*

Two weeks. What was two weeks when she had needed a loving, strong father all of her life? Her character was shaped now, like a piece of clay. What could meeting him accomplish? For her, very little—closure perhaps, and forgiveness. But for the others it might mean a great deal. Then again, perhaps it would come to nothing except the stirring of leaves in a whirlwind, and after the whirlwind passes on, the leaves just settle back down.

And what do you want out of this? What do you expect, Scott? she wanted to ask. Was it Lucy? Whatever he wanted, he believed she could help bring it to pass.

"It's still not clear to me just why you think my presence is needed."

"Perhaps because I don't know myself," he said quietly. "I'm merely hoping. Hoping that in seeing you your father can make peace with himself and with his past...and that it will cause him to move in time to keep Lucy from making a serious mistake with her life."

Vanessa wasn't cynical, but she couldn't help smiling ruefully. "You either think I'm a miracle worker, Mr. Morgan, or a great catalyst for change. I'm neither."

"I think you might end up being both."

She looked away. Did she want to give so much of herself with so little promise of anything in return?

She thought of the Norwegian refugees and the child who had apparently lost her mother and father. They were representatives of the faces of thousands of others who would lose everything in the war that was breaking savagely across the face of Europe, and now, even London. Millions would give their lives. But it was the faces of two young RAF pilots that made it all understandable and human for her. Kylie would be taking to the skies soon dueling Luftwaffe pilots, as would her own young hero, Andy. If something happened to them…. The painful thought interrupted her for a moment. With so much to say and to forgive, how could she hold back on a request that just might bring one brief moment in which Kylie could embrace his father and become free of the pain and anger that bound him?

She looked over at Scott and noticed in the last of the light the frown of worry on his brow. She'd told him she would discuss going to Scotland with Kylie. Her mind was made up; she'd mention it tonight.

"All right, Scott."

He looked at her, his brown eyes questioning.

"I may be walking straight into trouble, but I'll go to Scotland and see Robert Miles."

Now that she had agreed to go, he was quite calm about it. He said easily, "As soon as I saw you, I knew I wouldn't be disappointed."

But would she be disappointed, even regretful? The path she took was like a bog full of quicksand. She would need to move with caution. Her good intentions placed her at risk. And the cold, hard eyes of Kerc Trevalyan were no illusion. Scott did not appear a fool or an alarmist. *He reminds me of a gypsy,* she had said of the caretaker. *A thieving, murderous gypsy,* Scott had echoed. What he'd meant by a thief she could envision. She recalled the man's frayed peacoat cuffs, the missing button, and the hands that worked harder and received less of a bounty for his labors. Yes— she could envision the resentful Kerc Trevalyan being tempted to be a thief. But whatever had Scott meant by "murderous"?

4

Vanessa was in the Warnstead home when the taxi pulled into the driveway. That would be Kylie and Andy. She hurried onto the terrace, avoiding small puddles and thinking that Mrs. Warnstead would be upset when she discovered someone had forgotten to replace the covers on the outdoor tables and chairs.

Vanessa went to the rail to look below. The rain had momentarily stopped, but the sky was still spread with a heavy layer of clouds. In the taxi's headlight beams she saw the two young men heading for the front door, heard the bell ring, and then heard muffled voices.

She waited on the darkened terrace. A moment later, through the double-wide doors, she saw them enter the brightly lit drawing room, charming and handsome in their RAF uniforms.

Kylie was the intense one, his riveting blue eyes full of reckless energy. Vanessa secretly worried that he would make a dangerously reckless flyer, but Andy assured her differently. "He's careful and calm," he had told her, "but he has the boldness it takes to challenge the German pilots. He'll do very well."

Kylie looked about, saw the doors open to the terrace, and came toward her. "Hey, sis. What are you doing out there in the rain? Hiding from Andy, probably. Don't blame you."

"What's this?" Andy called, pretending to be offended, but turning first to his father, Colonel Nelson Warnstead, who had just entered the room. Father and son spoke for a moment while Kylie stepped out with a smile and glanced up at the sky. "Looking for Messerschmitts?"

"They must have learned you put on an RAF uniform and made a beeline back to Berlin," she said just as lightly, but her heart was more serious than her face revealed. She put her arm through his. "It's starting to rain again."

He turned her toward the doors, but glanced about the shadowy terrace as if to see if Francis were out there. He had had a crush on Francis for months now, and Vanessa wondered how it would end. But Francis was so taken up with her work that she either didn't notice, or she wanted to make Kylie think she didn't.

"Where's the ministering angel?" he asked.

"Still down at the harbor, working with Dr. Elsdon." She saw his disappointment. On the evening of his graduation it would have been nice if Francis had shown she cared enough to be here, but it really wasn't fair to expect very much from her at a time like this. At least, that's what Vanessa kept telling Kylie.

She tried to soften his landing by saying: "Dr. Elsdon's health isn't doing so well, I'm told. He depends on Francis a great deal. Tonight there was another emergency. Did you hear about the refugees?"

"A tragic but old story now," he said. His meaning was clear. There would always be more refugees staggering in from Nazi assaults across Europe, but he would not always be here to share a dinner with her.

He appeared to shrug off his feelings as they returned to the drawing room.

Andy Warnstead, steady, quiet, and looking around for Vanessa, was helping himself to a bottle of Coca-Cola from a bucket of ice on the table. Kylie greeted Colonel Warnstead.

"Good evening, sir."

"Hello, Kylie. My congratulations."

"Thank you, sir. I look forward to serving in your command."

Mrs. Warnstead hesitated a moment in the doorway before coming in from the dining room, as if she were gearing herself up for something she did not feel. She was either very tired or depressed. Seeing Andy, who with Kylie beside him was exchanging friendly words with her husband, she managed a smile and a cheerful greeting for both young men in uniform.

An admirable effort, Vanessa decided, taking Mrs. Warnstead in. Andy had inherited her smile and bravery in the face of overwhelming odds.

"Hello, Mom," Andy said. "I told Kylie we're having roasted chicken tonight, so I couldn't get rid of him at the gate."

Everyone laughed. "Poor Kylie, and we're only having cold ham sandwiches," Mrs. Warnstead apologized. "Leftover ham from Sunday brunch at that," she warned with cheer, accepting a light kiss on her cheek from Andy and including Kylie in her welcoming motherly hug. "But we are having cardamom cake for dessert. I made it last night with you in mind, Kylie."

"The missing chicken is my fault," Vanessa confessed. "I forgot Mrs. Warnstead had asked me to stop at Pelham's on the way home."

"Pelham's?" Colonel Warnstead's gray brows shot up inquiringly toward his wife. He was a short, squarely built man of fifty, with a pipe.

Julia laughed. "Nelson, you've driven by the butcher's nearly every day for twenty years."

"Oh, *that* Pelham," and he winked at Vanessa. "Now I remember."

"I had planned on chicken for our celebration dinner tonight," Julia explained.

"Oh, well, we'll forgive her," Andy intervened, throwing a protective arm around Vanessa's shoulders. "I like cold ham sandwiches."

"Ah, love," his father commented with a twinkle in his eyes. "I remember when Andy threw tantrums at dinner if he didn't get what he wanted."

"None of that, Dad. You'll frighten her away."

They laughed, and Vanessa smiled, embarrassed and a little uneasy over how it was becoming customary for Andy's family to already think of her as a daughter-in-law.

"Saved by the bell," Andy said when the telephone jangled in the hall. "I was afraid the sins of my entire childhood were going to be laid bare before Vanessa."

"I'll get it," Mrs. Warnstead called over her shoulder as she hurried toward the hall. "It could be Francis."

As the exchange between Andy and the colonel turned into a more serious discussion of the war, Vanessa recognized and appreciated their healthy father and son relationship. Comfortable, respectful, accepting. The evenings she had enjoyed the most since coming to the Warnsteads were the times when she just sat back and listened to Andy and his father talking together on a variety of subjects, each offering differing opinions. Andy was independent, yet he could also seek advice when he needed it. And Vanessa had never yet seen Colonel Warnstead prop up his ego by insisting Andy show submission or by embarrassing him in front of her. Her admiration for the RAF colonel had grown.

What would it have been like if only—Vanessa stopped herself from wandering down the bitter path of dissatisfaction.

She had met Andy in New York two years ago when he'd gone there to visit mutual friends after graduating from the Royal Air Force Academy. They'd been writing, and sometimes telephoning, ever since. Then last December he'd arrived in Saratoga on leave.

He wanted her to meet his family, and Vanessa wanted to visit the place where she and Kylie were born. Vanessa also had come back to England because she'd wanted to find out if she loved Andy, and because Kylie, who had returned to England five years before to attend the Royal Air Force Academy, was soon to enter active duty.

She glanced toward her brother. He was looking on without comment the way he usually did when father and son were talking. One hand was in his pocket while the other held an iced bottle of cola. Vanessa, who knew Kylie better than anyone, could tell he felt a little uncomfortable in the homey atmosphere. Kylie was good at a lot of things, but family fellowship was not one of them. He was standing between the divan and the terrace as though he sought the open space in case he needed an emotional retreat.

What will he think about the invitation from his own father?

"Francis says we should all go ahead and have dinner without her," Mrs. Warnstead told them when she returned, avoiding glancing toward Kylie. "She's got her hands full right now, and Dr. Elsdon has more than he can handle." She frowned worriedly. "Maybe I should go down and help out."

The colonel walked over and put his arm around her tired shoulders, quietly but firmly reassuring her. "You're already doing all you can, Julia. There's such a thing as giving too much of one's self, you know. In the end, burning the candle at both ends doesn't help anyone, and it will put you off your feet."

Julia Warnstead warmed to her husband's concern. "If you really think I shouldn't, Nelson."

"I think we're all going to devour those ham sandwiches while we toast Kylie's graduation from flight school. And when Francis does get in tonight, I'm going to have a little talk with her about her own hours with Dr. Elsdon."

After a leisurely dinner followed by tea and cake, they gravitated back into the drawing room. It was nearing 9:30 when Kylie walked over to the large Crosley radio with a questioning look toward the colonel. "Do you mind, sir?"

"Not at all. You youngsters go ahead and enjoy the music. I'm going to take the newspaper to my chair in the next room."

"And I've letters to write," Julia said, who corresponded with relatives and friends in Australia and America. With a kiss on her husband's cheek, she added, "I'll join you a bit later, dear. I want to make up a plate of food for Francis when she comes home. She'll be starving by then."

When they were alone, Vanessa sat down on the divan near the terrace and Andy came up. They smiled at each other in comfortable silence while across the room Kylie fidgeted with the radio dial, trying to bring in his favorite program that at this hour played the music of Glenn Miller and Tommy Dorsey. When he found it he turned the volume up, but not enough to disturb the colonel in the next room. London's loveliest songbird, Vera Lynn, was singing words of fidelity and heartache between sweethearts separated by the war.

"What made you forget the chicken?"

Vanessa laughed quietly. It seemed so incongruous to bring the chicken up again during such a song. "Are you still disappointed over the ham sandwiches?" she teased.

His grin was contagious. "Not really. Just curious." He sat down beside her.

Her brows lifted. "About what?"

"You."

"Me? I didn't think any curious facts about me were left unanswered," she said, smiling at him.

"Meaning the last two months have been hard on you? Raked over the coals by my inquisitive family?" he laughed.

"Oh, no, I didn't mean that at all," Vanessa said. "The last two months have been—well, wonderful, if you want to know. Your parents are so special, Andy, and Francis is like a sister. It's just that—" She stopped. She wasn't sure what she meant to say.

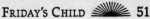

"It's just that it's time for the American girl to go home, where it's safe. From bombs, at least." His smile faded, and Vanessa laid a hand on his. He took it quickly, covering it with his own, while his eyes looked into hers.

"Perhaps it's best," he said reluctantly. "Dad thinks the Germans will attack us by air before attempting a land invasion. I'm going to be pretty busy in the sky, and with you back home in New York, I'd have one less thing to worry about. Unless," and his hand tightened, "you're willing to stay and become my—"

"Andy," she hastened softly, "let's not—"

"I know. You needn't say it. We must be sure. Only thing is, I'm already sure."

She looked down at their clasped hands and bit her lip. She felt the heat rise in her cheeks because she didn't know what to say without it hurting him. It was easier to say nothing, but was it fair to him?

"Don't worry," he said quietly. "We won't talk about it now. Let's discuss the mystery of the forgotten chicken."

She looked up amused. His eyes laughed at her, but there was a note of seriousness in them too.

"Very well, 'Mr. Holmes,'" she said with a dimpled smile. "What do you want to know?"

"First, I already know you're a very bright girl—besides being lovely to look at. And this bright girl just doesn't forget to pick up the chicken, especially when the dinner is in celebration of her brother's graduation from flying school. So, putting two and two together, I've deduced that something interesting must have happened to detour you from stopping at dear old Pelham's butcher shop."

"Very good indeed," she said, pretending to applaud his logical skills while still remaining evasive about Scotland, yet not knowing exactly why. She could only expect help from Andy who, like his father, was understanding and quick to offer support. There was so much about Andy Warnstead that told her she would be a fool to ever turn down his proposal. He would make the marriage work. Nor did she have a reason to conceal the news that Scott Morgan had brought her about Robert Miles.

"Well, what could have happened to deter me between the DP office and the butcher's?"

"Not much, granted it was an ordinary sort of day. Something did happen, though, didn't it?"

She had no choice now. She smiled and sighed at the same time. "Yes. You're right, as usual. A stranger was waiting for me just as I was leaving to come home this afternoon." She glanced toward Kylie. He was still standing by the radio, elbow resting on top, listening, eyes closed as though asleep. For a moment she was amused. He *had* fallen asleep standing there! He must have been up late last night with the squadron he'd been assigned to in London.

"Kylie doesn't know yet, but I've heard from our father," she said in a low voice. "He wants to see me. He's living in Scotland. I was thinking I'd go there for a few weeks before I return to New York. If I do return," she added thoughtfully.

"You mean Robert Miles, the beloved London Shakespearean actor? Hearing from him now is a bit of a shocker, isn't it? Did he say what he wanted, or is this just a sentimental journey with the war on and all?"

"That's just it. I don't really know. I told Mr. Morgan I would go for two weeks. He's going to arrange it with Robert by telephone tonight or tomorrow and be in touch with me."

"So, Mr. Morgan is the distraction who came between you and our chicken."

"Yes. He works for…for Robert Miles." She had a difficult time saying "my father." "I'm going to tell Kylie tonight."

"Seems like the right decision to go see him. What's there to lose?"

"Strange, isn't it?" she mused.

"What is?"

"Oh, how something as tragic as a war can close so many doors, yet still open new ones."

"If it's 'strange' as you put it, it's because our human nature doesn't expect suffering and pain to bring gifts of opportunity," Andy said.

"Yes, we want to run from such things."

He smiled. "It would be odd if we didn't." When she didn't answer, he squeezed her hand and asked, "So what's bothering you? How Kylie will take it?"

She sighed, plucking at her pretty gold bracelet.

"He's always resented his father. I don't know whether he'll approve of my visit, but I'd like to go, I think, not just for my sake, but for his."

Andy looked serene and confident. He stood, and taking her hand, pulled her up. Then he took both her hands in his.

"I wouldn't be apprehensive about throwing him a curveball right now, if that's what's troubling you. He can handle it. His nerves can be icy. Want my suggestion? Tell him. Give him the right to meet his father. What he does with it is his business. These are times we don't want to waste."

She knew what he meant. The obvious was on everyone's mind. Who knew what the next twenty-four hours would bring forth? That, of course, was true of every generation, but it was brought to light with painful clarity as the list of dead and missing grew longer with each passing day.

Yes, Andy was right. And Scott Morgan had said much the same thing. Tomorrow was never guaranteed. *We are a special generation,* she thought, *chosen to endure, and to confront suffering and death.*

"Doesn't war and the brevity of life encourage us to forgive and go on? It has a way of boiling things down to their essential nature. In a way it makes life simpler, clearer. The stakes are all laid out, and few people are deceived into mistaking life as an endless game of play and waste."

"Very philosophical," Andy said with a smile.

They drew apart as Kylie walked up.

"They're playing your song," Kylie said with a smile as he walked leisurely out onto the terrace, where the rain was coming down so finely that it was more of a mist.

Andy smiled at her and opened his arms. She came to him and they danced quietly to "Why'd Ya Make Me Fall in Love?"

Francis arrived sooner than expected, and she removed her heeled pumps as soon as she came through the door. "Why I wear these I'll never know. Hello, everyone." She glanced about too casually, until she saw Kylie come in from the terrace. "Sorry I'm late."

As everyone came to greet her and inquire about the wounded Norwegians, Kylie pulled out a chair for her. She sank into it gratefully, but kept talking to the colonel and Mrs. Warnstead, who now joined the young people.

"They've been brought to the hospital, but they can't keep them. They'll check them, then release them to Dr. Elsdon." She looked at her father. "Dad, isn't there anything you can do to get Parliament to set aside land outside London for a bigger clinic and hostel?"

"I'll try, but that's out of my jurisdiction."

"She's right. Do try, dear," Mrs. Warnstead urged. "Sarah said Lord George was the man to see about it. I've written him a letter, but it would be more effective if you gave it to him when he next visits the squadron."

"I'll do what I can."

Kylie brought Francis a cola. She accepted it with an absent smile, nor did she appear to notice when he sat down in a chair beside her.

"Anything on the little girl?" Vanessa asked Francis.

"What little girl?" Kylie asked.

Francis turned, as if aware of him for the first time. She explained what had happened and how none of the other refugees knew who she was or how she got aboard the boat that was rescued in the Channel.

"And she's deaf?" Kylie asked.

"We think so. Further evaluations can be done."

Vanessa was thinking again about the strange, unfriendly behavior of Kerc Trevalyan. She would have mentioned him except it would require telling Kylie about their father in front of everyone, and she wanted to wait for that until they were alone.

"After things calmed down a little, several of the Norwegians said they thought she belonged to one of the women who were killed in the attack."

"That appears most likely," Mrs. Warnstead said sadly. "Poor child. Where is she now, Francis?"

Francis leaned her head tiredly against the back of her chair and enjoyed the soda Kylie had given her. "She's with Dr. Elsdon at the hospital. They're doing some tests on her. It seems strange that she doesn't cry."

"She must be in shock," Mrs. Warnstead said.

"She might have been on the boat when the other refugees boarded," Kylie told Francis.

"But then her mother would have been right there with her."

"Not necessarily. If someone placed her on board, say, and didn't return in time, or..." he shrugged.

"Didn't want to return you mean?" Francis frowned thoughtfully. "Well...maybe...it's possible, I suppose."

"But wouldn't she have carried on when her mother didn't return as the boat was leaving?" Vanessa wondered.

"Beats me," Kylie said, standing up restlessly. He put his hands in his pockets and gazed down at Francis. "How about something to eat? Your mother kept a plate warm for you in the kitchen."

"Maybe later," Francis said, smiling up at him. "I'm just too tired to eat now."

"That's the trouble," the colonel said. "You and your mother are both doing way too much."

"Somebody has to, Dad."

Vanessa felt uncomfortable. She wasn't doing half as much to help as Francis and Mrs. Warnstead.

Francis smiled affectionately at her father. "That idea of working too hard goes for you too, right, Mum?"

"It's my duty," Colonel Warnstead said easily, then looked at his watch. "It's almost time for the news on the BBC."

Each day across Britain, people gathered together at the hours of the chief radio messages: eight o'clock, one o'clock, and nine o'clock, to hear the reports from London, Paris, and Berlin.

"It's coming on now, Dad," Andy said, turning up the volume.

After Dunkirk it shouldn't have surprised anyone that Germany would storm around the Maginot Line into France with little between them and the road to Paris but the French army commanders, who were sadly without hope. England had saved the stranded British Expeditionary Force (BEF) from the beaches of Dunkirk while being bombed to smithereens by the Luftwaffe as the German army moved forward for the slaughter. And yet! Or as the Christians were saying after national prayer in St. Paul's Cathedral, "But, God!" Though trapped with the sea before them, the Germans behind, and the Luftwaffe above, God had heard and answered the prayers of His people, and "somehow," as the British would say it, almost the whole of her fighting force had been rescued by her sea power, using great fighting ships as well as a multitude of small fishing vessels. The British army had been brought home to the shores of England early in June by the tens of thousands!

All of their fighting equipment, however, had been left behind. France then stood nearly alone. Her pessimistic leaders were certain they could not hold the German army back, and that even if they attempted to, nothing would be accomplished except covering the road to Paris knee-high with the bodies of young French soldiers. They would take a stand at the border defenses. Should the Germans break through, France would appoint Petain as their president, and he would sue for peace with Hitler. All would be over.

And it was over. The Nazi German *Blitzkrieg*—the lightning war—smashed through the defenses in only a few hours, and the German armored divisions were quickly advancing on the French soil that had just been softened up by Stuka dive bombers.

Colonel Warnstead took out his map as he always did after the news and traced the Nazi advance. Tonight, however, the changing fronts brought even more of a dismaying qualm to Vanessa's spirits as the colonel traced the French army's retreat. It had been sickening enough to see Poland fall after a gallant fight with no other country to help, and then to watch Holland, Norway, Finland, and Belgium—but France!

Andy read her expression, for it must have been on all their minds that if France fell to Hitler it was but a short distance across the Channel to England. With most of Europe already in their clutches, the Germans could turn their attention upon Britain.

Andy gave her a grim smile and placed his arm around her shoulders, as if to say: *Well, France might not fall.* But down deep, she believed that he doubted it.

"Dad, is there nothing England can do to save France?" Francis asked in a rather hopeless plea as though speaking to a physician about a terminally ill patient.

"We must save England," he countered.

Vanessa felt that in speaking those four words he had said what they all secretly knew and feared: that Britain would soon feel the full onslaught of the wrath of Nazi Germany.

"For all intents and purposes, France was lost months ago," he continued, "when the political and military leaders decided they would resist Hitler only to a certain point. When the enemy knows the limits of your endurance, you can be sure he'll push to get there."

Kylie said thoughtfully: "A country dies when its people choose comfort and escape from suffering in place of fighting to preserve their freedom."

"Yes, and when a people compromise with evil long enough, they lose the spiritual and mental clarity necessary to become determined to resist. And that," the colonel said thoughtfully, looking at his pipe, "is what England must not do. Churchill is right. We must never compromise an inch. We must stand against anything Hitler may throw at us." He looked at them with his steely gaze. "Because if we give him any expectation that we may talk peace terms if things get rough enough, we will soon be lowering the Union Jack and hoisting a swastika over Buckingham Palace."

Andy rallied to his father. "Churchill said we must fight on alone, if necessary. We have an advantage that France does not; we are surrounded by the seas."

"And we must keep the seas open or we're sunk," the colonel said.

"What about the French Fleet?" Kylie asked.

"Yes, surely they'll join us," Mrs. Warnstead said hopefully. "They'll see there is no other hope of stopping Hitler except by aligning with England."

The colonel studied the map again. He shook his head doubtfully. He was prone to paint the French Naval Minister, Weygand, as a man of small passion. "He won't risk it. I don't think any of the French leadership likes England, except Reynaud."

"I had such hope Reynaud could rally his forces—"

"We all had hope in Reynaud," the colonel said. "But there is gossip that he has a secret mistress who wants France to yield to Germany."

Vanessa and Francis exchanged quick glances.

"You don't think—," began Mrs. Warnstead, but the colonel shrugged his heavy shoulders. "Neither Weygand nor the map seem very encouraging to me."

"Nor to me either, Dad," Andy said.

Kylie grinned suddenly, a little fiercely, and clasped a friendly hand on Andy's shoulder. "Then it will be up to the RAF to hold the ruddy Germans at bay."

Vanessa knew that smile, and her heart beat a little faster with worry.

"Looks as if I'll get to tangle with the Luftwaffe sooner than I thought. Can't wait to see the Nazis spiraling downward in flames."

Vanessa kept silent, though thoughts of outcry and fear welled up in her heart. She noted the unexpected look of dismay on Francis' face as she sat across the room from Kylie. *Kylie,* thought Vanessa, *would have been glad to see that expression, but he is looking instead at the map with the colonel and Andy.*

In spite of Vanessa's hopes for brave little England, she did not see how, apart from God's mercy and deliverance, that this island could hold up a defiant flag of freedom much longer. She feared the Nazis would soon be parachuting soldiers into the countryside to engage in sabotage in preparation for an invasion from the Channel. That left her in a quandary. Should she go home as Andy now wanted her to do? Or should she stay with these determined people? If she returned to New York now she saw herself as deserting friends in time of crisis, but perhaps she was using mere emotion instead of wisdom.

There was little doubt that the cruel realities of this war would now be aimed at London as never before. What limits were there to Nazi power now that they had pillaged Europe of its food, its manpower, its gold, and all of its best resources? All was now at Berlin's fiendish disposal. And Hitler's *Wehrmacht* had the added prestige of crashing through the French defenses.

"What can stop them?" she found herself thinking aloud, questioning no one in particular. But it brought a response. They all looked at her.

"England will stop them," Andy said.

And God, she thought, looking out across the open terrace to where the lingering shade of lavender blue twilight blanketed the entire sky.

≈≈≈

It wasn't until the next morning that Vanessa found opportunity to speak alone with Kylie about their father. The colonel had been called to his office early and Andy had gone with him. Mrs. Warnstead and Francis had gone with Dr. Elsdon to meet with a group of wealthy women of the aristocracy who had agreed to hear about the need for property for the private Christian clinic-retreat, and Vanessa, on her way to the DP office, had ridden with Kylie to his squadron.

It wasn't the perfect time to broach him on the matter because he was already in a rush, but she was to meet Scott for brunch at Piccadilly Circus and he would be expecting an answer. Besides, Kylie was always in a rush with ten important things stirring in his mind. He had always been that way. Even when growing up in Manhattan, he'd been a bundle of restless energy.

They were alone, seated in the taxi, being driven to the squadron quarters.

"Are you sure whatever this is about can't wait?"

"It would, if I wasn't meeting Mr. Morgan this morning."

His brows lifted. "Mr. Morgan? He's the lead-in, I gather, to which I'm supposed to ask, 'Who is Mr. Morgan?'"

"Um…yes, actually. He works for Robert Miles."

A small bomb may as well have exploded inside the taxi.

"Our father," she said too quietly, still meeting his gaze.

"I know," he said icily.

"Yes...," she said lamely, and she fussed with her fingers, checking her careful manicure.

"This fellow Morgan works for him?"

This fellow. A sure sign that Kylie held no regard for this bearer of news from their father.

"Yes. He's a writer, helping Robert with research on a Gowrie family history book."

"Well, of course he wouldn't be writing his biography," he scoffed. "That would take the prize, wouldn't it? I wonder if he'd include how he abandoned two small children for his stage career while his wife had to work to support them?"

Vanessa was looking at her nails and biting her lip. She felt all of the poison in Kylie's words just as painfully and angrily as did he.

"But now isn't the time to go over those old ruts," she said, looking at him. "The fact is, he's asked to see me. He wants me to come to his estate in Scotland for a few weeks. That's all we need to discuss right now, Kylie. The invitation, and whether I accept."

"Of course you won't accept. Who does he think he is? He's turned his back to us all these years, and now he wants to meet you?"

"He wants to meet *us.*"

His mouth hardened, and for an instant she envisioned Kerc Trevalyan. "You can tell Morgan for me that—better yet, where is he staying? I'll tell him myself."

Her hand shot out, gripping his tense arm. For a moment she could almost feel the power reaching out in a thrust to the upper jaw of Scott Morgan.

"Kylie, please..."

"He has guts to pull something like this, doesn't he? After all these years, just to snap his ruddy fingers and expect us to go running to him? It's a little late to be playing 'Papa,' isn't it?"

She sighed inwardly. "I'm not sure that's on his mind."

"What is on his mind at this late date? A confession?"

She winced. "That's what I want to find out. Mr. Morgan didn't fully explain. I don't think he even knows himself. But he likes Robert. He feels we should give him a fair chance—"

"Fair chance?" his anger boiled in the depths of his eyes. "The only fair chance I'll give Robert Miles is a warning."

She glanced at him, hoping he wasn't too upset. "Mr. Morgan said he wasn't in good health."

"Conscience caught up with him, did it?" He gave a short laugh. "Good."

"I'm going for a few weeks, Kylie," she managed gently, but with a determination he knew. His gaze smoldered.

"Maybe you'd better explain," he said in a tight voice.

Vanessa attempted to be frank, though she progressed uneasily as she told him the details of Scott's calling on her at the clinic yesterday. "He—Robert—has asked to see me first."

"Ah, yes. Father and daughter sentimental rubbish and all that. I suppose he thinks he'll have a better chance softening you up than me."

"Give me a little credit, Kylie," she said heatedly. "I'm not a blubbering child, waiting for a pat on the head—"

"Sorry." He flashed a grin. "I know you're not, sis. You've always had the better head when it comes to taking things calmly. I just don't want him to take advantage of you, that's all. And say what you like, it's not going to be easy for you to resist the actor's charm when he decides to pour it down upon you."

"I won't let him do that to me, to us," she said stiffly, but her heart knew a qualm. Kylie wasn't too far afield when it came to her sentimental desire for a father. It was unrealistic after all these years, nor could Robert give her what she'd been denied while growing up, but the longing still remained a danger if not harnessed within appropriate boundaries.

"He wants to level the rocky slope we're all three about to embark upon," he said. "He probably thinks you can help him do

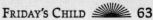

it, but he's wrong there. He's unrealistic if he thinks all it takes is his beck and call to—where was it, Scotland?"

"Yes. Mull."

"That's an island, isn't it? Don't tell me he owns it."

"It's a lovely island, I'm told. And no, he doesn't own it. Scottish people have been living on it for generations. Except for a few newcomers, mostly well-known individuals looking for privacy, it's very clannish, I think. Mr. Morgan said that Norah's last name, Benton, was a stage name. Her real last name was Gowrie, and her father left her Gowrie House in his will. It dates to the 1600s when James I became king of England."

Kylie did not look impressed. "Well, if the great Robert Miles thinks all he need do is say he's sorry and salve his conscience for what he did to us, he's more deluded than I imagined. Maybe that's it, he's gone senile."

"Kylie, please—"

"No mere apology can make up for what he did."

"You've made that perfectly clear."

Vanessa didn't need Kylie to shine the glaring light on the pain of abandonment by their father. She knew as well as he the pain caused by Robert's selfish decisions.

"Nor can he mend the damage by leaving either of us money when he dies," Kylie stated. "That's another mistake men like him fall into. Throwing money at their conscience to make it go away. Maybe it won't eat at him as badly if he can bribe the beggars at his gate by sending out a Christmas goose."

"I'm not expecting to receive anything tangible from him," she said. "I wouldn't take it any more than you would."

"I'm glad to hear that. Then why even discuss it? Why not just have Morgan return to Robert and inform him that his fatherly invitation is about two decades too late?"

"Because—"

Vanessa couldn't go on, perhaps because she didn't know all the answers herself. Too late. What devastating words...too late.

The door is shut and bolted from the inside. All the knocking, pleading, and hysterics in the whole world won't turn the clock back one minute. When life was over, it was too late. All the things left undone. All the deeds meant to be done. Too late. Too late to say "I love you." Too late to ask forgiveness. Too late—

"So he's ill, is he? Dear Daddy," he mocked. "We know you abandoned us and Mother to enhance your stage career, and it didn't matter to you whether we starved or cried ourselves to sleep at night...whether you loved us or not. We've come now to tell you that your deathbed confession is gratefully accepted by both us and God. Die in peace, my good man. How you have lived and what you didn't do really won't matter anyway. Abracadabra!"

She turned on him. "It's true he owes a debt to us that he will never be able to fulfill, but he's not our enemy. He'll need to live and die with that failure, and we will need to leave any revenge completely in God's hands. And you needn't tell me how to feel! I know."

He let a breath escape. "Sure you do. Probably better than me." He looked out the window.

She said more quietly: "One can't stay angry forever without it doing something to one's own heart. Anger and bitterness, even when justified, bite like an adder in the end. Anger must be guarded. It too easily turns to hate, then to self-destruction. Forgiveness frees the injured as much as the one forgiven."

"I can't forgive him."

His voice was so calm now, and so flat and final that all hope left her heart. The taxi stopped before the squadron entrance.

"At first I told Mr. Morgan I wouldn't go to Scotland, but I've decided I've little to lose, and perhaps something to gain—"

"Money? Blast his tainted money! Have you no more self-respect than that?"

"Is that what you think?"

"Well, it's obvious the old man has a bundle, isn't it? Londoners have paid plenty through the years to see him strutting about the stage mouthing Shakespeare. Now that he's about to leave his worldly goods behind, I suspect he's going to write you a big check to atone for all his selfish sins."

"I'm not going for money, or anything else he might wish to give me."

"Then, tell me, why are you going, Vanessa?"

For a moment they simply stared at one another. All words were lost to her, then she managed, "I'm going to listen."

"Listen?" He sounded as if she were impossible to understand.

"Yes. I want to know why he left us," she blurted out.

"But it doesn't take long, psychological investigations on the doc's couch to know the answer to that! Did you ever see a picture of the actress he left Mother for?"

Vanessa, dismayed, looked away as if that didn't matter.

"To Robert Miles it mattered," he said with disdain. "And she was the daughter of a well-known playwright."

Was it that simple? That cheap?

"There's got to be more...," she murmured.

"You think that, sis, because you have honor. You have a virtuous mind. But Robert Miles the *actor* responded to life on an animal level. I'll bet every important decision he ever made was based on what it would get him."

"Then why did Mother marry him?"

"Good question," he said dryly as he opened the car door. "She must have been looking for something. Looking in the wrong places, as they say. Looking to the wrong people to meet her needs. Putting her confidence in a broken vessel. I've got to run or I'll be grounded for a month!"

She leaned across the seat, her eyes searching his face.

"I'm going to Scotland."

"And you think he'll tell you the truth?"

"I'll make up my own mind, Kylie. Just as I'm making it up now. But I was hoping you'd understand."

"Understand...I understand that by rushing to his call you're betraying us. Everything we went through together. The three of us. And you're willing to throw it away just to hear what sentimental lies he can spume forth with a Shakespearean tongue."

"I'm not betraying you or the memory of Mother. Perhaps I'm trying to lay to rest once and for all the bitter legacy we've been carrying about for years. Mum is dead now. You and I must make our own lives. Neither of us are children any longer. I don't want the future weighed down with bitterness and hatred."

He looked at her, no emotion showing. "I don't hate him. I don't feel anything. He's merely an actor from a bygone generation. He probably surrounds himself with pictures and scrapbooks of his momentary greatness in the stage lights."

If she believed that, there would be no reason to go to Scotland.

"Kylie?"

The dead look in his eyes and handsome young face destroyed what she was about to say. She sighed.

"Nothing," she whispered. "Take care."

He smiled, gave her a casual salute, and ran into the building. She looked after him. *Dearest heavenly Father...please...*

A military vehicle honked loudly behind them. She closed the taxi door, and as the driver sped forward she called: "Piccadilly Circus."

5

The pigeons paid little attention to the London traffic rumbling by close to the sidewalks. Vanessa got out of her taxi and walked with other pedestrians between stopped vehicles in heavy traffic across two streets of the many that intersected at Piccadilly Circus. She reached the square and paused briefly below the statue of Eros while glancing around the city. It wasn't long before she spotted Scott Morgan coming up the steps from the underground railway station. He looked as serene as ever in his casual but name-brand tweeds and hat.

Scott saw her waiting and lifted a hand.

"Good morning," he called.

He smiled as he walked up, then noted her expression. "Dark news about France, isn't it? The fighting is going beastly for the soldiers at Verdun."

Verdun was known for the horrendous battle between the French and Germans during World War I. France had won the war, but at a great and terrible price. The French had fought with honor in white gloves while the Germans turned mammoth artillery upon them, slaughtering them without mercy. France, in the spirit of Napoleon, had stood alone.

"Is it true," she asked absently as they walked slowly away, "that in the Louvre gardens there is a grotesque statue the French nation put up after their victory in 1918?"

"Ah, so you know of it? Yes. It's called La Victoire." Scott shook his head in disbelief. "It's a trivial little stone statue alien to the true valiant spirit of the French soldier."

"Put up to honor their dead from the war?"

"Not for honor, but something very different. The artist seems to have deliberately represented his country's victory not as a noble woman, but as a prostitute. The best I can tell it was as though France felt that they had sold their soldiers cheaply. It insults and belittles their honor. It seems as though the price they paid for their victory was so great, that afterward they considered compromise and surrender to tyranny to be a better virtue than the honor of their hard-won liberty."

She was indignant. "Do the new generations of young men and women really believe that?"

He looked at her thoughtfully. "Certainly not you, but many now in French leadership are pacifists."

"No wonder then, after La Victoire, that the sons of those World War I soldiers don't think it's worth sacrificing themselves to face the onslaught of planes and tanks pouring across their border. If they fight and die, perhaps little more than a new trivial statue will be raised to celebrate their effort!"

"The French situation is more complex than that," he said, taking her elbow as they dashed across a side street toward a café. "The soldiers of the previous war were promised a new life. It never came. France is now cynical—cynical of the British for not being there thickly enough in the French trenches, cynical of any new promises Churchill is making them right now, and perhaps even cynical of themselves. Ah, the French! Sometimes magnificent, sometimes frustrating, most of the time, both."

The French soldiers who died at Verdun did not die for such a *victoire* as the shameless little statue implied. Of this, Vanessa was sure. Down deep in their hearts, she thought the loyal Frenchmen must know it too.

They entered the warm café, which smelled deliciously of fresh bakery goods, tea, and coffee. As they stood appraising the pastries on display behind the glass counter, he said casually: "I sense it didn't go well with your brother. I'm sorry."

"You can tell? I'd hoped to conceal my feelings."

"He disapproves of your visit?"

"This is one time when a bit of compromise might help the situation."

"But you haven't changed your mind because of his disapproval?"

She noted the hopefulness in his tone and looked at him. His warm brown eyes were alive with interest.

"No, I haven't changed my mind. I've my own reasons for wanting to see—Robert."

"Good." He smiled, showing more of his suave charm. "I like a woman who knows her own mind and acts upon it."

She could have told him it didn't matter what he liked in a woman, because she wasn't his, nor was she going to be in the future, but that would have been unnecessary and haughty on her part.

They seated themselves by a window facing the cars and pedestrians, all rushing to and fro on what must have been important business. Scott, in complete contrast to the scene outside, interlaced his fingers and rested his hands on the table, watching her quietly.

"I called your father last night."

He seemed to wait for her response.

"Yes?"

"He wants us to come to the Isle of Mull as soon as possible. When would that be convenient for you?"

Now that the plans were laid, she felt a little more unsettled in her decision than she had in the taxi with Kylie. It was becoming real now, the face-to-face meeting with her father in his own home.

She took a moment to add milk to her tea. "You weren't concerned that I might change my mind by this morning?"

"I took you at your word. You said you'd come, and I was sure this hotshot brother of yours wouldn't alter your determination."

She stirred slowly and avoided his eyes. It was rather disconcerting to have a man, nearly a stranger, settle on his own ideas of who you were inside that came close to the truth.

"What did my father say?"

He tried his coffee. "He was very pleased you'd accepted his invitation."

She had never told Kylie or her mother, but Vanessa had read up on everything she could find on Robert Miles and the second woman he'd married, Norah Benton. When Vanessa had been in high school, the New York theatrical paper and showbiz magazines had been full of stories of his career in London, and also gossip about his personal life. He was very "protectively jealous," the gossip columnists wrote, of his "lovely Norah," who gave up her acting career when she had their child, Lucy.

Vanessa had felt aggrieved over her father's love for another woman, especially Norah Benton. Vanessa hadn't thought the actress had half the character of her mother. As yet, Scott hadn't said much about her, and she asked him about it.

"What Norah thought doesn't matter," he said quietly. "She's no longer living. Did you read about her death? It was in most of the theatrical papers, here and in New York."

"I gave up reading about actors and actresses after high school," she said. "It was depressing to hear about one marriage after another ending in divorce."

There was disapproval in his eyes, or was it sadness? "Well, at least Robert and Norah stayed together."

He said this as though she were proven wrong in her assessment of the theatrical elite.

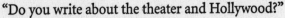

"Do you write about the theater and Hollywood?"

"Not Hollywood. I've mainly done research on the historical theater. Shakespeare, mostly, but not limited to that."

"Not research on actors and actresses?"

He gave her a quick look, his face blank. "Oh, sometimes. Not often. Mostly research on the parts they played, or the playwrights themselves and what motivated them on a certain subject. Research papers of this kind are published for serious drama schools and university classes. It didn't pay all that well, so I began freelancing. Your father hired me two years ago after he read something I'd written on a play he starred in during 1936. I think I mentioned yesterday he was writing a family legacy on the Gowrie family of Scotland."

"Yes."

"It's his first, and probably his last as well. So he's anxious that it's done professionally."

She looked at him and thought how pleasantly relaxed he now seemed. She found that in his company, she too became less tense.

"You went to work for my father after Norah died? Then you didn't know her?"

He pushed his cup away. "Did I imply I came to work for Robert after she died? I'm sorry, I didn't mean to suggest it. I worked for both of them six months before her death. And I've stayed on at your father's wishes."

"Oh. Then you did know her."

"Of course. We all dined together and got on fairly well. Except that—well, that doesn't matter now."

The relaxed mood now seemed as though it could vanish almost instantly.

"Needless to say we all—those of us who had come to know and appreciate her—have taken her loss hard. But really, none of this applies to your visit. Robert wants to see you for personal reasons of his own, and while I understand his feelings at this time,

I'm not one to pry. And your father isn't the sort to put up with prying from anyone if he doesn't want it."

"When you say his feelings 'at this time,' do you mean that he is more open because of his health problems as well as the war?"

He smiled, but the friendliness had left his eyes and impatience now flickered, showing her that Scott Morgan could become touchy when he thought she was out of bounds.

"Yes both, by all means. I don't want to hurry you along, but the sooner I can make arrangements for our journey to Scotland, the better."

"Yes, please do. I'm quite finished, thank you." She reached for her pocketbook and snapped it open, glancing in a small mirror to check her makeup. She caught a glimpse of someone behind them near the door that startled her.

Scott stood, left some change on the table, and went to pay at the cash register.

Vanessa turned in her seat just in time to see the man going out the door. Kerc Trevalyan? Why would he be following her and Scott? It couldn't be a coincidence, because she was quite certain that he had been watching them in the café, and when he'd seen Scott go to the cash register to pay, had chosen that moment to make his exit so as not to be noticed on their way out. Through the café window she watched the man striding away toward a newsstand down the street.

She snapped her pocketbook closed and rose from her chair, taking up her jacket. Scott came back, and they left the café. On the sidewalk she looked up at him.

"Goodbye. Thanks for the brunch. It's a pleasant day, and I think I'll walk from here."

"All the way to the DP clinic?"

"I've some shopping to do," she said lightly.

He laughed. "The working hours of the volunteer. And you had me feeling sorry for you. Well, all right then. Robert has concerns that travel restrictions may soon apply. He wants us to set out as soon as possible. If I can arrange tickets on the train to Glasgow for tomorrow, can you be ready?"

She hadn't thought she would depart so soon, but now that her mind was fully decided, there was no reason to delay. "Yes. I'll tell Mrs. Warnstead when I see her this afternoon. The family's been urging me to return to New York before the war makes travel too difficult. With what's happening in France, they'll likely approve of my visit to meet my father in Scotland." All of them, that is, except Kylie. And even he knew her well enough to realize her resolve would not be easily derailed once her mind was made up. She'd write him as soon as she got to the island and try to soothe matters.

"Scotland isn't likely to be much safer than England," he said. "Nazi U-boats prowl off the Atlantic coast. And if there is an invasion of Britain, as we all fear, the coast of Scotland and Ireland are danger points."

It seemed as though no place in Europe was safe from Nazi terror and aggression. "Trouble awaits us all, I'm afraid," she said. She held out her hand.

Scott smiled, and his sensible warnings seemed to evaporate. "But I've a notion you won't be sorry you came to Gowrie House, Vanessa—I can call you that, can't I?"

"Yes..." and she withdrew the hand he had held a moment too long.

Whether or not trouble awaited her during her visit to see her father remained to be seen. It was growing clear to her that trouble hadn't arrived with the invitation from her father so much as it had yesterday afternoon on the wharf when she'd met Kerc Trevalyan.

They parted on the sidewalk with Scott's promise to call her that evening at the Warnstead home. He would try to arrange tickets to Glasgow.

Vanessa glanced down the street toward the newsstand. She turned and walked in that direction. When she arrived, the fisherman was gone. Surely she hadn't imagined seeing him in the café? His image was indelibly stuck in her mind. There hadn't been any doubt about the unfriendliness toward her at the warehouse yesterday; it still made her skin crawl remembering. She frowned. Even his dark roguish looks were sinister. He reminded her of a pirate.

Buying a copy of the *Times* and folding it beneath her arm, she left the newsstand and walked briskly down the sidewalk wondering if he were watching her pass from inside some shop. Perhaps he intended to follow her. Uneasy, she quickened her steps. She saw a taxi and hailed it over to the side of the curb. Quickly she got in back. "Harrods," she said, glancing over her shoulder in the direction from which she had come. She had lost him—or he had never been following her in the first place. She leaned back into the seat, frowning again. She opened the paper and the bold black headlines of France's woes jumped out at her. Grimly she read the stories of the French government's flight from Paris and saw that Italy had declared war on England. President Roosevelt's words about Nazi Germany's invasion of France repeated themselves in her mind for the rest of the ride through downtown London: "The hand that held the dagger has stuck it into the back of its neighbor!"

PART TWO

Scotland

6

The Isle of Mull was not far across the Atlantic from the coast of Scotland. The single-sail boat had left the mainland at noon. Vanessa, who had boarded at Oban with Scott, was sitting in the boat's well trying to keep somewhat dry as the chilling sea spray wet her face. The wind whipped her golden-brown hair beneath the scarf that matched her gray-green eyes. She was staring intently in what she believed was the direction of the island's promontory, anticipating the lifting of the dense mist so she could see what Scott was describing—"There's a massive black rock jutting out over the water called Devil's Cliff."

She shivered in the bracing wind, blinking against the startling icy spray. The salty brine tasted like tears on her lips.

"There it is," came his avid voice. He pointed. "Can you see it?"

She squinted against the wind in the direction of Duart Castle and the lighthouse to make out the face of the rock thrusting up boldly over the waters of the sea.

"Foreboding, isn't it?" Kerc said.

Kerc had boarded at Oban before she and Scott. Vanessa had been troubled at his presence, refusing to believe it could be mere coincidence. Kerc had spoken little. "It's because we're *foreigners*," Scott had whispered to her. "The Scots think of the British as intruders." She had smothered a smile. Not that there was anything amusing about Kerc. Her suspicion that he was following her grew stronger. She'd mentioned this to Scott, but he had dismissed her concerns. "He had little choice but to board a ferry after his boat was damaged in the German attack. He left it at Portsmouth for repairs."

Even so, how had he arranged to be at Oban and take the small boat to Mull at the same time as she? Was he trying to make her change her mind and go back to London?

He was standing a few feet away, one arm hugging the mast. She noticed that outdoors in the light he looked younger than she remembered him in the shadows of the warehouse, probably several years less than Scott.

Until this moment Kerc had given the impression of being unaware of anyone else on the boat, and even less aware of the wind, which occasionally carried a splash of seawater. He'd kept his back toward them, looking instead at the wheeling white gulls overhead. There was something about him she didn't like, and it had nothing at all to do with his status as caretaker.

He still wore the same rough clothes, but this time he had added a pair of wide sunglasses, presumably as a shield from the sea spray, there being a lack of sunshine. This young Scotsman's rough and swarthy appearance matched his scuffed boots and mood of hostility. There was no denying his earthy good looks, but how could her half sister see anything "magical" about his care of the rose garden?

Vanessa didn't respond to his comment about Devil's Cliff. She looked away and left it to Scott to either answer or ignore him.

Let him stand there by the mast if he wanted to. His feet were steady in an inch of swishing water while she and Scott turned a little queasy. He appeared to be as at home on the Atlantic as he was in the garden. She believed he was standing just to embarrass Scott, who looked as though he might be on the verge of feeling seasick.

Scott's brown eyes were speculative. "Oh, I don't know," he said with a trace of congeniality. "I've seen that cliff a hundred times since coming here from Edinburgh. It doesn't look foreboding to me. It's probably just the name Devil's Cliff. It's the sort of thing the Scottish Islanders like to create tales about to frighten newcomers—especially Londoners." He smiled. "Around this area of Scotland, when it's all wispy and fogged in at night, superstitious folktales abound around the hearth. They help pass the long evenings." He looked down at Vanessa, smiling indulgently. "That's probably all there is to it."

She wondered if there was any insinuation that the caretaker spent too much time spooking Lucy with Scottish tales.

"Aye, that's part of it," Kerc said. "Though reality is often at the bottom of what gets the flavor of 'island superstition,' as you call it."

Vanessa looked at Scott, folding her arms against the cold wind and hunching her chin deeper under her coat collar trying to stay warm. So this was Scotland's summer!

"How are the trout biting around the streams and lakes?" Scott asked. "I was thinking of inviting Miss Miles out for a bit of fishing while she's here."

"Biting fine." Still holding onto the mast with one arm, he asked: "Need to hire a boat?"

Vanessa glanced uneasily at Scott. *No*, her eyes said.

"We can use her father's if we decide to go out on the lakes," Scott said. "Miss Miles will be staying at his estate for a few weeks."

Vanessa could feel the caretaker's stare. She looked straight ahead, offering no information, remembering his suggestion that she not come to Gowrie House, and wishing Scott hadn't mentioned her plans. She was relieved when Kerc changed the subject back to the rock.

"Devil's Cliff lives up to its name. Many a grim Spaniard made his watery grave hereabouts when a galleon was sunk near Tobermory."

Vanessa turned her head and watched him through squinting lashes as the cold wind blew into her face. She particularly noticed his speech when he said "aboot" for "about." It was rather attractive.

Scott grinned, the wind touching his dark gold hair. "When was that, a century or two ago?"

"Thereabouts," he repeated sagely. "In 1588, to be exact." Noticing Vanessa's thoughtful glance, he reached into his shabby peacoat and took out a stick of chewing gum.

"We don't need to worry about pirates now," Scott said, amused. Then his thoughts must have sobered him. He frowned. "It's the ruddy Germans. Soon they'll be sitting just across the English Channel threatening both England and Scotland."

Kerc gestured his capped head toward the cliff where the lighthouse stood. "Someone was killed on Devil's Cliff just a few weeks ago," he said, ignoring Scott's reference to the war.

Vanessa's skin tingled. She looked toward the rock. Blowing mist curled and swirled like whitish gray serpents.

"Did someone fall while climbing it?" she asked, breaking her silence. Was her imagination running amok, or was there a twinge of satisfaction to his smile?

"So it's said," Kerc responded.

Vanessa's slight gasp elicited a concerned glance her way from Scott.

"So it's said? What else would it be?" she asked.

But Scott shrugged his dismissal. "Forget it, my dear. Gossip, that's all. You know how it goes in these parts. Come, Kerc," he said shortly. "You're upsetting the young lady."

"Sorry, Miss Miles. Wasn't intending it."

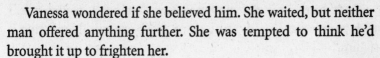

Vanessa wondered if she believed him. She waited, but neither man offered anything further. She was tempted to think he'd brought it up to frighten her.

Captain Duncan removed his pipe from his mouth and spoke for just the second time since leaving the mainland. "Aye, there was a write-up in the paper about it—she slipped. Said she was going there to meet her boyfriend."

Kerc looked down at the bearded captain. "What does the paper know about it?"

"What do any of us know about it?" the captain asked quietly.

The scream of the gulls following the boat into the bay sounded like a feminine shriek. Vanessa's eyes swerved to the rock. When she looked back at Kerc, he'd walked to the other end of the boat and turned his shoulder toward them. There he stood, gazing out on the gray, choppy sea.

She took a moment to study the boat captain, an ordinary looking man somewhere in his sixties, placid, with his duckbill cap and pipe. He was the living image of a typical Scottish captain in a sea painting.

Scott leaned a little closer to her, hands in his jacket pockets. The wind tossed his hair. "Don't let Kerc upset you," he said in a low voice. "I warned you about him, remember? I told you he was the surly type. The island inspector ruled the girl's death accidental. That should be enough to satisfy any of us. If there were more to it, the authorities from Glasgow or Edinburgh would be here."

"Who was she, do you know?"

"No." He hunched his shoulders against the chilly wind, looking toward the rock. "I've not really had a chance to get to know the regulars on the island. Your father keeps me pretty busy."

"Did the caretaker know her?"

"I've wondered that myself. She was a local. The daughter of a tavern keeper, I think the paper said."

Scott turned his glance toward Kerc. "Rather a strange one. I wish your father would dismiss him. Maybe you could mention it to him."

Her brows lifted. "Me? I'm hardly in a position to tell Robert Miles whom he should have on his employee list. I would think he'd be inclined to listen to you."

The corners of his mouth creased, hinting his concerned displeasure. "Your father is so preoccupied with his biography that he doesn't bother with complaints about his employees. Then again, Kerc appears to be a fixture at Gowrie House. He's been treading the turf there nearly all his life."

"You mean Robert has gotten used to him?"

"It's tradition. The way the upper class think about their servants. It's almost an old-fashioned master/slave sort of relationship, typical of the old days of fiefdoms. Esquires, you know, and all that sort of thing. Face it, live-in help on the island is hard to come by. Most of the workers either come from Glasgow or London. These islanders are a proud people. Many of them have businesses of their own, or are fishermen. The young girls marry, or are sent to Edinburgh to college, and most don't return."

Vanessa thought of the young woman who had gone out to meet her boyfriend on Devil's Cliff. "A tavern maid," Scott had said in a dismissive tone. For a moment, looking out at the mist, Vanessa wondered about the girl, what she'd been like, what were her hopes and dreams. Did she have any? Certainly, all young women did. Perhaps her biggest dream was wrapped up in the man she'd gone to meet in secret. Now why had she thought it must be a clandestine meeting? To think so had seemed natural, but it mightn't have been that way at all. Maybe they'd intended to watch the sea, holding hands and walking along the cliff's path, making happy plans for after the war.

She looked once more at the black jutting rock. Kerc had questioned the paper's conclusion that the tavern girl had slipped, evoking a contrary response from both the boat captain and

Scott. It was likely the two men had contradicted him, not wishing to upset her, which left her estimation of Kerc where it had been before: He didn't mind upsetting her because he didn't want her at the estate. Well, he was doing a good job of it.

The gusts of tart, spine-tingling wind curled the edges of the waves into gray froth, giving the sea a hostile look. On Duart Point she glimpsed a lighthouse and heard a bell. She guessed it came from somewhere very near the formidable black rock. Strange, that the lighthouse looked sinister to her, the very opposite of its purpose of guidance and comfort. The wispy fog swirled along like lost cobwebs.

"The lighthouse is historic," Scott commented. "People visit it for outdoor picnics in the summer."

She didn't respond. *There's really no reason, other than the war, to feel melancholy,* Vanessa reminded herself, putting the brakes on her runaway emotions. Her relationship with Andy Warnstead was progressing as well as could be expected during such a time as this; and, while something as serious as marriage hadn't yet entered their plans, they both took it for granted that an engagement waited in the wings. And now, the most stunning circumstance of all, the request to come meet her father. All was not dark and sinister. How could it be when she had a wonderful heavenly Father to hope and trust in?

The trip had been pleasant enough too. Scott had arranged for her to take the train from London, spend the evening at an inn in Glasgow, and then this morning he'd rented an automobile to bring them to Oban on the mainland. And now they had almost arrived on Mull.

But this summer day is neither warm nor bright, she thought, wishing for the fragrance of wild heather. So far, both in London and Scotland, the weather was as dour as the withering spirits of all Europe under the assault of the invading German army. The city of Paris was in turmoil, like a forsaken queen, her streets congested by a massive exodus.

But this day on Mull knew an undisturbed peace. They had passed Duart Castle guarding the approach to the Sound of Mull and entered the island's quiet loch where the water was shallow. Scott said that on a clear sunny day the bay's quiet currents would foam gently over the shore, and the water was the color of topaz. The captain eased the boat along the wharf. Scott gestured toward land. "A wonderfully peaceful scene, isn't it? Just look at all those neat little rows of whitewashed cottages. Life here is traditional and tranquil most of the time. The families go back for more generations than I'd care to keep track."

She learned that the cottages belonged to local fishermen and their families. She could see further back, past the cottages, toward the meadowed hills where there were more small houses, or "crofts" as Scott said they were called. She imagined warm sweet shortbread biscuits and tea waiting beside stone hearths where fires would sputter a welcome to the returning fishermen, husbands, and fathers. *A life worth living,* she thought nostalgically, *and worth dying to preserve.*

"Well, here we are," Scott told her cheerfully a few moments later. "Welcome to Mull."

Vanessa stepped ashore, looking about her on the wharf. In spite of this particularly cold gray day the heather was in bloom. She could see one rough hillside that was covered with a flowering quilt the color of reddish purple.

"It's delightful," she said. The heather should be sweet, but standing on the beach, the sea breeze was all she could smell: the salty brine of the sea and someone's catch of fish.

There were two fishermen mending nets who barely gave them a glance, but two small boys on the jetty stared curiously. A small dog stretched lazily, then sat waiting to see what might happen next. Gulls circled expectantly, hoping some tasty tidbits would be tossed their way. The worn jetty creaked and groaned with complaints beneath her feet.

From the corner of her eye she saw Kerc Trevalyan leap easily from the side of the boat onto the landing planks and, without a glance their way, stride off on his own. She watched him cautiously as he left the wharf and made his way toward a grassy hill. There was a brown dirt road which cut across to the other side of the hill through the heather, and looked as though it might circle back around toward a rocky slope facing the sea.

Her bags of luggage and Scott's two suitcases were stowed on the wharf, and when she wondered how they could carry it all the way into the village, he told her that one of the locals named Billy, who at times worked at the Gowrie House stables, would bring it up to the house.

"There aren't many automobiles. The village is small, and most of the narrow streets are very steep. The locals all walk, just as the generations did before them. Change occurs slowly here. There's no reason for it to be otherwise. But even here the war's influence may be felt. A few of the young men have already joined the BEF. Most likely, if they survive the fighting and return after the war, they'll be so different," he said sadly, "that they'll give up fishing the way their fathers did."

She walked along beside him up the street and away from the loch. "Does that disappoint you?"

He looked at her with a sudden smile. "That they give up fishing? Well, yes. When new ways replace old traditions, some things are not as pleasant as before. But then, I'm not from this Scottish fishing village. I'm American, the same as you."

"No Scottish ancestors who liked to catch fish?" she asked with a smile.

"Well, maybe for sport. There was an uncle who taught at Edinburgh University, but that was before I was born."

She paused on the climb to rest and look back. The mist was rising in places and she could see some distant hills and a small patch of blue sky. The loch, with its various-sized boats and vessels tied next to the wooden jetty, looked picturesque enough to have on a postcard to send to the Warnsteads in London, but not even this beautiful scene would draw Kylie.

"I suppose I should have asked if you minded the walk. Around here, it's the main transportation. That, and cycling."

"I like to walk. Especially after a boat ride," she said cheerfully, though feeling slightly unsteady.

"It's not far to the house now. The gate entrance is up the road, behind that hill. They'll place you in a room facing the bay and the lighthouse. There's a great view. It's not always misty like this. The afternoons are clear in the summer, but the mist rolls in again at night."

They came to the road and followed it around a hill that was covered in green.

"It's a small, gradual climb. Your father walks it most days, so you can see it isn't difficult. There are stones on the road, though, so if you'll permit—" and he casually took her arm to lead the way.

The wind switched directions, and the swirling mist that had settled close to the ground was lifting and blowing away, revealing tall grasses that rippled gracefully. Amid them there were splashy mounds of summer flowers growing among the rough and marshy land.

It's delightful here, Vanessa was thinking, lost in the quiet space and gentle winds smelling now of heather as well as the sea.

When they reached the top of the narrow dirt roadway, a large, mostly flat meadowland faced the sea. Inland, there were more gently rolling mounds of wild purplish red heather. As the wind came rolling across the fields the poignant fragrance was breathtaking.

They had come to the end of the dirt road. One section forked left and seemed to circle back around toward the loch. The right section wound past a wide field of bracken. There, on an elongated tongue of land above the restless gray sea, Vanessa got her first view of Gowrie House.

"A bit awesome, isn't it?" Scott said when she remained silent, just taking in the sight.

She stood admiring the estate until she saw someone walking across the heathered field as though having come from the loch. From this distance she couldn't be sure but she guessed it was Kerc. The dirt road he'd taken must have had a shortcut through the brackened hills. His head turned in their direction, but he didn't stop, nor did he indicate that he noticed them. He strode on, and presently she heard the distant, impatient whining of dogs. A few moments later, two large animals came bounding through the heather to meet him.

She glanced toward Scott to see his reaction. He was frowning. She expected a comment, but he remained silent.

"There's a shortcut from the harbor?" she asked.

"He knows every inch of soil around here. As do those ruffian dogs of his. I don't trust my way around those fields. They can prove dangerous."

"Why is that?"

Scott looked away from Kerc, his brown eyes screening his earlier thoughts. "For one thing, my dear, if you don't know your way, it's easy to get lost. Much of that area quickly turns into marsh. There's more than one bog out there, I'm told. A sheep wandered off into one just last week and was swallowed up."

"How awful. Does it happen often?"

"Often enough, I'm sorry to say."

Vanessa shuddered at the idea. Evidently, the caretaker knew where the bogs were. He was crossing the moor with an unhesitant stride, the dogs running happily at his heels. She glanced at Scott again. "He doesn't appear to be worried about it."

"No. As I told you, he grew up here. He went away for a few years, doing what, who knows? I only know that much about him because the old girl, Iris, likes to chat." He smiled.

"Iris?" They were walking up the narrow dirt road approaching the gate to the estate's grounds.

"The cook. She's some relative of Kerc's and devoted to your father. She thinks he's the greatest actor who ever lived."

She pressed on with her questions about the caretaker, careful to keep her true concerns hidden. She didn't want to get Kerc in trouble with her father until she knew more about him.

"His mother worked in the house as a culinary maid, I think. She had him out of wedlock. You know the type. She was also a bit crackers, I'm told. Not all there, if you know what I mean."

Vanessa remained silent. Oh, dear. Was that why he behaved strangely? She folded her arms against the chilling sea wind.

"I'm sorry to hear that. Does his mother still work in the house?"

"No. She died when Kerc was just a little boy." Scott's fingers tightened on her arm as he steered her away from the edge of the road. He changed the subject. "Well, what do you think of the house?"

Vanessa looked up at an old Scottish baronial castle built of gray stone, complete with high windows, turrets, and a stone balustrade. The traditional lion statuary with the addition of falcons, the beloved bird of feudal lords since before the Middle Ages, was tinted green with moss where it stood guard at the partially open gate.

Kerc must have passed this way. Where were the two large dogs?

For all the interest Gowrie House generated in certain historical quarters, Vanessa found it rather grim with an austere lordliness; and impregnable, even arrogant, in its ability to weather the stormy Atlantic since the 1600s.

"Its original owner was Earl Gowrie, an ally of King James I. Though Norah had an older brother, her father left the estate to her because Vernon and his wife, Theo, were childless. It has been thought for years that Lucy would inherit the estate upon the death of Robert. Every summer your father would come here to vacation with Norah and Lucy. When he retired from his acting career, he moved here permanently. Norah also adored the estate, especially its intriguing history. She spent months researching her family roots. Lucy would come here to be with her parents when school was out. She attended a fine college in Switzerland. Upon graduating she came back to make this her home. Lucy has always loved it here."

Vanessa didn't want to think about the special times Norah and Lucy had enjoyed here with her father while she and Kylie were excluded. *I shouldn't be selfish, I know,* she thought sadly, *but it's so hard to let go of the pain and loss.*

"We couldn't afford vacations," she commented, not knowing what she expected him to say, or even if she wanted him to say anything. "Mother would bring us to Coney Island on the Fourth of July. That was it."

Scott remained loyal to Robert Miles, and perhaps Norah as well, by not showing his feelings.

"Well, you're seeing Scotland now," he responded cheerfully, as though it made up for an absent father.

It wasn't the same. Adulthood changed things considerably, but she held back her comment. She had no real wish to discuss her grievances with Scott. He wasn't really on her side and she knew it. There was no cause to think he had changed now that they had arrived. His thoughts, she believed, were with her half sister, though she hoped she was wrong.

She had noticed that whenever he spoke of Lucy there came a gentleness in his voice. She stole a glance at him. The light, sunny hair, the pleasant brown eyes, and the quiet handsomeness of his face would make it easy to fall for Scott Morgan. Not that she had any need to become enamored. *Of course not,* she thought hurriedly. There was Andy Warnstead: any girl's dream of what a charming and dashing RAF pilot should be. She glanced again toward Scott, who, in his late twenties seemed mature and even a little fatherly toward her. Was maturity something she found attractive in a man because she had missed it while growing up?

Emotional volatility and a firebrand personality were tendencies she could do without. Her man must be steady, calm, comfortably predictable, and loyal. Whatever Lucy was looking for in a man, Scott had implied she'd found it in someone else, but he'd not yet explained what that man was like.

The house stood on a windy hillock overlooking a glen that sloped gracefully toward granite cliffs and the choppy sea fringed with white foam. Westward there were more mountains, but the sea was in view toward the south and east ends of the island. All seemed touched with the sweetness of peace. Was it an illusion? There came a hum of the wind through mounds of tiny flowers—periwinkle, canary, and rose hues—showering Vanessa with a belief that all the world with its bombs and burning buildings existed only in distorted imaginations. But then she noticed a croft, or bungalow as she knew it, at the far end of the glen behind the house. Vanessa saw the front door open and the caretaker step out.

She ventured a brief glance in Kerc's direction. He watched her as he had before, his hands shoved in his coat pockets, the wind tossing the coal black shock of hair across his forehead. "A bit crackers." Starkly cold, Scott's words blew across her soul. The Scotsman seemed to her a calculating force of steely anger just waiting to be unleashed at a time of his own choosing.

7

Vanessa imagined the curtained windows staring down at her blankly, uncaring. The stone steps running up to the Scottish mansion climbed to a heavy mahogany door. On either side sat big blue pots with red geraniums. The gleaming brass knocker glared imperiously down at her, discouraging her from disrupting its smug solitude.

So this was the mansion owned by Robert Miles, the acclaimed Shakespearean actor—a stranger.

She was willing to try to build a bridge across her painful past, but while the goal was noble, was it realistic? The question continued to tug at her heart. Had God sent her here to bring about reconciliation before the war made it impossible?

She shoved her mittened hands deeper into her coat pockets and took a deep breath. For a moment she had an impulse to turn and hurry back to the jetty and ask Captain Duncan to return her to the mainland.

Scott broke the spell. "Well, shall we brave the dragon's lair?"

Vanessa glanced at him. He smiled.

She stepped inside a huge hall, larger and wider than even the room at the Glasgow Inn where she'd stayed last night.

"I'll tell Robert you're here," he said, and he was walking toward a sweeping staircase when a woman's voice said, "My father's asleep. I'd rather you didn't disturb him right now, Scott."

Vanessa looked up to the top of the stairs. The girl, a few years younger than herself, was obviously her half sister, Lucy, the daughter of actress Norah Benton.

Lucy had taken after her mother. She was tall, dark haired, and sophisticated. Vanessa felt the measuring once-over her half sister gave her. If there'd been any doubt whether or not she was wanted here, Lucy's cool but polite dismissal was plain enough.

"Hello, Lucy," Scott said casually. "This is your half sister, Vanessa."

"Of course. Welcome to Gowrie House, Vanessa. Please come up. I'll show you to your room." Lucy turned away. "The housekeeper has the afternoon off. Scott, do you have Vanessa's luggage?"

Scott shot Vanessa a glance, as if wondering how she would react to the indifferent reception. "It's down at the wharf. I'll send Billy for it." He frowned. "Where is the boy, anyway? He's usually loitering around the front porch or under your feet whenever you don't need him."

Scott was taking charge, and with his hand on Vanessa's elbow, was politely urging her up the stairs. *As if he's afraid I'll change my mind about staying,* she thought, perturbed. She glanced at him, and he seemed to read her thoughts. He smiled, a challenge in his brown eyes. *Your father wants you here,* he seemed to say. He leaned toward her ear. "Don't run away just because Lucy hasn't decided yet."

That was exactly what Vanessa felt like doing. "I'm not the running away kind."

"I was banking on that."

For you or me? Vanessa wondered. She was still wondering about Scott's motive for wanting her here.

"Give her time," he was saying in a low voice. "She'll come around. She wants a sister badly."

Would she come around? Vanessa had doubts about how much Lucy wanted a sister to share Robert Miles with, even apart from sharing her inheritance. Not that Vanessa expected anything, but Lucy must be wondering what their father's plans were.

That Vanessa was an intruder was clear from Lucy's attitude, though she was being cordial. *Mere finishing-school manners*, Vanessa thought. *They mean little.*

"Billy's down at the stables," Lucy explained from over her shoulder as she led the way along the upstairs hall. It was warm with polished wood tones and gleaming with silvery wall mirrors housed in lattice-wood frames. "He's mesmerized by my new horse. He's been warned not to handle him until Jodrell has him trained."

"Jodrell?"

Vanessa noted something like surprise in Scott's voice. Then, again, it might have been disapproval, because Lucy, pausing and turning, looked at him with questioning brows. "Yes, *Jodrell*," she emphasized. "He's exceptional with horses. Everyone knows that."

"I suppose Theo asked him to help with the new horse," Scott said stiffly.

"And Father," she stated. "The estate needs someone like Jodrell to manage things now that Father is so distracted with that book."

Vanessa could see the tightness in Lucy's face when she mentioned the book.

Scott lapsed into silence. He shrugged. "It's none of my affair. Your family knows what it wants."

There was something more to his casual deference, for again Lucy glanced at him. Their eyes held. "Jodrell *is* part of the family," she stated, a splash of color coming to her cheeks. "And *I* wanted him here." Scott's mouth hardened. Vanessa, witnessing something she shared no part in, looked away, covering her embarrassment. *I should have stayed in London. Maybe Kylie was right.*

Lucy was saying now, "I think you'll be comfortable in here, Vanessa. This used to be my room until I moved to the third floor."

The bedroom was the feminine, pretty sort with muted blue blossoms on eggshell damask coverings and furnished with golden oak. There was a small terrace with a private stairway to the garden and a view of the sea toward the mainland.

"I hope you'll like it," Lucy said as though speaking to a business associate.

"Yes, thank you. It's quite lovely."

Vanessa walked to the terrace and looked out toward the distant lighthouse.

"As you'll soon discover, Lucy is a lover of horses," Scott told her. "There are wonderful animals here for riding, if that's of any interest to you. Lucy will be happy to set you up with one of her more gentle horses."

"Yes, do you ride?" Lucy drew aside the damask drapes to let in the light.

"I've done some riding in England, and a little in New York. Kylie and I used to go with college friends to the stables in upstate New York during Labor Day weekend."

"Kylie?" Lucy looked at her with blank dark eyes rimmed with lashes.

"My—our brother. He's in the RAF."

"Oh, yes. I'd forgotten." She turned to Scott, glancing at her watch. "I'm meeting Jodrell for dinner tonight on the mainland. He'll return with me tomorrow for an extended stay. You'll see that Vanessa is comfortable, won't you? Aunt Theo will be here as well."

Vanessa was still smarting over the indifference Lucy had shown to her own half brother. Then she became aware of a strained silence, and she turned from the window to see them looking at one another, something passing between them that made Vanessa feel sure of Scott's romantic interest in Lucy.

"You're going tonight?" Scott repeated.

"Yes, tonight." Lucy sounded defensive. "We've had this dinner planned at his cousin's house for a week. Theo was supposed to go with us, but she's decided to stay here. Jodrell and I will return Sunday afternoon." She turned toward Vanessa. "My aunt, Theo, will be here. And, naturally—Scott."

Lucy went out the bedroom door with Scott following. In the hall she remembered to look back at Vanessa. "If you want to ride tomorrow morning, Scott can arrange it. A jaunt around most of the island on a clear summer morning is wonderful. We do have clear days." She smiled for the first time, and her entire countenance changed to where she was not simply attractive, but pretty. The change on Scott's face was also noticeable as he watched her. A light seemed to have come on in his heart.

Lucy left them and went downstairs. Her muted voice was heard, followed by what sounded like a mild rebuke by someone—another woman? Aunt Theo? A moment later the front door shut and someone hurried across the graveled yard.

Trouble, Vanessa thought with an inner sigh. She hoped it wasn't over her arrival, but what else would it be?

If she had deceived herself into thinking that she would be welcomed into a close-knit family that until now had willingly excluded her, she was rudely mistaken. Lucy seemed to have no wish for a half sister coming into her life and bringing added complications at this late stage. She had her plans, seemed bent on following them to her own satisfaction, and no one, especially her father's daughter from a first marriage, was going to change things. That also included Scott, if anything could be determined from the tense exchange between them. It appeared as if Lucy was enamored with Jodrell.

She turned to Scott, who didn't appear concerned over her dilemma but his own. There was no mistaking the reality of his interest in Lucy. That would account for the restrained displeasure he'd shown when questioning Lucy about meeting Jodrell on the mainland. Vanessa felt a twinge of regret seeing his heart already bound. She stiffened her resolve against it. What business was it of hers? And what had she secretly expected—or hoped—from Scott Morgan?

"I can't help wondering if Robert is really asleep," she said unhappily. "Is this Lucy's way of keeping me from him for as long as possible?"

A flash of disapproval in his eyes set her back.

"Don't rush to judgment where Lucy's concerned, my dear. She's been through a lot recently. The death of her mother was a dreadful blow for her. They were very close."

Not a word about me, Vanessa thought. *Haven't I been through emotional pain too?* She opened her mouth to try and justify her doubts about Lucy's welcome, then caught herself in time to keep from blundering further. There would be little use in implying anything unfavorable about Lucy to Scott. If there'd been something mutual between them in the not-too-distant past, Lucy didn't feel that way anymore, unless she was deliberately trying to make Scott jealous.

Despite her wiser judgment, Vanessa wondered if she'd been hoping for something deeper to develop between herself and Scott. She felt a twinge of guilt when remembering that Andy was putting his life on the line every time he took his Hurricane up into the sky to face the Luftwaffe. Here in Scotland, however, the war seemed far away, even nonexistent. That, of course, was a false impression that time would counter.

"I'll find Billy and send him out to get the luggage," he said abruptly. He turned and left the hall.

Vanessa slowly closed the door, then stood alone in the silent room. She walked to a chair and sank into the cushion covered with ivory damask and clusters of violets.

I've made a dreadful mistake coming here, she told herself. *It's much too late for a meaningful relationship with either my father or sister.*

Even if she tried to build a bridge over the neglected past and reach out anew, there seemed to be no responsive chord on the other side. Lucy was a stranger, and she'd probably let Vanessa know she wasn't interested in someone her father had set aside many years ago.

Vanessa's dream of playing peacemaker between Kylie and their father had been wishful thinking. More than one obstacle barred her way through the welcoming gate. Even if she managed to pass through, would Kylie follow?

Don't be disappointed. What did you expect? The welcoming embrace of the father for his prodigal son?

But Robert Miles wasn't like the father in the Lord's parable. In fact, Robert was the one who had left for the far country. Worse yet, her father hadn't ever come to himself, deciding to return home. He had never given them a thought until a short time ago. *No, don't get angry. Those thoughts will only bring self-pity and resentment. Leave your wounds to the Great Physician.*

Yet her heart still ached with unfulfilled needs.

She fought from being taken captive by the all-too-familiar emotions that were tightening around her. She stood and walked around the room looking at the attractive furnishings, pausing at the window once more to look out. She concentrated on her steadfast Father above until her emotions began to settle like the restless sea that had been quieted by the voice of the Master. *Be still, and know that I am God.*

Yes, *Peace, be still. You are My child. And I will never leave you.*

He will never abandon me, even though I'm often too much trouble. She smiled to herself. She had always told Kylie when they were growing up that even if their earthly father didn't want them, the God of the universe did. But she knew that Jesus had not only wanted them, but had shown His love by leaving His place in glory to become the Savior who could touch the leper and say, "I am willing; be cleansed." And Jesus had taken all her sins and suffered willingly, then conquered death, so that she might be presented spotless before the presence of His glory with exceeding great joy. She knew that she had been adopted and made a joint heir with Christ. And in this present world He promised that the disappointments of life were not random winds of mindless fury. Circumstances were under His control. Every thorn had a valid reason for pricking. The events, both good and tragic, were in His hands, and He was using them for the good of those who love Him.

But though Vanessa could see no good in her father's abandonment, she knew that neither had Joseph seen any good from Potiphar's wife lying about his character and bringing about his incarceration in the Egyptian prison. What was that verse? Ah, yes... "But the Lord was with Joseph and showed him mercy."

Her own faith was also peering ahead through the fog. She could not see through it, nor make sense of it. But His Word, like a lamp, held light for each step. The journey was long, and she wasn't there yet. The end remained covered in mist. Would there be a rainbow at the journey's end for her? Ultimately, she knew the answer was yes.

She quoted to herself from the Old Testament book of Joel: "I will restore to you the years that the locust hath eaten."

If you know all this, she told herself firmly, *then act upon it. Don't run back to London like an insecure child. You're here, and by God's grace you shall stay to the end of whatever He has planned.*

8

The telephone jangled on the small desk in one corner of the bedroom. Vanessa waited, thinking someone would surely answer from below. But when it became clear that the phone line was direct to this room, she picked up the receiver. A voice whispered: "Vanessa? Come down to the garden!"

"Who is this?" she asked uneasily.

"Lucy. I need to talk with you alone."

The line disconnected. Vanessa listened to the dial tone, then replaced the receiver. Alone. Meaning—without Scott?

Strange. Vanessa crossed the flowered carpet to the window and looked below. The mist was beginning to thicken. She looked past a rocky pathway hedged with flowers leading away from the estate toward a woody section. Above the treetops, as Scott had mentioned earlier, she saw that on a clear day she would have a breathtaking view of the gray-blue sea, gentle hills, and farther in the distance near Devil's Cliff, the lighthouse painted white with a black circular roof. She stared at the dim outline of the lighthouse for a moment, wondering. Perhaps tomorrow she would walk toward Devil's Cliff and see it for herself.

Intrigued by her sister's unexpected request, Vanessa paused at the pretty vanity table just long enough to remove her comb from her handbag and run it through her hair, which was wind-tossed from the boat. Then she grabbed her jacket and left the room in search of Lucy.

She came down the last few steps of the polished mahogany staircase carpeted in a thick moss green. She might have become lost in what appeared to be a maze of chambers if she hadn't been fortunate enough to find a cleaning girl working in the entrance hall polishing a spindle-legged table.

The girl, bashful but anxious to please, told her there were several doors to the garden. The one on this side of the "hoose" was through the dining room.

Stepping into the garden, a damp, sea-laden breeze carried a fragrant whiff of herbs. Did Kerc grow herbs as well as roses? Somehow she couldn't imagine him interested in thyme and basil!

She walked a short distance and stopped on the path, startled. Lucy stepped out from behind some tall rhododendron bushes in pink bloom, looking back over her shoulder.

"Whom are we hiding from?" Vanessa asked uneasily, wondering if she wanted to play this game. She had no cause to be behaving as if she were trespassing on her father's property.

"No one," Lucy said with a stilted voice, avoiding her eyes. "Come this way." She moved out from the bushes and walked rapidly ahead.

Vanessa hesitated, and then followed, but Lucy had already rounded the bushes. Vanessa hurried on. She rounded the corner toward a low gate. Lucy paused, looked back, and beckoned for Vanessa to hurry. Vanessa passed through the gate and saw that the path left the garden and led off toward the trees. She went straight for perhaps a hundred feet, then turned sharply, steadily climbing at a comfortable angle into the trees. Was this a game of hide-and-seek? Lucy was nowhere in sight. The path must bring her out onto the low hill carpeted with heather that looked out over the loch.

But she was wrong. She stopped, looking about her. Where had Lucy disappeared to? She had to have gone ahead, up the unexpectedly steeper path. Vanessa followed, fighting against a rise of irritation.

The way began to take her away from the house in a northerly direction toward the brackish hills that overlooked the silent, isolated sea.

Vanessa drew her jacket around her. What was this all about? If her guess was right, this path led toward the lighthouse and Devil's Cliff. Her steps slowed as she debated whether to go on or to turn back and explain to Lucy later that she'd lost her. But Lucy couldn't be far away. There was no other well-marked trail. She could have cut through the woods, but she must realize Vanessa didn't know the way. Logic insisted Lucy would have waited until she came into view.

Vanessa looked away from the woods, up the path. Perhaps she intended to show her the lighthouse.

The afternoon darkened. Mist was continuing to roll in from the sea.

Gripped by the solitude, she had the uncanny notion that the mist was closing around her. She could almost imagine a python moving along the path and curling about her ankles. Somewhere in the distance came a foghorn...yes, the lighthouse on the black rock...

Perhaps because she was curious about Devil's Cliff and the lighthouse, or perhaps because she wanted to please her half sister, Vanessa started forward again up the trail hugging the narrowing hill and turning into a cliff that would soon circle around to face the sea.

Like her journey to Scotland, she felt she had come too far to turn back now. She pressed ahead. She had walked for a few minutes before the path took her away from the wood to where, as

Scott had told her on Captain Duncan's boat, there were rocky cliffs. There were places where you could reach the shore and watch the seals frolic, but the path was little used and could be difficult, even dangerous, if you didn't know what you were doing.

Shadowy treetops grew thicker and blotted out the gray sky. Eventually the trail took her away from the trees toward the sea, and then leveled out. Here, the mist grew denser. She was glad that she'd been wise enough to bring her jacket, but wished it had a hood. On sudden impulse she called: "Lucy! Where are you?"

Cautious now, when only silence came back to her on the damp breath of the swirling gray, she paused, unwilling to begin the trek across the open field that waited between her and the rolling meadow. The lighthouse must be just beyond the meadow, over the next mist-shrouded hillock.

She stood there at the end of the trail, the trees behind, the house to the south and out of view, and the meadow and hill ahead toward the sea. The solitude exaggerated the song of wind blowing across the meadow, and the distant surge of the sea, swelling against the rocks.

"Lucy!" she called.

There was a sound, but no answering voice. It was a mere tone that differentiated itself from the wind that was stirring the mist-covered heather among the bracken, a sound different from the sea and the distant gulls whose cries were carried to her. The sound came from behind, from the trees where she'd come from. She listened intently.

There it was again, not footsteps, not the wind, but a breathy sound—no—a snarl, vicious. She whirled to face the darkened trees. From out of the gray tendrils of fog came two large dogs, black like shadows. They stood guard with their noses lifted for the scent of an intruder, whiffing, looking at her, their lips pulled back showing white fangs.

Vanessa, who loved animals, froze. These dogs were not friendly, responsive pets. The look in their yellowish eyes told her they were to be taken seriously. They separated and began to circle her. Fear welled up in her heart as they came closer with low growls. A voice commanded: "Jacinth, Gemini, no!" The dogs halted in their tracks instantly as if a brick wall had sprung up before them.

Vanessa let out a sigh. She expected the tall figure who emerged from the mist to be Kerc, but it was someone she'd not seen before. He was tall, surpassing Kerc, and had a thick, muscled build. He wore a knee-length dark coat and hat and held a whip in a dark-gloved hand. A quick crack of the whip caused even Vanessa to step back, startled. The dogs trotted back toward the trees and sat down obediently, now and then whining. The man's face was square, with a short, well-trimmed black beard touched with gray. His deep-set eyes were a pale gray, like hoarfrost. His hawk nose flared into wide nostrils, and his ruddy lips at last melted into a sparse, almost sheepish grin.

"The dogs frightened you. I am sorry. They're not used to running into strangers hereabouts. You startled them."

Vanessa's heart beat faster from the scare, but also from the stranger's appearance. Although he smiled, his eyes were nervous.

She had the sudden impression that the dogs had not just come upon her, but that perhaps he'd been trailing her.

"You are—? If you don't mind me asking, lass."

She saw no reason to mind. "Vanessa Miles. I'm here to visit Robert Miles. I believe this land is part of his estate?" She kept her voice polite, but let him know she had the right to walk around without guard dogs terrifying her. They might have actually attacked if he hadn't been there to stop them.

His expression didn't change, but his bottom lip dragged impulsively, as if he couldn't control it. This response sent chills running up the back of her neck. His facial muscles momentarily contorted. Vanessa wanted to run. *It's the setting*, she reasoned. *Don't be a silly.* Then she remembered the tavern girl's death on the black rock, which might not be too far distant. She shoved her hands into her jacket pockets to keep them still.

"And you are?" Her voice was steady, surprising her with her own poise. She certainly didn't feel it. "Are you the lighthouse keeper?" She didn't know why she asked that, except the lighthouse was on her mind and somehow she could picture him there alone with his aggressive animals.

He gestured across the meadow to nowhere that she could see in the mist. "I live out there on the moor. Do you wish to see the lighthouse?"

"Not now, thank you." Her teeth chattered and she tried to control them. "I was looking for Lucy—Miss Miles. She came this way."

"Aye, Mr. Robert's daughter. She wouldn'a come this way, lass. There be quicksand out there. You best be careful yerself."

Quicksand! "But she must have come this—" She stopped. She sensed his unfriendliness. Like Kerc, this stranger resented her presence, she was sure of it, and had perhaps intended to give her a good scare with the dogs. She wondered too, if there really was quicksand. Scott had warned that there was muck in another direction.

"Mr. Robert's daughter wouldn't come this way," he insisted. The thin smile never left his tight lips, nor the watchfulness from his pale, piercing eyes beneath jutting black brows. Slowly, he came toward her, his heavy boots crunching the pebbles and stones. From behind him, she was aware of the excited whine of the dogs. Vanessa clenched her teeth to keep her imagination from running wild.

"You are afraid."

Vanessa stood her ground, though she may have been unwise to do so. The mist swirled along the ground like living, creeping things, moving around bushes, rocks, and the tall large stranger in black.

"Afraid? Should I be, Mr.—?"

"You do well to be frightened on this islet. There are many things to fear."

He looked down at her. His smile vanished.

"You mean the tavern girl?"

"Aye, so ye know about her, do 'ee?" he gestured behind the fog-bound hillocks in the direction of the sea. "The cliffs be steep. One misstep and ye'll as likely plunge to the rocks below as not. They be slippery."

Vanessa's fingers were clenched inside her pockets. "I've no intention of climbing Devil's Cliff in the fog or rain. I'll be careful."

He appeared to ignore her. "Then there be the muck 'n' mire. Always a danger to them who don't know the ways of the moor." He gestured his head and lowered his voice. "And then there be the goings-on in Gowrie House."

Vanessa stepped slowly away from him, feeling the wet mist on her face. It crept about them, playing around the mossy rocks and black stunted trees. She suspected that he was just waiting for her to ask about Gowrie House. She might have turned and left then, but she wanted to learn everything she could.

"Why should I be afraid?" she persisted, hoping that by staying she could gain a handle on the truth.

"Because if ye insist on going there, ye'll likely be in danger. Aye, like Maggie, said to slip from Devil's Cliff. Maybe an accident waits for you too, Miss Vanessa."

His teeth showed beneath his lip, and it reminded her of the snarl of the dogs.

Fear, fed by the curling whitish mist and the resentment in his eyes, began to close about her as she began to worry about this odd fellow with his strange words. He was trying to frighten her. Had Lucy put him up to it? What were her half sister's motives? A cold chill prickled the back of her neck as she thought that perhaps Lucy had led her in this direction knowing the man and his dogs would be here. Perhaps she even suspected she might panic and run into the moor, sinking in some quicksand pool—

She stopped herself. How could she allow herself to even imagine such things?

At that same moment her emotions were out of control, the dogs growled and the man suddenly moved toward her. She broke and ran—not toward the moor—but to the trail in the wood that led back to the house.

She managed to reach the trail in the trees. She could hear the dogs, but thankfully, they weren't immediately following. That she hadn't been quickly pounced on or cut off convinced her he'd held them back. He must be out to merely scare her, but that did little to help or comfort her now.

Vanessa raced ahead, nearly tripping over jutting rocks, half-buried in the soil, and old protruding roots. The hem of her skirt caught momentarily on a thorny vine. She jerked to free it, glancing backward over her shoulder and expecting to see the black-clothed figure and his dogs in crazed pursuit.

She ran on. She must escape this madman. Death waited behind every darkened shrub ready to spring out at her. With every crack of twig or cry of startled bird, her fears would leap. She was now fearing the man, not the dogs. The man who had followed the tavern girl to the rock perhaps?

The mist had become so thick that she could hardly see more than a few feet ahead as evening twilight was fast approaching. She stopped. Which way was the trail? She walked hurriedly now, the mist swirling, wetting her blouse, bedraggling her hair until moisture started to drip from the ends. She leaned against a big tree trunk, gasping, looking behind. Were they coming? She could hear little except the drumming of her heart. She pushed away from the tree and hurried on. The shadows fought her progress. Yes, they were still coming—she could hear the dogs and now and then the man's voice, giving orders.

Death may await you, just as it had Maggie. Murder? Was that what the man implied? Maybe that was why Scott had scoffed at Kerc's so-called "tale" about Devil's Cliff. Her thoughts raced on.

Darkness descended upon the woods. How long had she been running? Where was the trail? She had hopelessly lost it several minutes ago. Her lungs burned, her throat felt dry even in the dampness, and her eyes stung. She could see little ahead of her but thick mist. Her feet, tired and heavy, caught something that didn't budge. It was almost with resignation that she fell hard to her knees, trying to brace herself with her palms, but to her shock she was over an edge—a slope—and she felt only wet moss and leaves. She was starting to slide. "Lord, help me!"

She grasped frantically and her fingers brushed sharply against something—a shrub. She clenched hold. For a brief moment it held and cut her palm. She clutched it, grasping a slippery rock with her other hand. "Help me!" she screamed into the gray fog.

Her wrist couldn't hold much longer. She tried to find a foothold but felt nothing but slippery leaves. Her strength was fast ebbing. Her sweat mixed with dampness and ran through her lashes. She shut them tight. "Lord—please—"

"Ahhh!" Her numb fingers yielded without her permission. Down she bumped over the leafy embankment, sliding and scraping painfully until the side of her head smacked something hard before she rolled to a stop. Somehow she remained conscious.

Dazed, she lay still for a minute, her heart thudding. Had she broken any bones? She didn't think so and moved each limb slowly. Despite the frightening experience, it looked as though she was still in one piece. She stirred and then tried to sit up, discovering that she wasn't as strong as she thought.

She stifled a moan while managing to get to her knees. She waited, closing her eyes and trying to regain calm. *You're all right. You just fell. Rest and wait a moment. You'll make it in a little while. The Lord is with you, just as He promised. Don't be afraid of pain...*

Minutes passed by. In the distance she heard the dogs coming nearer and nearer until she heard them barking madly above the slope.

She was trapped like a poor rabbit.

Had the man arrived yet? She peered upward into the mist but could see very little.

She heard some falling pebbles rolling over the leaves. Her breath came quickly, and she said nothing. He might not see her and leave with the dogs. But that could mean she'd be here until morning, if the mist ever cleared enough for her to get back on the trail to the house. She had no idea how far out of her way she was. Somehow she would manage to climb back up the slope. Then again, Scott might miss her and come searching. That might not be until after dinner, or until Lucy's conscience began to bother her, if it did. Vanessa's mouth tightened. How could she do this to her?

The sharp barking of the dogs filled her ears. A hand torch switched on and swept across the bushes and weeds.

"You down there, lass?" came his hoarse call. Then to the whining dogs: "She must be. Look here at the embankment."

Vanessa winced. No! He was coming down—she could hear him and the dogs. She struggled blindly to her feet, took several fumbling steps and tripped again, and this time merciful blackness descended upon her.

9

Vanessa could hear the whine of the dogs. She blinked as a pale yellow light hovered above her. Where was it coming from? Her blurred vision cleared. She saw the stranger staring down at her, holding a lantern over her head. She was lying on some sort of cot. "Aye, so ye be coming around good now."

With one glimpse of his face, her heart began to beat again like a drum. Where was she? She turned her throbbing head cautiously. She was in a cottage. How did she get here? A fire crackled in the small hearth before which the two dogs lay comfortably, their pink tongues showing, their eyes bright. They appeared to be anything but ferocious beasts out to run her off a cliff. There was a wholesome smell of supper cooking, but at the moment it nauseated her. Her brain was still teetering on edge, beckoning her back to the oblivion of sleep.

Was that a door she heard opening? A gust of chill wind blew in, wet with mist. The dogs stood excitedly, tails whipping. A small breathless gasp was about to escape her lips but she held it back. Kerc! She didn't know whether to be relieved at his presence or even more concerned. How fitting that both these odious men should know one another! She had no reason to trust either of them. Her curiosity spiraled. She saw her chance to investigate without them knowing she was awake. After what had occurred, and the stranger's malicious warnings, she told herself she'd be wise to learn all she could. She closed her eyelids, opening them just barely enough to see what they were doing, watching the curious, nervous manner of the stranger as Kerc stood at the door.

Kerc had stopped abruptly when he caught sight of her on the cot. His startled reaction convinced her of his genuine surprise. Did this mean he hadn't been involved in what she now believed was a deliberate attempt, perhaps by Lucy and the stranger with the dogs, to harm her, or at the least, send her racing back to London? Or was Kerc's surprise because he'd thought she'd plunged to her death down the ravine, just as the tavern girl had fallen from Devil's Cliff? Vanessa wasn't forgetting what Scott had told her in London about the admiration Lucy held for Kerc over his success with roses. Perhaps they had other mutual interests. But if he hadn't known she was here, the other man, whoever he was, must have managed to bring her here on his own. She couldn't be very far from the ravine where she'd fallen. Kerc was standing in the open doorway with gray mist swirling outside, holding a pail, and looking over at her as though she were a mirage.

One of the dogs broke the spell by whining an excited greeting. Kerc elbowed the door shut with a bang and faced the other man.

"What's *she* doing here like *that*?" His demanding tone was surprisingly as cool, clipped, and British as Andy's could be when angry. What had happened to his clever little Scottish brogue?

"Dogs spooked her like a hind. The lass took off running 'fore I could stop her. She slipped off'n embankment. Must'a been the thick mist blinding her."

"What were they doing away from the kennel?" Kerc rebuked.

"Ye know them dogs, laddie. They've a mind of their own. They got out again. Jacinth be a cunning one. An' Gemini won't be at peace till she's with him. Jacinth picked up a scent that turned out to be the lass here."

"How badly is she hurt? Broken bones, sprains?"

"Nae, nothing. A few bumps, some scratches."

"Does she know you brought her here?"

"Nae. Was out like a cold goose. Aye, she don't know what hit her, is my guess."

"And she's still out?" came Kerc's cautious tone.

"Sure of it. Thought she was waking, but she's out again."

Vanessa heard Kerc's tread cross the floor to where she was lying on the small bunk. Now came the test. If only she could manage to be very still and calm. She sensed his scrutiny.

The moment seemed too long. She tried to concentrate on Andy. If she flushed with embarrassment, it would be all over. She must look a sorrowful sight. Torn skirt and blouse, ripped stockings, hair bedraggled and muddy.

"You were a fool to bring her here, Scarron," he breathed fiercely.

Vanessa winced inside over his displeasure. It would be far more dreadful now if he discovered she was playing possum. Whatever motivated the man called Scarron, it apparently did not agree with Kerc's mood or plans.

"I dinnae know what else to do, laddie. T'was no other place to bring 'er. Time I got back here, got a rope and a mule and got her out of the gully to the trail, I could'a hardly see two feet ahead. Should'a have left her?"

"You might have used your head and gone straight to Gowrie House. This was the last place to bring her!"

"Fog's too thick, as much as anything I've seen in years. Then there was the dogs."

"You say they were out?"

"Found 'em sniffing about the lighthouse." There was an uncertain moment, one she was sure was loaded with tension. It convinced her Scarron meant to imply something by mentioning the lighthouse. "It didn't take the lass long to start snooping," he added thoughtfully.

"I might be to blame for some of that. I shouldn't have—" Kerc stopped.

He shouldn't have what?

"It's too late now," he said shortly.

She read the displeasure in his voice. Why didn't he want her near the lighthouse? Because of Devil's Cliff and the girl Scarron had called Maggie?

She again sensed his gaze. Was he wondering if she were really unconscious?

"We can't keep her here. One of us will need to go up to the house for help. Scott Morgan, maybe. He enjoys playing the hero."

"He's been snooping round lately too."

"Yes. I could carry her on the mule, I suppose."

"'Tis a mile."

Kerc was silent.

Scarron said in a husky voice. "A pretty thing, isn't she?"

"Hand me that blanket."

Vanessa's heart stopped, then pounded in her throat as a moment later she felt the quilt being placed over her. She didn't move when Kerc lifted her hand and took her pulse.

"Aye, she's sound asleep, all right," Scarron said, as if trying to reassure him. "Hasn't stirred since I carried her in."

Kerc remained strangely silent. He let go of her wrist but did not move away.

"What was she doing up on the trail? Did she explain?"

"She be looking for Miss Lucy. So she says."

"Lucy!" Kerc's voice reflected his surprise.

"That was all I got out of her. Then the dogs afrighted her an' off she went into the mist like an apparition."

"Lucy," Kerc repeated thoughtfully. "I wonder if she was serious or just saying that to cover her tracks. You didn't see Lucy or anyone else, did you? Scott, maybe?"

"Dinnae see nobody but the lass. Stop your worrying, Kerc. She be all right. Just a few bumps and bruises and scratches. Might

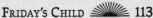

be more'n enough to get her to forget Gowrie House and take off back to merry ol' England."

"If it could accomplish that..."

"But ye don't think it will?" Scarron said uneasily.

"She's persistent, this one, even if she is 'a wee pretty thing' as you say."

Scarron chuckled. "Aye, she stood her ground a while longer than most, all right. T'was only when Jacinth showed his teeth that she bolted—"

"Enough," he gritted.

"I was just explaining—"

"I know what you were trying to do. Don't let it happen again. As for her sprouting wings and flying back to London, we can't count on that. She smells money and land. Scott made sure of that. And Robert will wave it under her pretty nose like bait. That makes for danger, but I won't surrender my plans, either."

"Aye, ye've come too far for surrender. What's to be done then?"

"I've got to think of some way to get rid of her, but it won't be easy. Have you ever met a woman yet who'd turn her back on a fortune? No, it will take more than a tumble down an embankment to send our American heroine back to the States."

"That, too, might be arranged, but 'tis a pity this one be so pretty," Scarron murmured.

"Pretty girls are a dime a dozen," Kerc said indifferently.

Scarron chuckled. "For you, maybe."

Vanessa's heart raced like a scared rabbit's. If she could continue making them think she was unconscious, she could perhaps wait until they both went out again. Then, if she walked slowly, even if she had to hobble, she could make it back to the house and find Scott. She would tell him everything and by morning the police from Edinburgh would—

"We've wasted enough time. Take the dogs to the kennel. See they're not running loose again."

Vanessa heard Kerc walk to the door. "The mist is lifting. After you put away the dogs, go up to the house. Get someone down this way with a stretcher."

"Aye."

What was Scarron doing taking orders from Kerc, the younger of the two? It would seem both men would be on equal terms as workers on the estate.

Scarron went to the door and whistled. The dogs got up and followed him out, trailing after his boots grinding across the dirt.

Through her lashes she watched Kerc walk to the sink, set the pail down, and wash his hands. She suspected he'd caught a fish. He removed his damp jacket and woolen cap and hung them on a hook on the wall, then he turned to look at her. He walked to the foot of the bunk. Vanessa's heart paused, then thumped nervously.

"You can stop pretending now," he said.

Silence enveloped her. For a tense moment she didn't move and went on pretending. How had he guessed she was awake when Scarron hadn't?

Vanessa allowed a breath to escape her lips and opened her eyes. She shot a glance toward the closed door wondering if she could make a bolt for it, but she knew the attempt would be futile. Every bone and muscle in her body was aching. Her gaze came back to the caretaker.

She became aware of how disconcerting his stare could be, with a look that might have meant anything. His dark hair, thick and curling slightly, fell across his forehead. He shoved his hands in his pockets and scanned her briefly.

"Was Scarron right? No broken bones, sprains?"

"Yes, I think so. I mean…I'm…I'm all right…I think. I can sit up—in that chair by that table, if you don't mind." It bothered her that she was in somebody's bed.

She raised herself to both elbows, then sat up, trying not to show how stiff and sore she was.

"I'm sorry this happened to you, Miss Miles, but you shouldn't have gone off on your own, snooping."

"I wasn't snooping," she corrected with a stiff voice.

He didn't appear convinced. He frowned. "Can you put weight on your ankles?"

She tried, gingerly. "You sound like a doctor," she murmured.

"Aye, you could use one, to be sure."

His strong hands took hold of hers. She avoided his eyes and tried to pull away as quickly as she could, trying to not sway. He ignored her reluctance. "You're as slippery as a fish."

"Yes, my ankles are all right. That chair will do..."

He edged her toward the beat-up old chair, and she sat down slowly, holding to the edge of the table. When she glanced at him, he was still watching her, pensively.

"You might have broken your neck."

"I'm already quite aware of that. I was deliberately chased by those dogs, *your* dogs."

He looked down at her for a steady moment, musing. "Those dogs don't chase people. You must have been very frightened and started imagining things."

"Yes, I was frightened, and no, I don't think I'm imagining anything."

"Miss Miles, there are dangers here at Mull. You had best return to London where you belong."

It was not just a suggestion. She remained silent for a moment, thoughtfully considering him and what he was about. "Do you think I'm in the habit of causing dogs to chase me? And therefore for my own safety I should leave Scotland at once?"

He ignored her question. "Are you in severe pain?"

"No." She rubbed her shoulder. "Just sore and shaken. I think I can walk now."

"You can't even walk to the door, Miss Miles. I suspect it's worse than you say."

"I tell you I'm fine now. I had a little scare, that's all. It won't change my plans." She ignored the mild challenge that sparked in his eyes.

"Just like a woman." She struggled to her feet, bent on leaving his unpleasant company at once, but she stood too quickly and became dizzy.

He steadied her. "You see? You won't get far."

"It's dreadful here. I'm leaving—anything is better than being here."

"Don't be silly. You might imagine yourself Little Red Riding Hood, but I'm not the Big Bad Wolf."

"Aren't you?" She pulled her wrist away from his strong tanned hand and rubbed it.

"You heard me send Scarron for help. Be patient. I don't fancy your being here any more than you want to be."

"You've made that clear."

"I meant to," he said calmly. "But as we don't have a choice, I'd advise some cooperation."

"What happened to your thick Scottish brogue?" she challenged, her eyes narrowing thoughtfully. "Listening to you now, Mr. Trevalyan, I'd vow you were as British as the king."

"Well, now, it just goes to show, doesn't it? I was born and raised in Scotland. And if you prefer the lovely flavor of me native tongue I can accommodate ye very well, lassie."

"I assure you it means nothing to me," she said loftily. "I just found the sudden change rather curious. Usually people with accents revert backward when forgetting themselves, not the other way around."

"It may be you're a wee bit curious about too many things, Miss Miles."

"You don't like me much do you, Mr. Trevalyan?" she asked, pointedly.

No surprise showed. "Not particularly, no."

Her eyes widened. "If you had manners, you would have denied it."

A glimmer reflected in his eyes. "Would you want me to lie, Miss Miles?"

The arrogance he displayed!

"Of course not. But…why?" she asked almost apologetically. "I mean—why do you dislike me? I want to know! It isn't often I meet a stranger who shows such personal disregard for me. And face it, you've felt that way ever since you saw me at the wharf."

"Any explanations can wait, considering. There's a scratch on your face. And on your arms and legs too. You'd best wash in the basin over there. Some of those bramble bushes can cause an awful itch and swelling if they aren't treated right away. Scarron keeps some ointment in that drawer."

Vanessa glanced down at her torn and muddy skirt, her ripped stockings, and at the scratches that were indeed red and beginning to swell. She raised a trembling hand to smooth her tangled hair from her face. "It can wait till I'm safely back at the house," she said stiffly.

"Suit yourself. But you're as safe here with me as you'd be with Scott Morgan."

That statement struck her as surprising and odd. "Am I? You don't like me for some reason—you won't explain why—and yet you expect me to believe that?"

"You can believe what you want. You will anyway. But you're a nurse, aren't you? Common sense says you'd do well to do something about those scrapes."

"Why do you think I'm a nurse?"

"I saw you with Miss Warnstead at the warehouse—with the little girl."

She saw no reason to explain otherwise. She decided to change the subject. "That dreadful man…Scarron. Why would my father hire him?"

He looked at her. "I didn't say he worked for Mr. Miles." A quiet look came to his face. "Scarron Carstair is his name. Scarron's an older cousin of mine. I've a dozen or more of 'em around these parts. None go by the name Trevalyan, though. Just me."

Just why he did, and they did not, Kerc didn't explain and she didn't care to ask. *He tried to kill me*, she wanted to say, but stopped herself in time. If Scarron was his cousin, then Kerc wouldn't listen to her. He'd already admitted he didn't like her. There was no more reason to trust Kerc than Scarron. They were a nasty lot, and probably the rest of his kin were too. Fighting clansmen. She'd wait and discuss the matter with Scott. She'd tell him about Scarron's threat and the mention of the tavern girl. She should have called him at once. She glanced about for a telephone.

Kerc followed her gaze and appeared to guess her thoughts. "He doesn't have a telephone. He can't afford one. Otherwise I'd have called up to the house. We're all not as rich as Robert Miles," he said, with a tinge of goading.

He went to the cupboard, searched, and uncorked a bottle he found and whiffed. "Smells like shark bait," he murmured. He popped the cork back in. "We'll settle for something else. You're an American, aren't you? I suspect you'd like coffee, but there isn't anything except tea."

"Tea—will be fine," she managed, adding, "thank you."

He cast her a glance, hesitated, then said, "I really am sorry about the dogs. You heard Scarron. They escaped."

Had they really escaped? Or had something been arranged with Lucy to frighten her, and the incident had just gotten out of hand? But Kerc had looked surprised when he came through the door and saw her. Too many questions ran through her mind.

Kerc fussed with the stove until he got the old burner lit. Now that his back was toward her she studied him cautiously, thoughtfully. "Is this your cottage?" she asked.

"Could be, but I don't live here."

"How did you know I wasn't unconscious?"

"I didn't, until the end. Your lashes fluttered too much, and your heartbeat seemed fast." He dropped loose tea in a pan. "If you were wise you wouldn't have come here."

"Another threat? I've had more than my share today."

"I don't go threatening women. It was a simple statement."

"Oh? Were you following me and Scott in London?"

He cast her a glance, his dark lashes thinning.

"I saw you in the café at Piccadilly Circus."

He smiled faintly. "I know you did. Aye, I did follow you. I wanted to know who you were meeting. Meddling can be dangerous when some view it as a plan to steal what they want."

She supposed he was speaking of her father's inheritance. "You've said that twice. About my 'snooping and meddling.' I don't know what makes you think that's what brings me here, but you're wrong. I've *personal* reasons for coming to see Robert Miles, and they have nothing at all to do with his estate."

Kerc didn't look convinced, and it riled her for some reason to think he thought she was a conniver. "If anyone is meddling, I suppose it's you—and the nasty Scarron. I'm sorry, he is your cousin, but I don't trust him—or you."

"Your privilege, lass. Then, again, could be you're making a mistake trusting those up in the house."

Lucy, perhaps, because it was true that she probably was worried about the Miles estate and about another half sister and brother unexpectedly showing up in the scheme of things at her father's wishes. Still, there was no cause not to trust Scott, or even her father, unless he planned to use her as a threat to manipulate Lucy into doing what he wanted. And if that turned out to be the case, Vanessa wouldn't allow herself to be used to coerce others. She'd already made that clear to Scott in London before agreeing to come to Scotland.

"If Robert Miles expects my presence to threaten the inheritance of others in his family, I'll have no part in it," she said.

Kerc studied her, his robust dark gaze making her uneasy. Again, she believed he didn't understand her, or didn't care to bother, and this was irksome. She said crossly, her head pounding with pain, "Anyway, Mr. Trevalyan, I don't see that it's any of your affair what goes on up at the house. And that includes my visit from London."

"Then again, maybe it is. A man has a right to protect those he loves. And maybe I don't accept his ownership of Gowrie House as even being legal."

Her thought went immediately to Lucy and what Scott had hinted of in London. Then was it true that she was asked to come here to help build a wall between the wealthy estate owner's daughter and the handsome-but-poor caretaker—to make Lucy change her mind about Kerc? What about the man called Jodrell? Scott had intimated that Lucy was engaged to him.

Could that explain why Kerc disliked her, and why Lucy had led her on the path to Scarron and the dogs—perhaps not to harm her as it had, but merely frighten her?

Vanessa leaned her forehead against her hands and closed her eyes. "It hurts too much to think..."

"I'm sorry."

He sounded genuine, and it mollified her a little. *Stop feeling sorry for yourself*, she thought. Searching for sympathy from good-looking men like Scott—and Kerc—was dangerous.

Oh, Andy, I wish you were here.

"You'll feel better once you drink this," Kerc said, setting a mug of tea in front of her. "Scarron has headache powders, but we'd best wait for the doc."

She wouldn't have taken any powders anyway, even if he had meant to help her.

A few minutes later, finished with her tea, she stood from the chair and made her way slowly to the water basin. She glanced in his direction, but he had his back toward her. He had a knife out and was cleaning a big silvery fish. She assumed it was for his supper, and Scarron's.

With both hands she poured fresh water from a pitcher into the bowl and slowly washed her face, hands, and arms. With a wet cloth she cleaned the scratches on her legs and knees, and finding the ointment he'd mentioned, she rubbed some on, keeping an eye on him as she did. He ignored her. No, he didn't like her at all. Well, it was mutual. She looked in the small mirror above the basin and saw a worried, unhappy girl with damp scraggly hair. She winced. Vanity, despite the struggle for higher motivations, won out. She saw a comb sitting there and used it to make her hair presentable. She wound its length tightly into a knot and used the few pins she still had to keep it in place. With the cloth she tried to clean the mud from her torn skirt and blouse, but she had little success. Exhausted, she limped back to the table and sat down.

"Is there any more tea?" she asked meekly.

Without a word he poured what was left into her cup from the pan. As the minutes slipped by she actually began to feel a little better, but her fingers were stiff and swollen.

"You need ice," he commented.

She looked at the swelling with dismay. She hoped it would not interfere with her plans.

"I'm surprised you care."

He shrugged. "Always did believe in plain politeness. Maybe now you'll have to go back to London," he observed.

Yes, that would work out just the way the three of them had planned, she thought.

"Why do you have so many dogs?" she accused.

She saw him hesitate. "I don't."

"But the other dogs, the ones I saw you with when Scott and I arrived this afternoon were sheepdogs, a reddish brown color. Those that chased me were Dobermans."

His jaw flexed. "They shouldn't have chased you. They wouldn't, unless—" He stopped.

"Unless your cousin told them to?" she asked unhappily.

"They're still in training, used for guarding."

"Guarding what? You said he doesn't work for the estate."

He frowned. "I'll get to the bottom of why they got loose, Miss Miles. Drink your tea while it's hot."

She masked a shiver thinking of the tavern girl named Maggie. Had Kerc known Maggie? She wanted to ask him, but thought he likely wouldn't say much as long as he mistrusted her.

"What were you doing looking for Lucy out here?" he asked.

She noticed that he'd used Lucy's first name. She wondered if he asked that only to see if she thought they were plotting together to send her away.

"I was looking for her because she led me this direction. I wouldn't have come otherwise. I was in my room when the telephone rang. She told me to come down to the garden. When I arrived she ran away, beckoning me to follow."

Kerc continued studying her. Did he believe her? Naturally, he'd side with Lucy. Even Scarron had told him she was snooping near the lighthouse.

"Did you see her?" she asked pointedly.

"No."

"She behaved rudely. Could she have wanted to lead me to your cousin and the dogs?" she asked suddenly, breaking her own earlier decision not to mention her suspicion to Kerc.

To her surprise he didn't immediately respond, but instead walked over to the door, opened it, and looked out into the mist that was blowing back toward the sea. He closed the door again, turned, and faced her, unsmiling.

"I won't answer that, because I don't know. I'll look into it. If I find out either of them tried to scare you with the dogs, I'll make certain it doesn't happen again."

His gaze was disturbing, and she found her eyes wavering. She found satisfaction in having him coming to her defense against their plot, if there had been one. Then apparently, Kerc wasn't involved; at least, not with the dogs.

She looked away at her hand, concentrating on the scratch. He was right—there was going to be an allergic reaction to the bushes.

"If Lucy was rude it's because she's worried. She doesn't approve of your father asking you here. The threat of disinheriting her in your favor, as you should be able to understand, is enough to upset anyone in her position."

"Now you sound like Scott Morgan. Any mention of Lucy seems to bring every bachelor in the county to her defense."

He smiled. "Scott's in love with her."

That comment, she supposed, was meant to explain Scott's defense back at the house, but did it explain Kerc's? She wasn't about to ask him. "I've told you, I haven't come here for an inheritance. All of her worry is wasted."

"Why did you come?" he asked suddenly, unexpectedly blunt.

Her brows raised in surprise. "At my father's invitation. I'm hoping to, well..." Kerc wouldn't understand. And he disliked her, so why explain? "It doesn't matter," she said wearily. "But if I thought she had anything to do with what happened to me this afternoon—"

"It had to be an accident. Lucy must have lost you in the mist. She probably went back to the house, thinking you did too."

She wondered if he believed that, or if like Scott, he was making excuses. Scott had seemed to think Lucy's interest in Kerc was based on his success with roses and Scottish folklore, but as Vanessa had the opportunity to study Kerc up close, she now wondered if it was as simple as that. Kerc, despite his relatively low station in life, was as masculine a man as could be desired. She couldn't imagine that Lucy hadn't noticed. *Well, I'm not going to notice.*

"Exactly how did it happen?" he asked.

"What?"

"Your slide down the embankment."

"You heard your cousin. The dogs were behind me a good while. I tried to run back to the mansion, but it was foggy and I grew tired. I stumbled and slipped down a hillside. It was slippery with wet leaves. I'm going to mention all this to Scott Morgan."

His eyes came to hers. "It's not possible for you to have run from the dogs 'a good while' as you say. They would have reached you in seconds."

"Well, Scarron was with them, maybe holding them back with his commands, but they were chasing me, sounding very ferocious."

"What do you expect Scott to do about it? He's the one who blundered bringing you to the island."

"It sounds as if you don't like Mr. Morgan any more than you approve of me. I don't suppose you'll bother to explain why?"

"You're right. I don't like him. He brought you here not because he cares about your father, or about reconciling, but for reasons that help Scott. He's selfish to the core. He'd lie himself black in the face, if necessary."

"And you think I'm in with him, is that it? In whatever he hopes to accomplish?"

"Aye. Curious about that part. You may be plotting together to get Mr. Miles to leave you his inheritance. You and Scott could even be business partners, ready to split the money and each go your separate ways. He perhaps to a more grateful Lucy, and you to your Andy in London."

She was surprised he knew about Andy. He must have heard it from Francis that afternoon at the wharf.

Vanessa stood tiredly. "So that's what you think. That I've come here for money and property."

"Sure, now. Why else? You can't have any interest in a father whose actions said loudly and clearly he didn't care what happened to you or your brother. Scott must have convinced you Mr. Miles would leave you a chunk of his money if you cooperated."

"I should be furious. You're just like Kylie. If my own brother, whom I am very close to, accused me of the same—coming for money—I shouldn't expect anything different from a stranger. But you're wrong! Not that it's any of your business. The truth is, I am a daughter of Robert Miles—as much of a daughter as Lucy. It was Lucy's mother who stole him away from me and my mother! I've nothing to feel guilty or ashamed about."

"If a man loves a woman the way he should, he's not going to run off with someone else just because she's prettier. But I don't want to discuss Mrs. Miles—either of 'em. If you didn't come for what you could get—and I'm still not convinced—you could have come for revenge. Maybe both."

"Never mind revenge. I've been taught to leave injustice to God."

"Rightly so. But is that what's planned?"

"Planned? *Nothing* is planned. Not with Scott Morgan, not with anyone. And why should any of this concern you? I've a notion you don't like Robert Miles any more than the rest of us, except perhaps Lucy."

"Yes, you might say that."

She sat down again, wearily. He was just like Scott. "Looks as if my half sister has run away with everyone's heart. Unfortunately, only one of you can have her."

He didn't answer that. He didn't appear as if he'd heard, or if he had, he'd shrugged it off.

"You've had enough scares for one night, Miss Miles. You ought to return to New York. That's where you're from, isn't it? The war will worsen, and you don't want to get stuck in London when the Luftwaffe starts its terror campaign and bombing. That's another reason to go now. New York is where you belong, not Mull. You're an American. If you had this estate, you wouldn't know the first thing to do with it. Most likely you'd waste it, or sell it to buy more pretty clothes and things. You don't belong to Scotland. You sure don't belong to the estate. And the estate won't be belonging to you if I can stop it."

Despite her pain she threw her napkin down, pushed back her chair, and stood again, holding to the edge of the table. She looked at him, hurt and angry, tears springing to her tired eyes.

"You don't know a thing about what you're saying. Not a thing. And you certainly don't know or understand me. Not that I care if you do. Not at all. But I'm sick of everyone threatening me and making my visit here miserable. For your information, sir, I will not be frightened away. Not by you and your nasty dogs, not by your madman cousin, not by Lucy's cold shoulder, nor by anything else any of you can throw at me. I'm staying. And I'm going to accomplish what I came for."

He looked surprised by her outburst.

"I may be foolish," she said, "but I'll make it clear and simple. I'm here to see Robert Miles—my father. And I won't leave until what he's asked me here for is settled. If that disturbs you and Lucy, well, I'm sorry. But I'm not the running-away type."

He looked at her evenly for a long, analytical minute. "So I see. And sometimes you're very much like your father. He's stubborn too. That might get you into more trouble than you realize."

Her mounting frustration spent, she wondered at her folly in even trying to explain to him.

"I've run once today when your dogs were sent to scare me, but I won't be frightened into running back to London by your words."

He tilted his head and surveyed her. There was nothing in his face to suggest that she had won or lost. "Then there's nothing more to be said."

"No. I suppose there isn't."

He opened the door and looked out. "Mist is lifting. I'll see what's keeping your rescue party." He went for his coat and his cap, watching her as he put them on. "Don't think you've convinced me with all your pretty courage, Miss Miles. If anything, you've given me more to wonder about. It can wait, though. I'm never far away. I'm either working in the garden or doing other chores around the place. You can be sure we'll talk again."

"I won't be holding my breath, but neither shall I run and hide. You see, there's a lot I want to know too. Including more about Devil's Cliff."

"Stay away from the rock. Better stick with tea parties in the garden. That way, you won't ruin any more silk stockings." He scanned her, stepped out, and closed the door.

Vanessa folded her arms and, swallowing back the lump in her throat, sank down in the hard chair. What a scamp! Just who did he think he was?

10

Vanessa could hear them approaching. Voices and hurried footsteps sounded through the damp mist, and then the front door opened and Scott was standing there, his face anxious. He rushed to her side as she stood up from the chair.

"Vanessa, you're not badly hurt? Thank God! I didn't know what to expect when Scarron came to the door asking for a stretcher. No broken bones?"

She assured him she was all right and permitted his arm around her, though she was aware of Kerc's watchful stare. She resented Kerc's gaze, knowing that he thought she and Scott had schemed to win Robert's inheritance from Lucy.

The raven haired girl unexpectedly came up to the table, her eyes wide with concern.

"Vanessa, I'm so sorry this happened! I thought you were right behind me on the trail. Then the mist came in suddenly, and next thing I knew you'd lagged behind. I turned back, calling you, but you didn't answer."

Vanessa fought waves of irritation. She thought Lucy's explanation was crafted especially for Scott's ears.

"I called too. Obviously we didn't hear one another."

"You must stay away from the moor. It can be dangerous if you don't know where you're going." Lucy smiled. "But you're safe; that's what matters. It looks as though nothing serious happened. Aunt Theo's called for Dr. MacGregor. He should be at the house by the time we get back." She took control, turning first to Scarron, who hung back, ordering him to ready the makeshift stretcher, then to Scott, asking him to help Vanessa outdoors.

Vanessa was embarrassed by all the attention and what was beginning to be portrayed as her own silly blunder.

She vigorously protested the use of the stretcher, insisting she could walk if someone would just lend their arm for support, but Scott seemed genuinely concerned.

"My dear, let's not take any more chances until the doctor checks you out. We can't be sure you haven't sprained yourself."

"He's right," Lucy said. "It was a terrible thing to happen on the first day of your visit."

"It wouldn't have happened if your father didn't allow those killer dogs to run loose on his property," Scott said unhappily.

"They be not killer dogs." Kerc spoke up for the first time. "They be highly trained animals."

Vanessa shot him a glance, not because of the dogs but because the accent was back and very pronounced. Was he mocking what he thought Scott and the others thought about his education? She put nothing past him.

"Trained, yes, but trained for what?" Scott demanded. "Do you call chasing Miss Miles off a slippery embankment well-trained animals? Something must be done about them, Kerc."

"Jacinth got loose."

"Loose? How!"

"Scarron says someone left the kennel gate open."

"Left it open, how? And who would have done that?" He turned. "You, Scarron?"

"Nae, Mr. Morgan, b'aint be me, nor Kerc here."

"I say you're getting irresponsible."

"Oh, Scott, stop it. You sound like the chief inspector from Edinburgh," Lucy said with impatience.

"Maybe we should call him."

Vanessa glanced at him surprised, then at Kerc. Kerc, who watched Scott, appeared almost absent of concern. Then he looked at Lucy.

"Scott, nothing happened to Vanessa. Why stir up a hornet's nest?" Lucy said, frustrated. "With Father already ill, any further upsets may set him back. And he still has the ordeal of meeting Vanessa—" She stopped, turned her head quickly toward Vanessa, and had the grace to blush. "Sorry. I didn't mean it the way it sounded."

Yes, you did, Vanessa thought. She tightened her mouth to keep her lips from trembling, giving away emotions she wanted held in captivity. Her vulnerability could break forth when she was least prepared to handle it.

Kerc's dark head turned toward her, studying her.

Scott said, "Robert called Vanessa here because he wanted to see her."

Lucy looked at him. It may have been one of the few times recently that Scott had defended someone other than herself, and Lucy was clearly aware of the small change. There was an awkward moment, then she raised a hand and brushed her shiny dark hair from her shoulder in a habitual gesture.

"So you've told us many times, Scott."

Meaning what? That she didn't altogether trust what Scott told her?

Scott didn't back off this time. "As for Kerc's dogs, something could have happened. That's the point. You need to talk to your father about them, Lucy."

"Vanessa slipped on muddy leaves because she didn't know the area. The mist rolled in quickly. She said so herself. The dogs wouldn't have done anything if they had cornered her up a tree!"

"So says Kerc and Scarron. Why take chances? Kerc has the sheepdogs, why also the Dobermans?"

"They be good dogs," Kerc said mildly. "I'll not get rid of 'em, Mr. Morgan. An' maybe Miss Miles here," he gestured his head toward Vanessa, "has learned a hard lesson for the future about being here on Mull."

Scott looked at him, his face hardening. "What do you mean by that?"

Kerc added easily, "Weather and terrain can be risky. What else would I mean? We learned that's true a couple months ago."

The tavern girl up on Devil's Cliff in the thick mist?

Cousin Scarron remained mute and fidgety just outside the open door. Vanessa masked a shiver.

"All right, Scott. Have your way. I'll speak to my father about all this," Lucy said abruptly. She swung around toward Kerc. Her intonation changed to one of fondness and empathy. "I'll explain it was an accident. Don't worry about the dogs, Kerc."

Scott watched Lucy, then Kerc.

So this is the reason he doesn't like Kerc, Vanessa thought. *Lucy appears to step in to defend Kerc against Scott. Naturally, this would intensify any jealousy he felt when it came to her.* Vanessa also wondered why Lucy seemed benevolent toward him. The obvious reason was his good looks. Even the false impression Kerc gave of being rather slow and uneducated had its charm, but Vanessa had seen and experienced his quick, sizzling wit and precise English. Just what was Kerc trying to accomplish?

Vanessa decided to take the blame. "Please, let's stop all this quarreling. What happened to me is no one's fault in particular."

They all looked at her.

She sighed. "I must have made the wrong turn on the trail as Lucy suggests. If I hadn't run away when I saw the dogs, it's likely they wouldn't have chased me. Let's forget all this blaming, shall we? As everyone can see, I'm alive and well except for a few bramble scratches and torn clothing. Scarron's medicated cream has helped the scrapes, and I can buy a new pair of silk stockings in London."

The silence settled down like fur on a cat's back, uncertain at first, as everyone appeared to wait to see how others would respond. Only Kerc watched her thoughtfully, and she was surprised to see a momentary glimmer of admiration in those dark, earthy eyes. She looked away to Scott quickly. "I'd like to go now, please."

"Yes, certainly. If you're sure you want to drop all this—"

"I'm sure. I'll be here only two weeks. And because I've no intention of exploring the moor, Mr. Trevalyan's Dobermans should prove of no further concern."

"Still—," began Scott.

"You heard Vanessa," Lucy interrupted shortly. "She wants to go."

Vanessa ended matters herself by walking slowly toward the door. Her knees were rubbery, but she made it without help.

Scarron, standing in the misty shadows outside the door, kept back.

Two people were needed to carry the stretcher, and though Vanessa again protested that she could walk, she was thankful to be overruled by Scott. Scarron came to take one end and Scott the other. Lucy walked ahead carrying a lantern, its golden light eerily shining in the mist.

Vanessa surrendered to the stretcher and lay back, drawing the warm blanket up around her neck as moisture from the tree branches dripped coldly.

The house appeared rather ghostly in the tendrils of mist with the half-moon glowing orange between a clear section of sky and pointed roof. Light glowed in the windows, but shadows were moving swiftly across the garden and the trees swayed in the wind that had recently risen, sending the mist out to sea again. The garden, so well attended by Kerc, smelled faintly of roses, and jasmine grew along the embracers of the ancient wall to the side of the house.

Lucy entered the front door first and rushed on up the staircase, apparently to locate her aunt. The house seemed strangely silent when Vanessa entered the darkened hall with Scott.

"Soon you will be snug in your bed," he said comfortingly, with a smile.

"Right now, I wouldn't mind being a little snail pulling into its shell," she said. "I think I shall sleep till noon."

"Do that, my dear. If it's a sunny day tomorrow, you can have tea in the garden. I'll look for you. By then I'll have spoken with Robert again and arranged for you to see him." He smiled grimly. "It's not been a pleasant arrival for you."

"I didn't expect anything different, really. Who knows? Robert may even decide he's made a terrible blunder and send me back to London without seeing me."

"He won't do that. I spoke with him after you arrived this afternoon. He wants to see you, but he's just not quite up to it yet. Things are taking a little longer to fall into place. Eventually, they will. A good night's sleep will restore your courage."

He looked up toward the stairway where a light glimmered down like a shimmering waterfall. "Something is keeping Lucy. I'd better go up and see. Dr. MacGregor should have been here by now. I'll also tell Theo you're here, though she's probably retired to her room. She often doesn't come down for supper. Like Robert, she has a heart condition and tires easily. It was only discovered last week."

"When will I meet her?" Not that Vanessa was anxious.

"Most likely tomorrow, unless she and Lucy take an early boat to the mainland. Theo is rather rigid. She doesn't respond well to sudden changes. She'll want to meet you in a proper way. Tea and all that, and wearing her finery. That's the way she is. I think you'll like her."

"She was married to Norah's brother?"

"Yes, Vernon Gowrie. Actually, Theo was his second wife. The first Mrs. Gowrie died soon after the first war. He married Theo about ten years ago. Vernon was her second marriage as well. They were quite happy in a companionable sort of way until he developed a lung condition and died. When Norah died, Robert wanted Theo to stay on and be with his daughter."

He frowned to himself as some thought must have troubled him, then noticing Vanessa standing there, his frown deepened. "Here I am rattling on when you need care. I'm afraid I'm not much good for anything tonight. Do you want to go on up to your room, my dear? Or take a chair in the library?"

"The library?"

"Dr. MacGregor always uses the library when he comes to see Robert about his heart condition. Robert likes to work there where it's quiet. He was there for a short time this evening."

Vanessa was anxious for the privacy of her room, but if she must see the doctor, it seemed best to see him downstairs.

"The library will be fine."

"Good. I won't be but a moment."

He showed her into the lighted room, and then he closed the door and left.

Vanessa was exhausted as she moved over to a big brown leather chair and sank into it, staring disconsolately at her torn and soiled clothing. The runs in her silk stockings were even worse now. She'd mentioned buying some in London, but with the war on they were nearly impossible to find. Not that such a mundane matter concerned her at this time...her mind was just so tired with all that she had encountered today that she found solace in thinking about the inconsequential.

There was a huge display of books lining one wall from floor to ceiling. A spacious mahogany desk stood near a draperied window with the shades now drawn against the gloom. A study lamp and a stack of books sat beside the typewriter. The monumental stack of paper must be her father's manuscript. Vanessa had not yet asked Scott about the book that he'd said was about the history of the Gowrie family.

She went to the desk and noticed that the lid on the inkwell had been left off. She placed it back on to keep it from drying out. He couldn't have worked very long tonight. *His health must be affecting his progress*, she thought, feeling nothing. The things she looked at—the books, the typewriter, the stack of paper, a pipe, a half-used book of matches, a glass ashtray—were all items belonging to a stranger. She neither knew him, nor loved him, and she was sure the feeling was quite mutual. Yet, here she was at long last in the room where her father spent so much of his time. This was his chair, his box of shortbread biscuits, his favorite pipe.

Vanessa ran her swollen fingers gently along the back of the leather chair. It was cold to her touch. She drew her hand back and turned, noticing that one of the volumes lay open, as though he'd been reading a section that might apply to his work.

It was a history book; she hadn't expected anything different. From the looks of the pages and leather binding, however, it was a very old and expensive volume, most certainly out of print and possibly one of a kind. The lamp was still shining down, and she peered over to see what section he was reading.

It took a moment to decide that the author had been writing about Robert the Bruce, the man credited with the founding of Scotland. She skimmed down the page to where Queen Mary and her son James were briefly mentioned, and then to a related Earl of Gowrie.

Gowrie. Her father must be writing about the history of Norah's ancestral family. Yes, Vanessa could understand why. Scott had said how much her father had loved Norah, how broken he was over her death, and a family search into her past and the estate lands undoubtedly brought him nearer to her in his mind and heart. But of what value would a personal history book like this be to the general public? Or was it, perhaps, not the public that was on Robert's mind but Lucy? He may want to leave such a monumental work to her as a wedding present, and naturally there would be her children and grandchildren.

The door opened and she turned around quickly.

A white-haired man entered, tall and elegant, with ruffled brows and fair skin. His bearing and professional gaze, coupled with a dark satchel in hand, identified him.

"Miss Miles? I'm Dr. MacGregor. I understand you've taken quite a tumble."

"I'm afraid so." She smiled. "I'm a New Yorker, unaccustomed to your beautiful moors and heavy mists."

"From the looks of your clothing, it might have been much worse. You seem to have escaped with only a few bumps. We'll make certain. We want to be sure that the rest of your visit on Mull will be pleasant and safe."

11

Awakening late the following morning, Vanessa lay for several minutes wondering why the room was in shadows and so stuffy. Her head felt unaccountably heavy and dull. Noticing the half-empty glass of water, she remembered the tablet Dr. MacGregor had insisted she take. So that was it. The sleeping medicine had done its work, but it had also turned her into mush.

Maybe if she got moving it would help. Easing aside the covers, she stood. Except for some stiffness and a few bruises, she felt reasonably well and able to pursue the goals that had brought her to Scotland. All she needed was something to help wake her up. *A steaming mug of coffee would taste delicious right now,* she thought with a sigh. Never a tea drinker, even after almost three months she was still adjusting to afternoon tea.

She reached to the foot of the bed for her powder blue dressing gown. Someone, probably Scott, had turned the clock face to the wall to ensure she slept late. She was startled to learn it was half past one in the afternoon. By now, Lucy and her aunt would have departed for the mainland, and Scott would have met with her father to arrange their introduction. They were probably wondering if they might need to send the maid up to awaken her.

She went to the telephone and rang down to the kitchen for tea and scones.

"Oh, mum, a good mornin' to you. I would'a brought them sooner, but Mr. Morgan told me not to trouble you."

"It was kind of you to let me sleep. Is Mr. Morgan in the garden? Perhaps I'll join him—"

"Oh, no, mum. He done left the house very early indeed."

"Did he say when he'd return?"

"No, mum. Nary a word."

"Any other messages?" Vanessa was thinking of her father.

"No, mum."

Surely her father intended to meet with her today. She replaced the receiver. Two weeks wasn't that long, and to have another day of postponement was discouraging.

Patience was needed. *Leave matters to Scott,* she warned herself, *and wait for the Lord to work matters out on your behalf in His own timing.* Did she believe He would? She was tempted not to. He had allowed her father to abandon them, hadn't He? Was God really involved in His children's daily happenings? *Have faith in God, Vanessa Miles. Has He ever abandoned you? No, He is always faithful and true.*

Drawing back the curtains she saw that the day was a lovely one, with sunshine pouring down out of a gorgeous blue sky. She breathed in a deep breath of fresh air and forced herself to smile. All was not lost. She saw a mother duck and six little ducklings waddling down the garden path toward a pond where blackberry vines grew in nice, neat rows on a trellis. More of the caretaker's careful, precise work. The weeds were gone, the flowers were staked, the bushes all trimmed.

It would be a good time to sit in the sunshine and write letters to Andy, Francis, and Kylie. Perhaps Scott would show up later. Maybe he'd gone back to speak to Scarron or Kerc to lay down stricter rules about the dogs. Vanessa frowned. She hadn't said anything to either Scott or the caretaker last night about Scarron's veiled threats. There'd been too much to handle. There was time for that later. Maybe she'd speak to the caretaker first. Scott seemed to be looking for some cause to provoke her father into firing him, and Vanessa, no matter how wary she was of him, wanted nothing to do with his dismissal. She was remembering the missing button and frayed sleeves on his old coat, and the simple bungalow Scarron lived in. Chances were that the fish in the bucket last night was considered a choice meal, while she and those in the house could have dined on a succulent roast. And his fishing boat had been badly shot-up. It would probably take months of work with caretaker wages to afford repairs.

If your enemy hungers, feed him. If he thirsts, give him drink. Do not render evil for evil. No, she would accept the incident with the dogs as what he'd said it was—an accident. Hopefully, an accident that hadn't been planned by him, Scarron, or Lucy.

"I'll speak to him myself about his odious cousin," she murmured aloud, looking out toward the lighthouse.

She turned away from the window. Last night, except for a simple washing up, she'd gone straight to bed, putting a pillow over her head to shut out everything unpleasant. A bath and shampoo were definitely in order. It was then, as she walked past the white spindle-legged vanity table toward the bathroom, that she noticed them sitting there. She stopped.

A crystal vase housed the most luscious roses she'd ever seen.

She scooped up the vase and breathed in their heady scent. "Mmmm..." They were beautiful.

Scott or Lucy must have sent them up from the garden. They were probably meant to be a peace offering after her cool welcome yesterday. Or—her head turned toward the window again. No. Impossible. *"You don't like me very much, do you?" "Not particularly."*

They must have come from Scott.

The sound of someone working outside drifted to her on a light breath of air through the window. *Unless Kerc's conscience is troubling him,* she thought wryly. A peace offering for not protesting about his dogs yesterday, most likely. Well, even roses offered grudgingly meant she would get along better on the estate grounds for the next few weeks.

She walked back to the window, still holding the vase thick with roses. Kerc's hair showed shiny and dark beneath the sun's rays, and he wore rugged work clothes and boots. He was hard at work trimming the yews and paid not the slightest attention toward the house or to her window and terrace. If he had sent the roses, it might mean he had decided to be a little friendlier. This would give her opportunity to ask questions, not just about his strange cousin, but about the tavern girl, and even Norah, though it didn't seem likely a caretaker would know much about Robert's second wife. Scott would be the one to ask about Norah, and maybe Lucy.

She went back to the telephone and rang down to the kitchen. "Never mind about bringing tea to my room. I'll have it out in the garden—say in twenty minutes?"

She looked again at the roses, set the vase on the vanity table, and hurried to take her bath and ready herself for a day that just might include meeting Robert Miles.

She chose her mint green silky dress cinched at the waist with a white belt and gold buckle. She arranged her long hair loosely down her back and held the sides back with honey-colored combs that matched her hair. A bit of cream makeup covered the pinkness of the scratch on her face, just in case her father asked. A little mascara and lipstick brought her features to life. There was even a sparkle today in what Scott had called her "smoky green" eyes. Naturally, she wanted to look her best for any impromptu meeting. There was also Lucy's aunt to meet.

A few minutes later, she left her room and went downstairs and out into the garden, feeling almost her old self, except for a little soreness and stiffness in her knee as she walked.

≁≁≁

June in Scotland. What could be better? The damp and chilly boat ride of yesterday was becoming a distant memory. The heather was in rich bloom, the bees buzzed, and the sky was as blue as a jay's wing. The afternoon evoked strange longings and restless desires. The hedgerows, the tender blooming meadow grasses with dancing yellow flowers, and the lazy sweetness of the air washed away last night's misty apparitions of things dark and troubling. The thrushes were singing ecstatically in the hawthorn trees, which were bursting with bloom. Cowslips peeped up from beneath the hedges. The ducklings had waddled into the pond, following their "mum," and there was one large white swan with her own brood on the other side, while a blue heron concentrated on fishing for its lunch. The whispering breeze lifted the hem of her silky skirt and touched her hair affectionately. No wonder her father had settled here.

How could anything be wrong in all the world on a June day like this? Yet the war was being fought across the Channel, England was in jeopardy of being bombed to smithereens by the Luftwaffe, and Hitler still raged before his adoring audiences. And here in Scotland, despite her Pollyanna emotions this noontime, Vanessa was aware that she was not wanted by all who lived here. When the sun set, shadows of suspicion would come sidling in again from the moors.

The courtyard, facing the front garden, was paved with an unusual bluish flagstone. There were tables and chairs, with stone benches placed here and there for the best view of the rose garden. A two-seater swing beckoned one to daydream between two hemlocks growing beside the path that wound to the pond. Beyond the pond there was even more garden acreage, probably fruit trees and vegetables.

A great deal of work for someone, she thought. Kerc must put in long hours, but it was very well cared for. No wonder Lucy spoke of his "magical touch." *There is no magic wand,* she thought, *but calloused hands and sore muscles at the end of the day.* A great contrast from Scott's type of work, poring over history books and digging up research for her father.

She glanced across the flagstones to where a small wicker gate opened into the rose garden. From where she sat, she could see Kerc working.

He saw her too, she could sense it, although he hadn't looked up.

Vanessa chose a table and was about to sit down when he called quickly: "Best wait a second."

She turned. Kerc was striding toward her. "Chair's still wet. I hosed 'em down this morning." He had a worker's cloth and quickly dried the seat and table. "Pretty dress. I wouldn't want the ruin of more New York clothes."

She smiled ruefully. "Nor do I. Thank you. I'll soon be running out of things to wear if I'm not careful. But this dress didn't come from a New York store. I bought it at a church thrift shop in London. I already had the belt."

The corners of his mouth turned up. He made no comment.

She noted that his eyes were as rich and dark as chocolate, that the lashes were thick and full, and that the dark hair she had once thought unkempt and might smell like fish oil was as glossy and clean as her own. How wrong she'd been about his personal habits! Though his hair was perhaps a mite too long, it in no way detracted from his overall appeal. If she cared to ponder, which she did not, the caretaker outshone them all. Kerc had darkly handsome good looks that suggested something very intriguing.

She found herself glancing away from his disconcerting gaze because she didn't want him reading her thoughts.

"Um—thank you for catching me in time, Mr. Trevalyan."

The smile deepened and was electric. "First name will do, miss. Not often the caretaker's called mister. Especially by a daughter of the occupant of Gowrie House."

The humility seems a little overdone, she thought. *Why?*

She set the woven bag holding her writing things down on the table and busied herself with removing them. When he remained, she commented, "You take excellent care of the garden. It's quite something to look at." She turned full circle. "It's very big, isn't it?"

"Aye, but in the old days it was bigger than this. There used to be a hunting range. It's said even his majesty once came here as a guest of Earl Gowrie and went hunting for stag."

"King George?" she asked surprised.

He laughed. "King James of Scotland."

"Oh." She hastened: "I'm enjoying the garden tremendously this morning after—" She stopped, not wanting to let the grumbling tiger of dislike out of the cage just yet by bringing up last night. He seemed to guess, though.

"Aye, nothing like sunshine and songbirds to chase the misty ghosts away. Sometimes the fog gets thicker than pea soup. When it does, even those born here don't venture out on the moors."

She carefully laid out her writing materials. "Well, thank you for warning me about the pool of water in the chair. I didn't see it and would have ruined my dress if you hadn't said something."

His attitude had taken an about-face from last night and the times she'd met him in London and on the boat. The question was, why? Was his opinion of her changing? She couldn't help thinking of the old adage about honey catching more flies than vinegar. Did he see her as a fly to trap in his web of intrigue?

"I thought I'd have my tea here this morning," she explained for lack of anything else to say. Bringing up her suspicions about his cousin now seemed distasteful. Did the caretaker's opinion of her matter so much?

She had brought one of the roses with her and laid it on the table to enjoy. It was also a signal for him to mention where the flowers had come from if he chose. He didn't, although he couldn't have missed its glorious presence.

"I won't keep you. Just thought I'd see how you were today. Seems you're doing fine enough. Can hardly tell you took that tumble."

"My body remembers, I assure you, but thanks for asking."

He appeared in no particular hurry to leave. He removed his gloves and checked his thumb with a squint.

She remembered and said: "And your hand? Is it all right now?"

"My hand?"

"You had hurt it...gracious, was it only last Wednesday when you rescued the refugees? It seems a month ago!"

"Aye, so it was," he said dourly. "And so my boat sits at the London docks. It'll be awhile before repairs can be made."

"And your hand?"

"It's fine now." He shoved his hand into his pocket as if it were in his way.

There was no scowl in his features today as there had been that night. Something told her he was struggling to keep his dislike from completely ebbing away. He must still be suspicious of her and Scott. Then why this unexpected friendliness? As she looked at him, his own gaze faltered, drifting across her face and hair before landing on her writing materials.

"Writing to one of your boyfriends about your troubles here?"

One of her boyfriends. So he thought she had more than one? Not very flattering, considering she had come to London with the idea of deciding whether to become engaged to Andy. But Kerc wouldn't know about that, of course.

She twiddled the pen between her fingers. "Andy Warnstead."

"Colonel Warnstead's son?"

"Yes, you know him?" she asked, surprised.

"No. I heard about him when I made a trip to London about a month ago. I had to order some supplies, and Edinburgh didn't have what I wanted." He gestured his head toward the pad of paper. "If you make your RAF pilot worry about you, he might be distracted when he scrambles."

"Andy isn't the worrying kind. Besides, he encouraged me to come here."

"Did he?"

She wondered if Kerc thought Andy was part of a romantic triangle. Vanessa wanted to correct Kerc again, but another denial might convince him she was trying to hide something.

"Your pilot was probably hoping you'd sort out all the nettles growing these years between you and your father. Sounds sensible, at first." His eyes flickered and the old look came back. "But he doesn't know all the facts. He should'a stopped you."

"All the facts?" she repeated.

"About your cooperating with Scott Morgan to get the estate from your father."

She sighed. "I've told you, I am *not* conniving to gain the estate."

"Everyone else is, why wouldn't you? And why not with Scott, as he arranged your coming at this time, when your father's ill and dying."

She was offended, but held back. "We don't know that he's dying...he had a mild heart attack, so says Dr. MacGregor, but he could have many more years."

He shook his head. "He's an ill man."

"As for everyone else conniving for the estate, Mr. Trevalyan, does that also include you? Through marriage to Lucy, perhaps?"

He smiled. "Not much chance Miss Lucy would marry a caretaker. She doesn't mind being friends, since she doesn't have many she trusts. But she's marrying Jodrell, if some in her family have their way. 'Course, Scott's hoping to stop that from happening. I'd like to stop it too."

Vanessa took that to mean he had his own personal interest in Lucy despite his humble position.

"Then—if Scott's in love with Lucy, he and I wouldn't be conniving together as you claim."

"I didn't say you and Scott were lovers; I just said you two might be playing this game together so he ends up with Lucy."

"And if he and Lucy marry, and she ends up with the estate as seems quite probable since she's Robert's daughter, what do you think my motive would be in working with him?"

"First, you're his daughter too."

She felt the heat rise in her cheeks. "I'd rather not discuss that, please."

"I understand the reasons. As to what you'll get, money is what most people get. Mr. Miles has a bundle besides the property. Scott might have promised to give you a hefty share. For a working girl like yourself, that would sound pretty tempting, I dare say."

Vanessa fumed. "You think you have me all figured out, don't you?"

"You'd be surprised the things I know. I'm part of the scenery around here. Have been since I was a boy."

"Well, you're flat out wrong about me. Furthermore, I've given up trying to convince you." She was nettled. "You're likely to believe what suits your fancy. So if you'll excuse me," she said, turning away with dismissal, "I've some letters to write, and I'm sure you have work to do." She sat down primly, drew her pad of paper across the table, and refused to look at him. Such an impossible young man. He was as obstinate as a mule!

She fussed with her writing materials, but he didn't turn away. Instead, he changed the subject. "You expecting company? Scott, maybe?"

"After your innuendoes, do you expect me to tell you anything?"

"Not that I'd be interested, mind you, except he won't be joining you for tea."

She looked up, wondering.

"Be much later than teatime. You'd best go ahead and have it yourself. Be lucky if he's even here by suppertime."

"How do you know that?"

"He took Lucy across to the mainland. Miss Theo didn't go as she planned. Said she wasn't up to it today. So Lucy asked Scott. He jumped at the opportunity. He always does when she asks him to do something. Too bad he couldn't keep his time with you though, since you got ready for him, changing your dress and all. What would your pilot think about it?"

She flushed foolishly. "He wouldn't think anything. He knows me well. *And* trusts me. Anyway, Scott didn't stand me up, as you put it. We didn't have a date. Not the kind you're hinting of. Since he's the one who brought me here at my father's invitation, he also stands between us, arranging things."

"Lots to be arranged, I imagine."

She ignored his comment and looked at the rose, fingering it thoughtfully. "I suppose Scott told you he was taking Lucy to the mainland?"

"Not exactly."

"Didn't he ask you to pick the roses?"

"Scott wouldn't know a rose from a geranium. You thought he might have asked me to pick 'em and send 'em up because of your accident last night?"

That was what she had thought, but she wouldn't admit to it now.

"The roses are wonderful, by the way. Lucy is right. You do have a way with them."

The corners of his mouth deepened into a smile that took her off guard. She dropped her gaze quickly.

"It was Mr. Miles who asked me to pick the roses."

She caught a breath—her father? It came as a total surprise. "Oh!"

"You like them then?"

"Who wouldn't except someone who's color blind with a bad head cold."

He smiled. "There were other shades I could have picked; the pink ones are nice too. But the hot flame color and copper kind'a gets to me."

"Yes. Kind'a does." She smiled as she touched a velvety petal.

There was silence. She glanced up. He was looking away toward the old rose garden and gestured his head. "There's some very old roses in there. They been growing from stock and replantings since the 1600s. The first Earl Gowrie brought the cuttings from the mainland. Where he got 'em, no one knows. The servant class who knows more sometimes than those in the house says he got 'em from the garden of Queen Elizabeth. Earl Gowrie was a friend of Earl Robert Essex. There's romantic tales about Essex and the queen."

"Yes...but in the end she had his head removed at the Tower."

"Aye. Like a woman to turn on her man when she gets riled." He looked down on her and suddenly the smile was back. "You ought to have a look in the old garden while you're here sometime," he suggested easily.

"Yes. I shall." She hesitated a moment, and then asked, "So my father asked you to pick the roses and send them to me?"

"Aye, he did. He called my bungalow around five o'clock. I usually get up at four. He was worried about your fall and wanted to send the best roses."

She laid the luscious bloom across her palm, as if cradling the small head of an infant. "I thought they were from Scott."

"Aye, I know."

She looked up defensively. "Or Lucy. Lucy is the one who takes the greatest interest in the old rose garden, isn't she?"

"Both of us do. Those roses were almost dead when I came back as caretaker. Nobody's cared for them since I was a boy. I used to go there often with—" He paused abruptly, and then said, "Anyway, 'twas your father who asked me to choose some for you."

She nodded, saying nothing. Looking at the rose and smelling its fragrance brought a lump to her throat. It was a response she didn't want. She had repeatedly warned herself not to allow sentimentality to color her judgment. It was a nice gesture and that was all. A belated gesture. She remembered her graduation from high school and the corsages her friends wore, many given to them by their fathers. She had fought against a feeling of rejection then, but now she wanted it there to safeguard her from rushing off a cliff.

Kerc was saying: "He says he wants to have supper alone with you tonight. Not here on the estate. There's a fancy fish house in these parts."

Her heart skipped a beat despite her intentions. Alone with her father. How that would have made her happy as a child. Sitting together away from listening family ears and eyes was what she had hoped for. Scott's excursion with Lucy to the mainland had worked out for the best after all.

Kerc appeared to watch her indolently, but she sensed his alertness.

"What do you want me to tell him?"

"Tell him…yes."

He nodded. "Be on the other side of the house around six o'clock. He has an automobile. A Daimler. It's too big for most streets near town, but he likes to take it out on the country roads." He cast a glance toward the big house. "Effie is taking a long time with that tea."

"About last night," she began, "in your cottage—"

"It's not mine. It's Scarron's."

"Well, I have a few more questions I'd like to ask."

He shrugged, and his dark eyes turned flinty again. "Sure. Ask away."

"It's about your cousin."

"I thought it would be."

"I haven't said anything to Scott because I didn't want further trouble between you."

"Is that why you let things go last night?"

"Yes. I want no part of it."

"That's commendable."

"It's sensible. I didn't come here for trouble, though you're having a difficult time believing that."

"I'm beginning to."

Was he really? She decided to let it go and continued, "I hope to be a peacemaker. I've decided not to mention what he said to Scott or Robert. I realize you work for my father and, well, saying anything to him at this juncture probably wouldn't go well for you or your cousin."

She could feel his emotions take a step back from her. He looked at her blankly.

She felt embarrassed and glanced at the rose.

"Go on, Miss Miles. No need to be shy about my position here. Everyone knows what it is, including me. I was born and raised here of servant class. I don't know anything different."

"That's not what—"

"But that's what I am. So if you're trying to say you protected me, my dogs, and Scarron, I'd be a skunk if I didn't say I appreciate your silence, especially to Scott, since he and I don't get along."

She avoided his eyes. "That doesn't mean I won't mention your cousin to my father should I think it necessary later."

"You're generous, Miss Miles."

The soft-spoken voice might be genuine, but she had her doubts.

"That you're willing to play it fair with Scarron makes me wonder."

"About what?" she asked quickly.

"About you. Might be I wasn't right about you. Least, not in everything."

"Not in everything?" she said ruefully.

"Best we don't get into that now. Go ahead. You said you had a question or two."

"Not questions, exactly. I'm concerned about Scarron."

He watched her thoughtfully. "In what way? His control over the dogs? I was going to tell you that you don't need to worry anymore. I put a new bolt on the kennel gate this morning as soon as I got up. They can't get out. And I've spoken to Scarron."

"That's all very well, but it's what he said to me that's troubling. He hinted at some frightening things."

He scowled. "He did?"

"You look doubtful. Then you didn't put him up to it, to frighten me into leaving?"

"I've been open about not wanting you here, so that's no secret. No, I didn't tell him to threaten you. Is that what he did?"

"Yes." She told him what Scarron had said and was satisfied when he didn't immediately counter with a charge of his own or rush to defend his cousin. He was thoughtful, and a frown developed between his dark brows.

"He mentioned Maggie?"

"Yes. Did you know who she was?"

The silence and veiled look told her he did.

"Was she the girl who met her death by falling from Devil's Cliff?"

"Yes."

"Then you knew her?"

"She worked at the tavern on the wharf. Just about everybody saw her around."

It was an evasive answer, but she didn't press for more information, sensing he wouldn't give it.

"Why would your cousin say that if I insisted on coming here to the house, I'd be in danger too, same as Maggie?"

His frown deepened. "I'll talk to him. I'll find out. I didn't realize he'd said all this to you last night, or I wouldn't have—

you'd been through more of a trauma than I understood. Looks like an apology is in order, Miss Miles. I hope you'll accept it."

Surprised, she looked down at her rose. She didn't want him to know just how pleased she was, or that what he thought about her could matter so much.

"Thank you for the apology. I do accept it. But have you any idea why he'd say such things to me?"

If he did, Kerc wouldn't say so now. She could see, however, that he was agitated and trying to hold it back so she wouldn't notice.

"Sounds like Scarron might have built himself a new still somewhere. Looks like I'll need to hunt it down and destroy this one too. Don't pay any attention to him. I'll see you don't run into him again during your stay."

"You'll find out what he meant?"

"I'll talk to him. You can be sure of it."

From the hardness of his jawline she had no doubt. She may have been foolish to put so much store in Kerc's new behavior, but she felt a little easier.

"What do you know about Maggie's death?" she asked him. "On the boat you seemed to hint that things may not have been accidental."

"I'm sorry I mentioned it."

"Why?"

His dark eyes refused her probing question. But if he was sorry about using Maggie's death on the boat to frighten her from coming to see her father, as Vanessa believed he had, he didn't admit it.

"Because there's enough going on that's troubling without discussing what happened to Maggie. And now that you're here, and it's plain you intend to stay, the less you probe around about Devil's Cliff, the better off you'll be."

"Now you're sounding like Scarron," she said irritably.

"No," and his voice was calm and easy. "I'm not trying to frighten you away now. I'm trying to keep you out of trouble."

"I'll tell you what I told your cousin. I've no intention of climbing Devil's Cliff in the fog or rain."

If he was satisfied, he didn't show it.

"What could Scarron have meant about the goings-on in Gowrie House? Was he just trying to frighten me?"

Anger sparkled in his eyes, but for once it wasn't directed toward her.

"Scott had no sense to bring you here."

"Why!" She stood. "Apart from your idea that I was in compliance with him, is there something more? Some other reason why I shouldn't be here?" Suddenly a new thought struck her. "Exactly how *did* Norah die?"

"It's up to your father to tell you about his wife's death, not me. There's a lot of talk. It's fool's talk, most of it. Just tales."

"If I recall, Scott said the same thing about you and Devil's Cliff—and Maggie, but you spoke differently, then."

"I once said one too many things," he said irritably, shoving his hands in his pockets. "I'm sorry I did now. You can forget what I said, Miss Miles. About you—about Devil's Cliff, about the whole lot of it. Sometimes I take after my cousin. That's nothing to boast of, I dare say. But there you have it. It runs in the family blood. Exaggeration, old folklore, suspicion, the works. We're a poor lot, and you would be wise to stay away from us."

She didn't quite believe him, and she wondered if he wasn't just trying to hold her off because she'd stumbled on a trail that might lead to more than either of them had bargained for, straight to Devil's Cliff.

He stooped and picked up his cutting instrument. "I best be getting back to work. I'll tell Mr. Miles you'll be ready for supper with him." He gestured his head. "Here comes your morning tea at last. About time. It's after two o'clock." He gave her a smile and walked away, leaving her with unanswered questions and a dissatisfaction about the outcome of their conversation.

The maid came around the side of the house and down the walk toward the courtyard carrying the long-overdue tea tray. Vanessa saw the girl's eyes follow Kerc behind the yews. There was a rosy glow to her cheeks, like country apples, and her blue eyes looked a trifle unhappy. Then Vanessa saw the girl's glance take in her dress and shoes, as though owning them were the total answer to her life's problems. What a new dress and pair of shoes wouldn't do to turn a maid into an upper-class lady—and perhaps gain the attention of the caretaker? Vanessa didn't doubt but that Kerc would be the heartthrob of every young woman of the servant class downstairs. She imagined with little difficulty that he could also be of profound interest to both upper-class daughters upstairs.

"Afternoon, Miss Miles."

There was a full pot of tea with a cozy, a plate of freshly baked scones, sugar and cream, and country butter and honey.

"Be anything more, miss?"

"No. Thank you."

"Very well, miss." The maid curtsied and started to turn away when she stopped suddenly with embarrassment.

"I almost forgot this. 'Twas the cause for my being a little long in bringing the tray, miss. I do apologize."

She reached into her white apron and produced a sealed envelope. There was no smile, but a certain vague dislike in her pale eyes that stood too close together in an otherwise plain face. Was the dislike for her or the person who had delayed her in the kitchen?

Vanessa took the small envelope, and the maid minced hurriedly away, glancing over her shoulder toward the yews.

Vanessa drew her chair out and sat down. From her father? No, more than likely it was from Scott. He must have left it before he took Lucy to the mainland. He wouldn't have known that Kerc would explain.

But the letter wasn't from Scott or her father. It was from Theo.

12

Vanessa,

I would like very much to speak with you before you meet with Robert. There are things you should know that Scott isn't likely to tell you. I'll be down in the garden by 2:30.

Theo Gowrie

Vanessa glanced at her watch. It was nearly that time now. She read the words a second time, cautious. Kerc's rationale for mistrusting Scott hadn't been fully explained. But why did Theo mistrust him? Could she have a purpose quite her own?

Vanessa folded the slip of paper and placed it in her bag. It was too late to retreat, and it wouldn't be polite if she did. But she didn't care to become snagged in a net of family complications and jealousies that would distract her from her real purpose in coming. It was her father she must face tonight—and she needed all her emotional strength intact for that meeting. Family tensions, and the death of Maggie, were a different matter, though Kerc hadn't convinced her there wasn't something more that deserved investigation about the tavern girl.

He was right about one thing, though. The underlying problems that threatened to surface like some huge destructive iceberg were not hers. She would see her father, work to arrange a meeting with Kylie, and then return to America by way of London. A return to New York, even in hot, muggy July, was preferable to a brewing storm of family problems.

Theo Gowrie came walking around the yews that marked the boundary of the front garden. There was a man walking beside her who took her complaint calmly.

"I can't see that you've accomplished much in the last two weeks," Theo was saying. "At this rate the third floor won't be finished until my niece's first child is born. If it's more help you need—" Her voice faded as she stopped on the walk to face him. Vanessa could hear no more.

He stood nodding his head congenially as though Theo were discussing the trout season instead of complaining about his inadequate progress.

Scott had mentioned the carpentry work being done on the third floor, getting it ready for Lucy and Jodrell's marriage.

Kerc was still in the vicinity busily trimming, and she was sure he had noticed Theo's arrival.

Vanessa turned her attention to Lucy's aunt by marriage. She had somehow expected Theo to be another replica of Norah Gowrie Benton, but there was nothing of the cool, dark-haired, self-contained actress about Theo Gowrie.

Sadly, perhaps hauntingly so, Theo reminded her of someone in a blurred family photograph whose features had faded with time so that she was no longer clearly distinguishable. If there was anything about Theo that drew attention and singled her apart from others, it wasn't a reflection of her sister-in-law's beauty. Unfortunately, it was Theo's defect—one leg was a trifle shorter than the other. Yet even the slight difference was exaggerated by her quick, peculiar gait, as though impatient to surge ahead. It wasn't until Theo spoke that the inner flare of strong self-will emerged to overshadow the physical.

"Hello, Vanessa. May I join you for tea?"

"Why, yes, of course." She managed a smile, though she was a little nervous. "I haven't yet had a cup myself. Please..." Vanessa drew out a wrought iron chair for Theo, who took it gratefully, and then sat down across the white table from her, removing the tea cozy from the pot.

"I say, it seems Effie had enough sense to include another cup. I'm surprised she remembered. She goes around in a fog most of the time, poor thing. She's a bit barmy, you know."

No, Vanessa didn't know.

"Unfortunately, it runs in the family from generations back. The servant class at Gowrie House are about as old as the Gowries themselves...ah, how nice," she said taking the cup Vanessa had poured. "I've been so busy this morning, it's marvelous to sit and enjoy this."

Vanessa removed the linen cloth on the basket of freshly baked scones.

"Scones originated in Scotland, did you know?" Theo said.

No, Vanessa didn't know that either. There were lemon curd, blueberry, and cinnamon raisin. Theo waved a hand of dismissal. "Sugar makes me excitable."

Vanessa nodded sympathetically and chose a lemon curd. She refrained from adding a heaping teaspoon of sugar to her tea as usual.

"Mmm...you have an excellent cook here, Mrs. Gowrie. This is simply wonderful."

"Call me Theo, dear, everyone does. Iris made the scones; she's Effie's grandmother...and Kerc's too, for that matter." She looked across the yews at Kerc, who was kneeling over something in a flower bed.

So Effie and Kerc were cousins? Then she'd misjudged that look Effie had cast his way when she arrived with the tea tray. Barmy...hadn't she heard Scott mention something about that?

"Of course, the malady hasn't show up in Kerc," Theo was saying. "Not yet, anyway. Perhaps in his children. Most regrettable. Such a handsome boy. But his cousin Scarron..." Her voice eased off, and her eyes came to Vanessa. "Such a dreadful chap."

Was Kerc in line for some sort of mental malady? In such a virile young man it was disappointing. For some unknown reason her spirits sagged. Vanessa looked away from the handsome image of Kerc to the faded face of Theo. At times the sunlight shone on her spectacles, concealing her eyes.

"And Scott was terribly upset about your encounter with Kerc's dogs. Most hideous, to be sure."

"I'm feeling much better. It's an experience I'd prefer to forget, and I'd rather he didn't make a fuss about it."

"Why Kerc keeps them is anyone's guess. But Robert permits it, so fuss or no, there's not much chance he'll get rid of them. Although Kerc could sell them to a kennel in Edinburgh. They're thoroughbreds, I'm told, and worth something. Since he's trying to raise money to repair his fishing vessel, perhaps he should think about it. Why anyone would pay a handsome sum for a dog is beyond me. A dog is a dog, a 'mutt,' I think, is how you Americans put it."

A lover of animals of any sort, and not blaming the dogs, but Scarron, for permitting their aggressive behavior, Vanessa remained silent.

Theo shook her head. "Whether it's Kerc's dogs or other matters, Robert isn't himself recently. I'm worried about him. It's the reason I wanted to talk to you. I hope you don't mind?"

Vanessa hesitated only a moment. "No...of course not." She was beginning to alter her opinion of Theo's involvement in family matters. She seemed genuinely concerned about things, including Robert, and Vanessa wanted to assure her that she wasn't here on the estate to add to her worries. It was clear that Theo thought of herself as holding the diverse family together, including the servants.

"Is something wrong?" Vanessa asked, inviting Theo to explain.

"Not wrong, exactly, but certainly troubling. One doesn't know quite how to approach such a delicate matter. Naturally, I wouldn't want you to think we didn't approve of your meeting Robert."

Vanessa couldn't help but notice that she said "Robert" and not "your father." Perhaps it was unintentional, but it was oddly distressing just the same. "We?" Vanessa repeated. "You and Scott?"

Theo set her cup down. "Definitely not Scott, no, no. I speak of myself and Lucy. Scott is part of the problem, you understand. He's worked for Robert for so many years that he's practically become part of the family...or thinks he has. He has more access to him than any of the rest of us do, including his own daughter. Lucy is terribly put out about it. And now Scott—well, I don't mean to sound unpleasant. You do seem to be a lovely young woman. Even so, Scott has sprung quite a surprise upon us by bringing you here."

Vanessa drew in a small breath, trying to shield her heart from the unexpected barrage of little arrows. Maybe Theo didn't mean to hurt her, but the result was the same.

"You didn't know I was coming until yesterday when I arrived?"

"We knew a week ago. Robert informed Lucy she had a sister."

"She didn't know about me and Kylie until a week ago?" Vanessa asked incredulously.

"Oh, I think she knew. We all knew about Robert's first marriage, but it was all so unreal until just recently. Most regrettable, I dare say." She fanned herself briskly.

She made it sound as though her existence was a terminal illness just announced by the doctor. Vanessa's hands turned clammy.

And Scott had helped to bring about her visit, so he was viewed not merely as a catalyst for change, but an instigator. The irritation in her voice over Scott's access to Robert spoke volumes. Was the jealousy for herself or Lucy, whom she intimated was the injured party?

"Lucy's erratic behavior is a symptom of her distress—for instance, going to the mainland with Scott. It was foolish of her to do that. It will make Jodrell angry. He knows that Scott is trying to come between them. And Robert! He's consumed with the research for his manuscript to the point of neglecting his daughter. She's terribly put out by this."

Vanessa felt the sting, though it wasn't obvious by Theo's manner that she'd deliberately meant it. She seemed merely consumed with her own concerns that centered around Lucy.

Neglected. What did Lucy know of neglect from her father? *She can make such a statement in regard to Lucy because she doesn't consider me to be Robert's daughter in the sense that Lucy is*, Vanessa thought with a sudden surge of resentment.

It was on the tip of Vanessa's tongue to snap: Lucy ought to have experienced the neglect that I and Kylie did if she wants to moan about neglect.

Wisely, she refrained. *Set a watch, O Lord, before my mouth; keep the door of my lips.*

She committed her resentment to God instead. Only God's Spirit could tame her resentment and end the poison brewing in her heart. While Kylie would say something brutally honest when angered by hurt, Vanessa recognized the bitterness as a tool for the wicked one to tempt her to stumble.

Who is the man who desires life, and loves many days, that he may see good? Keep your tongue from evil, and your lips from speaking deceit. Depart from evil and do good; seek peace, and pursue it.

Theo Gowrie couldn't change the past, no one could, not even Robert Miles. Seeds sown, good or evil, were sure to yield a harvest. Only the grace and mercy of God could alter the results of unwise decisions. He hadn't promised to keep foolish seed sowing from producing thorns and brambles, but He did promise a bright future to those who trusted Him.

"I can understand her feelings," Vanessa heard herself saying, "but Lucy is an adult now. Marriage is just around the corner. Having grown up in his care, surely she can forgive her father at this late hour in his life for spending time on something that evidently means very much to him."

"Lucy doesn't see it that way. Robert's totally absorbed with the ancient history of Norah's family. It's—it's an unhealthy obsession, an inquisition on the details of everyone's past."

Strange words to use: unhealthy, inquisition. "Researching the history of the family estate, do you mean?"

"Gowrie House, yes. The earls and lords who built it. Those who lived here and died here. It's taking a toll on his health as well as robbing Lucy of his time. Lucy's spoken to him about it, and he says he has his reasons, and I don't doubt he means well. Still, he drives himself to illness. Oh, yes, I blame the work for his last heart attack. I've tried to speak to him, but Robert has a maddening way about him that can shut people and events out of his life. I suppose that's what made him such a great actor on the stage. Distractions couldn't deter him. But on the stage is one thing; in real life, it is something else. He worries me, my dear. One wonders if Robert may not be a bit mad himself."

Just why was Theo telling her all this? What could she expect to come of it?

Theo talked on and Vanessa began to wonder if what she wanted was merely a listening ear. If that were so, it was odd that she would choose her, a stranger, when Theo didn't really appreciate her being on the estate.

"It's actually Scott's book, not Robert's," Theo explained. "Scott came here some years ago and lived on the island, doing research on his own. He thought he had something and approached Robert about its possibilities. He knew him from work they'd done together in London on the stage before Robert retired. Robert took a fancy to him, as a man might do when he misses having a son. Norah asked Scott to move into the house so they would have more time to collaborate on research and writing."

"Then Norah was involved in the project?" Vanessa asked, mildly surprised.

"Oh, yes. She adored such things. Believed in old Scottish traditions and all that. Scott managed to worm himself into a very cozy spot in the family."

There was that viper of resentment again. Was there something more, something that went beyond personal resentment to fear?

"Robert's been dedicated to the idea ever since. Just as soon as he found out the house dated to King James I. Full of blood and gore. I admit the Gowries weren't a nice brood of folks from the old clan. But Robert is driven to do this book in memory of Norah. She thought it amusing and sometimes adventurous to dig up old skeletons from family history. I saw nothing amusing about it at all. I warned her it could be menacing, but she just laughed. Before her death she talked about it incessantly to Robert and Scott. I discouraged her, naturally. Why stir up old ghosts? Too much digging about merely uncovers unpleasant things. After all, they say we are all sinners, don't they? Well, sin abounds in the history of any family."

"True, but where sin abounds, God's grace can much more abound," Vanessa commented easily. "I'm sure not all the Gowrie family were scoundrels. There must be a few heroes and heroines mixed in somewhere. Perhaps it is these Robert is researching in memory of Norah."

"You're kind to say that, dear, but..." She shook her head, troubled. "The memory of Norah should be left to photographs and pleasant times. Just as I've done with Vernon." She looked at Vanessa. "Vernon was my husband," she explained. "He died nearly eight years ago, long before Norah."

"I'm sorry..."

"But Robert won't let go of his research. And Scott, I fear, only adds to the problem by encouraging him to remember Norah's anniversary with this book. It's in October," she said, a dismal note to her voice.

"I see, the book will commemorate their marriage." Vanessa couldn't take pleasure in a marriage that had robbed her mother of her husband and a provider.

"Marriage?" Theo said. "No, no, Norah's death. It will be two years this October."

Vanessa held her cup to her lips without drinking. It chilled her to think the book was to commemorate a death.

"This is all Scott's doing," Theo was saying. "He's nothing but trouble, that boy. He envisions himself as a possible heir to Robert's inheritance."

"Surely Robert wouldn't leave his money to Scott."

"No, he wouldn't. Scott knows it too. That's why he wants to marry Lucy. He nearly accomplished it too, until Lucy saw through his feigned affection. Then she met Jodrell."

Feigned affection? Was it? She hadn't thought so, but she knew very little of Scott's real motives, and far less than she had thought if all that Theo was telling her was true.

I shouldn't be listening to all this. It's gossip. But Vanessa felt glued to her chair, both baited and troubled.

"The house and land belong to Norah's daughter," Theo said quietly. "And whomever she marries."

Vanessa glanced across the yews toward Kerc. Kerc and Lucy were friends. Maybe Kerc too had some vain hope of getting Lucy away from Jodrell. Caretaker or not, Kerc would know better than most how to run an estate like Gowrie House. He had been amused when she mentioned his marriageable interest in Lucy, but had that just been a cover? And could she trust Kerc just because he'd been more polite this morning?

"Lucy will marry Jodrell. There's no changing that." Theo sounded certain. "It's all settled for the spring of next year. Jodrell is perfect for Gowrie House. And he adores the land, the horses, and most of all, Lucy. Lucy is my main concern, and whatever gives her the best future. You see, don't you, how Scott has outworn his welcome here?"

Vanessa could see he had outworn Theo's welcome. *Don't get involved,* she told herself. *There's no need to take sides between Scott and Theo.* Nor was it wise. The more she involved herself, the more entangled she'd become.

"Robert should dismiss him," Theo said plaintively. "But Robert's dependent on him. Ill health keeps him confined a good deal of the time. Something must be done, soon. Before October. For Robert's sake."

Vanessa looked at her. Theo again was staring at Kerc. He had finished trimming and was moving across the walkway to a plot of rosemary fragrant with tiny blue flowers.

"What you're telling me may very well be true, but I don't see what any of it has to do with me," Vanessa said quietly.

Theo removed her glasses. For the first time Vanessa looked into the widely spaced dove gray eyes. They were Theo's best feature and yet she allowed her thick, unattractive glasses to hide them so that they were hardly noticeable.

"My dear, it's quite clear, really. It was Scott who brought you here. And your presence can only mean more trouble. Oh, I'm not suggesting you should be blamed about the dogs or even for listening to Scott's tales about Robert wishing to see you. Nonetheless, don't you see?" She leaned closer toward the table as if she couldn't see Vanessa well enough.

Vanessa leaned back, tense again. Theo saw her as a threat, possibly to Lucy's inheritance. Just the way Kerc did.

"No," she said politely, but firmly. "I don't see that I'm a messenger of trouble. If there's unhappiness here, Miss Theo, it existed long before I arrived."

"I'm not blaming you, Vanessa. Goodness knows I sympathize with your situation. You couldn't have had a pleasant or secure childhood. But that isn't Lucy's fault, is it?"

"Of course not. Nor would I even think such a thing. We're sisters, even if she, like you, doesn't care to have me here even for two weeks. But neither do I see myself as a threat to her rights or her chance for happiness."

"Two weeks, even three—it doesn't matter. Time isn't the issue. The issue is Robert and his health. Not merely in a physical sense, but emotionally as well. It's been so ever since Norah died. That's why he's driven himself about this book. He hopes to appease his conscience because she wanted it so much when alive. Scott knows that, and he's throwing fuel on Robert's passion. But it's not healthy, I tell you. And now there's you."

"Robert asked me to come," Vanessa found herself saying defensively.

"Robert doesn't know what he truly wants. He's ridden with guilt over many things in his past. In his current state, he's an easy prey for selfish manipulation by others who don't have his best interests at heart."

Stung, Vanessa sat for a moment in pained silence, then, "Perhaps, Miss Theo, it's not I who wishes to take advantage of his burden of guilt, but others in and out of the family."

"My dear, I've offended you—"

"I didn't come here to harm. I've come to heal. To…to…"

Theo's look quenched what Vanessa intended to say.

"Yes, I know…to forgive."

Her tone made it sound cheap. Vanessa's pain turned to sudden anger.

"It's written all over you," Theo was saying quietly. "There's a struggle waging in your heart as well. It's that which concerns me. Because despite your good intentions, your anger could lash out at any moment. And when it does, it will be more than Robert who gets hurt. It will be Lucy and Jodrell."

Theo was right to some degree, but wrong too. Vanessa simply looked at her with frustrated emotions. There was nothing to say that would convince her she meant no harm. How, then, was she to bridge the gap between them?

My actions, in time, will show them.

But could that happen, when they all resented her very presence? All, that is, except Scott and Robert himself. It was her father who would ultimately decide, and she would see him tonight. Did Theo know about their dinner plans? Vanessa didn't think so, otherwise she would have mentioned it.

"Let me say, dear, that you were not the only one I had in mind when I mentioned selfish manipulation," Theo said.

Of course she meant to include Scott, and perhaps others Vanessa knew nothing about.

"If you really do want to help Robert's peace of mind, there is something you might do," Theo told her unexpectedly. "You could join me and Lucy in convincing him to abandon his decision to unveil the book in October. He should perhaps take an extended vacation. That would do more to heal his nagging conscience than your arranging a meeting with your brother."

"If he won't listen to you and Lucy, he'd hardly listen to me."

"Perhaps he would. Your voice might be just the thing to help convince him he's pushing us all toward something both unpleasant and best left forgotten." She started to say more, but then made a little gesture of hopelessness.

"I'm sorry," Vanessa hastened. "I didn't mean to upset you."

"No—no, I'm all right, dear." She pushed herself up from the chair and stood for a moment getting her bearings. She caught a glimpse of Kerc and lifted a hand.

"Kerc? Kerc!"

He looked over at them, set his gardening instruments down, and walked around the bushes toward them.

When he came up to the table, Theo had one hand on the back of the chair and the other at the back of her neck. "Help me to the house...and tell Robert—tell him I must see him at once. In my room, please." She turned away from Vanessa with a rigid back and clung to Kerc's strong arm.

Vanessa stood helpless, dismayed by the dark, sizzling look of disapproval coming from Kerc. His look questioned her. *Now what did you do?* it seemed to challenge.

Vanessa watched until they disappeared behind the rhododendron bushes along the walkway at the side of the house.

Her heart thumped unhappily. Theo had been unfair. And Kerc would think intimidation had been used on her instead of the other way around.

No matter. She was going through with the meeting with her father that night.

In the silence that settled after their departure, the breeze rippled through the flowers and stirred the edges of the white lacy napkins on the tea tray. Suddenly, Vanessa felt another presence in the garden beside her own. Her imagination was so strong that she turned and looked behind her.

The crepe myrtle stirred, its blossoms scattering across the flagstones. From beyond the wicker gate, the old rose garden beckoned with the faint fragrance of many roses in bloom.

Yes, there *was* someone watching her...she could see him standing to one side of the gate in the shade of a rambling rose tree.

Vanessa walked toward the gate. "Hello there."

No answer met her casual greeting. In fact, no one was standing there as she had thought. She saw a tall broom leaning against the rose tree and decided her eyes had played a trick on her. Well, she wanted to see the roses from the court of King James anyway. Kerc had said they were labeled and dated.

She pushed the gate open and went through, entering the rosy paradise.

She hadn't gone far on the charming, curving stone walk when a man unexpectedly stood up from a stone bench between two tapered bushes covered with white rosebuds. She stopped. She knew this man.

"Hello, Vanessa," he said in a careful but friendly voice. "Allow me to introduce myself. I'm Robert Miles, your father."

Vanessa stood staring back. There was nothing else to do but face him, though she would have preferred time to adjust and prepare her emotions. This had come suddenly, too suddenly, and she felt overwhelmed with the poignancy of the moment.

She took a long breath to settle her thudding heart and walked slowly to meet her father.

13

This is my father. Vanessa's heart repeated the words several times. An excited breathlessness had come over her, then a certain nervousness that left her shaking. My father...Dad. Dad! She wanted to taste the word on her tongue, but her mind rejected it. Her heart longed to respond, but hurts blocked the path to freedom with hurdles too old and too entrenched to easily be cast aside. The hurts were like thorns that had grown into her flesh, becoming so much a part of her that they could not easily be removed without surgery.

She didn't trust herself to speak. She was afraid her voice would tremble and the sound would bring on an avalanche of tears. She thought of Joseph revealing himself to his brothers in the Egyptian court. Yet this was different. His brothers had sold him as a slave out of envy and jealousy because they didn't want him around to compete with Jacob's love and inheritance. But Jacob had not sold his son. For a father not to want you was more cruel than the rejection of immature, selfish half brothers.

Vanessa stared at Robert Miles. She waited, expecting some internal recognition of the man who was part of her. How often she'd heard smiling people saying to her friends, "You have your father's eyes" or "You have his smile."

Vanessa waited for her heart to respond, but nothing happened inside her. The kinship she had expected to engulf her had taken up wings and fled. She felt like a statue in a garden, staring at another statue, while the playful wind scattered rose petals about their feet as if trying to woo them to life.

She would have known her father's face in a crowd easily because she had studied it for so many years on the covers of theatrical magazines. The features were older, the handsome jawline beginning to sag, the strong lines of his brow a little more deeply lined, the golden blond hair the color of her own streaked with gray, and yet there was no mistaking the tall, slim man who had once been adored by thousands of starry-eyed fans.

Vanessa held her breath, waiting for lightning to strike her with a great flurry of star-spangled emotions. This man was her father.

He too studied her in silence, his expression guarded. What was he looking for? Her mother? Himself? Anger? Forgiveness? When he had stared long enough and Vanessa remained rooted to the pathway, his shoulders sagged a little, and he left the rose arbor and came toward her. She didn't know what to expect, but he stopped close at hand and searched her eyes. After a moment he sighed, then merely gestured to the stone bench. When she sat down, he walked to the pond and stood with his back toward her, his hands shoved in his pockets and his head bent, looking at the great white swan making a graceful circle that sent ripples through the water.

She sat still. The moment was completely lacking the dramatic flourish she had envisioned so often as a child and young adolescent. In her daydreams the meeting was aflame with anger, remorse, joy, pleadings, forgiveness, revenge, and tears. And always, everything ended settled and at rest, with hands clasped, his arm around her shoulder. She had imagined him saying, "I'm so proud of you, my daughter. My heart breaks to think I've missed seeing you grow up into such a fine young woman."

The silence between them became oppressive. Her heart began to thud painfully. Was he expecting a torrent of accusations to be hurled?

He had been the one to ask her here to his home. She had obliged his request, so he must be the first to speak. No matter what, she wouldn't turn and run just because the first meeting was disappointing and her childish hopes and dreams seemed to be withering on the vine.

I had no expectations when I came here, she reminded herself. *We both are mature enough to realize that the past cannot be recovered, nor will all the regrets in the world undo one minute of days gone by.* Her childhood and youth had been lived; his corresponding years had been spent on what he had decided would bring him satisfaction. He had made his choices, and she still had her future before her. Now what?

Vanessa had garrisoned herself against the onslaught sure to come from suppressed longings, when his actions had denied both of them a normal father/daughter relationship. *You've denied me so much that can never be restored. What's left to give me and Kylie except your apology? You've given everything that really mattered to Lucy.*

But she said none of these things aloud. The moment merely revealed what had been lost, not what could be gained.

Instead of accusations, her damp hand crumpled a fold of her skirt, and she too stared at the graceful swan. The things God did were beautiful. The things sinful man did bore marred reflections upon the water.

He turned from the pond to face her, his hands still in his pockets, feet apart in a defensive stance, a clouded look of unhappiness upon his face.

"Thank you for coming, Vanessa."

"I did it for Kylie. If you would meet with him and explain why you abandoned us, it might help him to cope with the bitterness he feels toward you."

His eyes closed for a moment. "I understand coming here must have been painful for you."

"No more painful, perhaps, than growing up in New York knowing you didn't want us."

"Please. That's not completely true. I suppose your mother told you that."

She stood quickly. "Do not start attacking her. You're in no position to throw stones."

"I have no intention of throwing stones. I had hoped you would refrain from accusations until you know all the truth."

"And what is the truth?"

"You can only find out and accept the truth if you're willing to listen, to wait."

"It's late for listening."

"Yes...very late," came his quiet, musing voice. "But you did come. That encourages me. I hope to explain about your mother. She deliberately kept you from me."

If he thought he could turn her against her mother, no amount of time would convince her. She had known her mother well, but she did not know, and perhaps would never truly know, this stranger with sad eyes. She sighed and sat down again.

"I'm willing to listen," she said. "That's partly why I'm here. I won't be manipulated, though. I don't expect anything from you now, so you needn't think you owe me anything, least of all anything of an emotional nature."

"I understand your anger. You should know I didn't give you and Kylie up because I wanted it that way. I wrote both of you many times."

He had written to them?

He reached over to an end of the bench, picked up a stack of envelopes held together with string, and slowly held them out to her. When she didn't move, he dropped them on the bench. "She never gave them to you. They're all marked 'Return to Sender.' They came back to me in London. Year after year they came back. There were other things too—birthday presents, Christmas presents—she sent them all back without opening them."

Vanessa's eyes closed with pain.

"She never even hinted of this, did she?"

Vanessa blinked back tears and set her jaw to maintain self-control. She stared ahead at the pond, unable to meet his gaze, unable to reach out and pick up the thick stack of old mail. Even to touch the envelopes now would bring on her tears, and tears must wait for when she was alone with God.

"I called the New York flat more times than I can tell you. Mary...your mother...told me I wasn't welcome; that I'd ruined her life, yours, and Kylie's. She said if I troubled her anymore she'd move and not let me know where she was. This was meant to frighten me, and it did."

"But did you ever come to the flat?" she asked at last. "If you had actually come and knocked on the door...or...oh, there were ways to let me and Kylie know you wanted us. You could have tried harder, but...but you didn't. That's what...hurts. You walked away from us..."

He released a long breath and sat down tiredly on the bench with the envelopes between them, untouched. He sat forward, fingers interlaced, staring moodily at the pond.

"I won't deny it. I could have forced the issue with her. I could have tried harder to get both of you. I'd have probably won the court case, because of who I was, but Norah convinced me a legal fight would only end up hurting you."

"That's just an excuse for doing nothing. We were hurt anyway."

"It would have been all over the papers. No matter what I did, Mary would look like the poor victim."

"So that was it? You were worried more about your career—and Norah Benton's? She was the 'other' woman, the one who stole you away. And it wouldn't have been good for your career if the story had hit the papers. That's what Kylie's said all along. I'd hoped there might be something more."

"There was something more. I'd married Norah by then. She was expecting Lucy."

"I see..."

"No, you don't see," he said sadly. "At the time it was about my career, yes. I'm the first one to admit I've made terrible mistakes, but I knew I wouldn't get anywhere with Mary. She liked the role of being the victim a little too much."

"Well, wasn't she?"

"Yes, because there was nothing she liked more. If she could have volunteered to be a martyr, she would have been one."

Vanessa had never heard anyone speak like this about her mother before. For a moment she analyzed the accusation to see if there was any truth in it. There were many times when her mother had shown traits of passivity, and even though she'd believed in God and encouraged Kylie and herself to go to Sunday school, she never went. She accepted fortune and fate as having cast lots for the trials of life rather than the sovereign, good hand of God. Yet in many other ways her mother had been strong.

"She worked harder than anyone I've known, first as a cleaning woman in New York offices, and later in the theater again designing wardrobes. I don't think she loved playing a martyr."

He lowered his head. "I didn't know about the cleaning woman job."

"That's what Kylie is bitter about most of all. What she went through because you put your own desires ahead of everyone else and ran off with another woman."

"I'm sure I fill the villain role easily enough with Kylie, but it wasn't as simple as he may think. Your mother was planning a divorce before I ever met Norah. She hated my career. Despised it, in fact. She hated my friends, the life we lived. She intended to leave me early on, until she found out she was going to have you."

For a moment she didn't have anything to say. He just sat there, looking old and tired, and her heart smote her. "I'm not blaming you for everything," she said gently. "I'm sure she failed you in many ways. We're all only human. If you had just kept in contact with me and Kylie..." Her words fell short.

"I have my own bitter feelings, my regrets. That's the reason I wanted to see you, to meet Kylie—while there remains still a small opportunity to act. If Mary had been fair, if she'd tried to explain our failing marriage to both of you...but she didn't, of course, why would she? That might remove me from the role of villain."

"Still, you could have pursued your wish to see me and Kylie."

"Yes," he said sadly. "I had the money to fight."

"And we had none."

"She wouldn't accept it from me."

"Do you blame her? You—"

He stood quickly, a flush coming to his weathered face. "Yes, I blame her. She might have despised me all she wanted after what happened, but she had no right to deny you and Kylie!"

She jumped to her feet, heart thundering, hands clenched. "It wasn't Mother who denied us. It was you! *You* who abandoned us. *You* who ran away with another woman. *You* who—" She stopped suddenly, dismayed, a trembling hand flying to her mouth. Tears welled in her eyes and splashed down her cheeks. She had promised herself she wouldn't lash out in bitterness. She had come here to serve the purposes of God. And now!

Pained at her failure, she turned away, choking on her tears. "I'm sorry—"

"Oh, Vanessa," he groaned helplessly. "I didn't want this to happen. I didn't want to bring you here to experience tears again!"

She shook her head, sniffing loudly, searching in her pocket for a handkerchief. "No...I'll get over it. I always have."

"No one truly gets over deep hurt without working through it. You have merely covered it up. And I'm to blame."

"It…it won't happen again. I didn't intend to accuse you. That's not why I made the trip."

"I know you didn't," came his shaky voice. "Scott told me what you're like. I put a lot of trust in him. He's got a good head on his shoulders, both he and Kerc. Too bad they don't get along."

Kerc!

"I could sense a gentle spirit in you the moment you came into the garden. Ah, poor Vanessa, we're off to a sad beginning. Perhaps we should let it go now."

She turned, stricken. "You…you want me to return to…"

"No, that's not what I meant." Then—a small brittle smile developed. "I still want that dinner with you tonight. I meant I think we've talked enough for now. We needn't discuss it all at once. The emotions we both feel are much too deep and burdensome for that. Our relationship must grow slowly."

"I don't expect that. I came because—"

"Because of Kylie."

"Yes."

"If anyone can arrange a meeting between us, it's you, Vanessa. But I'd hoped that you and I could also learn to accept one another."

I don't want anything from you. It's too late for any of that, she wanted to cry. Far better to have no dreams than to see them destroyed in seconds. The man before her was not the fairy-tale image she'd had as a child of her father, the grand and noble Robert Miles. She had judged him only from the photographs of his theater days. He, like herself, was mere flesh and blood, full of weaknesses, sins, and good intentions gone awry. This man looking at her was vulnerable to angry words, and he was reaching out to her in his own inadequacy. He wanted forgiveness. Why? Why did it matter to him now? She closed her eyes and sighed.

She was startled when she heard a small, painful gasp come from his lips. Opening her eyes, she saw his hand go to his chest. He moved feebly to the bench.

Vanessa's eyes widened in fear. "No…Father…"

Another heart attack—and she had brought it on—

What to do? *Oh, God, help me, help us!*

She ran for the gate, flinging it open and rushing blindly across the beautiful lawn toward the main garden, her feet flying, her own bruised heart pounding with fear and anguish, unaware of her pains from yesterday's fall.

My fault, her mind accused. *I upset him too much.*

"Kerc! Kerc!" she shouted.

In what seemed mere moments he appeared from farther down the garden.

She pointed back toward the old rose garden. "It's Robert," she cried in dismay. "He's collapsed! A heart attack, I think—"

He dropped his gardening tools and ran to her, catching her shoulder. "Where?"

"N-near the pond, over at the bench. Do something!" she cried.

His grip tightened as if to command her full attention. "Listen. Go to the house. Tell Theo to call Doc MacGregor. Then have Effie take you to his room. There's medication on his desk. She'll know. Bring it quickly. Got it?"

She nodded, but her knees were weak. Guilt and shame sapped her of strength. "My fault—"

"Snap out of it, Vanessa." He gave her a shake. "Hurry!"

She ran toward the house feeling as though her heart would burst from its pounding. *If he dies now I'll never forgive myself. Never…*

∼∼∼

The drawing room was furnished with expensive Persian carpets and heavy, outdated furniture that was covered with rich gold velvet and Victorian fringe. Light flickered in through the dormer windows draped with amber brocade touched with rose hues. Though the atmosphere was dignified and serene, the events of the afternoon had shaken Vanessa far more deeply than she cared to admit. She sat on an oval chair staring toward the double doors that opened into the hall, waiting for the dreaded sound of footsteps. Dr. MacGregor lived in a bungalow not far from Gowrie House, and he'd arrived within five minutes of Theo's telephone call. He'd been upstairs with Robert for over an hour now, and still there was no news.

Kerc stood by the window looking out. He'd said nothing in the last ten minutes. Theo restlessly paced the carpet, her heeled pumps making no sound, but her skirt rustled, and the beads she wore around her slender white throat kept clacking as they rubbed together. Vanessa tried to pray, yet her words were disjointed and repetitious, and she soon ceased. Her palm clutched the carved arm of the chair so tightly she could feel the scroll design digging into her skin.

How could it happen now? I'll suffer for this incident as long as I live. Theo already blames me. Kerc hasn't said anything, but his eyes have suggested he blames me too. Why else would he look at me that way? So measuringly? And what will Lucy say when she gets home tomorrow, and Scott? No sooner do I arrive than Robert suffers another heart attack and dies—

Theo ceased her pacing and turned on her, her square face precise, her tone, edgy.

"I was afraid something of this nature would happen when you confronted him. I told you so in the garden. Yet you wouldn't listen. You pushed ahead, heedless of our feelings, with no regard whatsoever for the interruption you've brought into our lives by coming here. You'll never understand Robert. I asked you not to see him now! What did you say to upset him so?"

Vanessa was too dazed to answer her.

Kerc turned his head quickly and looked at Vanessa, frowning. His dark eyes and his dramatic brows made a straight line across his forehead, as though he were considering something that surprised him.

Vanessa heard footsteps coming at last, and her anxious gaze swerved from the distraught woman to the white double doors.

"If he dies, you're to blame. But perhaps that's what you wanted."

Vanessa stood. "*Wanted?* How can you say such cruel things? It is greed and jealousy that are cruel instruments in the hands of schemers."

"Someone is coming," Kerc said. Theo turned as the doors opened, and Vanessa sank back into the chair like a condemned prisoner facing the verdict of the jury.

Dr. MacGregor looked tired and stern as he glanced at the three of them gathered there, then he walked up to Theo. "Better sit down, Theo."

Her feeble hand went to her chest as she searched his face. "Then—?"

"He's alive, but his chances aren't good."

Theo let out a little moan and allowed MacGregor to ease her into a chair.

Vanessa's head lowered. She sat still, gritting her teeth to keep back the tears.

Kerc said quietly: "How long, Doc, do you think?"

"That's hard to say. He's resting quietly. He may have a few weeks, even a month, or mere days. I've done what's possible."

"Shouldn't he be taken to a hospital?" Kerc asked.

"He doesn't want to go. Insists what time he has left, he wants to spend at home." He looked over at Vanessa. "Miss Miles?"

Vanessa forced herself to look up and was surprised by the sympathy in the doctor's somber gaze.

"He wants to see you."

Theo let out a choked sound, but the doctor laid a restraining hand on her shoulder. "Let it be, Theo. Robert has all his wits. He knows what he's doing. It would be worse on him if I denied him his wishes. I don't want him frustrated." He looked again at Vanessa. "Can you meet with him without getting him upset?"

"Yes...of course I can, but perhaps Theo is right and I shouldn't…"

"It's what Robert wants that matters right now, Miss Miles. I've told him I'd arrange it for later this evening if he promises to rest quietly this afternoon." He looked at his watch. "If you won't mind, Theo, I'd like to stay here for the rest of the evening."

"You can, certainly. I'll have the room next door to Robert's made ready." She pushed herself up weakly. "You must be hungry. Tea is probably being kept warm. I don't feel much like eating myself, but the rest of you, do go in and Effie and Iris will take care of you."

"I want you to rest too," MacGregor told her firmly. "I'm giving you a sedative and you're going up to your room."

"I must call Edinburgh and tell Lucy what's happened. She's due back tomorrow with Jodrell, but perhaps they can manage to come sooner."

"If Lucy does come," MacGregor said wryly, "it would be best if she doesn't see him." And when Theo looked at him, shocked, he said: "Robert's had enough excitement for one day. We don't need Lucy in his room in a fit of tears."

"I'll call, if you like, Miss Theo," Kerc said.

"Would you? Thank you, Kerc. The number's right here on the table."

Dr. MacGregor led Theo away and Kerc walked to the telephone and picked it up. After dialing he turned and looked at Vanessa.

"Better have some tea. You're pale. You need to keep up your strength and resolve, because I think I know what Robert will ask of you when you see him later."

Vanessa searched his face. He appeared calm, but there was an intensity to his eyes that always disconcerted her.

"I can't eat now," she murmured, turning away. "I wish I hadn't come. You were right. Everyone was right, including Kylie."

"Your father doesn't feel that way," said Kerc. "He doesn't agree with Miss Theo's criticism. If he did, he wouldn't want to see you again. That's what matters at the moment, isn't it?"

"And your criticism?"

"What the caretaker thinks don't matter much, does it?" he said with affirmation in his tone. "At least take some coffee. I know for a fact Effie made some especially for you." He turned to the receiver when a voice must have said something. "Yes? Hello, Lucy. Kerc, here. Is Scott around?"

Vanessa left the room, pausing uncertainly. She needed time to think. There was so much to decide. With a prayer on her heart, she went into the sunny dining room where a light meal typical of teatime waited on a side counter next to a silver tea service. Effie was standing there with a likable smile on her face.

"Kerc says ye be wanting some coffee, so I got some grounds at the market yesterday. Would ye like a cup now?"

Despite her unhappiness, Vanessa managed a smile. "That was kind of you and Kerc, Effie, thank you. Yes, I'd love a cup. I'll take it out on the terrace."

Effie looked pleased. "Aye, miss, I'll bring it out to ye."

14

Vanessa sipped her coffee on the terrace while leaning against one of the honeysuckle-covered pillars. She was watching the distant gray sea and the hills where the lighthouse stood when Kerc said casually: "Lucy's asked me to pick them up in your father's boat. It'll be quicker than waiting for a ferry. I'll be gone tonight. But Doc MacGregor is staying in the room next to Mr. Miles."

Vanessa turned and looked at him. "How is Lucy taking the news?"

"As expected."

"That's not what I meant, and I think you know it."

"Aye, I do. She doesn't know you were with him yet. She will, though. Theo's talking to her now. It's likely she'll blame you," he said in an uninterested tone.

She flinched, and Kerc watched her reaction with thoughtfulness. "I wouldn't worry. As long as Mr. Miles wants you here there's not much either Lucy or Theo can do about it."

Vanessa said in a small, shaken voice: "That's easy for you to say. You weren't there when it happened. No one blames you. But it looks as if I—"

She couldn't go on, and she turned away to look out toward the lighthouse.

"You can feel pleased Mr. Miles is fully on your side. He doesn't think it was your fault, and he ought to know. He told Doc he wants you to stay."

Yes, that was a soothing balm to her heart. "But it's clear that Theo thinks I planned for this to happen. Revenge, I suppose. She certainly couldn't think his death would profit me otherwise." She leaned back against the pillar. "What do you think?"

He spoke after a thoughtful moment, "I don't believe you intended to provoke him. I might have considered that possibility when I first met you."

"And you don't now?"

"No."

"What's changed your mind, may I ask?"

His gaze studied her face, and she wished she hadn't asked.

"What I took for phony innocence is looking more genuine. I think you were honestly afraid when you called for help in the garden. If you hated him and wanted revenge the way Miss Theo thinks, you could have delayed getting help. It would be all over for Mr. Miles. All you needed to do was leave. No one saw you in the garden, including me, and I was nearby working. True, you might have thought to do that and changed your mind at the last moment and yelled for help, but Mr. Miles would likely know it. And when Miss Theo turned on you just now in the other room, you were close to real tears."

Her eyes faltered. She was satisfied he had the insight to see what Theo had not. She turned to go past him into the dining room when his hand rested on her arm, stopping her.

"You've convinced Robert you're genuine. You have his confidence and his pride in you. You could, if you wanted, get just about anything from him before it's over." Kerc's voice changed. "He has lots of plans. Plans that concern you and Kylie."

She looked at him puzzled, trying to read behind that voice. For once his dark gaze was bland, and his face a blank page.

"The only thing I want from my father is that he die in God's peace. And if possible, make peace with Kylie as well. If that's too simple for you, I'm sorry. But that's the truth."

"I'm almost sure you'll get your opportunity to try where your brother's concerned."

"And will that upset you?" she asked pointedly.

"If Mr. Miles reconciles with his son? No. But I wouldn't want you to be disappointed about Gowrie House. It may not be his to give."

She couldn't help wondering what he meant. As yet she didn't fully understand his motives. Just what did he want? And why did he appear to question her father's rights over the estate he had inherited upon Norah's death?

Dr. MacGregor came into the dining room, unrolling his white shirtsleeves. He'd washed up for luncheon and was slipping into his coat jacket to sit down at the table.

He was frowning. "I'll need to delay Robert's request to see you, Miss Miles."

She tensed. Kerc said from behind her: "He's worsened then?"

"No. He's asleep. We shouldn't waken him at this point. I'm hoping he'll sleep through the night." He looked at her. "Perhaps tomorrow after lunch."

"Yes, Doctor, of course."

"You're on the way to the mainland for Lucy, Kerc?" MacGregor asked, pouring himself tea.

"Yes, sir. As soon as I get the boat ready. Anything I can get you from the hospital while I'm there?"

"Yes, I was about to request an errand. I'll give you a list of supplies and call to let them know you're stopping by to pick them up."

Vanessa left them and went into the hall. Effie came rushing from the back of the house, her cheeks flushed and her eyes wide. "Oh, miss, terrible news...on the BBC," she cried.

Her words brought Kerc and the doctor to the doorway. Facing her audience, Effie wrung her apron.

"T'was just on. I heard it with my own ears. The whole of London be under terrible bombing by hundreds of Nazi planes. Buildings be going up in fire and the Royal Air Force be fighting the Germans right over the city. They say many Londoners are dead, and more are buried alive under rubble."

Vanessa felt sickened. Her mind flashed at once to Andy and Kylie. They were in the fighting now, perhaps at this very moment. She rushed to the other side of the house where Effie had been working and a radio was still blaring out the devastating description of the ruthless attack. Dr. MacGregor came up beside her and Kerc stood behind them, with Effie clutching her dust cloth as though it were a shield.

Vanessa listened to the report. Her hands clenched. Were any pilots shot down? How many?

> Today a heavy onslaught of German bombers operating from French and Belgian airfields has been launched upon the city of London. In the South, almost all of our twenty-two RAF squadrons have been heroically engaging the German Air Force, many twice, some three times. German air losses at this time are estimated to be twice as great as our losses in Spitfires and Hurricanes...

"...losses in Spitfires and Hurricanes..."

Vanessa gasped. Her eyes shut as if by closing them she could shut out the dark news.

"Miss Miles?" It was the voice of the doctor, his hand on her arm. "Sit her down on the divan, Kerc. Effie? Bring my bag, will you?"

Vanessa felt herself being gently pushed into a soft seat and then Dr. MacGregor was giving her something nasty to swallow. She became aware of being watched, and turning her head met Kerc's meditative gaze.

The doctor patted her arm. Vanessa glanced again at Kerc. His dark eyes suggested cool interest. She returned his look gravely and stood. "I'll be fine. I think I'll just go on up to my room."

"Certainly. My best wishes are with your friends and loved ones, Miss Miles. This is a dark and evil time," said Dr. MacGregor.

She thanked the doctor and walked past Kerc, who made no reply.

Vanessa didn't come down for dinner. When Effie knocked at her door, she said she was fine but wanted to have some time alone. She spent a long time at her window, staring out to sea. Andy and Kylie filled her thoughts, as did her father. When she finally did make her way to bed, she lay awake hour after hour. If something had gone wrong in the battle, wouldn't Francis have sent her a wire by now from London? It was difficult to get through on the telephone. Vanessa had tried and received a busy signal. Thank God she could pray. There was never a busy signal from the Lord.

The slow hours crept by before she finally fell into a light sleep quoting the ninety-first psalm: *He that dwelleth in the secret place of the Most High shall abide under the shadow of the Almighty...*

She didn't sleep long, nor soundly. Dawn was casting its first light on the lawns and trees, turning them silver white when she went out to her terrace. Dark shadows remained among the bushes and trees. She dressed quickly, and taking her Bible with her, she left her room and went downstairs.

The delicious aroma of breakfast being cooked tempted her. She stopped a moment in the bright kitchen to get a cup of tea from Iris, and then she left the house and walked toward the fields of wild heather. She wanted to be alone to pour out her heart before God and find strength and wisdom in the pages of the small Bible in her jacket pocket.

The breeze was cool at this early hour, and she was glad she'd brought her woolen pullover. She soon found the narrow road she'd asked Iris about in the kitchen. The road would bring her to the western section of the island that was mostly isolated.

As she walked she enjoyed the fragrance of heather and sea. The silence was so deep she could almost hear it. The endless murmur of the sea was lost in a sloping moorland covered in bracken and stunted shrubs where even a bird's cry was dampened. She saw few houses, but these became hidden. Even the trees became sparse, with spindly branches reaching like blackened fingers toward the east.

She came to an elongated stretch of dry beach sand. The sea was at low tide, but it wouldn't remain that way for long. At both ends of the beach she could see black rocks, like shark's teeth, thrusting their points up through the water. She removed her walking shoes and socks and walked barefoot through the coarse dry sand, then she sat down on one of the protruding rocks close to shore.

The horizon had turned from its earlier shell pink with tinges of watery blue to a light gold, heralding a warm summer day.

She sat on the rock for over an hour just watching the Atlantic waves. Low tide had left the rocks and sandy shore exposed. Soon cold waves would sweep in, covering everything except the tops of the rocks.

Vanessa watched small grayish sandpipers busily at work. Through God's creative wisdom the little birds instinctively knew their best feeding time was fast approaching its end. As the incoming waves reached further up the dry sand, the spindly legged pipers ran along the wet bubbling foam searching as diligently for hermit crabs as a miner searches for gold.

There are so many lessons to learn from God's handiwork, she thought, chin in hand, as she sat bracing herself against the damp wind. Like the little sandpiper, she too must redeem her time. She was accountable before God to use her opportunities to accomplish the goal that had brought her here. The surging dark waters of war and family misunderstandings were moving in to engulf her path, and the paths of loved ones. "Redeeming the time because the days are evil," the apostle Paul had written to the Ephesians. While it is yet day, plant, water, and harvest.

She must engage in prayer for her father and for Kylie and Andy, relying on God's promises and warnings, embracing them in her heart. Her father's soul lay in the balance, ready to slip out into eternity. Kylie and Andy were both believers in Christ, but their lives on earth could be taken by God in war at any moment. Opportunities came and went with the wind. The harvest would be gathered. Winter was coming.

She shivered in the chilling wind. After reading from her Bible and praying, almost before she realized it the gray waves were beginning to splash around the rock she was sitting upon. As they rushed back to sea, she jumped down and ran toward dry sand. Replacing her socks and shoes, she found the path that took her back toward Gowrie House.

Her heart was quieter for having spent the time with her heavenly Father. She had found new hope and strength to continue her difficult task. Perhaps her call would get through to London today.

As she neared the front of the house, Lucy was just arriving with Scott, Kerc, and another man whom she hadn't seen before. *This must be Jodrell,* she thought, *whom Robert and Theo want Lucy to marry.*

One look at Lucy's tense face warned her that, in a worried and unhappy mood, her sister would have little patience for what she must consider Vanessa's troubling presence in Gowrie House.

When Vanessa caught up with the foursome on their way through the garden toward the front of the house, she halted, feeling as though she'd run smack into a rocky wall.

Lucy's eyes lighted upon her. Vanessa could feel the resentment emanating from her edgy demeanor.

She blames me for what happened to Robert, she thought. The road to reconciliation was not merely riddled with obstacles; she sensed that a dead end loomed ahead.

15

Scott left the others and walked to meet Vanessa. Her eyes evaded Lucy's confronting gaze. It would do no good to try to discuss it with her now. Whatever Theo had told Lucy on the telephone last evening, Lucy accepted it. If Vanessa thought she had started to build a relationship with her half sister, she now had nothing.

She was grateful for Scott's support as he came up. The friendship in his kind brown eyes soothed her emotions. She might have succumbed to his sympathy by feeling sorry for herself if she hadn't also been aware of Kerc's dark gaze. Unlike Scott, he did not offer pity. *If he thinks I'm going to shrink away, he's wrong.* She lifted her chin slightly and walked forward to face the little foxes of Gowrie House.

"I'm sorry it turned out like this," Scott said in a quiet tone as he walked beside her. "Don't blame yourself, my dear. Robert was ill before you ever arrived. We came as soon as Kerc could bring us over. Is Dr. MacGregor staying here?"

"Yes, but I haven't seen him this morning. Before I retired to my room last night he warned us we shouldn't expect too much."

Scott squeezed her hand with the suggestion of courage. "Hopefully he'll know more by now." He ushered her up the walkway to the front porch as the others were entering the house.

Theo was in the hallway with Lucy and Jodrell when Vanessa passed Kerc on the front step. Scott ignored him, but Kerc didn't seem inclined to be passed over. He caught Vanessa's glance and wouldn't let go.

"I need to speak to you for a minute, Miss Miles."

She paused.

"Can't it wait?" Scott interrupted. "Miss Miles is worried about her father and needs rest. Don't you need to secure Mr. Miles' boat?"

The rebuke toward a hired hand couldn't be missed by anyone listening, least of all by Kerc. Yet Kerc's gaze showed nothing as he looked at Scott. When he turned his head toward Vanessa, his voice was servant-polite.

"It'll take only a minute, miss."

"Yes, of course," she hastened, embarrassed and troubled by Scott's unnecessary rudeness.

A faint turn of Kerc's mouth told her he was not put off by Scott. He stepped aside, and she followed. He reached into his pocket and brought out the packet of letters her father had given her in the rose garden. "I found them on the stone bench. I figured you've been too upset to remember you'd left them."

"Oh—you're quite right." She took them and smiled. "Thank you, Kerc."

He gestured his head politely, backed down the steps, and then walked away, presumably toward the boat dock.

Scott joined her, frowning after him. "He's an irritating young fellow. Forgets his position too often to be accidental. Something's on his mind that bothers me."

"He was only being helpful," she said.

He turned with a slightly speculative look, and he didn't seem pleased with her comment aimed in Kerc's defense.

"Let's go inside," he said. "Lucy's worried half sick. And Vanessa, don't allow her response to this get to you."

"I'll try."

The others were all in the drawing room when Vanessa and Scott entered quietly through the double white doors and heard the doctor explaining to Lucy what had happened to her father and how he was progressing.

"It would have been much worse if Kerc and Vanessa hadn't acted quickly. Robert received his medication before I arrived. He's going to improve."

Lucy shot Vanessa an angry look. "How can you say that when it was Vanessa who brought on his attack?"

"Lucy, this is hardly the moment to hurl accusations," Theo said, forgetting she'd done the same the night before.

"Theo's always right. Come and sit down, luv," Jodrell babied Lucy, taking hold of her. Lucy melted like jelly into tears.

Scott frowned at Jodrell.

"If my father dies, I'll never forgive her," Lucy choked.

"Now, my dear child, you must pull yourself together," Dr. MacGregor told her firmly. "From the looks of Robert this morning, he has a fair chance. The next few days are critical, but we're doing everything for him we possibly can."

Jodrell was comforting Lucy, and Scott watched in stiff-lipped silence, his hands shoved in his trouser pockets. He walked over to the window and looked out.

Vanessa sat down, all but ignored by everyone.

"When can I see him?" Lucy asked, wiping her eyes.

"Not until your emotions are under control," MacGregor announced with unapologetic sternness. "The worst thing *any* of you can do is upset him. Tonight is likely, if he remains in stable condition."

Lucy shot Vanessa another icy look. "It's not his family who's upset him, or wishes to."

Scott turned from the window and looked across the room at Lucy. "Accusations won't improve Robert's condition, and they're unfair to Vanessa. She came here in good faith at his request."

His defense took Vanessa by surprise. Usually he rushed to support Lucy's every whim. She suspected his rebuke had more to do with his anger over Jodrell than with defending her.

Vanessa stood. "It's all right, Scott. Lucy's very upset. It's expected she would be."

"I don't need you to come to my defense." Lucy threw off Jodrell's hand and jumped to her feet, her eyes fired with anger. She looked at Scott with equal animosity. "I'm not so sure my father *did* send for her."

"We all know better than that," Scott replied. "Including Theo. Isn't that right, Theo?"

Theo wrung her pale hands and looked imploringly at Jodrell.

"Lucy, luv," Jodrell soothed, "let me take you up to your room. Dr. MacGregor will let you know when you can see your father."

Lucy walked toward Scott. "If he sent for her, you had something to do with it. Perhaps you had something to gain."

A moment of strained silence circulated about the room.

"That's nonsense, Lucy. You're talking this way because you're upset. You need to do as Jodrell suggests. Rest in your room until it's safe to see your father."

Jodrell came and took her arm. "For once Scott and I agree. He's right, darling. All this rancor accomplishes nothing."

Lucy pulled her arm free and walked up to Vanessa. Her cheeks were splotched pink and her eyes were feverish with excitement. "How much money would it take for you to go away and stay away?"

Vanessa stepped back as though Lucy had slapped her. They stared at one another, but Lucy's lips tightened with determination.

Vanessa turned her back, closing her eyes, her heart throbbing with pain.

Lucy whirled around to face the others. "I know you all think I'm behaving beastly," she cried. "Well, I don't. Because I know why she's really here, to get my father's money if she can. He means nothing to her. None of us mean anything to her. She ought to be sent away at once!"

"Lucy, *enough!*" Theo said, a hand at her heart. She sank weakly into a chair.

Jodrell took firm hold of Lucy's arm and led her across the room to the stairway as the girl broke down. A moment later Theo stood and walked slowly up behind Vanessa. Vanessa tensed, not knowing what to expect from this volatile family. Theo's trembling hand patted her arm gently. Shocked by this, Vanessa turned and looked at her.

"Robert would be very upset and disappointed with Lucy's behavior, my dear. My own hasn't been commendable either. You're taking all this very well, I must say. It prompts me to feel ashamed."

"Thank you, Theo. I'm sorry it's turned out like this. I had hoped..."

"Yes," she said wearily, "I know what you probably hoped, but I fear only more trouble will come out of this." She turned and left the room.

The doctor emitted a deep, troubling sigh. "I too apologize for Lucy's manners, Miss Miles. The girl is beside herself. She'll come to her senses in a few days. Lucy has always been high-strung. I hope such unpleasant remarks won't affect your decision to stay." He followed after Theo, catching up with her on the stairs and taking her arm attentively.

Scott lounged miserably at the window, looking as though he'd just returned from a funeral.

"Well?" she asked. "Did we make a mistake in London when we decided on this visit?"

He kept his moody gaze on the outside garden. "I don't know. Robert will need to determine that."

Vanessa felt unexpected pity. Scott was losing the woman he loved, and there wasn't anything he could do about it except stand by and watch it happening.

That afternoon after lunch, Vanessa tried again to reach London by telephone. At last she got through to Mrs. Warnstead at the DP office on Grimmes Street. Hearing her voice again lifted Vanessa's heart.

Yes, Mrs. Warnstead told her, as of the last hour they were all safe. No, she hadn't heard from either Andy or Kylie, but the colonel was practically living at the underground RAF command station in the heart of London and had informed her both men were well and in fighting spirits. Mrs. Warnstead had spoken to him late last night after the horrific bombing spree by the Nazis. The pilots had checked in, and both Andy and Kylie were accounted for at Biggin Hill Squadron.

Vanessa's relief soared like wings, yet with satisfaction came increased worry. The more missions they flew, the more chances they would be hit.

The static was crackling again. Vanessa hastened: "How's Francis?"

"What, dear?"

"I said—is Francis well?" she said loudly.

"She's exhausted. When the German planes came over London it was terrifying. There were roof fires, buildings down, people rushing everywhere. So many senseless injuries. It's beastly hard on the old and very young. The prime minister is asking for more shelters to be opened up, and he's visiting the injured in hospitals. The need for hospitals! I dare say, I've not the foggiest notion what we're going to do if things get worse, and from what we're hearing, the worst is yet to come. Dr. Elsdon is holding prayer vigils on the streets of the city and working himself into exhaustion. He's nearing seventy, you know. What a saint of God! He puts me to shame. We've also terrible news about the house we rented for our offices—the owner has reclaimed it for other necessary war uses. And our little orphanage by the wharf is overflowing. It's God's grace that keeps us open."

"Yes. Tell everyone I'm praying for them. My heart is with you—each one of you."

"We know that, Vanessa dear."

"And if you see Andy and Kylie, tell them—"

"What did you say?"

"I said tell them—"

"Dear, the line is fading. I can't hear you at all—"

The crackling noise took command and the line was soon dead. Vanessa found that she was gripping the phone so tightly that her fingers were pink when she set the receiver back into its cradle.

"Tell them I love them," she murmured aloud.

For the remainder of the afternoon Vanessa felt restless and troubled and turned again and again to the Lord. She ought to be there with Francis and Mrs. Warnstead. She ought to be helping with the injured or working at the orphanage. She needed to talk to Kylie about Robert. But what could be done now, anyway? How could Kylie come here for a few days to see Robert even if he wanted to? And their father couldn't go to London. Not now.

She went to dinner that night feeling as if she were trapped in a box that was closing in upon her an inch at a time. She tried to remind herself that the God of the Red Sea and the Jordan River was her God too. He was the God of impossibilities. The Mighty One who could make a way through the wilderness and spread a table of feasting for thousands in the hot desert sand. As long as that was true, her hope could fly high.

Little had changed in Lucy's attitude by dinnertime. She was still morose, though Jodrell and Theo must have convinced her to keep her resentments over Vanessa to herself. Her eyes were red-rimmed from crying, and she hardly touched her food.

If Vanessa could convince Lucy she wanted good for Robert and didn't expect to share his inheritance, it would probably calm the girl down, but until she was willing to listen, no amount of denial would help. Vanessa reconsidered leaving Gowrie House for London, but having learned yesterday from Dr. MacGregor that her father didn't blame her for his attack and wanted her to stay, she postponed the decision to depart. She must take it a step at a time.

The mood at the dinner table was somber. London was once more under German attack. Everyone was jittery and tense and had lapsed into secret thoughts, except Jodrell.

"That horse, luv, is a magnificent creature," he told Lucy. "I intend to start with her first thing in the morning. With you riding her in September at the show, there's small chance you'll not get the blue ribbon this time 'round."

Lucy appeared not even to hear. She was using her fork to absently toy with the cut green beans on her plate. Now and then she looked coldly at Vanessa, who tried to ignore her displeasure. Scott noticed, and he was more attentive toward Vanessa than usual. This merely seemed to harden Lucy's dislike toward her.

When Vanessa first saw Jodrell, she'd been too troubled by Lucy's coolness to notice much about him. Tonight as he sat across from her at the table, she had a clear view of the man Lucy intended to marry. Somehow she'd expected the pretty Lucy to have favored a younger man than Jodrell, who appeared to be in his midthirties. Vanessa had even thought that Lucy may have turned Scott down because of his age and literary endeavors. Evidently this was not the case, unless Lucy's decision about Jodrell had something to do with Aunt Theo.

Jodrell was tall, well over six feet, and wiry, with sinewy arms and muscles in his neck, reminding her of the cartoon figure Popeye. Except for a curving mouth that smiled too much and the restless blinking of his watery gray eyes, his face was pallid and bore lines of weathered discontent.

A wide silver chain bracelet held her attention. It was too large for his wrist, and he kept lifting his hand so that it would slide back to his forearm. The action was distracting, and Vanessa noticed that Scott seemed annoyed by it. The bracelet must have been a gift to Jodrell, probably from Lucy, because there was an engraved heart with a pair of initials in the center, which she guessed were "J" and "L."

"Before Vanessa leaves for America, we should properly show her the island, don't you think, Lucy?" Jodrell was saying congenially. "And there's no better way to see it than by way of a horseback ride and picnic. On a clear day the view's unbeatable. What d'ya say, everybody? What about next Saturday?" He looked at Vanessa. "Lucy owns some good riding horses. Buttons would be perfect for you. She's a gentle thing, safe enough for a child to ride. Isn't that right, Lucy?"

"Oh, Jodrell, this is hardly the time to be discussing festivities," Lucy scolded, setting her fork down abruptly.

"Times of stress seem best to me," he countered. "I'll wager Robert would want you ladies to forget your worries and see to it Vanessa here has one good outing while she's at Gowrie House. I'll even wager by next Saturday Robert will be feeling so much better he'll be up and about his room working on his book."

Theo sighed. "He's probably right about the diversion, Lucy. A pleasant distraction would do us all a bit of good."

"Aunt Theo, with my father in the condition he's in, who can think of picnics?"

Theo looked apologetic. "I agree, it does sound rather heartless, but Jodrell was merely thinking of your tattered nerves, and of all of us. Setting worries aside for a day can do wonders for a burdened heart."

"I'm sure I needn't be the excuse for an outing on the island," Vanessa spoke up mildly. "Honestly, I'm not much for horseback riding anyway. If I were inclined toward a picnic, though, it would be at the old lighthouse near Devil's Cliff."

Vanessa was aware of the catch of silence, like a paused breath, when she'd mentioned the lighthouse. Lucy was looking at her without resentment for the first time since they'd sat down to dinner.

"Why are you curious about the lighthouse?" Lucy inquired bluntly.

"It's historic. That always interests me. And the view from it must be magnificent on a clear day."

"It's breathtaking," Scott said congenially. He looked over at Theo. "There's a picnic area somewhere around the lighthouse, isn't there, Theo?"

"Yes, but I'm not sure it would be a suitable place now. Not after—" she paused. "Not after the accident."

Jodrell turned to Theo. "Accident? Don't tell me we've had German U-boats right off the coast of our island?"

"No, of course not," Theo said with a snap in her voice, showing she didn't approve of his having brought up the picnic to begin with.

"There was a woman who worked at the tavern," Lucy told Vanessa pointedly, ignoring Theo's wishes. "She fell to her death a few weeks ago." She turned to Jodrell. "Didn't you read about it in the papers?"

"In Edinburgh?" Jodrell's brows lifted. "What goes on here is of little interest to the mainland. The papers are filled with news of the war."

"Maggie must have gone to the picnic area to meet a boyfriend," Lucy said, and she looked at Scott with a sardonic smile. "Don't *you* think so, Scott?"

Scott focused his attention on his meal and made no comment.

Now, what was that about? Vanessa wondered, glancing from Lucy to Scott.

Jodrell turned his head with apparent interest. "Maggie? Was that the girl who died? You don't mean the Carstair girl, by any chance?"

Theo tossed her white napkin down on the table. "This is a beastly topic. Must we? What were you saying about a horseback outing, Jodrell?"

"I was saying that it might prove awfully jolly if we could arrange something entertaining for our charming American guest." He looked at Vanessa. "Though calling her a guest may be too formal. Half sister, isn't it?" he asked Lucy with a little smile.

Lucy's mouth thinned. She looked toward the dining room door. "What's keeping Dr. MacGregor anyway? He should know something by now."

Theo turned her silver head toward the doorway. "I believe I hear him coming down the stairs."

Vanessa gripped her napkin on her lap as Dr. MacGregor entered through the doorway from the outer hall. She tried to read his face.

"How is he, James?" Theo asked MacGregor quietly.

"I'll go out on a limb, Theo, and say he's doing a wee bit better. He's alert. And he insists he's strong enough for a visit, but it must be a short one."

Lucy stood up from her chair, but MacGregor's brows tufted together a fraction. "It is Robert's wish that Vanessa go up to his room first."

A slight intake of breath came from Lucy.

Vanessa was aware of the guarded look that came her way from Jodrell. Even Scott appeared curiously surprised by the news.

Didn't her father realize that his request to see her first would merely make them more suspicious of her presence? Vanessa considered suggesting Lucy go up first, but the doctor was saying, "It's best we don't frustrate his wishes. You will see him after breakfast tomorrow, Lucy. As for you, Miss Miles, I don't want you to stay long."

For an uncomfortable moment she found herself the focus of their scrutiny. Theo was politely restrained, but subtle displeasure showed in her eyes.

Lucy first looked confused and then surprised. But it was Dr. MacGregor's meditative stare that troubled Vanessa most. He had nothing to gain or lose by her presence here in Gowrie House; still, he seemed cautious of her motives.

Could he have believed Theo's earlier accusations about deliberately upsetting Robert in the old rose garden? The thought was disappointing. She liked the dignified Scotsman and wanted him to think well of her.

"Well, well," Jodrell was saying under his breath. He turned his head toward Lucy. His little smile seemed to say, *I warned you about this unexpected half sister of yours. See, looks as if I was right.*

Vanessa rose from her seat, and Scott was pulling her chair back. He smiled encouragingly. "Better go on up, Vanessa. Robert wouldn't have insisted if he thought you were responsible for his setback."

"Well put," Jodrell quipped.

Scott looked at him. "There was never any real doubt."

Vanessa knew it was simple kindness on Scott's part that prompted his attention, but it didn't go over well with Lucy. As Vanessa turned to leave the room, the younger girl also stood and accused: "Father may not blame you, but I do. You just walk into our lives and upset everything and expect to take him over."

"I could never take your place with Robert even if I wanted to, and I don't."

"Then why are you here troubling us all?"

"Lucy—," began Scott.

"Stay out of it, Scott. It's quite apparent where your interests lie." She looked back at Vanessa. "You're not wanted here. Can't you just go away and stop trying to interfere? Not even Robert really wanted you to come. It was Scott's crazy idea." She looked at him again. "We might want to ask why. Maybe both of you together expect to take advantage of him when he's ill and feeling guilty over the past."

It sounded like something Kerc had accused her of previously. Vanessa wondered if Lucy might not have heard it from Kerc himself.

"I'm going to keep you and Scott from succeeding in your plot to steal Gowrie House!" Lucy said.

"Don't be foolish," Scott said sharply. "It isn't true that Robert didn't want her here. And her coming has nothing to do with money or the estate."

"Please, I didn't mean to distress anyone by coming," Vanessa protested.

Lucy looked at her with frustration, then making an effort to control herself, she started to say something more, even as new tears welled in her eyes. She turned furiously and hurried out onto the terrace and down the steps into the court, her dressy heels clacking down the stairwell.

Scott turned to go after her, but Jodrell's cool voice interrupted.

"You heard my fiancée, Mr. Morgan. She asked you to stay out of this family misunderstanding. I'll ask you to do the same. And if anyone should go after Lucy, it's me." He pushed his chair aside, said something low and indistinguishable to Theo, then walked briskly from the room to the terrace. "Lucy?" he called over the rail, and the sound of his confident footsteps followed him down into the silent garden.

Theo looked after them anxiously. "This simply can't go on. Lucy's never behaved this way before."

"Lucy's never had to worry about her position in Robert's will before," Dr. MacGregor stated. He looked at Vanessa sternly. "Regardless of what you say, young lady, it's not likely your father will cut you out of his inheritance now that you've come here."

"I've tried to make it clear, Doctor, that I don't want anything!"

His brows lifted. "It may not be want you want, or expect, but what Robert decides. You'll need to overlook Lucy's poor behavior. Give her time to adjust to the fact that she has a sister and brother to share her father with now. She won't like it, but she'll accept the obvious in time."

"If only I could make her understand I mean her no harm," Vanessa fretted. She turned helplessly to Theo. "If you could arrange a meeting between Lucy and me, perhaps we could come to some agreement."

Theo had grown quiet and thoughtful and was watching Dr. MacGregor as though she hadn't heard a word Vanessa said.

"You must speak to Robert about this dangerous game he's willing to play, James. He's the only one who can end it. Insisting on seeing Vanessa tonight instead of Lucy was a foolish, hurtful thing to do. Lucy rushed all the way from Edinburgh to get here in time, and he might as well have rebuffed her verbally."

Dangerous game? Vanessa wondered.

"Robert alone knows his own heart," Dr. MacGregor said with a touch of acidity in his voice. "As we all know, when Robert insists on something, he usually gets his way."

"As soon as I see my father tonight and arrange for his meeting with Kylie, I'm leaving for London."

Theo looked hopeful, and Scott's jaw clamped.

"With the bombing of London, there's little chance you can get Kylie relieved from duty to come here to see his father." Scott turned to MacGregor. "It will be up to Robert to go to London." He added quietly, "If he recovers."

"There will be small chance of his going to London anytime soon," the doctor said shortly. "If he recovers, it will still mean a month or more, at least. And that's being optimistic."

"I won't give up on Kylie being permitted to visit Scotland," Vanessa persisted. "Colonel Warnstead is his commanding officer. If anything can be arranged, the colonel will see to it."

"Perhaps if Dr. MacGregor wrote a letter to the colonel explaining Robert's condition, Kylie might be released for a week to see him," Scott suggested.

Vanessa looked hopefully at the doctor. She hadn't considered that; was it feasible?

Dr. MacGregor arched his brows. "That is a possibility." He looked at Theo. "What would you think of that, Theo? The young airman could meet his father and all this could be put behind us."

Theo looked grim and exhausted as she sat there in her black dinner dress, her gray eyes fixed on MacGregor.

"If you think it's best, James, then I suppose we could try. I could speak to Lucy about this too. If she can be assured neither Vanessa nor her brother mean her or Robert any injury, then yes, this might work."

"Good," Scott said. "The sooner this is done and over, the sooner peace can return to Gowrie House. You'll write the letter to Colonel Warnstead, Doctor?"

"If Theo and Lucy agree, yes. And of course, that includes Robert's going along with this as well. I know he was hoping to go with Vanessa back to London to meet Kylie."

This was the first time Vanessa heard that her father had expected to return with her. All along she had expected Kylie to come to Gowrie House.

"Then I'll speak to Lucy tomorrow," Theo relented. "She's too upset now. The best thing is for Jodrell to talk to her. She listens to him."

Scott's silence spoke louder than anything he might have said.

"Come along, Miss Miles. By now, Robert will be wondering what's keeping you," said MacGregor, ending the conversation.

Once in the hall, walking toward the staircase, the doctor took hold of her arm. "Whatever you say to Robert, young lady, don't trouble him about what just occurred with Lucy. He has one too many burdens on his mind as is."

"No, of course I wouldn't do anything to upset him now, Dr. MacGregor."

He nodded approvingly. "Robert's room is the second from the right. If you need me, I'll be in the dining room. I could use some tea and dinner, believe me."

"Thank you for everything you're doing."

He looked at her for a long moment, then nodded and left her on the staircase.

She watched him walk back across the hall to the dining room. She heard Scott's voice, then silence. Vanessa turned quickly and hurried up the steps.

The door to her father's room stood slightly ajar, and after hesitating a moment, she pushed it open and saw a huge bed and lamps glowing softly on bedside stands. She entered quietly, shutting the heavy door. She walked over to where he lay.

There was an upholstered salmon-colored wing chair drawn up close to the bed, and she eased herself down into it, trying to quiet her thumping heart. Her father's eyes were closed, and his face looked drawn and ashen. She leaned forward. What should she call him?

She moistened her dry lips. "Father?" she whispered. "It's me—Vanessa. You asked to see me?"

16

Robert's eyes flickered open, gray-green eyes much like her own, and despite his illness they were alert and questioning.

"What did MacGregor tell you?" came his low, weakened voice.

She swallowed, her throat dry. "Nothing much, except to not tire you."

"No, I mean about why I wanted to see you."

"Not a thing. Was he supposed to tell me something?"

A weak breath escaped through his lips. He shook his head and gestured to the chair. "Come closer, please."

She scooted the chair nearer to the bed and leaned forward, waiting expectantly for whatever it was he wanted to tell her. She began to think there was something else disturbing him.

"What happened in the garden would have come sooner or later. It wasn't your fault. Don't look so upset. I knew I wasn't a well man when I agreed with Scott to ask you to come."

"Then it was you who wanted me to come?" she asked cautiously. "Not Scott?"

"Scott mentioned the notion to me after my last attack, but I'd been entertaining the idea for months. My health was warning me I'd better do it now. He knew I wanted to meet you and Kylie and took the first step, knowing I was afraid to try."

"You? Afraid?" she asked doubtfully.

"Afraid you would laugh in my face. I wouldn't have blamed you if you had. I've no claim on you, you see. I'd given that up many years ago and knew it as well as anyone. There are some precious things a man sacrifices to folly and loses forever. There are decisions made in life that forfeit a happy ending, and not all the tears and regrets in the world can change the outcome."

She instantly thought of Jacob and his twin, Esau. Esau sold his birthright for a mere bowl of stew, because he said he was starving to death. Afterward, he deeply regretted the loss, but it was too late, "though he sought it carefully with tears."

"But I came," she whispered. "While the past cannot be relived, and tomorrow is uncertain, we do have these moments."

"You came, but Kylie—" His voice ebbed off in a tired breath.

"I can't promise I can convince him to come," she assured him quickly, "but I'm going to try. Scott mentioned the possibility of Colonel Warnstead authorizing a short leave for Kylie to visit you since you're so ill. Dr. MacGregor offered to write a letter to the colonel. I'll take it with me to London."

That appeared to please him and a flicker showed in his eyes. "Did you bring a photograph of him?"

"Yes. It's in my room. I'll ask Effie to put it on your breakfast tray."

"I suppose he's a rascal."

A small smile formed on her mouth. "At times."

"He's not like you. You're the angel in the family. I've no problem guessing that." He sighed. "I've missed a lot, haven't I?"

She was determined tears would not come. It wouldn't be good for either of them right now. "So have we," she said gently.

He reached a hand toward her.

Vanessa clasped it at once. There was no time for self-pity over the past. "We never did get to all those questions you had, did we?" he lamented.

"Tomorrow is another day," she heard herself saying.

His smile was tired. "Optimistic, aren't you? You didn't learn faith, hope, and love from Mary unless she changed radically. And that faith wasn't inherited from me either."

She saw an opportunity and didn't hesitate. "Anyone who believes in the promises of Scripture cannot be a pessimist."

"Ah," his brows lifted with deeper satisfaction.

"The first book of the Bible has Adam and Eve cast from the Garden of Eden, and the last book closes with mankind redeemed and dwelling in Christ's presence in the New Jerusalem. Since God's story ends in eternal joy for those who love Him, we've got to be optimists!"

"I should have known you'd be a devout believer in Christ. Good. That makes things much easier…"

She looked at him, surprised. Could it possibly be—? "Why is that?"

"Another day I'll answer that. You wouldn't believe me now. It makes it easier for me because it means I can count on you."

"Is that meant as a compliment?"

"Yes, Vanessa. There's something I need you to do. It's important. I can't ask Lucy or Theo or anyone else to help. Not even Scott."

Confused, she hesitated, then: "I'll leave for London tomorrow if Dr. MacGregor writes the letter to Colonel Warnstead."

"That isn't what I was going to request of you just now. There's something else I want you to do. Tonight."

Tonight? Her curiosity was piqued. "I'll…try, if it's feasible. What is it?" She thought he might mention something about soothing Lucy, that perhaps he had overheard some of what happened downstairs since his door had been partly open when she came up. Voices carried when they were filled with frustration or anger.

She remembered what the doctor had told her about not upsetting him over Lucy, so she waited patiently for her father to explain.

"You're the outsider, and for now that's the best thing that could happen. It's safer that you are."

"I've never thought being the 'outsider' where my father was concerned of any particular benefit. Why should it make things safer?"

His fingers squeezed hers gently. "I wasn't thinking of that unhappy aspect of your being an outsider...I was thinking of Gowrie House. About your being a stranger to the unpleasant undercurrents swirling around me, the land, the inheritance. They all want it, you see. They each have their own particular reason. Each would be the first to insist their cause is the nobler one." His eyes flickered with some far-off thought that brought a determined hardness to his now-haggard face. "Yet I *will* see that justice is done."

Vanessa didn't like the sound of things and moved uneasily in her chair, aware that he still clutched her hand as though afraid to let it go, as though she might vanish. The eagerness on her father's part brought a strange satisfaction, yet sorrow too. She kept thinking that his grasp should have been there when her insecure, childish hand had needed it the most. Vanessa, the insecure little girl afraid of her own shadow at school. They'd been lonely hands too, when she reached her teen years and had no strong father to support her when she'd taken her first adult steps. But God had given her this moment in time to relish. She thought of Paul's words in Philippians, "I have learned in whatever state I am to be content...I have learned both to abound and to suffer need. I can do all things through Christ who strengthens me."

Yes, I even learn contentment at getting to know my father only on his deathbed if that is God's best for me.

"They bicker at one another like a bunch of circling crows in a cornfield," he was saying.

Vanessa smiled wryly.

"Theo, although she isn't a Gowrie by blood, feels she has every right to the estate because she was married to Vernon."

"Yes, she told me about Norah's older brother."

"Vernon met Theo in Edinburgh one summer. She loves Gowrie House. You'd think she'd be pleased about this book I'm doing in memory of Norah, but she is dead-set against it. She has personal reasons for that, of course."

Vanessa remembered Theo's reasons for showing disapproval over the book, but wondered if they were the same ones her father was thinking of.

"Theo was proud of her marriage to Vernon Gowrie. She became upset with the research Scott dug up unmasking a few of the ancestors as scoundrels and knaves. She thinks information of that sort should remain buried."

"But those people lived so long ago. What they did has no effect on the family now. Why should it matter?"

"That's just it. It matters a great deal when the present heirs are traced back to the real Gowries of Scotland. Gaps in the lineage could be important."

"Are you suggesting there's some question about who the present family members are?"

"No. They're Gowries, all right. That is, Norah and Vernon were. Theo married into the family bloodline. Lucy is a Gowrie too. Theo simply wants any mayhem that has gone on through the generations when the estate was passed on to be deleted."

"And you obviously don't agree," Vanessa said quietly.

"If history isn't authentic—and accurate—what good is it to anyone? Besides, Norah wanted everything out in the open."

"And Theo would like to own Gowrie House?"

"Norah inherited the estate upon her father's death. Upon her death, the house became mine alone. Theo believes I will pass it on to Lucy, and she hopes to gain control through her. Theo treats Lucy like a daughter."

"Yes, I noticed she was quite attached to Lucy."

"There's no doubt of it. From the time she was about ten years old, Lucy grew up as much under Theo as she did Norah. Norah was often busy in historical societies." A frown puckered his pale brow. "That was a mistake on our part. So many mistakes..."

Vanessa leaned toward him and said quietly: "Perhaps we had best not discuss these things now, Father."

"No, no, we must, Vanessa. Time is as short as the warmth of a winter afternoon. Theo is fond of Lucy, yes. To the point of planning her marriage to Jodrell."

She studied his face. "I thought it was you who wanted Lucy to marry Jodrell. He arrived this morning, you know."

"Yes, to keep Lucy happy, to train her new horse from Ireland. Hmm...I suppose I did want her to marry Jodrell at one time."

Had he changed his mind? If so, why?

He looked thoughtful, regretful. "It's unfortunate for Scott that he fell for Lucy. She became angry with him over my book—and another woman. Lucy wanted Scott to give up his research and tell me he could no longer assist me. Theo put her up to it. Scott wouldn't do it. Lucy still distrusts him over the other woman and turned her back on him. That's what Theo wanted. Theo then introduced Lucy to Jodrell at one of the summer horse shows in Ireland last year."

"Have you changed your mind about Lucy marrying Jodrell?"

"Let's say I'm not as comfortable with the idea as I was even a month ago. Naturally, Lucy won't listen to me. She goes out of her way to show her independence. It's as if she wants to goad me and Scott with Jodrell. Why, I don't know. I suppose it's my work on the book. I'm worried about her. She's always been impulsive. I'm afraid she takes after me in that regard. If she really loves Jodrell, then I wouldn't worry so much, yet I don't think she knows her own heart. She'll make a lifelong mistake if she marries him just to spite Scott."

Vanessa was thinking of his first marriage to her mother. Did he now think it unwise to have left her for Norah Gowrie? If he did, he was avoiding it.

"I'd like to befriend Lucy, but she resents my being here. I wish you wouldn't say or do anything that makes her feel I'm a threat to her security."

His eyes twinkled tiredly. "Are you telling me you don't want to be my heiress?"

Startled, she drew back. She finally decided he must be testing her, that he had no intention of putting her before Lucy.

"I've no desire to become heiress. For one thing, it wouldn't be right."

"Why not? Don't I owe you and Kylie something? After all, from the standpoint of sons and daughters, you two reaped nothing and Lucy got everything. Maybe it's time to tip the scales."

"No, Father, please don't do that. I've told you—and I meant it—I didn't come for money. Nor does Kylie want anything."

"I've guessed what Kylie wants," he murmured. "He'd like to tell me in no uncertain terms that he hates me…"

She was remembering their last conversation inside the taxi.

"…and that he'll not accept anything from me," he said. "Is that how you feel too?"

"You spoke of owing us something. That kind of debt cannot be paid off with money; it can only be forgiven."

He was quiet. Then—"You think I need to be forgiven?"

She looked at him. "Don't you? For that matter, don't we all?"

"Then you're willing to forgive, to wipe the slate clean. Kylie is not. That's it, isn't it?"

"Yes, something like that. When I came, I admit it wasn't for your sake or mine, but for his. A daughter desperately needs her father, and I certainly missed not having mine. Nothing can change the past, I know that. I don't expect anything, although I'd enjoy being friends with you and Lucy. But Kylie is different." Her voice changed. "He's bitter. He's angry, even though he knows what God says about it. He struggles. Anger like this will damage him if he allows it to continue. That's why I hoped that healing could begin."

"Yes," he mused. "That is one burden of the soul I can still influence, perhaps. I shall try. The war, the brevity of life. Waiting until these dark scourges afflict us doesn't say much for some of us, does it? To think that it takes war and death and loss to convince us to act on what's right."

"No, it doesn't say much for our wisdom," she said. "God's Word tells us not to be like the horse and the mule who must be led by a bit and bridle. Cultivating a relationship with the Lord makes the heart sensitive to His nearness so that all it takes is the glance of His eye to direct our paths. But it's often in our nature to be slow and as stubborn as a mule," she said, smiling.

"It's also our nature not to see our sins, but to blame others."

"Yes, that too." She was thinking unexpectedly of her mother. Did her mother share no blame in the tragic ending of her marriage?

She was dead now. Vanessa would never know.

"When we're young and strong, we cannot imagine ourselves old, or see the end in view. We want to follow the yellow brick road, winding on forever amid blooming flowers and blue skies. But when the road's end is in sight, and the mist settles in, we grieve for wasted years, for lost opportunities, for what might have been," he said to himself, still holding onto her hand.

"Surely those very lost opportunities are what will convict the unbeliever. Far better to see the end coming and be aware of our need for trusting the Savior than to be suddenly cut off without remedy. He is acting in mercy when He gives us time to see our weakness and need. He gives us new opportunities to reach out to Him. Part of that will be the healing of relationships."

"Yes, you are right. And the foolish man? What does he do? Press his foot against the throttle and race ahead into the mist?" he asked with a twisted smile.

"The fool doesn't worry about it."

"You think then that this old man can yet heal any wounds he's caused and make some amends?"

She looked at him for a long moment. "Yes, Father. But there's only one Great Physician. Only One who can make amends to God for our mistakes and our sins. Recognizing our need and setting aside pride is a great beginning."

"'The fear of the Lord is the beginning of wisdom,'" he murmured. "Proverbs, isn't it? A new path can lead to a satisfying ending if we take it. Yes. Do you think there could be a better ending for me?" he asked quietly.

The lump in her throat was painful. "With God? Yes. With me, yes too. With Kylie? Maybe not with Kylie—but who knows? Greater miracles have happened."

"And you think we need a miracle."

"I'll settle for an opportunity to bring that letter to the colonel and have Kylie released on a few days' leave."

"An opportunity," he repeated the word thoughtfully. "To try and make things more palatable." He smiled wistfully. "Are you a peacemaker, Vanessa?" But he didn't expect her to answer, for he went on, musing to himself: "Remember what Jesus said to those who gathered to listen to Him on the mountain? 'Blessed are the peacemakers: for they shall be called the children of God.'"

She remained silent. He looked at her and drew in a breath. "We'll talk again about these things. There is the other matter. The task I mentioned. It's important."

"I'm listening. What is it you need me to do?"

He paused, thinking to himself, then: "Are you aware that there's an old historical rectory on the estate?"

"No. I haven't really seen much of the grounds yet. I did notice the lighthouse."

"The rectory is about a five-minute walk from this house."

"You mean there's a minister, or as the British would say, a vicar?"

"He's retired now, but when his health and age permit, he holds Sunday morning services for a few of us who like to attend. The vicar calls Kerc and then Kerc either telephones the parishioners or walks to their bungalows to let them know. Lucy intends her marriage to be held at the church, carrying on an ancestral tradition dating to the marriage of the first earl. Kerc takes care of the vicar's garden as well. He does a lot of things for him. They get on well together."

He paused and looked at her.

Vanessa waited, very much interested.

"There's a very old parish registry kept in the chapel, along with a book written by the first Earl Gowrie. It's called a confessional, rather in line with Augustine's *Confessions*, except Earl Gowrie was a dark and sinister rogue who never changed. He died a haggling old man."

She shuddered.

"It's that old volume of Gowrie's I want you to get for me. And the volume from the parish registry from 1853 through 1922. There's also my folder of historical research notes locked in the desk. I need all three."

"You're asking me to go to the church and get these items for you?"

"Yes. And it's imperative no one see you. Will you do it?"

She didn't know what to say. "But—is it lawful?"

"Quite." His mouth twitched. "I own this land, remember?"

"Yes, but the church—"

"The vicar is a friend of mine. He will understand."

Still, she hesitated. "Why don't you want anyone to see me?"

"I've tried to explain how the family is at odds over who should inherit. If anyone could eliminate evidence that would compromise their getting everything in the end—well, you see?"

She did, and her skin crawled. "Surely old historical records would be under lock and key," she whispered.

"The key is under my pillow. I intended to get them myself after I left you in the garden, but unfortunately..."

Guilt filled her heart. She would almost certainly need to make amends and get them herself, except the idea continued to trouble her.

"You want to safeguard the records?" she asked.

"Yes. Someone may wish to destroy them for reasons of their own."

Someone in the immediate family. The thought was chilling.

"Will you go, Vanessa?"

"Yes, if you think it's important."

"Important, yes. That information will also be put in the family history I'm writing. I want those old records preserved in case someone decides to destroy them."

"I don't quite understand all this, Father, but I'll do as you request. Shall I bring them straight here? It will be late then. What if Dr. MacGregor doesn't allow me back in to see you?"

"No, don't bring them here," he said hurriedly. "Not in my condition."

"You don't actually think—," she began, amazed.

"That someone would enter my room and take them if they knew? I've no doubt they would. If someone thought I was asleep, or thought—" He did not finish his sentence, but added decidedly, "It's best to not tempt them."

She lapsed into silence. Who, besides her father, would want them desperately enough to try and steal them? Was he ill and imagining all this? He looked alert and sober-minded.

"Then no one else knows these materials are in the church?" she whispered.

"Undoubtedly they've guessed. I've been working down in the vestry. I've tried to keep it a secret. If they knew for sure, I doubt these items would last through the night without being destroyed."

"Will you tell me what information they contain that's so important?"

"Yes, in time. You can read it in the book I'm writing when it's printed." He sighed and released her hand. "The key," he said, "is under my pillow. Take it and wait until everyone is asleep. As I said, it's important no one see you go there. I wouldn't request this of you, except I can't go myself. You've convinced me you're the only one in the household who isn't plotting to gain control. That and your loving and giving attitude assure me I've someone I can fully trust."

A flush warmed her cheeks. At last! Genuine praise from her father! *Careful, or you'll make a fool of yourself.*

She stood and reached beneath the pillow and found a ring with two keys attached. She slipped it inside her pocket.

"Which direction to the church?"

"It's near the family burial ground. Go through the garden gate. It's past the caretaker's cottage, the vegetable garden, and the pond. When you come near the pond, take the stone walkway that branches left toward the graveyard. Before you reach it, you'll see the old family church building near a stand of trees. The door is always unlocked, so you'll have no trouble there. But once inside, you'll need the first key for the vestry door. The second key is for the vicar's old desk. My folder is locked inside. The key also unlocks the grillwork on the library shelf. Gowrie's confessional is on the eighth shelf, five books over."

She nodded, indicating that she understood. There were footsteps outside the bedroom door announcing Dr. MacGregor. Her time with her father was over.

"You should have no trouble," he said in a low voice as the door opened. "There's a full moon tonight."

17

The moon was shining through the boughs of the apple trees when Vanessa neared the bend that snaked past the caretaker's cottage. She could see a faint glow of light from Kerc's open window and hear music from a radio station in London that was playing, soft and low. The instrumental tugged at her heart as it brought back memories of dancing with Andy just last week at the Warnstead home. So this is where Kerc lived.

She hadn't expected him to still be awake, because he rose so early. She would have thought a man of physical labor to be fast asleep at this hour. She skirted quietly past his yard, noticing the neatly trimmed fruit trees, the vegetable garden in the back of the cottage, and a fluffy white cat curled up at his door.

She hurried on. In only a few moments she was in the shadow of some tall cypress trees, where the path to the church rounded another corner and brought her in sight of the pond, glimmering like glass beneath the silvery moonglow. She heard little as she went past—just the rustle of tall grasses and leaves as a duck slipped from a nest with her ducklings to swim toward the safety of the middle of the pond. Frogs plopped into the water. The lacy branches of a big willow trailed gracefully along the water's edge, sending gentle ripples. *This is a night for romance and soft music, not for sneaking along the walkway on a clandestine mission,* she thought ruefully.

Her feet trod the muffled path that was partly covered with moss until she reached the wooden gate that opened onto the churchyard. To the left, a path wound toward the Gowrie burial plot dating from the 1600s. She wondered halfheartedly if the marker of the original founder of Gowrie House, the earl, was there. "A sinister dark rogue," her father had called him.

She walked past yew trees to the church, which stood like a tall shadow against the moon-brightened sky. Here, she paused. A white cross gleamed as a refuge amid the darkness and offered her a sense of belonging. She went up the porch steps unafraid of the silence and shadows around her and grasped the iron ring on the door. The church was always open, her father had said. And so it was. The door opened silently on well-oiled hinges. More of Kerc's work?

It was almost dark inside except for one low-wattage lamp that burned down the center aisle near the altar. She shut the door quietly and stood for a moment getting her bearings.

Ancient smells came to meet her, none of them unpleasant, and all of them speaking to her senses of well-worn pews, of candle wax, of old hymnals, and of sweet flowers left in their vases from Sunday morning worship.

Moonlight shone through the stained-glass window behind the altar, hinting of red, blue, and gold when tomorrow's sunshine would beat upon the glasswork.

Where was the vestry?

She reached a hand to the light switches on the wall beside the door, but halted. No, she'd better not flood the church with light. Her father had been insistent that no one notice her. Although the church couldn't be seen from the house windows because of the tall stand of trees, the caretaker's cottage was near enough for Kerc to see a glow should he happen to look out a window. He might come to check on what was going on, since the vicar wasn't likely to be here on a Monday night at a quarter past ten.

The last thing she wanted was a run-in with Kerc and the need to come up with an explanation for being here at this hour.

When she neared the chancel, she went to the altar steps, paused, and lit a large, white candle. From above, the dim glow reflected off the rainbow colors of the stained-glass window's representation of Christ, the Good Shepherd, holding an injured lamb in His arm.

Before assuming the task for which her father had sent her, she sat down on a front pew and spent several minutes in prayer and meditation upon the Divine Shepherd's saving and keeping power. She prayed again for her father, for Kylie and Andy, and for her friends undergoing the bombing in London. Whatever the future held for her, for all of them, she could trust the Good Shepherd who gave His life for His sheep.

Slowly she stood up from the pew, and lighting a smaller candle from the one already burning on the altar, she rehooked the cord across the chancel rail and walked to what she believed must be the vestry door.

The door was locked, just as her father had said. She wondered why he had a copy of the vicar's keys. She supposed it was because Gowrie House had always maintained the church and paid an extra goodwill pittance to the retired vicar. That her father had been coming here to use the vestry as a place to work seemed a little strange to her. Yet, perhaps, it wasn't strange at all.

Did Scott know that her father came here to work on his own? She wanted to reject the unsettling thought that her father didn't trust Scott with some of the information he'd discovered on his own. If that were true, why didn't he?

Inside the vestry, the vicar's desk faced a row of windows. She set the candle down and used the second key to unlock the upper drawer and lift out a thick portfolio folder that was sealed.

She found she was standing quite still, frowning at the sealed folder, disturbed by what her father said some might do to obtain the records.

She was pondering when she noticed what she first mistook to be square boxes stacked on the floor beside the desk. Closer inspection with the candle proved them not to be boxes, but the old parish registries.

She knelt and briefly went through them. The registry that her father wanted, 1853 through 1922, was not there. He must have left it in the desk, or somewhere else in the room. Her search, however, turned up nothing.

Had the retired vicar found it and put it back in the vault? No, he would have kept all the registries together.

What was in the registries? Nothing except old names and dates of baptisms, marriages, and births and deaths dating from the time of King James. Certainly, the registries didn't come close to the value of several church items she'd noticed near the altar. There was a Communion cup and a cross that looked as if it was from the Norman period. *They ought to be under lock and key*, she thought.

She laid the thick portfolio down on the desk and turned her full attention to the tall library case that loomed like a square giant in the dimness. The volumes were protected behind a grill, but the second key on the chain would also open its lock, he'd said. The volume her father wanted would be on the eighth shelf.

She drew the small library ladder over to the case and mounted with candle in hand. The key turned in the lock, and she pulled back the grill.

The books looked to be quite old, many of them first editions, leather bound and engraved with gold. Some were priceless. Most of the works dated to the 1700s, but several were early 1600s. Unlike the registries, these would be worth a great deal of money if they were sold to a rare book collector on the London market. The volume she searched for, *The Confession of His Lordship, Earl*

Stuart Gowrie, had been printed in France during the exile of King Charles II when Cromwell ruled England. It should have been easy to spot.

As she stood on the small ladder holding the flame high, titles and names of authors glimmered in gold. There was an edition of *Paradise Lost* by John Milton, as well as early Shakespeare, but the leather bound volume written by Earl Gowrie was not there. Could it also be missing along with the parish registry? An empty space stared back at her without explanation.

She was almost sure the book had been removed recently, perhaps this very day, because there was a fine layer of undisturbed dust everywhere on the shelf except the space where the volume had once been.

But her father had said it was here, so it must be somewhere, perhaps placed in the wrong slot.

A thorough search with the candle produced nothing but disappointment. The volume was nowhere on the library shelves. She stared at the gaping space again. Who could have removed it without her father's key to the grillwork? There was no tampering with the lock, no scratch marks in the black paint or bent metal to indicate forced entry.

Logic insisted the book was somewhere around close at hand. The vestry door had been locked when she arrived. So had the vicar's desk and the library shelves. Who else would have a duplicate key? The vicar, of course, but he was trustworthy, and why would he bother to take it after all these years?

Her father may have placed it elsewhere and forgotten. She sighed. She would need to spend more time searching the vestry. She glanced over her shoulder down at the desk. It might be in one of the other drawers. If she returned to the house without it, he would be very disappointed. At least she had his folder.

Vanessa raised the candle and searched the shelves a second time to make certain her eyes hadn't skipped over it. Satisfied the volume wasn't there, she was in the process of closing the grill and locking it again when a vague apprehension awakened her senses to noises outside the room. She paused. She couldn't have explained why she felt so suddenly disquieted, except a surreptitious sound had come from outside the vestry windows in the churchyard.

The effect on her senses was as chilling as someone's breath on the back of her neck, causing her skin to prickle.

You're imagining something quite Gothic, she told herself. *Next thing, you'll be imagining an uncanny creak coming from a crypt—a black cloak billowing in the wind as something moves noiselessly among the yew trees.*

She smiled at her imagination, turned the key in the lock, and was about to climb down from the ladder when her smile vanished. Someone *was* out there watching her through the windows.

The windows didn't have drapes. She feared to turn her head, afraid of what she might see through the glass pane. On impulse she blew the flame out on the candle to shield herself with darkness from someone's prying eyes. As shadows rushed to encircle her, she came down the ladder. Heart thumping, she turned to the windows.

She peered through the pane. Nothing. Nothing except the outline of the yew trees flanking the graveyard. Nearer at hand there were furry outlines of man-size bushes and below the windows foxgloves were growing tall. She noticed that the wind had risen while she'd been busy in the vestry, and she supposed she might have mistaken bushes shaking, or branches dropping leaves, for nefarious footsteps.

Her father had been right about the full moon.

The moon, God's comforting lesser light to rule the night, was silvery bright and would shower her walk back to Gowrie House with its friendly glow.

But it wasn't the shining moon that would ultimately safeguard her steps. "I will fear no evil, for You are with me." The Good Shepherd faithfully leads His sheep through dangerous trails to green pastures and gentle waters.

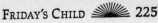

Even so, despite her deliberate concentration on the Lord, her wariness grew, as though she were being warned to avoid risk and flee the night.

She returned to the desk, snatched up her father's folder, and fumbled with the key, trying to lock the desk drawer. Her fingers shook and the key wouldn't go in. She heard a slight noise from behind her, inside the sanctuary. Anyone could have come inside, of course, because the church door remained unlocked, welcoming both saint and sinner. She tried to calm her frantic heart. It might be just the wind rattling some old timbers.

The key turned, and the desk locked. She dropped the key into her pocket, then turned to face the sanctuary.

She could see the one candle she'd lit when she first came inside, flickering on the altar. If someone had entered and was sitting among the pews—

She glanced behind her, toward the vestry windows. For the first time she noticed a small side door that opened onto the churchyard. Relief swelled her heart. Of course! The vicar *always* had a private entry. She could slip out quietly and avoid the sanctuary door altogether. The candle on the altar was securely placed on metal and would go out by itself.

She closed the vestry door to the sanctuary, locked it, and then went to the vicar's outer door. She turned the knob. It opened. She escaped into the silent night.

Wind and moonlit shadows surrounded her. She eased away, avoiding the flower bed of foxgloves Kerc must have planted for the vicar. She kept close to the walkway, then nearing the stand of yew trees that separated the graveyard from the churchyard, she rushed through the small gate and ran until she came within sight of the pond. Here, she paused to catch her breath.

Something about the beauty of the water, the calm of the ducks, and the throaty croak of the frogs was reassuring. She hurried on toward the house. When she neared Kerc's bungalow, she saw that the dim light in the open window had been turned off and the music had ceased. Holding the folder tightly beneath her arm, she crept past, then ran. She hadn't gone far when she heard the unmistakable click of his door closing softly. Had it been open a crack when she ran past? She now wished she'd taken a closer look. Or had he been following her from the church? Or had he just now decided to look outside?

She darted aside into the rhododendrons and found uncomfortable refuge in the burrow of darkness. She quieted her breathing as she listened for his footsteps following her along the walkway.

Wind rustling leaves covered any stealthy sound. She turned her ear toward the path, scarcely breathing.

She must have waited a full minute, plenty of time for him to walk past her hiding place. She felt a sick disappointment. *It must have been Kerc latching his door after returning from watching me in the church.*

Suddenly, from behind her the bushes rustled. She whipped about and saw a figure lunge for her. She would have screamed except his hand came down hard over her mouth, and he grabbed her roughly, his other hand knocking the folder from her grasp. As quickly as the attack came, it was over. He shoved her backward into the rhododendrons, bent, and then was plunging toward the high-walled garden. He stopped. She heard a startled breath come from him. Someone else was standing in his path. From the sound of things a brief but fierce struggle ensued. She heard a thumping "whack," as if someone was hit with a heavy branch, then one of them fell hard into the shrubs. The victor tore heedlessly ahead, clambering over the garden wall. A cat screeched, then it lunged over the wall and ran off toward the pond.

Silence settled like a net. A moment later, the soft wind could be heard again in the tops of the apple trees touched with the silvery moon glow.

18

Vanessa crawled from the bushes as Kerc came up catching his breath and holding one hand to the side of his head. She stared at him, relief flooding her heart. *Then it wasn't Kerc.*

"Are you hurt?" he asked.

"Not exactly...but you are..."

"That hunk of branch he hit me with served him better than a sledgehammer." He reached his free hand down and pulled her up. "Did you see who he was?"

"M-me? No—he just came from nowhere, from behind me. Oooh—my elbow! But you...you must have seen who it was."

"No. He had something like a ski mask over his face. Is your elbow skinned?"

"Yes, I...I thought it was you at first." She didn't realize her deep wariness, even now, until hearing her own voice.

"You think I go around pushing girls into prickly bushes, Miss Miles?"

"No," she said sheepishly, "I suppose not." But her voice stiffened when she thought about that ruffian, whoever he was, and looked at the tear on her sleeve.

"Your luck's running low in Scotland, it seems. Got more bruises here than most girls do in a lifetime. I'd say it was a good time to sail back to London...except for the bombing."

Vanessa glanced at him. He gestured his head toward the bungalow. His calm voice might have been discussing the weather. Considering what they had just both been through, it was surprising.

"No sense in standing here," he commented. "I was about to have some tea. You might as well have a cup too. We need to talk about this."

She hesitated, eyeing him. But his light had been out...*about to have tea?* It couldn't have been him that pushed her, could it? Not with the bruise on his head, unless he was faking. If she accepted that cup of tea, she'd get a chance to see that bruise in the light. Even if she didn't trust him completely about some things, Kerc was showing a more pleasant side of himself that was, well, rather attractive. Not that it was exactly the proper hour for tea. Had he really been making tea, or was he just too curious about what she'd been up to? Well, maybe she'd learn something at the caretaker's little bungalow.

"I'd like a cup. If it's no extra trouble, of course. I wouldn't want to be in the way during your midnight teatime."

"No trouble at all. Anyway, you'd best give me the facts on what happened so I can report it."

So that was it. She'd been right. He was curious. Well, who wouldn't be?

"Report it?" she asked, shooting him a glance as they walked slowly back to his bungalow. He was dabbing his head with a handkerchief, and she was checking her other elbow. "That chap really bashed me." He paused. "My brain's out of socket."

She covered a smile over his description. "I'm terribly sorry. I'm not a registered nurse, but I know a bit about this. Have you anything to put on the cut? And we need ice."

"Aye, there's iodine in the cupboard. But no ice. And I won't have you chasing back to the house for it. I'll survive. I'm always hitting or cutting myself. I'm used to it."

"When you said report it, did you mean to the police? Because you see, I'd rather we didn't make too much of a fuss over this."

He looked at her a long minute. "Someone attacked you while you were walking along the garden path, and you don't want to report it? Is that wise, Miss Miles?"

"Perhaps it was—an accident?"

"Little chance of that."

"Anyway, I'd rather we didn't say anything just now."

"Odd of you, if you ask me." He looked at her. "Then you think you know who he was?"

"No," she said quickly. "I said that I didn't."

"Maybe. But it's the only reason I can think of as to why you don't want the bobbies brought in."

"It would upset my father. He's so ill. I'm afraid it might make him take a turn for the worse. It's something we can't afford to do right now."

"Aye, I get it. You're not sure it wasn't someone in the family, and you want to shield them."

Put like that, she was appalled. "But, Kerc, it can't be someone from the house. It just can't be." The thought was dismaying, but she wouldn't admit the full implication even to herself.

"Whoever he was, he gave you a rough going. Pushing you in the bushes like that and hurting you. Look at your sleeve. It's torn and got blood on it. That's the second outfit you ruined here. You're going to be out of a wardrobe before long."

She glanced at him, thinking she noted a hint of restrained amusement, but he looked innocent. "I didn't get it half as bad as you. Do you have anything for a headache? If you won't let me go for ice, you're sure to get one."

"Probably will anyhow. No use worrying yourself." They arrived at the bungalow. "Here, come inside, Miss Miles." He opened the door and stood back. "There's a constable," he said, reverting back to the discussion of the police. "I could call him. Still, he'd need to come from the mainland."

"He wouldn't make it until tomorrow anyway."

"When I said report it, I also meant informing Miss Theo. Like you said, with Mr. Miles ill and all, we can't be troubling him about this. Does that suit you?"

She was still a little dazed over what had happened, but she found herself agreeing. "I suppose so. Even Theo will be terribly upset. She was tonight when Lucy ran from the dining room and Jodrell went after her."

"Yes, Lucy came here before Jodrell showed up."

So Lucy had run to Kerc. Vanessa wondered what Jodrell thought about that. Lucy was often seeking Kerc to lay her burdens on him.

"I'm afraid Theo will blame me again if there's any more trouble reported. She did about Lucy being upset tonight at dinner," Vanessa said lamentably.

"So Lucy said." His matter-of-fact tone told her little of what he thought about Lucy's grievances.

Vanessa sidestepped the issue of her sister. "Dr. MacGregor says Robert mustn't become upset."

"The doc's staying at the house, is he?"

"Yes, I'm told he's a friend of Robert's."

"He is."

"Is Theo likely to trouble my father if she learns what happened?"

"Hard to tell. She can be as cool as a cucumber. Independent too."

"Then again, tonight she was quite upset." She watched him, trying to gain information from his reactions.

"Because Mr. Miles asked to see you instead of Lucy."

"Yes. You see my point about keeping quiet for now. Especially if they find out why I was out so late at the church. I was on an errand for my father."

"And Mr. Miles didn't want the others to know."

She looked at him suspiciously. How did he know? "Um, yes. He was quite emphatic about that."

Including you, she thought, but it was a little late to say that now. Like it or not, Kerc was involved.

She entered the bungalow and went into the kitchen. It was spotless, and everything as neat as a pin. She remembered how wrong she'd been about him in the beginning. He must have appeared so that afternoon in London because of the terrible circumstance of having his fishing vessel attacked while rescuing as many of the Norwegian survivors as he could. Actually, what he had done had been heroic.

One small lamp was still burning. There was a radio sitting on the open windowsill, but it was off now. So that was why she had been able to hear music playing when she'd walked by. Despite all this, she wouldn't be convinced of his innocence too easily.

He came in and shut the door. She turned to look at him in the light. He met her gaze head-on. There was no use denying his charm. Since she was fair herself, she'd always preferred men with dark hair. Kerc was tanned from all his outdoor work, and it looked well on him.

If he guessed what she was thinking, he gave no evidence as he pulled out a second chair from the corner. "Have a seat, Miss Miles." He went to the cupboard for another cup.

"I bet you take your tea with sugar and milk."

"Just sugar will do, thank you." She sank into the chair, her legs a little weak from her fright. She'd come out of the attack with nothing more than a skinned elbow and a torn sleeve. Not bad, considering.

"You'll have to content yourself with honey," he said.

"Honey will be delicious. You're up awfully late, aren't you? I hear you working by five in the morning." She looked at her watch for emphasis.

"Do I disturb your sleep?"

"Oh—no, I wasn't complaining."

"I'm off tomorrow."

"I see."

"I usually leave for the mainland when I'm off, but there's nothing I need this time. Anyway, I have to save before I'll be going to London to see about my fishing boat."

He set two cups down and poured hot tea.

As calm as can be, she thought, studying his bent head. Where was that bruise? At least he really had made some tea.

"You don't remind me of a tea drinker," she said.

"Never touch coffee. Gives me the jitters."

Did anything ever give him the jitters?

Yes, she thought wryly, *probably me, when he was feeling unfriendly towards me.*

"Thanks for the tea. You must be altering your opinion of my being a shrewd and conniving woman out to steal Gowrie House along with Scott."

That evoked a ruffle in the calm waters. He looked up briefly, a flicker in his dark pupils, but he didn't respond.

He set a container of honey on the table with a spoon. "So I decided not to go to the mainland this time. Thought I'd go pole fishing tomorrow on the other side of the island. It's quiet out there by the rocks. And the seals and otters are fun to watch."

"Seals and otters?" She smiled with interest for the first time.

"You like them? Most women do. Especially those playful baby otters with long whiskers and huge soft brown eyes. A man ought to learn something from that, but I don't know what exactly."

She didn't respond as she leaned forward and spooned some honey into her cup.

"Anyway, they make pleasant enough company for an afternoon." He went to the sink and wet a cloth, holding it to the side of his head. He squinted. "That is, if my head's not throbbing. I was going to walk there. It's pleasant this time of year."

She stood apologetically. There was a bruise after all, and the cloth was pink with blood. "Your head—I'm sorry. I'd forgotten all about it. Do sit down, Kerc. Let me clean the spot and put something on it. Where did you say you kept the iodine?"

"In that lower cupboard right there. No need to trouble yourself, though."

"Please, I'd feel terrible if I didn't try."

Vanessa went to search, and he hooked a foot around the leg of a chair and hitched it forward, sitting down.

She came back with the small bottle. "This is going to sting."

She pushed his hair gently out of the way. It was clean and as fresh smelling as the wind coming through the window from the apple orchard…

"Ouch!"

"Sorry," she murmured guiltily. *Pay attention to what you're doing,* she thought. "There. All done. It's a dreadful bump. You really should have an ice pack."

"I've learned to live without ice. Without a lot of things, actually. The simple life, they call it. Those who call it that don't know much about doin' it. Nothing simple about it."

"No, I suppose not," she said quietly. "Still, you appear to like your work."

"It has its problems."

She wondered why he stayed. He appeared to have more than a fair amount of intelligence. She had already suspected that his speech patterns were a little exaggerated, though for what reason she couldn't guess. His restrained yet confident manner automatically attracted girls like Lucy to run to him with their woes. She could see why. He was easy to talk with when he wasn't being outright briny. She still believed he was staying on because of interest in Lucy. Maybe he thought he could yet change her mind about marriage to Jodrell.

She took the bottle of iodine and the box of cotton back to the cupboard. "Was that you watching me outside the church tonight?" she asked unexpectedly, keeping her tone unaccusing and hoping to catch him off guard if he were the one.

"Now why would I be down at the churchyard this time of night?"

"I don't know. I only know that I was there, and that someone else may have been there as well, though I can't prove it. It was just a feeling I had. As though I were being watched through the vestry windows."

"Can't help thinking it was whoever pounced on you like a sparrow hawk. It's none of my business why you went, but after what's happened I think you should explain. You're not still thinking it was me just now who pushed you?"

"No. Unless you enjoy hitting your own head."

"Rather difficult to do. If so, I wouldn't risk sitting here in my bungalow alone with myself. Not if I'm that barmy."

She couldn't help but smile at that. "Agreed. And there's no denying there were the two of you in that fight," she said.

"Aye. It wasn't a fight, though. I'd have whipped him if it was. He was trying to get that branch. Fully concentrating, he was. And all I wanted was to grab what he'd stolen from you and hide it. Then get that ski mask off. I was working on the first, but it gave him the advantage with that branch. That will teach me not to leave tree trimmings on the ground next time."

The folder...she had hoped that she wouldn't have to explain it to him. How was she going to tell her father that it was missing? Would he still trust her?

"Oh, my folder, I must have dropped it."

"Sure, what else would it be? He was watching you through the vestry windows and followed after you and pushed you down to get it."

What could she do now? She remembered the Lord's parable about the woman that had lost one of her ten precious coins.

"Don't look so worried. I have it safe."

"You have it!"

"Got it right here."

To her utter surprise he reached inside his shirt. "I got used to carrying papers like this when I was a boy. Never failed to rain soon as the teacher dismissed the class." He smiled.

Vanessa stared happily at her father's work still sealed safely and secretly inside the folder.

Kerc watched her face. "There's no mistaking he was after this. I don't suppose you know why?"

She came to her chair, looking from the folder back to him. "It's nothing I can discuss now. It has something to do with what my father said in his room tonight."

He didn't hand the folder over to her but was weighing it in his hand as though its heaviness would answer the question of its importance. Did Kerc know what was in it? Was he just trying to learn how much she knew? No, he couldn't know, not unless her father had confided in him. Through Lucy maybe? Did Lucy know what was in it? Maybe.

She continued, "Someone seemed determined to get hold of it."

"This must be his research papers."

"Yes. How did you know that?"

"Because I've seen him walk down to the church a dozen times the last few days. Ever since Scott went to London to bring you here. I knew he was working alone in the vestry on his book."

She frowned. "I wonder who else knows?"

"Hard to say. It's no secret about that family history book he's set on writing in Miss Norah's memory, though he didn't tell Scott he was researching on his own. That's a bit curious, I dare say. I'd be down there working, and Mr. Miles would take breaks and come out and talk to me. Ask me all kinds of questions about Gowrie House."

Somehow that surprised her, then she remembered that Kerc had been born here, raised here, and would know a great deal from another perspective.

"You went away from here a few years ago, my father said. Why did you come back?"

He didn't answer at first, just watched her as if deciding what he wanted to say.

"Meaning—I could have done better for myself elsewhere? Aye, you're right. I could have. I've even thought of emigrating to America. But land gets in your blood. It can be like a woman, hard to give up, to forget."

Could he be thinking of Lucy? Was Kerc like the others in the family whom her father mentioned who wanted Gowrie House? What was it he had said on the terrace about not being disappointed if she expected to inherit? Surely he didn't think that he could ever own it? Through marriage to Lucy, perhaps. Kerc too loved the land, but she couldn't help thinking his interest was for another reason, but perhaps only because he tended to become attached to the things he worked with. She wanted to ask him about his family and how he'd grown up here, but now wasn't the time.

"The real question is why somebody wanted this folder," he said. "Seems like whoever it was decided Mr. Miles' illness gave them opportunity."

"To steal it you mean?"

"Well, why else would they lay in wait for you to come along that path?"

She thought back to her father's concern about Gowrie House. Should she mention it to Kerc? It wasn't a secret since Kerc once accused her and Scott of working together to steal the estate. He had hinted that he no longer believed that about her, but he hadn't changed toward Scott.

She needed someone to confide in, and he had come to her rescue tonight on the path. He was being friendly too, although he might have his own reasons that had little to do with liking or trusting her.

Finding his level gaze as speculative as her own, she relented.

"There could be one of two reasons why someone wanted the information," she admitted. "From what Robert told me tonight, everyone wants Gowrie House and would do just about anything to get it when he dies. You were partly right about Scott. He wants the estate too." She became a little more careful in her explanation, "So, there must be something in my father's research that's important to one of them."

He watched her. "Could be. There's another reason too."

He had torn off a piece of bread from a loaf and was smearing honey on it. "Let's say the information didn't favor any of them, and your father knew this but was going ahead and writing the family history anyway, because it's what Miss Norah wanted before her death. You can see how if someone knew this, or even suspected it to be true, they might get desperate enough to stop the work from coming to light. I say there isn't one of them who wouldn't stoop to keeping the truth hidden if it meant they'd get the estate for themselves."

Vanessa watched him. So he *did* know more than he'd previously let on.

"Hope I haven't frightened you," he said.

"You mean...my father could make known something about the family that might put their inheritance at risk?"

"Why not? Makes sense. That's a pretty big risk to them, don't you think?"

"I'll say. A very big risk." She was remembering what her father said about Theo. "But the Gowries have owned this land for hundreds of years."

"The old earl had relatives, didn't he? And he had an enemy, to be sure. Was it a cousin? Can't quite recall at the moment—anyway, they fought a duel right outside this bungalow."

"Over Gowrie House?"

"No one's ever said. Maybe most of them don't know the reason. There is one of those historic signs on the spot where Earl Gowrie's cousin died, giving bits of information for guests to read and enjoy. I remember liking the duel story. As boys we used to play swords."

Vanessa slowly sipped her tea as she thought about the far-reaching events of history. Robert seemed anxious to bring the past to light.

"Was it Mr. Miles' idea or yours," he asked, "to go to the church so late tonight?"

"He didn't want anyone to see me go. He said there would be a full moon to light my way. I was to keep the materials in my room until he was strong enough to safeguard them himself. He suspected that they wouldn't be safe in his room, and he didn't seem a bit shocked by the idea of someone entering to take them. He took it as matter of fact."

"Maybe he knows them too well," he said dryly.

"Kerc, a volume of the parish registry is missing. The one dating from 1853 through 1922. See on the folder? The same dates are written across the front."

"Aye, I see it, with the question mark after it."

"That's odd, don't you think?"

"Aye, does seem odd all right."

"The book written by Earl Gowrie is missing as well."

"It is?"

"Doesn't it seem logical that the person who tried to steal the folder tonight also took the registry and book?"

"I doubt it was the same person."

"Well, why not? It's plain to me," she protested.

"Because whoever it was tonight could have stolen the folder the same time he took the registry and the old earl's volume. But he didn't. Could be that they're two different people with different agendas."

"That's assuming whoever took the registry and book also knew the folder was locked in the drawer," she argued.

"Aye, but there wasn't anyone who didn't know, I'm thinking."

"But can we be sure of that?"

"I think so. That's why Mr. Miles wanted you to go there unseen. If no one knew about his work, there'd be no cause to worry about who saw you. You could have gone in the morning. Like you said, he didn't put it past any of them to take the information."

"Yes...I see what you mean. They may have known, then." She frowned.

"But whoever it was waited for the right time. Your father's attack coming as it did probably convinced them to make their move. They might have concluded he wouldn't make it anyway and that now was the time to steal his folder."

"They could have taken it before now."

"But he'd have known. And don't forget your coming here has also upset things for them. They don't know what Mr. Miles will do about his will."

"I've said I wouldn't—"

"But they don't believe you. They're judging you by how they'd respond in your place. If they'd broken into the drawer while Mr. Miles was still well and strong, he'd know right away and confront them. They acted tonight because they had opportunity."

"But someone—even if it isn't the same person who acted tonight—took the registry and the book without my father knowing."

"Maybe they thought he didn't know what was in the registry."

"Yes—that's quite possible."

"The book, they might have thought he was through with it. It had the worst old English rhymes I'd ever heard. Sounded more like German."

She looked at him quickly. "You've seen the book?"

He stretched easily. "Sure, why not? The vicar showed it to me once. Even had my name in it, he said."

She sat up straight. "Your name!"

He smiled at her surprise. "Aye. He was the old earl's bodyguard. His name was Kerc. After he killed the earl's enemy, he took his daughter as wife. Needless to say the earl was furious. I often wondered what happened."

"Yes...Well, I wish I could have seen who was watching me."

"Wish I'd seen you go. Chances are I'd have caught a glimpse of him."

She frowned. "Who could it have been? You didn't notice anything suspicious about him?"

He looked at her laconically. "Might be Scott."

She leaned back against her chair, her mouth tightening.

"Aye," he said, "I thought you'd reject that straight off."

"I'd feel badly, of course, but I don't think it was him."

"Just goes to show how emotions get in the way of things. Why shouldn't it be Scott? He's got it bad for Lucy, doesn't he? If he could think of a way to get Gowrie House, he'd have a good chance to beat out Jodrell."

"And it could be the other way around too," she said defensively.

"It could. And there's a lot going for Jodrell, seeing as how Miss Theo treats him like kin. But Jodrell already holds the winning hand where Lucy's concerned. That marriage is set."

"Lucy could change her mind. Don't forget that women have been known to do so."

"I wouldn't be doing that. I never underestimate them. In my opinion Lucy would do well to change her mind about Jodrell.

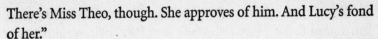

There's Miss Theo, though. She approves of him. And Lucy's fond of her."

Naturally Kerc would want Lucy to change her mind about Jodrell. Scott too must have been a problem to his hopes at one time.

"Did you see much of the old book written by the earl?" she asked.

"I skimmed it when I was in the vestry that day talking to the vicar. That was before he retired. It was pretty dull stuff."

"I'd heard Earl Gowrie was quite a figure in his time."

"Oh, sure. There was always overdone talk about him when I was growing up. From the exaggerations I'd heard, he might just as well have been the king himself. He was a sinister sort of rogue, fond of the usual ways of the flesh. Women, mostly. He supported King James and served in the palace in London for some years. When Charles was beheaded, he went into exile with Charles II. Went to France or thereabouts. He married someone there. Some London lady with real class, I heard." He finished his tea and poured a second cup. "More?"

"Thank you. You've no idea where it could be now?"

"The book?" he asked casually.

"Yes," she said patiently.

"I gave it back to the vicar and saw him place it on the library shelf behind the grillwork."

"Yes, I understand, but—"

"You said Mr. Miles told you it was locked up. He gave you the key."

"Yes, I have it here."

"Whoever took the book most likely took the registry too, and took them for the same reason. It either helps or hinders someone's right to inherit. You don't think I'd take them from the vestry, do you?"

"You might, if you had a good reason, but I don't think so. You'd need to be a Gowrie to be the rightful heir, wouldn't you? And there's little chance of that."

"No chance. I always thought Trevalyan sounded better than Gowrie anyway."

She smiled. "It does. Oh, well, Kerc, as you said, you don't care much for reading."

"Not those old books, anyway."

"I'm sure the volume will show up. Robert may have mislaid it himself. When I tell him it wasn't in its regular place, maybe he'll remember what he did with it."

"It is good that he trusts you, Vanessa, or he could think you were keeping them."

"He called for me because he's convinced I didn't come here to wrangle the estate from him," she explained. She wanted to believe that trust was growing between herself and her father, a trust that would last beyond the few days remaining in her visit.

"He wanted you to keep the folder and the book in your room. Aye, I understand, but after what's happened, it's a mistake to do it now. There's no cause to say whoever wanted it so badly won't try to get it again. Until Mr. Miles is better able to guard it himself, I'm thinking it's better off with me than you. What do you think?"

Aware of his bland but level gaze, she wavered. "Well...I'm not sure, Kerc. Robert did specifically ask that I keep them."

"If Mr. Miles knew what happened awhile ago, he'd likely change his mind about it. He was pretty worried about what the dogs did to you. Think what his response would be if he knew someone played a bit dangerously with you again tonight."

"He'd be very upset, yes."

"Look, you've naught to worry about. The folder is sealed. I'd not likely get it open without either you or your father knowing. And since you're sure there's nothing in here that affects me, I'm the logical one to protect it for him. I'm not on his list to inherit Gowrie House."

"Yes, you're right about that. Well, all right. I admit that after that scare, I'm not happy about taking on the responsibility of its safekeeping. I'll tell him when I see him tomorrow."

He looked satisfied. "I'll sleep a bit better too. Better lock that terrace door to your bedroom."

She smiled ruefully. "I intend to do just that." She stood. "I'd better go now. Thanks for the tea, Kerc."

"You're welcome." He stood too. "I'll walk you back to the house."

"I'm sure I'll be safe now. After running into you, he'll be more cautious next time. He was almost unmasked."

"Aye, but I'll walk you back just the same."

"But your head must be aching dreadfully."

He smiled pleasantly and stretched. "I feel like a walk. And I'm not particularly tired."

There was little left to say. In this instance she was rather glad he could be resolute.

The moon was still high, shedding its silvery glow along the walkway when they left the bungalow. A few moments later Gowrie House came into view, awash with summer moonbeams. There was a welcoming glow in her bedroom window.

They had said very little on the short walk and now at the gate, as he opened it to let her pass through, he said: "If you'd like to see the seals tomorrow, I'll be going around ten o'clock."

"I'd like that. But isn't ten rather late for you?"

He smiled. "I could have said eight o'clock, but I figured you wouldn't want to get up that early."

"You're right. I wouldn't." She laughed. "Good night, Kerc."

She left him at the gate, hurried across the court, and rushed up the steps to her terrace. Once there amid familiar potted plants of pink carnations, she looked back. She could just see his tall figure closing the gate and walking back to his bungalow.

She opened the door to her bedroom and entered to warmth and safety. Safety? Was it safe? It was almost impossible to think that anyone inside the house would actually put her in danger because of some research papers, yet she knew it boiled down to much more than that. Her father had warned that his room wasn't a safe place to keep them. Maybe Kerc was right. She'd made a wise decision in turning the folder over to him. That nasty bump on his head vindicated him. She smiled to herself as she closed and bolted the terrace doors, shutting out the dangers of the night and the spicy fragrance of Kerc's carnations.

19

Vanessa was up early and came downstairs to find Dr. Mac-Gregor spreading berry jam on a scone. He was cheerful, and he looked as though he too had slept well.

"I've good news for you, Miss Miles. Your father rested undisturbed through the night."

"I wonder if I could see him for a few minutes before I leave. I'll be out most of the day. I'm going fishing with Kerc."

He smiled. "Ah, a wonderful morning for it. I envy you. Even so, I'd prefer you didn't disturb your father this early. Is it important enough to awaken him now?" His concern told her he didn't think so.

She thought it wise not to mention her father's research papers or the missing volume by Earl Gowrie.

"Not if he's sleeping soundly. I…um…have a photograph of my brother, Kylie. My father asked to see it last night. I told him I'd send it up on his breakfast tray, but as he's asleep, I'll wait until this afternoon."

"I'll see Robert before then. If you like, I'll give him the photograph."

"That would be fine. I have it here." She handed over a recent picture of Kylie in his flight uniform, standing before his Hurricane.

He nodded approvingly. "Robert will be proud. Nice-looking fellow. I can see your father in him. I suppose you're anxious to get to London with my letter to Colonel Warnstead. Did you mention it to Robert last night?"

"Yes. He suggested we do it as soon as we can."

"Theo will talk with Lucy today. I'll do what I can to tip the scales in your favor. I should be able to write the letter this afternoon. A telephone chat with the colonel won't hurt either if I can get through to London," he added with a scowl.

"I appreciate this, Dr. MacGregor. There is one thing more. Would you tell him he was right about last night?"

There was a strange moment of silence. "About last night?"

"Yes. There *was* a full moon."

The doctor looked after her as she went out the door.

It was still too early to meet Kerc. She had planned it this way. There would be plenty of time to come back and meet him at ten o'clock by the gate.

The birds were up singing and the flowers were beginning to warm and open to the sun's rays. It would be a star-spangled day, perfect for seal watching, fishing, and for making her plans to return to London. Things may not be going as badly as they had seemed last night in the darkness.

She went through the garden gate and took the same path she had used yesterday morning to bring her to the heather-covered slope facing the lighthouse and the sea.

It didn't take more than ten minutes to reach the sandy beach. The slab of smooth rock at the water's edge waited, inviting her to a time alone with her heavenly Father and the true Book He had given to all mankind.

Some minutes later, she was perched on the warm rock next to the sea with a large sun hat shading her face and her Bible on her lap.

∿∿∿

The sun grew warmer and the hum of bees louder. She looked up and across the meadow toward the low rolling hills touched by light blue sky. The taller grasses blew gently in the sea breeze. Gulls circled and their distant cries could just be heard. Someone was walking the narrow dirt road in the direction of the light-house—someone whose stride had become familiar. Why was Kerc going toward the lighthouse when he was to meet her by ten o'clock? A glance at her watch told her it was now a quarter after nine. Had he changed his mind about fishing?

She watched. Someone else was coming from the same road toward him. From this far distance she couldn't tell who it was. His cousin Scarron, perhaps? But as the two met and talked, she could see the other man was not as tall as Scarron.

Vanessa watched them until they went up the hill toward the lighthouse and disappeared from view.

Vanessa was still considering this when a pleasant voice behind her called: "Cheerio! MacGregor said you'd gone fishing with Kerc."

"Oh, good morning, Scott." She closed her Bible and smiled. "I'm to meet him at ten o'clock."

"MacGregor said you came this way. I'm in luck to find you. I was afraid the two of you had already gone off on your jaunt. There's been a change in plans. At least Lucy seems to think so."

He perched on the rock beside her and looked with interest toward the dirt road winding into the hills. Unlike the doctor she'd seen at breakfast who had appeared well rested, Scott had tired lines under his eyes as though he hadn't slept much.

"Delightful day for a picnic and a little fishing. Since your father's recovering so well, everyone wants to take advantage of the sunshine to go up to the picnic grounds near the lighthouse while MacGregor keeps watch on Robert. Even Theo's coming.

For someone who frowns on ants, flies, and mosquitoes, Lucy performed quite a feat in getting her to come."

"How did Lucy know I was going fishing with Kerc?" she asked dubiously. Anything her sister unexpectedly planned must be scrutinized with caution. Why had her mood changed so quickly from last night's near hysteria?

"MacGregor told her, I think. He said a relaxing day would be good for everyone. Have to be careful about 'all work and no play,' you know. Lucy thinks we have a small victory to celebrate with Robert sitting up in bed. MacGregor says it might not have been an attack after all."

So that was the cause for Lucy's happier mood. Well, Vanessa didn't blame her for that. It was an answer to prayer. "Go to the lighthouse, you say?"

He nodded toward the hills, drawing his knee up on the rock and resting his arm across it. "There's a pretty spot with grass and trees. The grounds are managed by the lighthouse keeper. That's where the trail leads up to Devil's Cliff." He looked at her. "Jodrell mentioned it last night, remember?"

"Yes. Everyone was a bit reluctant at first."

"Things have changed for the better."

So it seemed. At least where her father was concerned. Naturally, no one knew about the incident on the way back from the church—except the culprit. "Well, I can't argue against it being a beautiful day for a picnic. When are we leaving?"

"In an hour or so. Just as soon as Effie and the others working in the kitchen make up the food. They're a bit put out by it. Not enough time to make the right things, the cook said." He smiled. "How is your relationship progressing with Robert?"

"Well enough. We're on the right path, anyway. And he does want to see Kylie. I gave him a picture this morning."

"That's another reason Lucy wants to have this picnic. MacGregor seems to have convinced her and Theo to have Kylie come here to see your father. If you want, we can make the trip to

London starting tomorrow or the next day. I'll ask Kerc to have the motorboat ready to bring us to the mainland."

Vanessa marveled over the sudden congenial atmosphere. Was it all due to her father's improvement? Or was someone satisfied they now had all the evidence in their possession that might preclude them from the inheritance?

There could be another reason behind Lucy's change besides Robert's improvement. Perhaps it was just that Vanessa would be leaving soon.

Scott was watching her, and she tottered on the edge of telling him about last night's incident. For a moment she could almost convince herself the entire escapade hadn't happened at all, but her sore elbow bore witness to her being wrong. How was Kerc's head today? Would anyone notice? Not if he wore a hat. *Whoever it was, it couldn't have been Scott!*

He smiled and a sandy brow lifted. "Such a scowl for a pretty girl on a sunny summer day! Something troubling you, Vanessa dear?"

She blurted— "Why is there such a secret about Maggie?"

He looked at her blankly. "Maggie?"

"Yes. The girl who they say fell to her death on the rocks. Jodrell mentioned her last night. Maggie Carstair."

He didn't answer at once. For a moment the fog seemed to be drifting in, shutting out the sunshine.

"The more I've thought about it, the more certain I am I want to know about her. I could go to the tavern and talk to the owner, I suppose." She wouldn't, but the suggestion was enough to make Scott cautious.

"What's the sense of doing so? You didn't know her. She was no relation to you. Why get involved? After the dogs, I'd think you'd want to stay clear of anything that could upset you."

"Or upset someone else?"

He didn't answer.

"What is it about this particular girl that makes everyone wish to avoid talking about her? The village is small enough so everyone must have seen her about at one time, or even knew her. Do you know who her parents are?"

He looked at her a long steady moment, then turned that hard gaze out toward the sea. The steady buzzing of the bees and the wind through the grasses circled around them.

"If we're cautious, it's because Maggie worked here at Gowrie House until she went to the tavern. Her death caused quite a ripple, I can assure you. It isn't quite true that the constable glossed over the ugly incident the way Kerc implied on the boat. The constable gave us a very difficult time, especially me."

She studied the side of his face, seeing him looking flushed. "You?" she asked quietly.

"I'd spent some time with her," he said stiffly. "She was a pretty girl. She had Kerc's fine looks. Maggie was related to him."

That came as a shock. "I see," she said dully.

"It's not the way you seem to think. I merely took her out to dinner. That's all. But Lucy found out. It's the main reason she turned against me and toward Jodrell."

"Did it ever occur to you, Scott, that a woman wants to believe the man she's in love with is faithful and true to her?"

"Of course. And I was. It wasn't until she started paying attention to Jodrell that I asked Maggie to dinner."

"If you're still in love with Lucy, I'd advise you to tell her all this. She may think the worst. And the girl's death doesn't help." She looked at him sharply. "You weren't with her the night she fell, by any chance?"

"No, thank God! I went to bed early. That's what I told the constable, and I still stick to that story because it's true."

He looked so adamant that she couldn't question his honesty. "She must have had other boyfriends if she was so pretty. Did the authorities question them?"

"Oh, sure. No one was let off. The thing is, she didn't have that many boyfriends. Maggie was a decent girl. Kerc saw to that. He resented me seeing her."

She looked at him quickly. He shook his head. "No, nothing like that. She was like a younger sister to him. He didn't approve of her working in the tavern. He was right. It was a terrible mistake—for her. Whoever she left with that night after work could have been anyone from the mainland. Seamen come and go, and so do soldiers now that the war's on. The strange thing is, no one remembers seeing anyone unusual at the tavern that night."

"And she didn't leave with anyone?"

"No. She left alone, early. She told the owner she had a friend coming."

A friend. "On the boat you gave no hint you knew her," she accused mildly.

"Because I knew Kerc was trying to draw me out. He didn't like me being with you, I think. It was a warning." He flushed. "As if he thought I'd harmed Maggie."

So was that the real underlying reason for the tension between the two men? "You say she worked in Gowrie House?"

"Yes, as a parlor maid. She was born here, same as Kerc, Scarron, Billy, the whole bunch of them. They're all related in one way or another."

"Then, about Maggie, do you think she was murdered? Because on the boat you said it was an accident."

He let out a deep, troubled breath. "I wish I knew, Vanessa. All the clues lead to a dead end for the authorities. The case is still open, but there seems to be nowhere to go on it. Kerc is still more than suspicious. He believes she was murdered," he said so quietly that she hardly heard him.

Vanessa was remembering how worried Kerc had been last night about the incident on the path. Maybe it should be reported. But were the separate incidents related at all? What happened to Maggie Carstair might have nothing to do with Gowrie House.

The minutes dragged by in thoughtful silence.

"So now you know why I didn't want to talk about Maggie. From the look of your face, I was right. The ugly details have spoiled your mood."

She stirred. "I'll try not to let it spill over on anyone else. We'd better go, or we'll be late."

"I'm supposed to take you to the stables so Jodrell can fix you up with the right mount. We're all taking horses. Lucy insisted. Have you done much riding? I think you told me you haven't."

"I'll manage if the horse is gentle. Jodrell mentioned one named Buttons."

He took her hand and pulled her from the rock. He winced suddenly as he did so.

"Are you all right?" Vanessa asked, wondering.

"Yes, I'm fine. Just a few sore muscles." He smiled slightly, as if embarrassed. "The boat lurched a little on the sea coming back from the mainland, and I took a quick tumble to the deck." He seemed anxious to change the subject. "Regarding Buttons, Jodrell is the expert on horses, so I think we should leave the decision to him. Shall we go? It's a fifteen-minute walk from here to the stables."

The Gowrie stables were well stocked and newly reconstructed. Vanessa could see why Jodrell, whose business was raising and training horses, would find the estate a pleasure to manage, and own, if he married Lucy. There was money to be made here, even she could see that.

Jodrell had already chosen horses for the various riders, including Aunt Theo, and the animals were lined up and saddled when she arrived with Scott. Lucy and Aunt Theo weren't there yet.

"Good morning, Vanessa," he called pleasantly. "Looks like we'll get that picnic after all."

So Jodrell was in a friendly mood. Was it genuine, or was he covering up?

"You'll enjoy the old lighthouse," he told her. "Goes all the way back more'n a hundred years. Did Kerc tell you about it?"

"No, what about Kerc?" she prodded with a smile.

"Oh, his old cousin Carew runs it. So Kerc knows all about it. I see him going up there often enough, even late at night...seems a bit strange, though. Taking those dogs out for a run so late."

"He works such long hours," she said. "Maybe it's the only time he can spend with them."

He looked at her, a glint of curiosity in his eyes. She turned away to pet her horse so he couldn't read her thoughts. Why was Jodrell spying on Kerc? Or had he just *happened* to notice the late-night walks with the Dobermans?

"She looks gentle enough," she said of Buttons.

"Oh, she's that, all right. Too old to do much. But she's a fine girl. Aren't you, Buttons?" He rubbed her nose. "We're all attached to her, so we keep her. Lucy won't hear of putting her away."

"I don't blame her at all."

"Yes, that lighthouse is still operating the way it did in the old days," he continued.

"And Kerc's cousin runs it?" She was thinking of the man she'd seen on the dirt road.

"He's got more cousins around here than I can keep track of," said Jodrell. "I hear you had a run-in with one of them. Scarron's an odd one, all right. I've thought him a little barmy myself."

"Let's not get on that topic," Scott interrupted a bit shortly. "Is this my horse, Jodrell?"

"Think you can handle him?" Jodrell asked in an undertone of malicious humor.

Scott shot him a wry glance. "What did you do, old fellow, put a burr under his saddle?"

Jodrell laughed unpleasantly. "Too bad I didn't think of that. No, if you take a tumble, it's your horsemanship, so don't blame me."

"Tell me more about who manages the lighthouse, Jodrell," she said, changing the topic and hoping to come between the two snarling lions. Lucy, the prize, wasn't even here yet. A pleasant day? Maybe.

"The old man and his wife, 'Miss Mary,' as everyone calls her, have the lighthouse keeper's cottage up there. Lucy says they've managed things for as far back as she can remember. Here, let me help you up. Nothing unpleasant can happen riding this one I guarantee it."

She settled herself in the saddle and then looked down at him from beneath her hat. "I'll remember that," she said with a laugh. She noticed scratches on Jodrell's right hand as she took the reins from him. She looked away quickly lest he observe her glance.

Scott had sore muscles this morning when they'd gotten up off the rock. Either one of them might have been in a scuffle last night with Kerc.

Jodrell squinted up at Scott, now astride a big gray gelding. "By the way, Scott, Lucy found your cap in the garden this morning. She left it in the hall for you. So it was you I heard last night."

Vanessa tensed slightly and heard Scott say, "Oh? What do you mean?"

"Didn't you go out last night?"

Scott's mouth tightened. "Go out?" he repeated impatiently. "After everyone retired, do you mean? No. Why should you ask that?"

"I thought I heard you leave your room. It must have been after 10:30."

"I read until midnight and then slept like a log. What's with you, Jodrell? If I did go out, what difference would it make to you?"

"No difference at all. But Billy said he heard something unusual in the garden. Thought he might have seen someone running. Did you see him?"

Scott frowned. "No. I told you I didn't leave my room. What are you suggesting?"

"Nary a thing. Calm down. Why are you so jumpy? It was just a question. Theo says some of the older boys from town have been a little too rowdy lately, cutting through the grounds to get to the beach. I just thought you might have seen something to back up Billy, is all."

"How could I? I wasn't out last night."

Jodrell shrugged. "Okay. Sorry I brought it up. You must've dropped your cap earlier. Hey, here come Lucy and Theo." He walked to meet them.

Scott's face was hard with anger and something else as he watched Lucy come up to Jodrell and loop her arm through his. "I want to ride my new horse," she was saying.

"You can't, luv, Strawberry isn't ready yet. I'll need a month with her, at least."

She made a pretty pouting face. "Oh, very well. Then at least let me ride Dolphin."

"I've already saddled him. Morning, Theo dear. You're looking grand."

"Good morning, Jodrell. How did I ever allow you and Lucy to talk me into this?"

"Now, now, you heard what MacGregor said. A picnic is the perfect remedy for highly-strung nerves. Did you tell Effie to include berry cobbler?"

"I did. They're coming in the motorcar with the food. I do hope this outing isn't a mistake. I hate to leave Robert even though James says he'll be fine."

"With a doctor at his beck and call, what could happen?"

"I suppose you're right. Good morning, Vanessa, Scott. Very sensible of you, dear, to bring a big hat," she said to Vanessa. "The sun will be hot today. Well? Is everyone ready for the ride? Come along, Lucy."

"Where is Kerc?" Lucy asked, glancing about, but particularly at Vanessa with a speculative glint in her eyes.

Vanessa kept a blank face, and after a moment Jodrell said: "He was already gone from his bungalow when I came to the stables. I'd stopped by to see him about arranging a boat tomorrow for Vanessa."

"Oh, well. He'll show up when he's ready," Lucy said. "Coming, Jodrell darling?" She glanced coolly toward Scott to make sure he heard the word of endearment. He had, and his gaze was unpleasantly fixed on Jodrell.

Vanessa sighed.

20

The morning was warm, blue, and brilliant as the horses walked single file along the narrow trail that wound gently uphill through a purplish-blue lake of fragrance, mounded here and there with bracken and oddly shaped dark rocks.

At Jodrell's suggestion, Vanessa rode safely in the middle, with Theo behind her, and he and Lucy in the lead. Scott followed behind Theo. There was still no sign of Kerc or a hint that he'd even show up. Effie and Billy had gone ahead in the motorcar, preparing the picnic grounds.

"There's the old lighthouse," Scott announced, breaking the silence.

Topping the rocky rise, the Firth of Lorn, wide and pleasantly gray-blue, was shimmering in the sunlight. Far out to sea was an incoming front of thick gray mist.

"It will come creeping in by sunset," Scott suggested.

"At least the day will be enjoyable," Theo said.

Vanessa was looking toward the white-and-black lighthouse, thinking it didn't appear old and dilapidated at all but the prized object of someone's hearty affection. The oval roof and lookout were freshly painted white, and the handrails to the door, a shiny black.

The keeper's bungalow stood perhaps a hundred or so yards away with a well-groomed lawn and a row of wind-strengthened cypress bent to interesting ghostly shapes. Red geraniums flocked the stone walkway up to the black oval door, where a brass knocker was lovingly polished.

She wondered about the lighthouse keeper, Carew. If the cottage upkeep was any indication of what he was like, then he was not another snarly Scarron. Flowers were expertly cared for, and plump white ducks waddled contentedly across a patch of blue-green sea grass in search of their own picnic lunch.

The public grounds were another five minutes ahead. The picnic area was a flat sandy square rimmed with cypress that faced the rocks and sea. An iron rail encircled the cliff's edge that overlooked a steep drop to the rocks and waves below, the boulders showing shiny gray as the sea splashed and foamed around them.

Vanessa left the others at the picnic tables and walked across the grounds to the rail. A narrow strip of sandy, rocky soil led outward and around the hill. A sign read: "Trail overlook to Devil's Cliff. Caution. Loose rock."

She was leaning on the rail staring up at the infamous path, imagining Maggie in the thick mist climbing in the dark. No, a mere accident didn't make much sense. Why would the girl go up there in heavy fog? Could she have climbed up earlier and stayed too late, the fog trapping her? Had someone been with her? Had she missed an important step at the top? In a moment Maggie had fallen and her companion, unable to help her in that needed second, had watched in horror and guilt as she plunged below to her death. Unless…he'd pushed her.

"As you Americans say, a penny for your thoughts. Or are they worth much more?"

She whirled, jumpy. Kerc stood watching her with a guarded expression. "Didn't mean to startle you."

"Oh, hello, Kerc. Where did you come from?"

"The keeper's bungalow up the road. Lucy told me we were all supposed to meet here for a picnic lunch. Looks like our fishing got pushed aside. I hope you didn't mind. I thought it might be best for you, considering their past behavior, that you accept the olive branch."

"Is that what this picnic is, a peace offering?" she asked. Lucy hadn't shown any particular friendliness at the stables. Only Theo had spoken to her.

"Let's hope so. I told her when she called me this morning that she was blessed to have a sister like you. If she has any sense, she'll try to build some sort of a relationship."

"Thank you, but I'm afraid I'm still the unwanted guest. Lucy, I'm sure, is more concerned about getting the ordeal over with and forgotten than anything else. Once Kylie meets Robert, that will be the end of it, so they hope. And they could be right."

"Is that what you want?"

It was the first time Kerc had showed any interest in what she wanted, and it surprised her.

"I don't know yet. I'm getting on fairly well with my father, but..."

"I understand. I went through something of what you're facing when I was growing up. My father packed his suitcases one day after my mother died, left me with Scarron's family, and went exploring Africa. He never came back."

"Did he die there?" she asked gently.

"Either there, or somewhere like it. He was a great one for adventure, but he never cared much for responsibilities at home."

She looked at him curiously as he leaned against the rail, looking out to sea, the breeze blowing his dark hair and the collar of his shirt. She noticed, against her will, the handsome profile—

He turned and she quickly looked away. If he caught a glimpse of her thoughts, he gave no clue. He gestured his head toward the trail. "Not a pleasant hike, if that's what you're thinking about doing later. Especially with those sandals you've got on."

"I wasn't intending to walk up there. I do want to see the lighthouse later, though."

He reached into his pocket and held up a big key. He smiled. "After lunch? There's an old bell there, about a hundred years old. We don't use it now. We have electricity here and a rotating beacon. I bet you'd like to see the lamp."

He was right. "Well, I'd love to see them both." Her eyes were irresistibly drawn back to the rock. "That trail…I was wondering why Maggie would choose that route to meet a boyfriend."

His expression changed, hardened. He seemed to weigh her words with cautious interest.

She looked out to the sea again and held to the rail. "If I'd been Maggie, I'd have insisted on a pleasanter spot for a rendezvous."

"Such as?"

"The sandy shore by the sea. That big rock suits me well."

"Aye, I know it. I saw you there this morning."

Her eyes came swiftly to his. He looked amused. "Couldn't miss you, Miss Miles. Not in that pretty sun hat with a red ribbon."

She looked away. "I didn't think you noticed me."

"I know you didn't. You're probably wondering who the man I met was."

"Well—yes, I did. That was before I knew about the change in plans, and I wondered why you were going to the lighthouse when we were to meet at ten by the gate. I thought you'd forgotten."

"Forgotten? Not likely. Not meeting you, anyway."

The simple suggestion caused her heart to beat a little faster.

"The man was a friend. He's staying in the lighthouse cottage with Carew and Mary, cousins of mine."

That answered it well enough.

"What makes you think Maggie came here to meet a lover?"

She might learn even more if she let him know she knew that Maggie had been his cousin.

"That's just it," she said. "It doesn't make any sense that she'd come here with a romantic interest. And everyone at the tavern insists she left alone."

"How do you know that?" His dark eyes became intensely alert.

"Scott told me," she confessed quietly. She felt his penetrating stare. "He told me everything he knew about your cousin Maggie."

"He didn't know that much about her. He used her shoulder to cry on, is all. And she let him for reasons of her own. She wasn't a fool."

"No, I don't think she was either, not now. Not after Scott told me how you two were close. You talked good sense into her, he said."

"I'm surprised he noticed," he said dryly. He studied her. "He shouldn't have involved you. I dare say, you've been in enough situations since you got here. You don't need any more. The trouble with Scott is that he seeks too many shoulders to lean on. He ought to be upholding you, since he brought you into this. As for Lucy, he ought to be making it clear as water how he feels about her. Instead, he mopes about feeling sorry for his loss, but isn't man enough to go after her."

"He doesn't think he can win," she said defensively.

"He'll never know till he tries. I never thought much of him for his reluctance. What kind of a man can love a girl the way he does Lucy and let her make the worst mistake of her life?"

"You mean Jodrell?" she asked surprised. She hadn't known Kerc felt that strongly about him.

"Aye. Jodrell," he said with thoughtful coolness. "He's got more than Lucy on his mind. Those horses are his first love. It wouldn't surprise me if he didn't want to marry her just to own that new purebred from Ireland. Strawberry, I think Lucy named her."

"Women don't always listen when a man starts lecturing them."

He smiled. "I can see that. They dig in their heels and refuse to submit. I wasn't speaking of lecturing Lucy. Just letting her know plain out that I was crazy about her, if I were Scott."

She glanced at him quickly. If *he* were Scott, and if *he* were crazy about Lucy—he'd let her know. Then did that mean Kerc wasn't interested in her?

"Well, doesn't she know that he cares?"

"If she's telling me the truth, she doesn't. She thinks his withdrawn manner is rejection because she's already made a mistake in letting her relationship with Jodrell reach the point of engagement. But engagements are just that, a time to make sure about a lifetime commitment. If it begins to look wrong, there's no shame in breaking it off. Much better a broken engagement than a difficult or broken marriage. Don't you think so?"

"Yes..." Somehow her mind traveled to Andy. "Quite my idea on the matter." She was looking down at her left hand where Andy had placed what they'd called a ring promising an engagement. The green peridots glittered in the sunlight.

Kerc reached over and to her surprise lifted her hand and looked at it. "Your RAF pilot? He's a pretty classy chap, I suppose."

Had she detected just a bit of testiness? She couldn't be sure. It might just have been his way of asking questions in that accent of his that she rather liked.

"Yes. Andy Warnstead."

"Usually engagement rings have diamonds."

"I think they do," she said quietly, pulling her hand away gently.

"Why green stones?"

"No particular reason. We just settled on green..."

Now, why did I say that? Why not tell him plain out that I'm not engaged? Somehow she knew that had been what he was trying to ask her without being obvious.

There was a moment of silence in which the door quietly shut between them. She had done this, but why? He had put out a slight feeler, and she had withdrawn.

She didn't look at him. After a few moments the discomfort passed. He said, "Scott sought Maggie out for the same reason he seeks you out. To unload his unhappiness about Lucy."

"He's not indecisive if that's what you're suggesting. He's had a definite mind of his own ever since I've met him in London. Don't forget he was the one who talked me into coming here."

"I'm not likely to forget that."

"Honestly, Kerc, it was my prodding that got him to open up about Maggie. He finally admitted he knew her, that she'd worked at Gowrie House."

"He talks too much."

"You're in a grumpy mood. Your head must be hurting you." She glanced at the hat that concealed the injury.

"Sorry. My head's fine. I had a worse bump than this when I fell from the rocks when I was a boy."

"Kerc? If you feel this way about him, then why did you let Scott get by with pretending he didn't know Maggie when we were on the boat coming over? Especially when he denied that the constable was suspicious of foul play?"

He turned and looked at her directly, thoughtfully for a minute, then said without embarrassment: "I'll admit that I wasn't really aiming my words at Scott, but at you. I wanted to scare you back to London."

She folded her arms. "I see. That's what I thought at the time."

"I know you did. You glared at me." He half smiled.

"Maybe you're still trying to 'scare' me back to London."

"Maybe. Not for the same reasons, though. Look, I apologize, Vanessa—Miss Miles."

"Vanessa." She smiled.

"I misunderstood you the first time we met. Like I said before, I thought you and Scott were plotting together. He, for Lucy, and you, for money. Your father didn't give you much of anything while growing up. I thought you talked yourself into vindicating your motives to get what you could now, by using his guilt. You're not that kind of a woman. I see that now. You have Christian character. Plenty of it."

Pleased, she looked away. "Whom do you think your cousin came here to meet?"

He considered. "I'll tell you what I told the constable. She had a good reason for coming here. Did you see that lighthouse keeper's cottage back there?"

"Yes. Scott said he was related to you as well."

"Aye. Carew and Mary are grandparents of Maggie. If she came here, it was to visit them and spend the night. She often did that on Saturday after she got off work."

"Then…you don't think…but you said on the boat you thought she'd been pushed."

"I still do," he said gravely, but withheld further comment.

"Then…" She struggled to understand. "You think she met someone here, perhaps by accident?"

He looked at her. "Or by appointment. Maybe both."

She frowned. How could it be both? She thought that suggestion over. "That leaves Scott out then, doesn't it?"

"I never thought he did it. I told the constable that. In talking to Carew and Mary, they both said Maggie went out around eleven o'clock to have a look at the sea. She never came back."

"The sea, on a foggy night?"

"Exactly my point."

"You think she had an appointment to meet someone?"

His hand rested gently on her shoulder. "Look, don't concern yourself with this. It's dangerous. More so than anything you've come up against so far. Let me say it has nothing to do with Gowrie House. I tell you this only so you'll leave it alone. Say nothing to Scott, or anyone else. Agreed?"

She was surprised, but nodded. "I won't share your views with anyone at the house."

"The constable is still investigating, despite what the papers say or what anyone else thinks, including Scott. We'll find the answer."

"We?" She looked at him curiously.

He shrugged and leaned against the rail again. "Naturally I'm interested. Maggie was kin. We were pretty close growing up, like siblings. She was three years older than me, actually. Yet I was closer to Maggie than Scarron. Scarron was already grown up when Maggie and I used to go down to the rocks here at low tide looking for starfish."

Her thoughts went to her brother. She knew what Kerc meant about closeness. She said suddenly, "I'm leaving for London tomorrow. Did Lucy tell you?"

"That they'll welcome Kylie? Yes."

"Dr. MacGregor is writing a letter to Colonel Warnstead, and he'll try telephoning as well. All I need do now," she said ruefully, "is convince Kylie to pay the visit."

"Hey, you two," Jodrell called, "what's the big secret you're hatching together? If you don't get over here, don't blame me if there's no more cold chicken—or berry cobbler!"

The remainder of the afternoon passed peacefully. After eating and relaxing, the small group spent some time exploring the area. Effie and Billy cleared the picnic things away while Kerc walked up to open the lighthouse. At the last minute Lucy said her ankle bothered her and that she must have twisted it climbing around the boulders. She preferred to stay behind. Aunt Theo groaned that she'd become stiff and sore from the ride and that her limp troubled her. She'd had more than enough outdoor activity for one day.

"Maybe we should all just finish our tea and start back," Scott said. "I don't like the looks of that fog bank. It appears to be moving toward shore sooner than we thought." He looked at his watch. "It's a quarter of four. We all know the history of the lighthouse anyway."

"Now, hold on, old chap. Vanessa doesn't know the history," Jodrell protested. "And she hasn't seen the lighthouse. If I remember right, that's what we all came up here for, wasn't it? Besides, Kerc's waiting up there to give his little speech."

"Then I'll bring her up," Scott said stiffly. "Someone needs to stay with Lucy and Theo."

"No one need stay with me," Lucy corrected him.

"And no one needs to bring me," Vanessa said cheerfully, standing and ending the debate. "I can take myself up to the lighthouse while the rest of you finish your tea. It's a short walk, and the trail is safe and easy to climb even in my sandals. I won't be long."

"There," Jodrell said decisively. "It's settled, my good man. Effie, pour the tea! I say, where did that girl disappear to now?"

"She's looking for Billy. I think he took the picnic things back down to the car," Theo said. "I'll pour tea, my dear."

"Then I'll go and check the horses," Jodrell said, and he went off, whistling.

Vanessa was leaving the picnic grounds when Scott came after her. "Vanessa, perhaps I'd better go with you after all."

She laughed. "Don't be silly, Scott. This isn't the wilds of Africa."

He frowned and glanced toward the trail to Devil's Cliff.

"I came alone all the way from New York, remember?" she said gently. "Go enjoy your tea!" She smiled, and added, "Look, Jodrell just left. Now's your opportunity to make Lucy feel *wanted*."

He smiled dourly. "She'll probably tell me to go away."

"Well, try." She lifted her hand and took off up the trail toward the lighthouse and cottage. The others were soon out of sight as she entered a tall stand of trees.

With the sun behind the treetops it looked later than it was, with shadows deepening among the rocks.

She walked along, musing over all that Kerc had told her before lunch. Why had he suggested Maggie may have met someone by accident? Who might that person have been? He had asked her to leave the matter alone. Perhaps she'd best do just that. She had quite enough to concern her.

Her thoughts lingered over Kerc's small compliments. She looked at her ring. In the shadows of the trees, the stones withheld their green sparkle. Had she been too cool toward him?

She stopped as a pebble got stuck in her sandal. As she paused to remove it, she became aware of the distant sounds of the sea on the rocks below, of the utter stillness among the trees, of a disquieting sense of once again being watched. Her spine stiffened. She turned quickly around, looking back down the path from where she'd come, thinking one of the others might have changed their mind and wished also to see the lighthouse. There was no one else on the path. Then she looked toward the trees. A figure darted out ahead of her.

21

Lucy came toward her and stood smiling, hands on hips. "I had to run all the way to overtake you."

Vanessa was relieved and yet curious about her behavior. "You startled me."

"Did I? It's all from that business about Maggie, I suppose. It's enough to give anyone the shivers."

"Did you change your mind about seeing the lighthouse?"

"No. There's something else I want to show you."

After the last time Lucy offered to be her guide, Vanessa was wary.

Lucy noticed. "Oh, you'll see the lighthouse. This will only take us a few minutes. Besides, the lighthouse is more picturesque at dusk when the light goes on. All that mist rolling in means it'll come on sooner. Do come, Vanessa. This way. There's a path that's shorter."

Lucy seemed as carefree as a young girl, and just as volatile, reminding Vanessa she needed to take precaution. "What happened to your sore ankle?"

"Oh, that." She waved a hand of dismissal. "I just said that. I wanted to get rid of them all and talk to you alone. Scott went off to take a walk, and when Aunt Theo closed her eyes to snatch a quick nap, I slipped away."

Lucy moved as if she were going to leave the path and climb into the trees.

Vanessa frowned. "It isn't necessary to lie in order to talk to me. I'll be glad to talk to you any time."

"Yes, Scott warned me you were extremely religious. Took your Christianity seriously, he said."

"Warned you?" Vanessa laughed. "I didn't know I'd affected him that way. We've hardly discussed Christianity."

"Oh, he didn't mean anything unkind. He likes you rather a lot, you know. So does Kerc."

"Kerc?" Vanessa asked. "How do you know that?"

Lucy chuckled. "Here, take my hand and I'll help pull you up the embankment. Those sandals!"

"Look, Lucy, I really do want to talk. But I'm not much in the mood right now to go scampering off on another unknown romp in the woods. The last time you led me on a merry chase, you disappeared and Scarron showed with the guard dogs."

"You don't believe I did that on purpose, do you?" she asked, her eyes wide and innocent.

Vanessa looked at her skeptically. "Well, didn't you?"

"No. The fog settled so quickly, I lost you." Seeing Vanessa's expression, she sighed. "All right, so you don't believe me. I promise it won't happen again. Do come! This is on the up-and-up."

Then, the other venture wasn't?

Vanessa turned away and glanced up the path leading toward the lighthouse. It would be far easier and less risky to pursue her own plans. Yet, she wanted to talk with her sister before returning to London and this could be the opportunity. *I may be foolish*, she thought, *but...*

She clasped Lucy's hand and climbed up the dirt embankment. "I hope it isn't far."

"Not far. Stay close."

"I intend to," Vanessa said dryly. "In fact—" She snatched hold of Lucy's belt. "I'm going to make sure you don't disappear this time."

Lucy laughed. "Hang on tight, then. Walking is a sport with me. I won a medal, you know."

"Really? Congratulations!"

"I'll show it to you sometime. I came in second. Aunt Theo says it's not feminine to win medals in outdoor activities."

"I don't think I agree with her. Well, maybe not in boxing, but..."

Lucy laughed.

"What did your father say about your medal?" Vanessa asked.

"You mean *our* father, don't you?"

Vanessa said nothing, and Lucy didn't appear to notice and went on: "He's so busy with that family legacy book that nothing I do makes much of an impression on him. Except when I displease him. Ah! He pays close attention to *that*."

"Only children do naughty things to get their parents' attention."

Lucy shrugged.

"You don't seem to approve of the book he's writing. Is it the content or the extra time that he's putting into it?"

Lucy avoided answering and glanced toward the sky. "We've got to hurry while the sun is still shining on the garden."

"The garden? You're bringing me to a flower garden?"

"Besides walking, it's my second favorite hobby. But not just any old flower will do, you see. They must have a medieval history."

"There are no 'just any old flowers.' They're all gorgeous and say something unique about their Creator."

"True. Anyway, this is the most delightful garden on the entire island. You'll see."

Lucy appeared to know exactly where they were going, and within a few minutes she'd led the two of them out of the trees into a sunny clearing. To Vanessa's surprise, the lighthouse bungalow she'd noticed riding up to the picnic grounds was just below them on a grassy knoll. The back garden faced the stand of trees from which she and Lucy had just emerged.

"Wait till you see Miss Mary's roses. She's simply smashing when it comes to having a green thumb. She's the one who taught Kerc how to get the old rose garden at Gowrie House producing again. Some of Miss Mary's roses are from clippings of bushes dating back to the seventeenth century."

Vanessa followed her slowly down the embankment, getting pebbles and stickers in her sandals. They went through the back gate.

"Don't worry. She doesn't mind at all. I come here often. She always has tea and sweet biscuits. Today, though, we won't bother her. I just want to show you the roses."

True to Lucy's word, Vanessa entered a delightful garden full of sunshine, twittering birds, and a royal blaze of flowers, all open, fragrant, and with an army of bees humming.

"The bees won't bother you unless you get aggressive with them. They prefer to work and be left alone, rather than to sting."

"Who told you that?" Vanessa asked warily.

"Kerc. He knows so much about horticulture and entomology. Did you know he—" She glanced at Vanessa and stopped. "There are twenty varieties of roses in every shade and fragrance." She waved an arm in a sweeping gesture, a delighted smile on her face.

There were musks, pinks, damasks, and white curling clusters that reminded Vanessa of grapes. There was a mammoth rose at least seven inches across. Lucy whispered: "Look at it. It came from a walled garden in France a hundred years ago! Still blooming."

The scent was tantalizing, and the effect had a rather fairy-tale allurement about it, so that if a garden fairy had popped up behind the petals and shot a tiny bow and arrow of gold dust at Vanessa, she wouldn't have been surprised.

"Stunning," she breathed, cupping the giant bloom between her palms and breathing in its aroma with delight.

"What do you think when you look at it?" Lucy asked with awe.

Vanessa closed her eyes. "I see Rapunzel's balcony. She's letting down her long hair from her bedroom window to let her lover climb the wall. And here he comes scaling her tower with this rose between his teeth. The rose is as big as the golden moon above."

Lucy laughed merrily. "You're as daft as I am. Only I can't see Jodrell scaling my walls," she said dryly. "He'd prefer to be brushing Strawberry in the stables."

"What about Scott?" Vanessa asked slyly.

"Scott's even worse. I don't think he has a romantic bone in his body." She turned, looking about. "This is my favorite spot." Lucy walked over and sank into a swing beneath the apple tree. "I used to come here when I was young and meet Kerc."

Vanessa straightened and shot her a look, but Lucy was basking in the dazzling array about her and didn't notice.

"We used to talk about everything," she said reminiscently. "He was a few years older, you see. He gave me lots of advice. Sometimes Maggie would join us. She had such a wonderful sense of humor."

"Were you infatuated with Kerc?" Vanessa asked her plainly.

Lucy looked at her, but there was no caution or resentment in her look. "Yes, for a short time. His looks, you know. Smashing. Like a romantic gypsy with a violin."

Vanessa's mouth curved, and she folded her arms.

"Infatuation didn't last long, though. He became the big brother I never had." She looked dubious. "And now, suddenly, I've got a real brother connected by blood." She shook her head in disbelief. "It's a staggering thought. One that takes time to sink in. At first it's so shocking. 'It can't be,' you say to yourself. Then, little by little, like small drops of water seeping into dry soil, it starts to become real. Kylie Miles. My brother. An RAF pilot. Amazing! I saw his picture this morning. He looks dashing. Your mother must've been pretty."

"My mother pretty?" Vanessa considered that a moment. "I never thought of her that way...not in the way your mother was. I resented the great Norah Benton when I was in high school. It was a terrible temptation. I struggled with dislike for years. It was my main prayer concern. I no longer feel that way. I feel more sad than anything else."

Lucy watched her thoughtfully. "I never thought of it that way. In fact, I never thought of your mother at all, or how she would feel about Daddy leaving her for my mother. I suppose she hated Norah."

"Hate destroys the one whose heart it controls. One becomes its slave. There's freedom in letting go, no matter how painful, in turning the thorns that pierce our hearts over to Jesus. If anyone knows what thorns feel like, what a spear through the heart feels like, it's the Savior."

Lucy watched her. "I wasn't raised in churchgoing, though I enjoyed the church on the estate when I was here on holiday."

"Yes, it's a lovely little church, but keeping holidays isn't the same thing as knowing Christ as your redeemer. Ritual often gets in the way of intimacy with God."

"When did you see the church?" Lucy asked curiously.

Vanessa reached over and lifted the drooping head of a buttercup. *I can't lie.* "Last night. I went there late." *Please, don't let her ask more questions and put me on the spot.*

Lucy continued to watch her inquisitively. Then she shrugged. "Anyway, the shock of having a sister and brother is wearing off, and the truth is beginning to sink in. You're here to stay."

Was that her statement of concern or a decision to accept the inevitable?

"I hadn't thought of staying permanently. I've said that before."

"Aunt Theo's convinced Father has plans that will supersede yours and Kylie's."

"I'm sorry she views my coming as a threat. It must be miserable to live your life, always afraid someone is going to steal away what matters most to you. What matters most to me can't be stolen."

"Money versus a relationship with Christ?"

"Yes. Anyway, I don't believe in making someone else's life miserable by forcing myself on them. Really, though, I'd like to become friends with you. There isn't anything Robert can give to me now. His life is nearly over, and I'm pretty settled in my ways. The time when I needed him is past. He wasn't there, and there's no going back. So...not that I wouldn't be friends with him," Vanessa hastened. "I don't mean that. But...well, you and Theo don't have anything to worry about, is what I'm trying to say. My greatest struggle is to get Kylie here to visit him."

Lucy held the ropes on the old swing and swayed gently to and fro, watching her curiously. "You know, I'm beginning to believe you."

"If you could accept that, it would be one happy memory I could take back with me to London. As for Theo—"

"She's hopeless," Lucy said wearily. "I dare say, nothing means as much to her as this estate. That's why she dislikes Scott so much. He wants it too."

"What right does he have?"

"None, by blood. His passion for Gowrie House, though, outweighs his love for anything—or anyone—else."

Vanessa recognized the bitterness in her tone as evidence she believed Scott's earlier interest in her may have stemmed from a greater love for the estate. No doubt learning of the supposed relationship with Maggie had merely served to strengthen that belief.

"Whether he does, I don't know. I do think he cares about you much more than he's able to show. He's quite miserable about Jodrell. Scott seems to have a difficult time showing his feelings."

For a brief moment Lucy looked as if she were hoping Vanessa were right, but then her lips thinned. "That isn't true. Scott wanted to marry me because of the money Father will leave me. Theo found out and told me."

How did Theo find out? Vanessa wanted to ask, but felt it was wiser not to be attacking the older woman. Whatever Theo had told Lucy, it had convinced her.

"Do you love Jodrell? I mean *really* love him? Enough to spend the rest of your life with him?"

"I don't know, but he's wonderful with horses. We both want to raise thoroughbreds on the estate someday. And Theo thinks the world of him."

"There's life beyond the stables," Vanessa said with a small smile. "No matter how good of a trainer he is, or how much you love horses, there's so much more in a marriage to agree upon. As for Theo, I know she means well. It's plain to see she really loves you. But it's not Theo who's going to marry Jodrell, but you. Why is she so set on your marrying him? Did she ever say?"

"For one thing she believes he'll be the best one to run Gowrie House when the time comes. She trusts him. And, of course, he's quite polite to her and does what she wants. They seem to think alike."

"And your father? Does he approve?" Though Vanessa already knew that Robert questioned Jodrell's sincerity, as did Kerc, she wanted to see what Lucy's reaction to her father's opinion would be.

Lucy's obstinate look settled on her face again. "He doesn't particularly like Jodrell, but then again, he's so taken up with that book he promised my mother he'd write, that he's not a fair judge of whether Jodrell and I would be good for one another or not."

"It's none of my affair, but I do hope you won't rush into marriage and end up regretting it a few years from now. Maybe you ought to give Scott another chance."

Lucy smiled wryly. "My sister the matchmaker?" She stood up from the swing and walked to the gate. "The mist is coming in. If we want to see the lighthouse, we'd better leave. It's not far. We can go through the gate and down this path."

"I wonder if Kerc's still there. He may have gone back to the picnic grounds to see what was keeping us."

Lucy said unexpectedly, "When you visited the church last night, did you happen to hear or see anything, well, unusual?"

Vanessa suddenly remembered Jodrell's comments to Scott at the stables. She should have mentioned it to Kerc, but she'd forgotten its importance until now. Who had told Lucy? Jodrell?

Taking Vanessa's silence to mean that she hadn't heard anything curious, Lucy dismissed the subject and opened the gate.

It just couldn't have been Scott last night on the path, Vanessa thought.

The mist swirled around them as their steps quickened across the graveled walkway in the direction of the lighthouse. They walked in silence for the next few minutes, each deep in her own thoughts, and then the lighthouse came into view, ethereal in the thickening gray except for the beacon of light flashing hope.

"Kerc must have turned it on, unless Carew came," Lucy commented, and she opened the door. Vanessa followed her into a circular receptacle. Except for two little windows, a small desk, and some notices posted on the wall, the spiral stairwell filled most of the small space. Vanessa sniffed turpentine and the ocean dampness that clung to everything. The silence, interrupted only by the motorized beacon above, sounded almost eerie. The interest and pleasure she had expected to enjoy in coming here were oddly missing, and instead, the hollow sound of their footsteps on wood sounded unpleasant.

Lucy, oblivious to what Vanessa sensed, led the way up the steps, calling cheerfully: "Kerc, guess who I brought!"

Vanessa held back, looking up past her sister toward the next flight of steps. Her palm rested on the polished banister. She drew her hand away and turned it palm up. What was this sticky wetness...

Her gaze dropped to the steps. There were more dark drops splotched on the wood. She recoiled.

"No, Lucy," she choked, "...don't go up there..."

Lucy stopped at the tone of alarm and looked down at her. Her face changed as she picked up Vanessa's dismay. Then she saw the stain on Vanessa's palm. Lucy's gaze lowered to the steps. She frowned. "Blood? Someone must be hurt. How?"

"Kerc?" Vanessa called up urgently. "Kerc, are you up there?"

Unpleasant silence pervaded.

Vanessa now went past Lucy and climbed quickly up the spiraling steps. It might not be anything at all. No use rushing to conclusions and allowing her nerves to jump out of her skin. A minor accident is all, yes, just a pricking of a thumb—

Reaching the upper chamber, she stopped in the doorway. Her gaze swept the small room. Nothing. Kerc was not there, nor was the old light keeper they called Carew.

Lucy sucked in her breath. "There—on the floor."

In the shadows nearest the wall, a man lay face downward, deathly still.

22

It's Scarron," whispered Lucy in bewilderment.

Vanessa was checking his pulse. "He's alive, but his heartbeat is very weak." She couldn't turn him over. He was too heavy. He was lying on his chest with one arm beneath him.

"What happened? Could he have fallen somehow?"

"It looks as though he's been shot, and his face is bruised."

Lucy gasped. "Shot?" she choked with unbelief. "But how? And who?"

Vanessa quickly removed her woolen pullover, folded it, and placed it under his head. "Hurry, Lucy, go for help. I'll stay with him and see what I can do. Was anyone at the cottage when we were there?"

"Yes, Miss Mary, for sure. She always takes a nap this time of day. But Carew may have already come here, discovered Scarron, and gone to report it. Someone's been here recently. The lamp is lit."

"Let's not take chances. There should also be a friend of Kerc's at—" No, maybe it wasn't wise to mention the man she'd seen Kerc meet early that morning on the road. Was he even at the bungalow as Kerc had said?

Lucy was looking at her expectantly. Vanessa said instead, "Even if someone's at the cottage, one of us will need to go back and tell the others."

"I'll go. I can run. Maybe Kerc is at the cottage now."

"Hurry, Lucy."

Vanessa heard Lucy's footsteps rushing down the stairwell. The door banged shut. Then silence filled every shadowy corner of the lighthouse. Vanessa tried to not think about it and turned her attention to Scarron. What was he doing up here? Had he come to meet the person who shot him? Would he have the strength to stagger up here afterward, trying to reach Kerc or Carew, his cousins? How long ago had this happened? She and Lucy hadn't heard the shot in the bungalow garden, or even at the picnic ground, if he'd been shot earlier.

Scarron tried to speak, his syllables sounding hoarse and garbled. The awful sound aroused her pity, and she bent over him, placing her palm on the back of his head, patting him gently. "It's all right, Scarron. It's only me, Vanessa Miles. I've sent for help."

His cracked and bleeding lips parted, and he tried to speak, growing more agitated by the moment.

"Closer," he rasped.

Thinking he was delirious, she tried to calm him by bringing her ear down toward his mouth. "Yes?"

"Lis…en…"

"Yes, I'm listening, Scarron. What is it? Who did this to you?"

His brogue was so thick, especially now, that she could hardly make out his wheezing speech. Something about Croft? Hook? Tell him. Aloud, she repeated what she could pick up.

"Aye…," he affirmed, "…tell 'im…"

"Who did this to you, Scarron?"

"Kerc…Kerc…" His eyes shut. He was gone. She bent there on her knees, horrified. He *could not* have meant Kerc. He just couldn't! It was a mistake; he had to have made a mistake. He was merely calling his cousin's name. Her heart pumped rapidly. She stared at him intently as if she could will the answers from his silent body.

His strange words tumbled around in her head, making no sense. She whispered them over and over again using the Scottish accent, until—"Of course. Not 'hook,' but 'book.' Book? And croft? The Scottish way of saying bungalow. 'Book and bungalow.'"

Vanessa stood. The missing book? In Scarron's bungalow? Tell "him." Kerc? Of course! She whirled toward the door, then restrained herself. Wait. Could someone else have been looking for the earl's book? Desperately enough to have confronted Scarron like this? Even take his life? Her hand went to her forehead. She couldn't believe one of them would do such a thing.

But someone had. That was the awful reality.

What if that someone had discovered that Scarron knew where the old volume written by Earl Gowrie was hidden? Then it might be too late. She turned around and looked down at him again. Whoever had done this to him could even now be on his way to Scarron's bungalow. Where was the stranger who supposedly was staying at Miss Mary's? Kerc had said he was a friend, but—

But Scarron wasn't the sort to talk just because he was threatened. That could account for his being dead now from a bullet wound. Then, if he hadn't confessed, it must mean the book was still hidden there, somewhere. Because Scarron had been anxious that she protect it. That she tell "him." She was to tell Kerc it was in the bungalow.

She rushed out the door and partway down the stairwell. Wait again. She stopped. What if the "him" were not Kerc? Could that be possible? And why should she assume he'd meant Kerc? If the book did turn out to be Earl Gowrie's confessional, then Scarron could just have easily been asking her to tell Robert Miles when he'd said to tell "him."

After all, to whom did the rare copy belong but to her father? It certainly didn't belong to Kerc, who held the caretaker's job. Who was to say Scarron and Kerc got on well together just because they were cousins and he cared for Kerc's strange dogs? And just why did Kerc see the need to keep guard dogs anyway? He had never actually explained that.

She stood frozen to the step trying to decide what to do. Then she continued down the first flight and was starting the second when the door burst open, and Kerc entered alone.

He stopped when he saw her on the steps above. She must have looked pale and shaken because he came bounding up, taking hold of her, his dark eyes impossible to read in the shadows on the steps.

"You're not hurt, are you?"

"No, but Scarron's been shot." He started up, but she grabbed his arm, her eyes searching his. "He's dead, Kerc. I'm…sorry."

He looked down at her for a moment in silence, then she felt his arm muscles relax. He looked up the steps. "Did he say who did it?" His voice was flat, anger brewing just beneath the restraint.

Kerc—Kerc, he had said.

Vanessa stared into the darkly handsome face looking at her intently. "I…I had a difficult time understanding his few words. Where's Lucy?"

"She went to tell the others. One of them will go for Doc MacGregor."

"Can't you call him from the cottage?"

He frowned. "The telephone line's been cut."

Her spine went rigid. Their eyes held. His silence confirmed her worst fear. She swallowed. Why would someone do this? Why such extremes? What was really at stake?

He shot past her and ran up the steps, and she remained where she was, looking up after him.

It was several minutes before he returned, slowly. He paused on a step looking down at her. "You were right. He's dead."

Her breath went out of her. She leaned back against the rail. He came down, his steps echoing, and stopped in front of her. "What did he tell you?"

Under his penetrating gaze, she nearly wavered. She remained silent.

He was watching her closely. "Well?" he urged.

"Where have you been all this time?" she finally asked.

"I waited for you and the others here. When no one came, I began to worry. I went back to the picnic grounds, and Scott told me you ran off. So did Lucy."

"I didn't run off. I started to come here but Lucy intercepted me. She wanted to…talk. We spent around twenty minutes in Miss Mary's back garden. Then, when the mist came in, we came here. The light was already burning, and we thought you or Carew were upstairs." She looked up and shuddered as the image of Scarron rose up before her eyes.

Kerc's warm strong hand touched her shoulder. "I'm sorry you found him looking like that. Did you see anything else you considered odd, see anyone, hear anything unusual?"

She raised a hand to her head. "We found Scarron just the way he is, except I couldn't turn him over. He was too heavy. I sent Lucy to the cottage."

"I was there."

Her eyes came to his again, searching. "You were in the cottage? When did you get back from the picnic grounds?"

"A few minutes ago. I went out to the garden. I suspected she'd bring you there. It's Lucy's favorite retreat."

She studied him for a long moment.

"What is it, Vanessa?" he asked softly, but wryly. "Do you think I'd beat up my cousin, and then put a bullet into him?"

Her eyes faltered with shame. "No," she rasped, "of course not."

"I'm sorry. I shouldn't have said that. The fact remains, however, that someone did."

"Why didn't one of us hear the gunshot?"

"Probably because of a silencer. Better go to the cottage. Miss Mary is making tea for everyone. The others will be here soon."

Kerc turned to go back to where Scarron's body was laid.

"Kerc...wait."

He looked down at her speculatively.

Her fingers tightened on the banister. "Why did Scarron come here now, when everyone was gone except you?"

"He must have been looking for me. Why do you ask the question like that? What are you trying to suggest?"

"That man I saw you meet this morning on the road. You said he was a friend."

"That's right."

"Where is he?"

His face became bland and told her nothing. "Maybe you can ask Miss Mary. He's her guest, and Carew's."

"But he is also your friend. You told me so."

"He is. But I don't keep him on a leash, Miss Miles. He's free to walk about and go anywhere he wants."

"Maybe the constable will have the answer." She turned and went down the steps.

She heard his footsteps behind her, felt his hand on her arm. "Wait a moment, please. You haven't explained. What do you mean to suggest by asking me these questions?"

She faced him evenly. "Isn't it obvious?"

"No. Nothing is obvious except that my cousin is dead, shot by someone with a silencer on his gun. Who did it and why is a question for the police—just as Maggie's death was."

"Could it be the work of the same person or persons who attacked me on the path last night?"

He looked at her sharply, but remained silent and pensive. "No. I don't think so."

He didn't explain why he was so adamant.

He stared down at her for a long moment until her breathing quieted.

"I had nothing to do with what happened to Scarron. The question is, why do you think so?"

"You don't seem terribly grieved."

His eyes sparked. "You're wrong."

She turned to go.

"Are you sure you don't have anything to tell me?"

She pretended bewilderment. "What do you mean?"

"You know what I mean, Miss Miles. Did he speak? Say anything to you? Tell you who it was or anything else?"

"Yes," she said dully. "He mentioned your name twice."

He lapsed into silence. She turned quickly and left him, afraid he'd read her eyes.

Outside, the gray mist met her and encircled her, wetting her skin and hair. She could hardly see the cottage, and wouldn't have, except for a golden light that flickered dimly in Miss Mary's windows. She walked in that direction, feeling as though she were lost amid the clouds. There was nothing to do now except wait for the others to arrive, including Dr. MacGregor and the constable.

There wasn't a sound as she moved along the ground toward the beckoning light.

How could Lucy find her way to the picnic grounds in this?

Kerc had been anxious to know if Scarron told her anything. Naturally he would be. So would the constable when he was finally notified.

And so would someone else be wondering if Scarron had said anything, unless they'd thought he was dead.

If her suspicions were true, someone else was worrying, because no matter what she'd said to Kerc in the lighthouse, she didn't think he would shoot his own cousin or anyone else. The stranger was another matter. Was Kerc cooperating with him?

≈≈≈

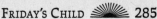

A good hour had passed since the party from the picnic grounds had arrived, full of questions and in shock over what had happened to Scarron. It had to have been an accident was the first thing everyone said. Theo was looking gray and bleak as she sat in a chair.

"What's keeping Jodrell and Dr. MacGregor?" Lucy asked uneasily. "They've had plenty of time to get here by now."

"Lucy, my handbag, please. My tablets are in it," Theo said.

"Who could have done it?" Lucy asked, looking ill and cold as she handed her aunt a fashionable alligator bag. "And why?" She looked almost accusingly from face to face from her place near Vanessa. Theo noticed the bond beginning to form between them and didn't look happy about it. That response saddened Vanessa.

"That's for the police to find out," Scott said gently.

Lucy turned to look at him, and then went on as though she hadn't heard. "Why didn't one of us hear the gunshot? We were all within range."

"A silencer," Scott echoed Kerc's earlier explanation to Vanessa. "Nor is there proof Scarron was shot up in the lighthouse. He could have made his way there seeking help."

"From anywhere?" Lucy said, looking tense and strained and wary. "With a silencer on the gun, could he have been shot near the picnic grounds?"

Scott watched her uneasily.

"Don't be absurd, Lucy dear," Theo said curtly. "That implies it might have been one of us."

"Well, couldn't it have been?" Lucy asked.

"Ridiculous. You're becoming hysterical. There was no reason for any of us to shoot Scarron. Besides, one of us would have heard the shot fired."

"That's just it, don't you see?" Lucy said with wide eyes. "The silencer would have muffled the sound enough so that it could be mistaken for a branch breaking in the woods."

"The use of a silencer tells us something important," Scott said.

Theo looked up, pallid and depressed. "What do you mean? Why should it?"

"It's plain, Miss Theo. It was well thought out. Someone is in the habit of carrying a gun and is careful enough to have a silencer. That tells me he or she isn't afraid to use it and probably has in the past."

"Mere conjecture. And you're upsetting Lucy with all this talk. I don't know why both of you wish to rush to that conclusion," Theo said with a trace of impatience.

"Who would want to kill Scarron?" Lucy said thoughtfully. "What did he know?"

"Lucy, *please!*"

"Who is staying at the house with Robert?" Vanessa asked.

"Yes," Lucy said worriedly. "I don't want Father left alone."

"He's not alone," Scott said, handing her some tea and easing her back down onto her chair. "The servants are there. We'll all be going back soon, anyway. How's your ankle?"

Lucy looked blank. "Ankle?" Then she must have remembered what she'd told him at the picnic grounds, because she had the grace to blush. "Oh—it's much better now."

Vanessa watched her a moment. Lucy liked to put on an act. When was she sincere and when was she not? Was she genuine now? Her fears certainly appeared real enough. Vanessa glanced cautiously at the small group gathered in Miss Mary's little parlor.

Billy Carstair, who appeared to be about nineteen, sat hunched in a corner on the floor saying nothing as he watched everything and everyone. Although Scarron had been Billy's cousin, he seemed closer to Kerc. He showed more wariness than he did grief.

Effie looked so upset that Vanessa feared she would soon burst into crying. That too could be an act. Vanessa had seen Effie behave in cool and calculating ways when it came to her cousin Kerc.

Scott was grim, Theo, frowning, and Lucy, afraid.

Miss Mary was a small gray-haired woman with a sweet and open way about her, but her face was drawn and tense now. Vanessa had helped her prepare tea and make cheese and bacon sandwiches before the others had arrived from the picnic grounds.

"Most of us know Scarron was a poker player," Theo said tiredly. "He could have owed someone a large amount of cash. Those sort of men are never far from being criminals. It's quite easy for them to resort to violence under the right set of circumstances. When Scarron couldn't pay up—well, they may have argued and the man lost his sanity and fired his gun."

Miss Mary looked over at her. "Cousin Scarron gave up poker a long while ago, Miss Theo."

Just then her husband, Carew, came in the front door with Kerc. Vanessa found herself taking a good look at Carew, weighing possibilities of guilt or innocence based on appearance, which she knew was wrong. She couldn't imagine the lighthouse keeper shooting Scarron any more than she could see Miss Mary doing it. He was a pleasant-looking man in his sixties with a thick white mustache and lively dark eyes. Yet he looked strong and agile for his age. He would be a match for Scarron, if it came to a struggle.

Vanessa watched Kerc gather his hat and jacket and walk back to the door. Was he leaving so soon?

Scott noticed too.

"Where are you going, Kerc?"

"For the constable."

Theo moaned. "We've all had more than enough of the police snooping into our lives over poor little Maggie. Now we must go through it once again with Scarron."

Kerc looked across the room at her. "I'm sorry, Miss Theo, but you know how it is. This is a matter for the authorities."

"Yes, yes, naturally I know we must call the constable. I don't have to like it though."

"None of us do," Scott said. "Kerc is right. We'd all be hauled up for hiding a crime if we didn't report it." He turned to Kerc. "It will take him time to get here from the mainland. Are you going to take the boat over tonight?"

"I was thinking I would."

"In this fog? It could be dangerous," Theo said unhappily.

"I'll manage, Miss Theo."

Scott walked toward him. "Maybe I should come with you."

"Not necessary. I've done it a hundred times. I've been caught in heavy mist when I was out with the fishing boat. The ladies, here, might need you."

"Why not telephone the mainland police from here in the bungalow? Carew has a telephone," Scott said.

"He can't," Vanessa said with a slight quaver to her voice. "The line was…was cut."

"Cut?" Scott turned toward her in shock.

Vanessa felt Kerc's sharp glance. Hadn't he wanted her to admit it? But they'd soon know it anyway.

Kerc opened the door to a wisp of fog. "Carew? Don't let anyone in the lighthouse till the police have had a search. Fact is, we'd best lock it up now. Toss me that key, will you? I'll do it on the way."

"Aye, lad."

"What's that supposed to mean?" Theo said testily. "You actually think one of us turned a gun on Scarron, and that we're going to go snooping around to cover up incriminating evidence?"

"It means we need to be careful, is all, Miss Theo," Kerc said quietly. "The police won't want anyone in that room or anywhere in the lighthouse until they've gone over it. That means every one of us. Including Carew."

"Does it include you?" Scott asked with a slight tinge of acidity to his voice, his momentary friendliness vanishing in the high tension of the moment.

Kerc favored him with a calm but cool appraisal. "Would you like to walk over with me to make sure I don't touch anything?"

"Don't be absurd, Scott," Theo chided. "Scarron was Kerc's cousin."

Vanessa could have also pointed out that Kerc already had an opportunity to remove something if he'd wanted to when she had waited below while he went up to see Scarron.

Carew tossed a ring of keys to Kerc. "Aye, lock it up, lad."

Kerc went out, shutting the door behind him.

Silence followed his leaving, then Miss Mary asked shakily if anyone wanted more tea, or perhaps a bit of coffee.

Vanessa slipped into the kitchen and went out the back door into the mist-shrouded garden. The roses she had enjoyed earlier with Lucy were now blanketed with eerie gray. Summer flowers had turned into a funeral bouquet.

She had to speak to Kerc alone. If he was going to see the constable, then she had better tell him what Scarron had said to her. Twilight shadows were settling. She went out through the gate and hurried in the direction of the lighthouse.

"Kerc?" she called.

He could be no more than two or three minutes ahead of her, but either the mist had swallowed him up, or he had not come this way after all. She hurried on, chilled by the damp ocean breeze.

The lighthouse was ahead, its welcoming light bravely penetrating the gloom.

"Kerc? Wait! Where are you?"

He was nowhere to be heard or seen. She couldn't have lost him, unless he walked faster than she thought. She rushed on and within a few moments was back at the door of the lighthouse. It was still unlocked. He must have gone up the steps to have a last look around, or maybe to cover Scarron's body with a blanket.

She entered and came to the steps winding upward. "Kerc? Are you up there?"

She waited, her hand on the banister, listening intently for his movements. There was no sound except the rotating light.

He wasn't here. Surely he would arrive any minute. He had said the door must be locked. But where was he?

She lingered at the bottom of the stairwell, growing more uneasy by the moment as the silence loomed. Outside she could hear the sounds of early evening settling and the doleful music of the sea below on the rocks.

Vanessa didn't move, partly because unexplainable fear suddenly gripped her and partly because she thought she heard a stealthy step above. He couldn't be up there unless he didn't want her to know it. That thought gave her a start and put more dread in her than anything else.

Was he up there looking for something? Scarron's jacket, perhaps, with something in one of the pockets? Maybe containing the information Scarron had managed to choke out to her. She was annoyed that her heart was thumping like a drum.

Somewhere above a board creaked. Then all at once her isolation closed in on her and the twilight outside was full of suspicious noises. Vanessa turned blindly and rushed for the door, flung it open, and ran.

She didn't stop until she tripped over a hidden rock buried in the sandy soil. As she went down, her rasping breathing filled her ears, and she lay there shivering.

Whether seconds ticked by or minutes, in the end it was the cry of a lone bird that spoke peace to her heart, bringing a measure of reason that ended her panic. The bird's cry echoed above in the mist. Was it lost? Had it stayed out too long trying to catch one last tidbit of food before settling safely for the night? Now, the fog and twilight had trapped it. Yet, despite its predicament, there was a note of confidence in its call. Then in the distance the answer came. Its mate? Calling sweetly, giving it direction. Soon, all was quiet again. The bird had flown to safety.

The Lord is my light and my salvation; whom shall I fear? The Lord is the strength of my life, of whom shall I be afraid?

Slowly she rose to her knees and brushed her damp hair from the sides of her face. She breathed deeply and slowly for a minute, and then calmly repinned her hair into its place and stood. She walked back toward the cottage.

When she arrived, Jodrell was coming from the horses tied to some ghostly-looking trees.

"Did you bring Dr. MacGregor?" she called.

"He's inside now. Where have you been?"

"Walking."

"Walking! In this weather?"

"Yes, of course. Why not? Come in, Jodrell. You look as if you could use some of Miss Mary's hot tea and sandwiches."

He came up, his face tense and strained. "Look here, Vanessa, if you're up to it, could you get back to Gowrie House on your own?"

She wondered at the odd question. "I suppose I could, why?"

"It's not that far, you know. And the fog is lifting. The wind's coming up."

She picked up the urgency in his voice. "What's worrying you?"

He glanced toward the cottage. "After Scarron was murdered, who wouldn't be feeling edgy? I'm concerned about Robert, for one thing. Bringing MacGregor here meant leaving him alone. True, it won't be for long, but I don't like it just the same. Doc seemed to think it was safe enough, and well, it probably is..."

Probably!

"I'd send Lucy, but she's too upset. She'd only get Robert in a tizzy. She thinks one of us did it."

Vanessa played dumb. "But why would any of us want to harm Scarron?"

"You're asking me? That's what the police will want to find out. He must have had something on one of us. Or...maybe he had some knowledge."

"Knowledge of what?" Her heart beat faster, but her voice was quiet, giving nothing away.

"If I knew that..."

"You mean you think Scarron may have been threatening someone? Asking for money?" she whispered into the mist.

He shrugged impatiently. "Who knows? It's just a thought. I got to thinking about Billy saying he saw someone running through the garden. Could he have seen Scarron?"

She looked at him blankly, but her mind was racing. Scarron running through the garden—Scarron hiding the book in his bungalow—could he have been after the folder as well?

His voice lowered. "You were there this morning at the stable. You heard Scott get all huffy over a few simple questions about last night. Why should that be, I wonder?"

If she even mentioned what happened on the pathway coming back from the church...

"Maybe it was Scott he'd come to meet," Jodrell said in a nervous voice.

"It couldn't mean anything as dark as all that, Jodrell. You're not accusing Scott of killing Scarron, are you?"

"When you put it like that, no. Sounds impossible. Someone did, sure enough."

What about you? she wanted to say. *How is it you heard Scott leave his room? What were you doing awake at that hour?* Instead, she redirected his thoughts to Lucy.

"If anything's troubling Scott, it's Lucy. You know he's in love with her. He's bound to be agitated over her engagement to you."

"Sure I know it. But Lucy won't have him—and Theo won't either."

"Why is it so important what Theo wants or thinks in the matter? It's Lucy's marriage and vow to fidelity for life."

His mouth turned into a humorless smile. "Because Lucy is wise enough to know how much Theo cares about her happiness.

She's like a mother to her. You don't know how hard Lucy took the death of Norah. Theo helped heal the void."

Vanessa could see she was getting in too deep. Jodrell obviously didn't appreciate her insight into the matter when it didn't align with his opinion.

"What does all this have to do with Robert being left alone at the house?"

"Just that Scott holds him responsible for Lucy's decision. Don't you see? I wouldn't put it past Scott to go there now, knowing Robert's alone, and argue that he do something to stop Lucy's marriage plans. He could upset him pretty badly. After what Robert has been through—understand?"

"But Scott is here in the cottage. At least, he was when I went out."

"When was that?"

She looked at her watch and frowned. "Almost twenty minutes ago."

"He's not here now. No one knows where he went, but he may have gone back to the house," Jodrell said unhappily.

Vanessa was thinking of the lighthouse. Could Scott have gotten there ahead of her? He'd been in the parlor when she'd slipped out the back door and gone through the garden. He would have had to leave through the front door, and then run to get there before her. Wouldn't he have caught up with Kerc?

The cottage door opened and the lamplight fell on the front step. Lucy was standing there. "Is that you, Jodrell?"

"Yes, luv, I'll be right there."

"What took you so long?"

He turned to Vanessa and said in a low voice. "Someone ought to be with Robert."

He walked quickly toward the cottage door and went inside.

Vanessa wrestled with her decisions. There was more than Robert to think of. Scarron's urgent words repeated themselves in her mind. Had he been delirious? Did he even realize to whom he was speaking? If the book he'd mentioned was the correct one, then how had he gotten hold of it? What had he intended to do with it? Someone else had wanted it badly enough to commit murder to claim it. "The heart is deceitful above all things, and desperately wicked," wrote the prophet Jeremiah. The human heart, apart from God, was capable of anything. And her father was alone...and the telephone line cut so that neither she nor Lucy could call him to see if all was well...

She went quickly to the cypress tree where Buttons was tied.

It wouldn't take long to go to Scarron's bungalow before returning to Gowrie House, but the idea of doing so left her skin tingling with apprehension. Was it wise? Would it be safe to go there? Possibly, since everyone was here at the bungalow. Everyone except Scott. And Kerc.

She couldn't help thinking of what Jodrell had said. Was it possible that one of them had slipped away at the picnic grounds unnoticed to meet Scarron in the trees?

After lunch Theo had said she needed a rest. Lucy had claimed she hurt her ankle and wanted to be left alone in her misery. She had come out of the trees ahead of Vanessa, a sure place to have met Scarron, but had there been enough time? Maybe, if she'd been determined about what she planned to do.

That left Jodrell, Scott, Billy, Carew, and Kerc.

Scott had gone for a walk alone after Lucy refused his company. Jodrell had said he was going to have a look at the horses. Billy had brought the picnic things to the motorcar. And Effie—where had she been? Had she gone with Billy? Vanessa couldn't remember. And Kerc—Kerc had been the first to leave and walk to the lighthouse. Plenty of time to meet Scarron. That left the stranger Kerc had met on the road early that morning. He remained an enigma, a mere shadow. He hadn't been at Miss Mary's when she'd arrived. Kerc had said he didn't know where he was. But when they talked earlier at the lookout over the sea, Kerc said the stranger, whom he'd called a friend, was staying at the bungalow with Carew and Miss Mary.

Perhaps the dark suspicious shadows hanging over them all were no more than isolated coincidences, but she could not deny that Scarron's last words to her had been about the book.

Jodrell had mentioned Scarron having some knowledge. Unknowingly, he may have spoken the truth. The book itself might be that special key unlocking knowledge that would change everything at Gowrie House.

With a squaring of her small jaw, she made up her mind. The book *must* be located and brought safely to her father before whoever killed Scarron got hold of it. There was no time to lose. The constable wasn't likely to arrive until morning, but Scarron's rasping whisper in her ear had nonetheless shouted of urgency.

Scarron's bungalow. The thought of it prickled her nerves and battled with his plea.

Knowing what she may be up against, Vanessa dealt sternly with her fears. Unloosing the horse's reins, she mounted the saddle and rode away into the tendrils of white mist.

23

The old horse knew her way and trotted confidently down the trail toward Gowrie House.

On the ride to the lighthouse that morning Vanessa remembered noticing the single track that led off to Scarron's bungalow. She had cringed when seeing it in the sunlight as she recalled the dogs and her conversation with Kerc. Now, in the misty dark, the bungalow was even more foreboding.

She slowed the horse to a stop, making certain of her direction. The trees all looked the same and so did the narrow trails. Moisture dripped from the overhanging branches. Buttons shook her mane. Vanessa reached over and patted her neck. "We're in this together, girl. Where's Scarron's bungalow, d'you know?"

Jodrell was right about the wind coming up. Little gusts stirred through the leaves on the branches and freed them of moisture. The sound did nothing to calm her jittery nerves.

This was the road she'd seen this morning, Vanessa decided, the way to Scarron's bungalow. She looked at her watch to gauge the time, then urged Buttons forward.

For some minutes Vanessa walked the horse along the track. It was wider here and looked well traveled. Finding what she was

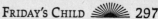

looking for, she followed on for several hundred yards before coming to the dark outline of the bungalow.

She dismounted and tied the horse to the nearest tree, then, squaring her shoulders, she walked up the steps to the front door. Here she waited, trying to muster courage to enter the darkness.

She tried the door cautiously, not surprised that her hand shook, and found it to be unlocked. She slowly entered and left it wide open until she lit a match and found her way to a lamp. She switched it on and the room brightened. She closed the door and stood surveying her surroundings. Things were much as she remembered: a small bunk bed and a commonplace table with two wooden chairs. There was also a sink, a small stove, some cupboards, and dirty dishes. The smell of fried trout still lingered unpleasantly. There were several boxes of his belongings stacked by the closet, and near the foot of the bed, a wooden chest.

Vanessa went to the chest first and lifted the heavy lid. The hinges creaked. She had the horrid notion that she was opening an ancient casket. Thankfully, it was just a storage bin with winter blankets, towels, and other odds and ends.

Where would he have hidden the book? She paused amid her search to look around her again, scanning for anything that might offer a secure hiding place.

The trees that huddled close beside the house creaked, and the wind crooned around the roof and its eaves. She felt cold and wet and suddenly the scanty bungalow, chilled and deathly silent, sent her skin crawling.

Steady, she told herself. *The angel of the Lord encamps around about those who fear Him. I'm not alone. And my mission here is to do good, not evil. What is there to fear?* "My times are in thy hand," she quoted aloud from the psalms. What a comforting thought! Every moment she lived and breathed was not only granted by her heavenly Father, but sustained until He alone decided differently. If she died here like Scarron, she could do so knowing that even a sinister person with murder as his intent could not take her life one moment sooner than allowed by a sovereign God.

With a sense of divine destiny and trust in God's presence, she went about her search forgetting the whining wind, the creaks, moans, groans, and the possibility that someone with wicked intent had followed her here for the same purpose: to obtain Earl Gowrie's confessional.

For fifteen minutes she searched and found nothing. Had she chased the wind?

She sat down on one of the hard-backed chairs and surveyed the small room again. She had looked everywhere. Everywhere except the obvious place. Unable to believe he would place the volume in the open on the small two-shelf bookcase, she had ignored it. She got up and went there, scanning the few meager titles. *Botany*, *Entomology*, and *Maureen Mahoney's Book of Irish Poems*.

She pulled out the first two. So! As she had thought. Textbooks from Edinburgh University and signed and dated a few years earlier by the student: Kerc Trevalyan.

"I knew it," she murmured under her breath. "He's been to a university."

She smiled wryly as she pulled out the book of Irish poems. Was this his too?

Her mood turned to surprised excitement. Mahoney's *Irish Poems* was a false book cover. It shielded instead the old leather-bound volume of Earl Gowrie's confessional. The parish registry dated 1853–1922 was located on the second shelf between the false folders of what looked like a picture album. Holding her two treasures as tightly as though they were bags of gold, Vanessa rushed for the front door. She paused, went to Scarron's closet and found a long hooded pullover. She slipped it on, turned off the lamp, and went out, closing the front door behind her.

The horse was patiently waiting by the tree. "We did it, Buttons," she said gleefully. "And now, to Gowrie House and my father."

The horse looked at her with one bright eye and shook her mane.

Vanessa mounted, placing the materials underneath the pullover for protection. Turning the reins, she headed back to the main trail.

~~~

The house was still and dark when she arrived. If Scott were here, he was keeping out of sight. Jodrell must have been mistaken.

She walked Buttons into the stable and dismounted. Not being much of a horsewoman, the best she could do was to remove the saddle, which she did awkwardly. Then she noticed a bag of oats and dumped some into a feed trough. Buttons took a mouthful and began to munch contentedly. She patted the horse's neck briefly and whispered, "That'll have to do until Jodrell or Lucy comes, old girl. Thanks for getting me here safely!"

The lights were burning low above the steps to her terrace. She rushed up and into her bedroom, turning on the lamp by the door. Before meeting her father, she changed into dry clothing and combed her damp hair into place. Then she went straight down the hall to her father's room, carrying the rare volume and parish registry wrapped in a woolen scarf. First, before sharing the good news, she had one or two questions she hoped he would answer.

A light shone beneath his door. She tapped. "Father? It's me, Vanessa. I must talk to you."

"Come in."

She entered, startled to see that he was out of bed and walking slowly about the large room. He looked very much the actor in a blue silk dressing gown, smoking his pipe.

"You're out of bed," she said surprised, closing the door behind her. She bolted the lock, just in case, and laid her small bundle on a nearby table. "Do you think it's wise? And smoking a pipe at this time isn't—" She caught herself quickly, but saw a look of satisfaction in his eyes, as though her daughterly concern pleased him. She pretended she didn't notice his reaction.

"I'm feeling much better," he assured her. "James doesn't think it was a heart attack after all." He eased himself into a comfortable-looking leather chair and crossed his legs at the knees. "How is Scarron?"

"You mean you don't know?" she said, daunted at the unwanted prospect of breaking the dark news of murder.

He looked surprised, picking up her concern at once. "Jodrell talked to James. I was left with the impression Scarron had fallen from the lighthouse steps and broken his leg."

She stood, uncertain, concerned that too much excitement might cause him harmful stress.

His perceptive gray-green eyes had already understood her worry. "It's all right, Vanessa," he urged her soberly. "Don't worry about causing a relapse. From the look on your face, it's worse than I had thought. Go ahead. I'll be all right. What happened?"

"Scarron was shot. He's dead."

He remained calm and hushed. Then: "Shot?" he asked doubtfully. "You mean he shot himself? Was it an accident?"

"No, not an accident. Scarron was murdered."

He made no response for a long moment, but sat deep in thought. Instead of shock or an outraged denial the way Theo had responded, he puffed his pipe and his foot swung restlessly. After a moment or two, he asked: "And what do you think?"

The question took her off guard. She sank a little breathlessly into a chair opposite him. "I think he was murdered too."

He nodded. "Then you'd better give me the details," he said crisply.

She told him the unpleasant facts of how she and Lucy discovered Scarron in the lighthouse.

He scowled. "A ruddy thing to happen to you both, finding the body like that. Lucy's more high-strung than you are. Is she taking the shock satisfactorily?"

She nodded. "Yes. Theo and Jodrell are with her at Miss Mary's bungalow."

"And yourself? You're holding up, I see. You didn't mention Scott being at the bungalow. Is that for a reason?"

A pause. "You mean he's not here?"

His brows shot up. "Why no, is he supposed to be?"

"I'm not sure exactly."

"I haven't heard anyone come home. Then, again, that's not to say he isn't somewhere about. I didn't hear you either. You must have come up the terrace steps through your room. What made you think he was here? Did he tell you he was coming?" he asked worriedly, as though something may have happened to Scott on the way.

"No, he didn't tell me. It was something Jodrell said, that Scott had left to come here. He must have been mistaken. Jodrell asked me to come back. He was worried Scott would trouble and upset you over Lucy."

"What about Lucy? You said she was holding up."

"She is, considering. Jodrell was worried that Scott might come to you insisting you intervene to end her engagement. Why Scott would choose this unsettling moment to do such a thing isn't clear to me. Jodrell didn't explain. He was so upset about you that I chanced the heavy mist. Thankfully I didn't stray too much. The horse knew the route. And, there was something else I needed to do right away," she said without explaining.

"Worried about me, Jodrell? You can forget that." He smiled with weary endurance. "The chap's more concerned about a loss of plans to turn the estate into a horse-breeding and show-training extravaganza. He believes marriage to Lucy will give him the keys to Gowrie House and the combination to a safe with a handsome financial endowment." His bluntness embarrassed her. "His love for horses outweighs devotion for Lucy. He fears I favor Scott as the better husband, and I do."

"Then you trust Scott," she said with secret relief, keeping her earlier concerns hidden.

He nodded, puffing his pipe. "Always did. We share interest in the theater, writing, history, that sort of thing. And he has a good head on his shoulders. He's a little prejudiced when it comes to Kerc, but that's because Scott doesn't understand him. He will, in time."

The mention of Kerc interested her. What was there to understand? Her father's unexpected defense of Kerc was intriguing. First, he had refused to tell Kerc to get rid of his dogs, making excuses for him. Then, when her father had been working on his research at the church, he'd deliberately sought Kerc out to chat with during the garden work.

"You like Kerc," she stated.

His gaze over the pipe was watchful. "Yes."

"Scott thinks Kerc is poisoning Lucy's mind with folklore about Gowrie House. He even suggested Kerc himself might have secret designs on Lucy."

"That's nonsense. Scott ought to know better, but jealousy does strange things to people. He's distrusted young Kerc from the moment they met. It's true Lucy once had a romantic interest in Kerc, but that was before either Scott or Jodrell entered the picture. Lucy was hardly into her teens at the time. She'd perch herself in the garden just to watch him work. It was amusing, really. She outgrew that, and they've become close friends."

"Yes, so she told me. You must approve, or you wouldn't have kept Kerc on as caretaker."

"I'm sure he's told you he was born here. This is his home. Except for the time he went away to school, he's worked on the estate since he was a small boy. He came back here three or four years ago. The island's in his blood."

"He went to the university in Edinburgh?"

He nodded. "Did well too. He doesn't need a caretaker's job. He studied agriculture and entomology."

She thought of the books in Scarron's bungalow. Scarron must have taken them from Kerc's cottage. But from where had Scarron gotten Earl Gowrie's volume and the registry?

"Who paid for Kerc's tuition? It must have been expensive." Her heart thumped.

He removed the pipe from between his teeth, his eyes showing no concern. "I did."

A small fear, not fully understood, sprouted and grew. "I see."

"I wonder if you really do," he said quietly, but made no further attempt to explain and changed the subject back to Scarron. "I suppose the constable has been called?"

"Kerc is seeing to that now." *At least, that's what he said he was doing,* she thought. It was also time to tell her father about the attack last night on her way back from visiting the church.

Upon hearing the details he grew angry.

"You've no idea who it might have been?"

"No. Nor does Kerc."

He shook his head in disbelief. "I never thought they'd go this far."

"They?"

"And the materials I sent you for?"

"Kerc is keeping the folder. He thought it would be safer with him."

He looked wary.

Her brows lifted. "But a moment ago you said you trusted him."

"I do. And it's time, past time, for the truth to step forward. It's just that I'd planned to wait until the book was printed. However, irreparable damage has already been done by delaying. If he finds out, so be it."

She tensely scrutinized his every word, trying to grasp his meaning.

He shook his head slowly. "I never imagined anyone would revert to physical violence to keep the truth buried. Thievery for financial gain, yes, but killing?" He shook his head again, disgusted, as though he didn't want to accept it. "There must be some other explanation for Scarron's death." He got up and walked to the window.

Vanessa was still thinking of what he'd said about Kerc finding out. Finding out what? A slow suspicion began to gain strength in her heart. Oh, no—

She got up slowly, her legs feeling wooden, and joined him at the window.

The mist-draped sea and the lighthouse was somewhere out there, now masked with gray. Her father stared in that direction as if seeing something. "There have been things going on by the lighthouse recently that are a little curious."

"Maggie's death?"

He looked at her unhappily. "So you know about that too."

"Kerc mentioned it, hoping it would send me running back to London," she said, perturbed.

"Did he?"

"At first he thought I might be here conniving with Scott to gain Gowrie House."

"Ah! Then he does understand. Far more, in fact, than I realized. I wonder—"

"What does Kerc understand, Father?" she asked urgently, taking hold of his arm.

He smiled wanly. "Patience. Tell me first what you know about Maggie."

She let out a breath. "Scott mentioned her too. It seems he dated her a few times."

"Yes, a mistake on his part. He was hoping to jolt Lucy, but it merely made her more suspicious of his intentions toward her."

"So he said."

"Maggie is another matter that cast long shadows, but I wasn't thinking of her. I was thinking of German U-boats when I said things have been going on near the lighthouse."

She looked at him startled. U-boats!

"There's been stories circulating. They grow by leaps and bounds as the war worsens. Talk of spies coming ashore in small rafts from German ships, or paratroopers dropping in. That sort of thing. It's rife in England as well."

"Is there any truth to it?"

He bit on his pipe and didn't say anything for a moment. "I'm beginning to think so."

"But you don't think Scarron's death had anything to do with the war," she said incredulously, waiting for his flat denial.

"No, not Scarron's, but maybe Maggie's."

She didn't know what to say to that. She looked away from him back toward the fog-laden Atlantic.

He looked grim. "Never mind that for now." He turned to face her. "What makes you think Scarron's death is linked to what happened to you last night?"

"For one thing, Earl Gowrie's book was missing from the vestry library. So was the parish registry."

"That's impossible," he said with alarm. "There are only two people who have the key to the library shelf, myself and the vicar."

She was glad now that she'd gone first to the bungalow. "I can't tell you how he got hold of them, because the bookshelf was locked when I went to the vestry. Nor was there any sign of burglary. But Scarron had them both. He'd hidden them in his bungalow. I've just come from there."

"Great Scot!"

"I'll get them for you." She went to the table where she'd laid them. He followed, frowning, bewildered and yet delighted.

"Scarron...," he breathed. "I can hardly believe it."

She told him Scarron's dying words and how she'd gone to his bungalow to locate them.

His brow furrowed with alarm. "Whoever killed him might have followed you. And after the incident with Kerc's dogs, you took a terrible risk, dear Vanessa."

"The dogs weren't around," she said. "I was pretty sure they wouldn't be. I took a chance on it, because I knew how important it was to find these books. Scarron must have meant you when he said to tell 'him' where they were. I can't quite figure out why he would steal them from you in the first place, though. Unless—"

She wouldn't say what was troubling her. That it was Kerc who had taken them, and that Scarron found out and seized the opportunity to hide them in his own bungalow until he could return them to her father. There was something about this conclusion that didn't bode well, like a puzzle piece that didn't quite fit, because if that were true, then Scarron proved more honorable than Kerc. Just how much was Kerc involved in all this?

"I think Kerc suspected something," she told her father. "He asked me if his cousin said anything. I put him off because I didn't quite trust him."

"Then he knows. Scarron didn't mean me, my dear, but Kerc."

She halted, alarmed.

He brought the book and registry over to a desk that he kept in one corner of his room and switched on a lamp. He pulled up his chair and sat down. "Yes," he was saying, relieved. "This is it, all right. Vanessa, you're a marvelous girl. If these had been destroyed by whoever killed Scarron...but they weren't, thanks to you."

"Destroyed? You mean Scarron was trying to protect them?"

"That I can't say. But we have them safely at last."

She walked over to the desk and watched anxiously as he put his glasses on and carefully leafed through the volume to see if all the pages were there. What was it all about?

"Aside from the book's value, why is it important?"

He thought for a moment, then—"A moment ago I told you it was past time for the truth to come out. The family history will be a disappointment to the others. Norah and I expected that, even some trouble to gain the rights to Gowrie House, but never murder."

"You're not saying Theo did it?" she gasped.

"No," he retorted grimly. "I can't say, because I don't really know. Nonetheless, I should have known murder was not merely possible, but probable. I haven't been a Shakespearean actor all these years for nothing," he said wryly. "Shakespeare knew human nature far better than most writers. Men have murdered for much less than an inheritance worth half a million pounds."

Half a million...

"Then it all *does* have to do with Gowrie House?"

"Ah, yes, indeed, it does, but it won't stop me from completing my purpose." He banged his fist on the desk, his jaw setting hard. "The cause is just and decent. Norah was right when she wanted to correct a wrong. She became very devoted to God in the last years of her life, you see. That faith motivated her to make changes. Faith in Christ always produces change. Remember Zacchaeus? 'If I have taken anything from any man by false accusation, I restore him fourfold.'"

The woman she had been raised to think of as another Jezebel had become devoted to God! This was a surprising revelation for Vanessa, yet not an unhappy one. She felt an emotional release that brought joy. Of all things! Norah Benton the famous actress had become a Christian. Oh, the great grace of God.

"It must have happened late in her life?"

He realized what she meant, yet took no offense.

"Yes. It was she who aroused renewed interest in the church here and worked with the vicar to begin services again. It was Norah's influence that awakened my own conscience toward the way I'd badly injured you and Kylie all these years. And it's the cause behind my writing this family history." He patted the volume. "My family legacy was Norah's brainchild. She did most of the research before she died. Scott helped, but it was mostly Norah. She was the force behind the project. And now I'm concluding it in her memory that the truth may be unveiled."

"What truth? Am I allowed to know?" she pleaded.

He smiled. "After what you've been through last night and today, yes, indeed. It's only fair you understand. Better sit down, though."

She drew up a chair, wondering, growing more uneasy. It had something to do with Kerc. She could feel it in her bones.

"First, I've desperately wronged you and Kylie," he began. "That you've come here at all, showing kindness and a willingness to give of yourself to establish some sort of peace and understanding between us is an example of Christ's command to love and forgive. And," he said gently, "I've more than my share to be forgiven for. It was Norah who brought me to Christ just before she passed on into His presence. It was then I saw how my life had been lived so selfishly, leaving the rubble of human emotions and broken hearts littering my path to professional success. I knew I wasn't far behind Norah in going to meet the Savior. Neither of us could ever restore what we took away in our younger, reckless years. Some things are so precious that, once broken or marred, they can never be put back together again without leaving a scar." Tears filled his eyes. "In our case, I'm afraid the sun is setting behind the mountain. We haven't a lot of time. I can never be the father you deserved, but I did want to confess my grievous sin of abandonment of you and Kylie. Not so much for my sake as for your emotional release, and my son's. I don't expect anything in return. It isn't fair to expect it—" His voice cracked.

"Oh," tears welled in her eyes and both sorrow and compassion filled her heart. "I—"

And to think she had wondered if she could ever be a witness to him of Christ's love. And Kylie—he'd bitterly resented the notion of a conversion toward the end of one's life, and even insisted such late conversions couldn't happen, that they weren't genuine. Well, Kylie was wrong. It had happened. Her father believed, and Christ's Spirit now lived in his heart.

God, she thought in awe, *is free to do as He wills. I must never try to put Him in a box by saying what He can and cannot do. Because He is Sovereign. He can save a man or woman on their deathbed, just as He saved the thief on the cross. Age and time don't matter. One must never presume upon His grace, yet one must never limit Him by doubts. God is the God of the impossible! God is the God of answered prayer. Kylie's bitterness has trapped his faith and kept his expectations low, yet God always accomplishes His purposes.*

Vanessa reached a hand across the desk and her father was quick to clasp it and squeeze tightly. Whether he smiled, or whether tears rolled down his lined cheeks, Vanessa couldn't tell, because the tears in her own eyes dimmed her view.

"Now we'll never be separated," he said. "We have eternity."

"Yes..."

It isn't much I can give you, Vanessa. All this poor stammering tongue can say is I'm sorry."

She smiled through her tears. "Sometimes 'I'm sorry' can be pretty big words when a man's life backs it up. I'm thinking yours does, and will continue to as long as He gives you breath. I always wondered what it would be like to call someone 'Dad.' I'll enjoy this gift God has given me, even for a little while. It's worth it."

He got up and came around the desk. "Vanessa, my poor girl—"

They embraced tightly.

It was some minutes later before her father was able to continue his explanation about Gowrie House and its heirs.

"You might wonder what all this has to do with the estate. It happens that Kerc also knows family rejection and loss. He is part of this family and...its heir."

No...the only part of his statement that bit were the words "part of this family." Her heart sank to her feet. Was Kerc a half brother? Oh, no!

She watched her father with dismay. A feeling of great loss, rather than gain, came tumbling down upon her head. Her hands gripped the arms of her chair, and she leaned forward.

"You're not saying that...that Kerc and I are related by blood?" she asked in a disappointed whisper.

24

Vanessa leaned forward in her chair, looking across the desk at her father with the rare volume written by Earl Gowrie between them. The worn gilt edges glinted beneath the lamplight and sparkled mischievously of age-old family secrets.

"Kerc grew up unwanted by the family as the illegitimate son of the parlor maid."

"Are you hinting that he and I are—," she said with a catch of her breath.

"No, no, I didn't mean to imply that at all. Gracious, I've enough sins in my life as it is without fathering Kerc. But he is related to Lucy through Norah's cousin, Cornel Trevalyan. Cornel was born and raised here until the First World War. He died some ten years ago."

Vanessa leaned back in the chair and watched her father, who frowned at his pipe and continued doggedly.

"Norah heard the story circulating about her cousin Cornel and the parlor maid, Edna Carstair, when she was still a stage actress. She shrugged it off. Even if it were true, it didn't concern her. Neither one of us were inclined to think much of it at that time in our lives. It wasn't until we retired from the theater and moved here that Norah, while working on the idea of developing a family history to leave as a legacy to the next generation, became interested in the story. By that time she had become a Christian, which changed her thinking. She now felt compelled to do something for Kerc. By then Kerc was in his early teens. Norah became friendly with him and set up a trust fund for his education.

"Looking back, I'm inclined to think her interest sparked Kerc's curiosity. It probably set him on the road to begin a serious search of his roots. Someone in Edna's family, Carew Carstair the lighthouse keeper, told him that Cornel was his father. I think he's been doing research ever since. When he returned a few years ago from Edinburgh, it may have been with the sole purpose of proving his rights. He talked to the vicar, who was his friend as a boy. Kerc had always put in the vicar's summer garden and trimmed his fruit trees. So they became conspirators," he said with a rueful smile.

"Then Norah never actually told Kerc who he was?" Vanessa asked breathlessly.

"No. There were reasons for that too. There was Norah's brother, Vernon to contend with. He always felt that even though he never had a child by Theo, he should have inherited Gowrie House after his father's death. After Vernon and Norah died, things settled down. Theo came to look upon Lucy as her own daughter, and through Lucy Theo could in essence inherit the estate by controlling whom Lucy would marry. Theo settled on Jodrell."

"Yes," Vanessa said, "I can see how the sudden introduction of Kerc would fan the flames of jealousy and fear." She was also thinking of herself and of the chill treatment she had received from Theo and Lucy when she'd first arrived. Thankfully, Lucy appeared to be slowly changing, but Theo...

"Then, just before her death, Norah came across an old letter Cornel Trevalyan had written to Edna Carstair, the parlor maid. In the letter he addressed her as 'Dear Wife.' That letter," her father said with a frown, "is missing. It disappeared the night of Norah's death. That's why Earl Gowrie's old book and the parish registry are so important. They are all the evidence we have left."

"You think someone burned the letter?"

He sighed and shook his head. "I've searched for it everywhere. That's what first brought me to the church vestry. Norah had worked in the vestry doing her writing and research. I thought she may have mislaid it there. She wasn't feeling well at the time. She could have forgotten where she'd put it, so I thought. I never found it. The vicar says he hasn't seen it, either. It was during that time I began continuing her work and found the earl's old volume. More recently, I came across the registry from 1853–1922. Even Norah hadn't come across these two books. They quite well lock up the truth about just who Kerc is. And that is the reason someone has tried to steal them."

"To destroy proof, the way they successfully did the letter."

He nodded and relit his pipe.

"So there you have it, Vanessa. Well, not quite all. The most important find is before us." He patted the book. "And it's to be included in the family legacy."

"And that is?" Vanessa asked with a catch in her voice.

"Certain proof that Cornel Trevalyan's son was *legitimately* born. Cornel did *not* have an illicit affair with Edna. He loved her dearly and married her. You can be sure no one in line for Gowrie House is inclined to allow anything of this nature to come to light. It means that Kerc, not Lucy, is next in line to inherit."

Vanessa stammered: "But—Norah was a Gowrie. Wouldn't Lucy inherit before the son of a Trevalyan cousin?"

"Ah, but that's the dark secret, my dear. I found it in Earl Gowrie's confessional!" He leaned across the desk, lifting his eyebrows. "The sinister Earl Gowrie confesses to having murdered his cousin Dougal Trevalyan for this estate. In the beginning, it was Trevalyan land."

A little shiver inched along the back of her neck. In the silence, the very walls creaked. They were alone in the great house with the last proof that would deny the others the inheritance. Scarron had been murdered that afternoon, he who had the proof in his bungalow. And to think she'd gone there for it, alone. If she'd known all this then, would she have had the nerve?

"You mean Gowrie House is actually *Trevalyan* House?"

He nodded, puffing his pipe. The smoke curled. "You see what is at stake?"

She had the sudden thought that her father's life could just as easily be at risk. "Father, you should have told Kerc sooner. You could have worked together. He could have protected you if..." She couldn't bring herself to say it aloud.

He was sober. "I know that now. Unfortunately it took Scarron's death for me to grasp how far someone will go." He opened his top drawer and drew out a semiautomatic pistol. He set it on the desk with a grimace. "I never expected anything to happen. I should have been more discerning about danger and evil. I suppose I depended a little too much on Scott."

Yes, so had she until Jodrell aroused her suspicions. Kerc, at least, was fully vindicated and would have no reason to harm her father or Scarron. That thought brought more satisfaction to her heart than she would have expected. Even if Kerc had been working on his own to prove his claim to be Cornel Trevalyan's legal son, he would have no reason to harm her father, because they could only enhance each other's goal. Scott, Jodrell, Theo, even Lucy—perhaps someone else—had everything to lose.

"Let's get back to the Earls Gowrie and Trevalyan, blood cousins and archenemies," he said.

Vanessa inched her chair a little closer.

"Earl Dougal Trevalyan was the legal first owner of this estate. And Earl Stuart Gowrie simply but ruthlessly claimed it after his demise. His power in the king's court was such that he could silence anyone who may have wanted to bring the truth to King James."

"How did he kill Trevalyan? Does he say in his book?"

"Ah, yes. He goes into fine detail. The famous duel here on the estate was not a fair sword fight at all. In fact, Trevalyan won the duel, flicked blood, and called it quits. He told Gowrie to leave the island and never return. When he turned his back to walk away, Gowrie shot Dougal with a pistol. He himself was already wounded, so he claimed to the servants that he'd won the duel. If anyone noticed that Earl Trevalyan had been shot in the back, no one was brave enough to call the sinister Gowrie a liar and a murderer. Eventually he called himself one in his confessional."

"Then," Vanessa said, "the Trevalyans are the rightful heirs."

"Yes. Naturally there's been a good deal of intermarriage since then. But justifiably, as you said moments ago, this should be called Trevalyan House, not Gowrie. If any of the descendants of cousins Dougal and Stuart have a right to its claim, they are the Trevalyans, and therefore the estate is Kerc's by right."

"Did Cornel have any idea he was the true owner?"

"Norah thinks he might have, but if he did, he never contested the matter. He traveled most of the time and didn't have much interest in the estate or the island. He left for the war and after that explored Africa."

She remembered Kerc mentioning Africa. "And Kerc's mother? Whatever happened to Edna Carstair?"

"She was a pretty girl, as Kerc's looks would imply. She wasn't educated beyond simple basics, but who knows what her capabilities really were had she been born the daughter of an aristocrat rather than of house servants? I give Cornel credit for marrying her. He must have truly loved her. And why not? The proof of that love is right here in this registry. They were married at the church. Here, have a look at their signatures."

He turned to the right year, 1912, and found the month September on the 14th day, when Edna Mary Carstair, 16 years, took her matrimonial vows before God to become the lawfully wedded wife of Cornel Trevalyan, 25.

Vanessa smiled. "What happened to Edna?"

"Cornel took her off to London. She died there a few years later. Cornel sent Kerc to Edna's relatives here on the estate. Kerc was raised with Scarron, Billy, Effie, and all the rest of them. The Carstairs are quite a clan. Kerc took a bit of rough teasing when as a lad he insisted on taking the name Trevalyan instead of Carstair. The family here in the house ignored it, believing he was illegitimate. And even some of the Carstairs thought he was just arrogant."

"And Maggie was another of his mother's relatives," she said quietly.

"Yes. Maggie worked here for about a year, then Theo accused her of stealing. Small change—things like that. Then, small pieces of jewelry. Maggie denied it all, but Theo insisted. I'm afraid I didn't want the trouble of trying to sort out the facts." He sighed. "Another of my mistakes. My only excuse is that it was soon after Norah's death. My emotions felt bankrupt. I couldn't deal with it."

"So you dismissed her?"

"Theo dismissed her."

"You sound sorry. Because of her death?"

"It's been on my conscience ever since it happened. I suppose it's because I actually believed Maggie to be innocent. She went to work in a tavern after that. The constable believed she went to the lighthouse to meet someone and either missed her footing in the thick mist that rolled in that night, or she took her own life. The man she came to meet most likely was someone who didn't want their relationship known."

This motive for Maggie's death, taking her life, was far different from what Kerc implied, but it was possible.

"Do you think she took her life?"

"What else could it be?" He looked at her almost pleadingly.

"Kerc once said that she might have been—pushed."

He groaned and rested his head against one palm. "Yes. He mentioned that possibility to me also. I've had many sleepless nights since."

"You can't blame yourself for everything, Father. If she took her life, she was responsible for that decision, not you. And it was Theo who dismissed her. Anyway, it may not have been that way at all. Kerc thinks there's something more to the whole incident."

"After Scarron, little would surprise me," he said, a strained note in his voice. He touched the old book. "Rather clever of Kerc to gain control of my folder," he said with a faintly wry smile. "If he's read it, he knows everything by now. He may know everything even without it. My notes will give him proof positive. Naturally, he'd want these two items," he said of the book and registry, "because they're mentioned in my notes, as was Cornel's letter to Edna calling her 'Dear Wife.'"

"The folder was sealed," she said.

"Kerc wouldn't hesitate to *unseal* it if he thought it would clear up the mysteries surrounding his birth. I don't fault him for that. If I were him, I'd have fought for my place in the sun too. I'm going to tell him everything tonight, if they ever get here." He looked at his watch. "The sooner the truth is brought into the open, the sooner his enemy will be disarmed. Nothing can stop it now. I intend to make them all witnesses."

"Scott doesn't know any of this, does he? I don't see how he can. There is mutual dislike there."

"He knows very little. I've handled the sensitive research myself, and left general research of island history to Scott. You know why he's cool toward Kerc."

"Yes, Lucy. She told me today she isn't sure about Jodrell. I think she'd be wiser to wait until her heart is made up about which man she really wants."

"If that's true, it's the best news I've had about Lucy in the year she's been engaged to Jodrell. Jodrell is a likable young man and talented with horses, but I wonder about him at times."

"She may see that yet herself, and call it off."

"You're coming here has been a blessing to us all, Vanessa."

She basked in the affectionate look he gave her. "I can truly say I'm glad I came, Father."

"One door is closing, and another is opening. Once Kerc knows the truth and the others are forced to accept the inevitable, we can turn our attention to Kylie. We'll let the constable handle the murder of Scarron Carstair."

~~~

Vanessa left her father in his room poring over Earl Gowrie's book and went down the dim, winding staircase, listening to her footsteps breaking the stillness. Although it was dark outside, there was still no sign of the others. Vanessa walked out onto the front porch to see if she could hear the horses and motorcar coming.

The wind had blown away most of the thick mist, and the moon could be seen rising above the sea, turning the distant hills and nearby trees into silver. The minutes slipped by. Why didn't the others come? Were they waiting at the lighthouse bungalow for the constable? Kerc had said he would need to take a boat to the mainland. It would take hours to go and come back. They weren't intending to stay there all that time, were they? She could telephone Lucy—no, the line was down.

Why had the telephone line been cut?

Someone had wanted to delay getting hold of the constable, or maybe they had *wanted* Kerc to go all the way to the mainland—

She stopped. Could Kerc now be the target? If they couldn't destroy the evidence, why not destroy the heir?

What had Theo said? "It could be dangerous." She thought at the time that Theo meant the thick mist, but mightn't there have been a more subtle meaning? And Scott, where was he if not at the bungalow with the others?

Vanessa's fingers tightened on the porch railing as she peered off onto the moonlit lawn toward the little dirt road leading to the harbor. He wouldn't have gone that way. Kerc would have taken a shortcut to the harbor across the bog-laden fields—

But Kerc was too careful, too aware of danger, not to be on guard in case someone was waiting to plan another "accident." It was too late to warn him. By now, if he'd taken a boat to the mainland, he'd already be far out to sea. There was nothing to do except wait.

At last she heard the distant sound of an engine. The sound grew louder, and presently the yellow glare of headlights lit up the yew trees and threw long black shadows across the drive. The engine stopped, and a few moments later Scott walked up the porch steps, followed by Theo, Lucy, and Dr. MacGregor.

Relief rushed through her. "Where's Jodrell?" she found herself asking rather sharply. And how was it Scott was with them? Maybe Jodrell had been wrong, and Scott had never left the bungalow. Why would Jodrell have told her he had?

"Coming with the horses," Scott said. "None of us felt much like riding back. Jodrell wanted to make sure they were brought home safely. You know Jodrell," he said, "the horses are more important to him than any of us."

"That's nonsense," Theo said from behind him. "Those horses are worth money. We can't afford to lose them on the moor the way McClelland's been losing sheep."

"Those horses know their way back blindfolded," Scott said.

He stopped by the hall door and looked at Vanessa with concern. "What made you leave like that and ride back alone? And without telling anyone? I was under the impression you weren't that comfortable riding. In the thick mist it might have been risky. We thought you might have gone after Kerc."

Vanessa was about to mention what Jodrell had told her when Theo interjected with what seemed exhausted patience, "Oh, come, Scott. Leave Vanessa alone. She can handle herself, I'm quite certain. Buttons is as docile as a baby lamb. You worry too much about the wrong things." She turned, looking out the open door. "Where's Lucy? Why is she still waiting by the motorcar? Go bring her indoors, Scott, for goodness sake."

Scott left them and went down the steps. Theo looked at Vanessa. "You look as though you could use some rest, Vanessa dear. Perhaps you should go on up to your room. There's nothing any of us can do tonight. We'll need to wait for Kerc to get back with the constable. I doubt that will happen until the early morning hours. The fog is blowing away, though. That will help him."

"Yes. I am tired, but I wanted to make sure everyone got back safely. Are Billy and Effie all right?"

"Oh, yes. They're in the kitchen clearing away the picnic things. I'm exhausted. I'm going straight to bed. How is Robert by the way?"

Dr. MacGregor had already gone upstairs to see him. Vanessa told her that Robert was doing much better.

"Probably nothing but a dreadful case of indigestion," Theo said crossly. "To think he put us all on the edge of a dreadful case of nerves! We even blamed you for a heart attack. Your stay hasn't turned out well, has it, poor girl. And now Scarron. It's dreadful, just too ghastly to think about." She climbed the stairs, her limp more noticeable when she was tired. Vanessa felt unexpected compassion. Poor Theo. She didn't have much to satisfy her heart. She had searched in all the wrong places to quench her soul's thirst.

Neither Scott nor Lucy came indoors right away, and Vanessa, realizing that Kerc wouldn't be coming soon, relinquished any thought of further discussion that night. She gladly took Theo's suggestion and went to her room. Sleep, for a little while, would mask all suspicions.

She was nearing her door, when Dr. MacGregor, coming from her father's room, called quietly: "One moment, Miss Miles, please."

His face was tired, but his crystal blue eyes were inquisitive as he studied her for what she believed were signs of emotional exhaustion.

"Robert is well on his way to a sound recovery. After what happened to Scarron Carstair, however, I wish I could say the same for the others," he stated with crisp efficiency. "I have something for you."

At first she thought he was going to recommend a sleeping tablet, but it was an envelope he handed to her, addressed to Colonel Warnstead. "I spoke to the colonel this afternoon. He is quite amenable to having your brother Kylie take a few days' leave to see Robert. Naturally, I had no idea your father would recover as he has. The colonel is under the impression Robert is near death. You can explain otherwise when you see him."

Vanessa thanked him for the letter and for his intervention. He held up a bottle of white tablets. "I'll be making my rounds to see the others and pass out a good night's sleep. You don't look distraught like Theo and Lucy, but would you like to have one?"

She smiled. "Thank you no, Doctor. I'm so sleepy I'll be out like a light as soon as my head hits the pillow."

"Good. Well, then, goodnight, my dear." He started to turn away, paused and looked at her from under his white brows. He cleared his throat. "I may be the doctor attending to Robert's health, but I wanted to thank you, Vanessa, for what you've done for him."

"Me?" she said, embarrassed and surprised. "I haven't done anything important."

"Oh, but you have," he said with a vague smile. "You have brought him the gift of peace in knowing you've forgiven the past. That, my dear, has done more for him than all the medicines and tonics I could prescribe."

She smiled. "Thank you. It's done me wonders as well." She clutched the letter, thinking of Kylie.

"The others could use a good dose of the same. I'll hand out these tablets, but it won't bring the lasting effect your coming has given to your father. Good night, young lady, sleep well." He patted her shoulder and walked down toward Theo's room.

Vanessa was smiling as she looked after him. His words had done more to encourage her than he knew. *Not everything is dark and gloomy*, she thought, opening the door and going into her room.

Nevertheless, she locked her door.

She looked at the envelope.

Her quest for peace was not yet complete.

25

It was past eight o'clock when Vanessa awoke to Effie's knocking on her door. Vanessa slid back the bolt and the girl entered with a tray, her eyes wary.

"Constable's arrived, miss. He's going to be talking to everyone this morning about poor Scarron."

"When did Kerc come?"

"Oh, he was already here before the sun rose, miss, and the constable was with him. They were taking breakfast in Kerc's bungalow before they ever come here to the main house."

It's going to be an unpleasant morning, Vanessa thought. Even so, the sun was shining and the breeze through her window brought the fragrance of roses and heather, and the pond glittered like a vast silvery-gray pearl. It was difficult to remember that dark and murderous things had occurred yesterday.

She dressed neatly in conservative blue and went downstairs to find Scott and Dr. MacGregor halfway through their breakfast out on the terrace. Theo was having hers in bed, as was her father, and neither Lucy nor Jodrell had showed yet. The ruddy-faced constable was having a cup of tea.

She became aware of being watched, and turning her head she saw Kerc standing to one side. She met his level gaze and noticed for the first time restrained interest. Had it always been there?

Vanessa greeted the men at the table as she poured herself a cup of tea, and then she casually walked up to where Kerc stood. She didn't look at him, but at the garden he kept so lovely.

"I was rude last night and wanted to apologize," she said quietly, so the others wouldn't hear. "I no longer think you had anything to do with Scarron's death. I'm sorry. My excuse, I suppose, is that I was very upset."

He took it in stride, as though he were used to her seeking him out and apologizing.

"You had a right to be upset. You walked in on a gruesome scene. I wasn't helpful. I only had one thing on my mind, and that was who killed him."

She looked at him gravely. "I don't suppose you've spoken to Robert yet?"

"No. Why? Is he wanting to see me?"

She smiled faintly. "Yes. He has a surprising announcement. Not just for you, but everyone else too."

He looked at her thoughtfully and his dark brows lifted a fraction. "I'd be interested to know what changed your mind about suspecting me, but whatever it was, it can wait." He gestured his head toward the constable. "You're in for a host of questions since you found my cousin. Think you're up to it?"

She nodded. "I'm not nervous, if that's what you mean. All I can do is tell him the truth."

"Scott said you rode off last night alone. That could have been dangerous. I saw how you handled Buttons earlier, and you weren't very good at it. You need riding lessons."

She began to get ruffled, then thought better of it. He didn't know yet where she'd gone or why. Because there was more concern in his gaze than mere criticism of her riding abilities, she smiled. "I'll...um...keep that in mind."

"Mind telling me why you left like that?"

"Jodrell told me he was worried about my father." She told him what Jodrell said about Scott going to Robert.

He frowned as he half-sat down on the rail. He looked over at the table, but Jodrell's chair was vacant.

"He was mistaken," she said, "Scott didn't leave." She looked at him searchingly. "I went to the lighthouse to talk. When I got there I called up, but there was no answer."

He returned her stare too blandly. "I didn't go there right away. There was something I wanted to do first. I came around twenty minutes later and locked it up."

"Then someone else was in there," she said in a low voice. "I distinctly heard footsteps."

His mood was dark. "You were smart not to go up. Someone was looking for something he'd lost. He didn't know I already had it in my pocket."

Surprised, she stopped herself from turning and looking suspiciously at the others. "Do you know who it was?"

"Aye, I do. I've already told the constable. Better have something to eat," he said calmly, redirecting their discussion. "It's going to be a long day."

Lucy arrived, unresponsive to anyone's "good morning," and Jodrell came behind her tight-lipped and frowning. Scott noticed and looked from one to the other, but Lucy avoided eye contact. Jodrell pulled out a chair for Lucy, who plunked herself down, unfolded her napkin, and reached for the pitcher of orange juice. Her hand shook a little as she poured.

"Trouble?" whispered Vanessa to Kerc.

He nodded slightly. "I've already talked to Lucy this morning. She came to see me at the bungalow. She's breaking her engagement to Jodrell. She must have told him."

"That will make Scott happy. And my father. I think he favors Scott."

"Hmm," he said. "Theo won't be happy. When are you leaving for London?"

"It was going to be soon. I don't see how I can go now, not with what's happened."

"Doc is a good friend of the constable. He was talking to him about you. Looks like the constable will let you leave to bring Kylie here to see your father. Think that letter to the colonel will help?"

That was good news. "I'm sure it will help get him leave. The hard part will be to convince Kylie to come."

By now the constable had finished his tea and he stood. The others began making their way into the drawing room, looking morose over the ordeal ahead. The constable, a large, heavy man with florid features and a balding head, looked back at them and nodded. Reluctantly, Vanessa followed, with Kerc holding the door open to let her pass. He smiled. "Don't worry. You're already dismissed as a suspect."

"Daddy," Lucy cried, rushing to Robert as he waited for them in the drawing room. "What are you doing up?"

"Good morning, Lucy darling," he said as he gave her a kiss on the cheek. "I'm doing much better as you can see. James says I'm allowed out of bed today, though it could have been under happier circumstances. Good morning, Peter," he said to the constable. "A tragic thing about Scarron."

"So it is, Robert, so it is. Where is Mrs. Gowrie?"

"Don't worry, Constable, I haven't run off across the border," Theo said with a trace of acidity in her tone. She entered the room and sat down in one of the chairs. "I suppose this ordeal will go on past luncheon. Effie?"

"Yes, mum?"

"Tell Iris we'll need extra settings at the table today. And bring in coffee. The constable prefers it to tea."

"Obliged, ma'am," the constable nodded toward her in deference.

"Peter," said Robert, when the others sat down, "if you'd permit me to speak before you begin asking questions of us all, I think I may be able to shed a great deal of light on what happened to Scarron Carstair."

In the sudden silence that followed, Vanessa became acutely aware of how shock and wariness had come over the faces of everyone there. Only Kerc showed neither surprise nor caution, but it was quite clear that even he was wondering, for he eyed her father closely.

"Daddy—how can you say that?" Lucy asked, troubled. "You weren't even at the picnic."

"I didn't need to be there to deduce some of the facts, my dear. I have in my hands—thanks to Vanessa—the motive for the crime."

For a moment, all eyes turned toward Vanessa. She kept hers on Robert.

"And opportunity for murder was present with all of you," he continued. When he produced Earl Gowrie's book and the parish registry, a slight intake of breath from someone—maybe more than one—was audible, and a chill descended over the room.

Vanessa quickly looked at Kerc to see if he recognized what her father held in his hands. The sharp glance he gave Robert was answer enough. Robert was looking at Kerc. "It's time the truth were known, Kerc. But even you don't know all the facts."

"Kerc!" Lucy cried, misinterpreting her father's words to mean his guilt. "Daddy, that's nonsense. Kerc wouldn't shoot his own cousin."

"No, he wouldn't," Robert said, "not even for an inheritance. I'm afraid I can't say that about everyone else in this room."

Theo looked drawn and white, and Scott was watching everyone with a wary frown. Jodrell came up behind Lucy's chair and laid a hand on her shoulder, but she shrugged it off, looking glum.

"You don't really think...you can't possibly...," stammered Theo. "Robert, this is madness. You must not go through with this..."

"Not madness, Theo, just plain old covetousness taken to its final step." He looked over at the caretaker. "This estate rightfully belongs to you, Kerc, but I've a notion you already know that."

"Aye, sir, that I do," he said quietly.

A startled gasp came from some around the room, and Effie, just bringing in the tray, nearly dropped it. She gaped at Kerc.

"I've been researching for some time now," Kerc admitted, "but I couldn't prove anything until the vicar showed me the earl's confessional. I knew then that Earl Gowrie killed his cousin, Dougal Trevalyan. Not just for the estate, but for a woman too. Her name was Kathleen McGuire. There's a historical marker on the spot where Gowrie was supposed to have dueled Trevalyan, but in the confessional he wrote before he died, he told how it was murder, cold and shameless."

"You're right," Robert said.

Theo's head sank back against the leather chair. She looked old, ill, and beaten. The others simply stared at Kerc.

Lucy said, "You mean...I'm not going to inherit Gowrie House?"

"No," Robert said. "Kerc is the son of your mother's cousin, Cornel Trevalyan."

"Oh!" Lucy cried. Suddenly she clapped her palms together. "That's wonderful!"

"Lucy," breathed Theo, stricken, "how can you?"

Lucy stood and turned to Jodrell. "Because now, maybe, I won't need to worry about men wanting to marry me for reasons other than love."

"Lucy—," Jodrell said in a strangled voice, "that's not the reason."

"Oh, yes it is." She looked at Theo, who had her forehead in hand, her eyes closed. "Isn't it the reason, Aunt Theo?" she demanded.

Theo sat very still.

Vanessa started to cross the room to her chair, but was surprised to feel Kerc's hand on her arm, restraining her. She looked at him. His eyes told her *not yet*.

"You wanted Jodrell to marry me because of the estate," Lucy told Theo again. "You've wanted it all these years. That's why you told me lies about Scott and Maggie. And they *were* lies. I know that now. Vanessa made me see sense for once in my life. I was about to throw away my life on a terrible mistake, and the saddest thing is that you'd have let me do it, just so Gowrie House would go to you and Jodrell. You didn't care about me, but Vanessa did. My sister. She's only been here a short time, and she's already taught us things we wouldn't have learned otherwise." She walked over to Kerc and threw her arms around him, crying. "I for one am glad Kerc is going to inherit. I'm free."

After a minute of stunned silence, Robert cleared his throat and looked at each one.

Theo spoke, bounding to her feet unexpectedly. "Lucy, you don't know what you're saying. This is nonsense! Norah was the rightful heiress of this estate. It naturally follows that you inherit after her. Kerc might be the son of that runabout maverick cousin of Norah's, but even Cornel didn't want an illegitimate son born of a parlor maid."

"That's not true," Vanessa heard her voice rise, shaking. "Tell her, Father. Tell them all what we found out last night!"

Kerc cast her a quick look. "Last night?"

She turned to him with a little smile. "Yes. Last night. Before Scarron died, he did speak and he gave me a message. I know I told you he didn't, and I'm sorry I held back, but I didn't completely trust you then. He told me where to find Earl Gowrie's book. It was in his bungalow. It was there, along with the parish registry, in his little bookcase."

"So that's where he hid them," Kerc said thoughtfully. "I knew he'd stolen them from the vicar. He sent me a message before the picnic to meet him at the lighthouse, but by the time I got there, he was dead."

"He sent you a message?" Robert asked.

"Aye, sir. I've already given it to the constable. In it he told me he had the book and registry. He was going to sell them for a thousand pounds to someone he claimed would be willing to pay the price. Scarron's dream was always to emigrate to New Zealand and buy some land of his own. Unfortunately, he thought money by blackmail would do the trick for him. But he must have taken a look at that book and registry and decided they were worth a good deal more than that. He got in touch with me instead."

"Then Scarron did mean you when he said tell 'him' where they're hidden," Vanessa said. "I thought he meant my father."

"Scarron must have looked through them and discovered you were the legal heir of Gowrie House," Robert said. "Since he was your cousin, he probably felt it wiser to get the money to emigrate from you."

"I don't believe any of this," Theo was saying furiously. "What are you doing, trying to rob your own little Lucy of the Gowrie inheritance?"

"It isn't Lucy who's being robbed; it was Kerc all these years. The truth must come out. Norah wanted it that way, and so do I, Theo."

"But he's not the *legal* son of Cornel Trevalyan! It will never hold up in a court of law."

"Oh, yes it will," Robert said. "In this registry is proof that Cornel married Edna Carstair. He married her before Kerc was conceived because he was in love with her. That was the truth that Norah discovered in her research. The truth that I'm including in the family legacy. And all of you are now witnesses. Fighting against it will do no good, Theo. I know you wanted this estate for your son, but you'll need to be content to live out your days here in peace as a guest in this house, if Kerc will allow that."

"Married—," Jodrell spat, looking at Theo with a red face. "How could you have made such a stupid mistake!"

"Jodrell—," Theo choked, dropping her face into her hands.

"Don't speak to your mother like that," Robert warned him sternly.

"Mother?" Lucy cried. She left Kerc and walked over to where Theo was sitting, a crumpled figure. "Jodrell is your son?"

"Yes," Robert said. "From her first marriage. She kept it a secret, knowing you'd see through her plans to own everything if you found out about Jodrell. Isn't that true, Theo?" he asked gently.

Jodrell snapped, "Yes, it's true. And we'd have done far better with the estate than Kerc here. I would have raised some of the best horses in all Scotland."

"There's no reason why you can't still raise horses here, if Kerc permits…," Robert began.

"I'm afraid there is a very good reason why that can't be, sir," Kerc said.

They all turned to look at him. Even Theo raised her head, her face stricken and gray.

"Jodrell killed Scarron."

Theo stood, turning a sickening white, then collapsed, hand at her heart. Vanessa rushed to catch her, as did Dr. MacGregor.

Jodrell fled the room, but outside the window they heard the sounds of a scuffle. Another policeman who had come with the constable had tackled him, wrestling him down to the ground. Jodrell's voice was heard shouting: "It was an accident! I didn't meant to shoot him! It was an accident…if he'd just told me where he'd hidden the things…but he wouldn't."

Scott went to help Dr. MacGregor carry Theo upstairs to her room. Lucy sat dazed on the divan, and Robert sat down beside her. She cried in his arms. "It's awful, awful—"

"It's all right now, dear, it's all over. For some of us at least, everything is going to be all right. In a world where mankind's sin still abounds, it's the best we can hope for until a new day comes. Go ahead and cry it out. It will do you good."

Vanessa stood watching, aching with distress. Then Kerc took her arm and gently led her out onto the terrace.

∿∿∿

The refreshing wind and the song of birds soothed her heart. There were still many beautiful things in the world worth fighting for.

"H-how did you know it was Jodrell?"

"I saw him go to the lighthouse last night, to search for his knife."

"His knife?" she looked at him, bewildered.

"The constable has it. He knows everything. He came just to stage this scene, hoping we could smoke Jodrell out. Little did we know your father would make it easier by his announcement. Yes, his knife. That's what he was searching for in the lighthouse when you heard him and thought it was me. I suspected Jodrell even then, because I found his knife clutched in Scarron's hand."

"You did! I didn't notice it. But, then, one of his hands was beneath him. He was so heavy I couldn't turn him over."

"He must have picked it up before dying, knowing I'd suspect Jodrell if I saw it. Jodrell used it to cut the telephone wire at Carew's house. He must have dropped it in the lighthouse during his struggle with Scarron. Jodrell cut the wire to give him more time to cover his tracks and make an alibi before the constable arrived."

"But...how could it have been Jodrell if I met him on the way back from the lighthouse to the bungalow? He came from the horses. That's when he talked about Scott."

"That's what had me curious, until Lucy told me this morning that Jodrell didn't arrive with Doc MacGregor. When Jodrell met you, he gave the impression he'd arrived with the Doc, didn't he?"

"He was lying?"

"Yes. He'd arrived before the doc. Lucy saw him through the window. No one ever thought to ask Doc MacGregor if he came alone. It turns out Jodrell left him on the trail with an excuse that he'd forgotten something."

"But if he was the one I heard in the lighthouse, how did he arrive back at the bungalow before I did?"

"Once you left, it would have been easy to outrun you, especially in the thick mist. He was there waiting when you came up."

"Yes...I see how that's possible. I tripped and sat there for a few minutes before I continued on. But why did he want me to come here last night to be with my father?"

"Oh, I suspect it was the best thing he could come up with to keep you from being suspicious of him. Blame Scott for everything. Make him look guilty."

"Yes—he accused him at the stables of dropping his hat in the garden the other night. He must have wanted me to think it was Scott who'd attacked me on the walkway."

"That was neither Scott nor Jodrell, but Scarron."

"Scarron!"

"Aye, he wanted your dad's folder. Scarron stole the books from the vicar's house when the old gentleman was out walking his dog."

"The vicar told you that? How did he know it was Scarron?"

"He saw him leaving. The day was chilly and the vicar turned back to get his cap before continuing his walk. He let me know right away. I talked to Scarron. He admitted it. When I found out he was the one who pushed you down, we had it out. He was going to bring me the book and registry when we met at the lighthouse later. But Jodrell must have found out first. When Scarron refused to tell him where he'd hidden them, Jodrell lost control of himself. One thing led to another, and well, you know what happened. I dare say, it was best he didn't bring them as he said he would. Jodrell would have gotten them."

"When I went to the vestry that night, the book and parish registry were missing. Did the vicar explain why he had the book at his house?"

Kerc smiled. "He had the book because I gave it to him to keep."

"You did," she said shocked.

"Sure. I wasn't about to let it fall into someone's hands who wanted to destroy all evidence of my claim. I wish I had also known about that registry."

"You mean you didn't?"

"No. You see, I believed I was illegitimate. It never occurred to me to look in it. Scarron must've seen your father in the vestry taking notes from it and decided it was valuable. It's certain proof of my parents' marriage. And to think it was there in the vestry all the time when I was growing up."

She smiled, looking warmly at him. "I'm so glad we recovered them."

"So am I, but you took a big risk in going to Scarron's bungalow last night. If Jodrell had suspected Scarron told you anything and followed you—well, thank God he didn't," he said reverently.

They were quiet, both leaning against the terrace railing watching the ducks waddle down to the pond and listening to the birds warbling their morning music.

"What will happen to Jodrell now, do you think?" she asked after a minute.

"He'll stand trial. I feel sorry for Theo. Though if my guess is right, she's the one who lit the fire under him to do all this. She probably had the thousand pounds to pay Scarron for turning the book over to Jodrell."

"What will they do to her if she was involved?"

He shook his head. "She's old and ill. She didn't look well at all when she collapsed in there. I'd say she's actually worse off than Mr. Miles when it comes to her heart. Maybe they'll go easy on her; let's hope so. She may have just been wrangling to have Jodrell marry Lucy. If that's her only part, then there's no crime there."

She turned and looked at him thoughtfully, then smiled. "Well, Mr. Trevalyan, what does it feel like to be master of Gowrie House?"

"Well, to tell the facts straight, I don't feel a bit different. I suspected it all along, though the marriage part came as a shock. A happy one. Always did hate the idea of being born on the wrong side of the blanket."

She flushed. "Well, you can forget all that. There was a letter too, written by your father to your mother. He called her 'Dear Wife,' and according to Robert, he loved her a great deal."

"He'd have to, wouldn't he? I mean, to marry a young parlor maid like that. Yet he didn't think much of me. He went off after she died in London and forgot I was ever born. I'd say he wasn't much of a man to brag about."

She sighed and plucked a blossom from the vine. "You've been vindicated anyway; it's all yours now. Do you have any plans?"

He leaned against a pillar. He shook his head thoughtfully, looking out at the garden. "Carry on, is all. Oh, after the war I've got plans, but right now things will stay much as they are."

"After the war?" she asked cautiously.

"Sure. I can't just stay here and enjoy myself as the new owner when the ruddy Germans are overrunning Europe. Next thing, they'll be here in Scotland. We'll need to stop them in England, since they've defeated France. It will be hard and difficult, and most likely take years to beat 'em back to Berlin."

"You're—are you joining the military, Kerc?"

He looked at her. "I wouldn't be able to stand myself ten years from now if I didn't."

She said nothing and found that she'd torn the flower to pieces without realizing it. She let it drop to the flagstones beneath the terrace.

"I'd think you'd cheer me on, Miss Miles. Your brother is in the RAF, and so is that flight lieutenant you're engaged to marry. What's his name?"

She thought he remembered but was merely reminding her to see her reaction.

"Andy Warnstead," she said quietly.

"Aye, that was it. I suspect you're pretty proud of them both. So, I'd at least think you'd tell me I was doing the right thing too."

She turned, bewildered about her depression and looked at him. "Don't tell me you too will fly one of those Hurricanes or Spitfires! If you do, your chances of ever being master of this estate have just been cut in half."

"Maybe. But it's a comfort to know my days are in God's hands, not in the hands of some Nazi soldier. Anyway, I'm not thinking of the air force. I've other interests."

She thought he meant the navy, but she didn't ask because the birdsong had stopped and, as she looked out to sea, it appeared as if fog were coming in again. Her heart too felt gray and bleak. She turned away.

Her father joined them. "There you are, Vanessa. I want to talk to you about that trip to London. You too, Kerc, if you would. Can you step in here for a few minutes?"

26

It was arranged that Vanessa would leave for London the following day. Kerc would arrange for a boat to bring her across to Oban and then she'd make her way to Edinburgh, where she'd catch the train to London. She had bidden her father goodbye the night before and expected to leave quietly and unnoticed. Therefore, it surprised her as she came downstairs early the next morning to find Lucy waiting. She looked as though she hadn't slept much and there was a sadness in her eyes that hadn't been there when Vanessa first arrived. The ordeal over Jodrell and the sorrow she must feel about her aunt had left its marks on the young face.

"I wanted to wish you a safe and good trip," Lucy said.

"Oh, well…thank you," Vanessa said, hiding her pleased surprise. Although they had come to some agreement in Miss Mary's garden the day of the picnic, Vanessa hadn't been sure just what their relationship as sisters would be in the future.

"The bombing of London is all over the news. You'll be careful, won't you?" Lucy said.

Vanessa took the hand extended toward her and smiled. "I'll be on the lookout. How is Theo?"

Lucy shook her head hopelessly. "Dr. MacGregor gave her a sedative last night. He's watching her carefully. She's taking it horribly bad about Jodrell—as we all are. It's...it's..." She had no words and closed her eyes, her dark lashes trembling.

Vanessa squeezed her sister's hand, letting her know she needn't explain, that she understood her devastation. Although Lucy hadn't been in love with Jodrell, she had thought she was for a time, and her heart must be aching.

"They're still questioning him," Lucy said weakly. "Father says he's confessed everything, but he insists Aunt Theo was not involved. Oh, it's too dreadful. Everything that's happened."

Vanessa used the unexpected open door God had given her. She opened her shoulder bag and dug inside for the small book of Psalms she often carried with her.

"I have something for you. I don't know how you'll feel about it, but I'd like to leave it with you, if you'll let me. The psalms have given me great hope and comfort through the years. I want you to enjoy the same fatherly love of God that I do."

Vanessa, taking Lucy's hand, opened it and placed the book of Psalms on her palm and enclosed her fingers about it. "All is not lost, Lucy. Not as long as the Lord Jesus is alive."

Lucy's lips trembled. She nodded and looked down at the portion of Scripture. A tear splashed on its worn white cover. She tried to brush it away, but Vanessa's hand stopped her.

"It's quite all right. My own have left some tearstains as well."

Lucy swallowed hard. "I have something for you and Kylie." She reached over to the hall table, picked up a thick envelope, and handed it to Vanessa.

"Good luck with Kylie. I do hope he'll come and see our father. I want to see him too. I've written asking him to come. Would you see that he gets it? There are some photographs inside."

"Yes, of course I will," Vanessa said, pleased.

Suddenly Lucy threw her arms around her. "I'm glad you had the courage to come to us, Vanessa. You've changed so many things for the better in such a short while. No matter what Kylie chooses, you'll come back, won't you? Please do!" She looked at her, smiling sadly through her tears. "Now that we're sisters we can't ever say goodbye again."

"Oh, Lucy, yes, yes, I'll come back again one day, even if Kylie feels that he can't. I may need to return to New York, but we'll stay in touch. And if I can't come back here to Scotland, maybe you can visit me in America."

"That will be grand, but Father will never want to lose you again now that he's found you."

Vanessa somehow managed a bright smile. "He'll have a hard time getting rid of me permanently." She hugged her tightly. "Goodbye, Lucy. I'll let you know about Kylie as soon as I can."

"Do! Have a safe trip."

Effie was waiting on the front step, looking a little shy. "Goodbye, miss. God be with ye. 'Twas good to meet ye." She hesitated, then thrust out some hastily picked roses from behind her back. "Ye do us all good, miss. Come back."

"Oh, Effie, they're lovely. Thank you! And—thanks for all those special cups of American coffee."

Effie laughed. "Ye take care, miss. Ye watch out for them Nazis."

"I will." Vanessa lifted her hand in farewell and went down the steps to where Kerc was waiting.

She stopped and looked at him as though mentally taking a last photograph. The breeze smelled fragrantly of the sea and flowers. No matter what Kerc might become in the future, she'd always remember him hard at work as the young caretaker, living in the humble bungalow and growing the most luscious roses she'd ever seen or would likely see again.

His younger cousin Billy had her luggage and was lounging against the gate waiting to escort her to the harbor. Vanessa offered her hand with the brightest smile she could muster. "Goodbye."

He smiled back at her in return. "I'll walk with you to the harbor."

"You needn't, you know. I don't want to keep you from anything important, Kerc."

"Not keeping me from a thing. Fact is, if you hadn't needed to go this morning, I could have seen you all the way to London. I'll be going myself in a week or two about the repairs on my boat."

Billy opened the gate and went ahead of them with her bags. Kerc and Vanessa followed him slowly.

"Oh, that's right. I'd forgotten your fishing boat. Well, at least now, as the new master of the house, you'll be able to see it's taken care of." She glanced at him. "I don't know how long it will take to arrange things with Colonel Warnstead about Kylie."

"What if Kylie refuses to come?"

"I don't know what I'll do then. I can't stay in London indefinitely."

"Mr. Miles isn't likely to be happy about you heading back to New York so soon."

"I'm glad it worked out as well as it did. I shall write him often."

"Writing's not the same thing as being with someone."

"No. It isn't."

"Maybe you ought to consider coming back and staying awhile even if Kylie doesn't come."

She glanced at him. "It's your estate now. I really have no right to come back."

But he didn't answer at first, and for an embarrassing moment she thought he wouldn't, that she had placed him in an uncomfortable spot.

He didn't look the least embarrassed or trapped. He smiled. "You'll be welcome anytime you'd like to come back, and next time the dogs won't chase you."

"Is that a promise?"

"You can count on it."

"About those dogs—"

"Aye, I was going to tell you about them." He stopped. Ahead, Billy seemed to guess there was no hurry. He set her bags down and leaned against a tree.

The harbor was in view and Captain Duncan was waiting, smoking his pipe.

The sea breeze was cool, but the sky was a clear blue and the hills were green.

"They're in training to become military patrol dogs. Scarron should never have fooled with them. He really wasn't their trainer. I was and still am."

"Patrol dogs?" she asked, wondering.

"London is worried about German agents being let offshore here by U-boats or other ships disguised as fishing boats from Ireland. Someone's been sending signals from the lighthouse and Devil's Cliff. I've been taking the dogs out each night whenever Carew sends me a signal that he thinks something suspicious might be up."

She remembered what her father had said about spies being smuggled into England.

"Oh," she said, amazed. "You're involved with the military and patrol this section of the beach?"

"Something like that. Remember the man you saw me meet on the road yesterday morning? The one you kept asking about?" he said rather wryly.

"Yes..."

"He's with the British War Department. He's gone now. He came about Maggie, and about some other plans we have laid out for the future."

Her eyes searched his. "He came about Maggie?"

"My cousin."

"Yes, I know, but what has she to do with it?"

"She was working with me. She had that job at the tavern just to spot newcomers. I was against it, of course. Didn't want her working in a place like that, but she had her own mind."

"Oh!"

"That night she was at Carew and Mary's bungalow, she went to meet a friend from the CID. He didn't show up. They don't know where he is. He may be dead. The man who met her may have been a German agent. She must have taken him by surprise. New information is pointing toward a German infiltrator. We're thinking Maggie gave her life in duty to her country."

She was astonished and said nothing.

"No one knows about this, so keep it to yourself, will you? I wanted you to understand. First, we thought Scott was involved smuggling the Jerries. He's not. Neither was Jodrell. But someone is helping to get the infiltrators safely to England and Northern Ireland. We're still working on that. We'll find whoever it is. I don't think it's anyone we know."

"Thank God it isn't Scott," she said reverently.

When he looked at her thoughtfully, she added, "For Lucy's sake. What will she do now, I wonder?"

"Scott will be staying on to help Mr. Miles finish his book. I've a notion things are already coming together between them."

"Can Scott get along with the new master of the house?" she asked with a brief smile.

His eyes glimmered. "I think he'll manage to be civil now. We both will. You have been good for all of us."

Vanessa enjoyed the moment of pleasure his compliment brought.

He looked down at the harbor. "Looks like Duncan's ready to cast off."

"Yes..." She was still thinking of the startling revelation about Kerc, Maggie, and the dogs.

He smiled. "See you in London."

"In London?" she asked a little dazed.

"Aye. My boat, remember? I thought maybe I could call on you at the Warnsteads' house to see if Kylie will be coming."

"Yes, please do. Goodbye, Kerc. Thank you for telling me—for trusting me."

"After mistrusting you the way I did and making things more miserable for you, I thought the least I could do was explain a little more about how it is. My apology about Scott and you conniving together. You're nothing like that. I had it all wrong that time."

"No apology needed. We both had it wrong."

His dark eyes held hers, and her heartbeat strangely quickened.

"Maybe next time we can get it right."

She held out her hand. "Goodbye."

He didn't take her hand, just smiled. "See you later in London." He turned and took his shortcut across the field and moor toward Gowrie House—now Trevalyan House.

She watched him go, thinking how well he fit into the lovely Scottish countryside with its blaze of heather and sky. Then, she turned away slowly and walked down to Captain Duncan's boat.

Suddenly her heart felt a little brighter. Not goodbye, just— "See you later."

God be with you till we meet again. What a difference those few words of assurance made to a heavy heart.

For parting Christians it was never goodbye. It was always, "We'll meet again!"

PART THREE

London

27

The outside of the Warnstead house had changed quite a bit in the week she'd spent in Scotland. The summer flower garden was dry and neglected and her favorite gardenia bush had ceased blooming. The windowpanes were all taped now and boards painted black were used at night during blackouts. Buckets of water and sand were stored within easy reach in case of fires from bombs. She learned that this was a practice all over London urged by the government. Every neighborhood had its fire brigade made up of the folk who lived there.

As for the city of London, it was filled with serious faces and determined wills. The people rallied to Winston Churchill as naturally as athletes to their coach. At first Vanessa was shocked to see the damage done from the German bombing raids. Then she grew outraged over the injustice of the Nazis. Daily there were new deaths and maimed bodies of the old, of women and children, and destructive fires that burned down the homes of the rich and poor alike.

Vanessa learned quickly to fit in with the rush of daily life while adopting the determination of the British people to stand firm against aggression. "We won't be bullied" was the unspoken motto. From her American heritage the motto would have been: "Give me liberty, or give me death." For Britain there would be no surrender to Hitler and his SS troops.

Vanessa's meeting with Colonel Warnstead went as well as expected. He already anticipated what was at stake and promised that Kylie would be given a few days and nights leave to visit his ailing father as soon as he requested it. Kylie, however, was in the thick of the air battle and his sleeping hours had become quite erratic. The same was true for Andy and the rest of the RAF pilots, who were making almost constant flights. The losses were heavy, but they were holding their own against the Luftwaffe. Each time Vanessa heard the sound of a British plane her heart would jump to her throat. *God be with each one of you and protect you,* was her daily prayer.

She hadn't been allowed to see Kylie yet, but Mrs. Warnstead told her the colonel was arranging for a night off, Andy included, so that they could all have dinner together at the house.

Not only was the military on constant alert, but the Warnsteads themselves were all overextended in their duties. There was hardly a day when someone wasn't missing from the breakfast or dinner table. It was a grimmer and wearier Mrs. Warnstead that Vanessa was working beside since leaving London with Scott for Mull. Her face mirrored her concerns for her husband and son, and for the DP headquarters.

"We're filled to capacity with refugees," she told Vanessa one morning when the warm weather chased them outdoors for their tea. "We've fifty children now, ranging in ages from three to fourteen. The church is doing everything it can to feed and clothe them, but unless we get a bigger facility soon, we'll need to turn them over to other orphanages."

"They won't get Bible training if we do," Vanessa said.

"That's what Dr. Elsdon fears. He's not just caring for their ailments, but he's holding daily Bible classes and praying with them. And I told you, didn't I, that the DP office is lost to us? It's going to be used now for army wives. London is overcrowded and getting worse every day."

Vanessa said nothing of returning to America and no one asked her intentions. They were so shorthanded that her help was grabbed up at once by a host of Londoners in need of assistance.

While waiting to see Kylie, she worked at the military hospital visiting the injured men, writing letters, running errands for them, and just keeping them company and making them smile. Soon, she began to spend more time in the RAF hospital headquarters than at the orphanage.

On Wednesdays she went with Francis to the orphanage and assisted her and Dr. Elsdon, doing smaller tasks that freed them to accomplish more important things. She read to the older children, sang with the little ones, and even improvised a puppet show to keep the children laughing. She made up a story about a willful lamb who wandered from its mother, got caught in a bog in Scotland, and was rescued at the last minute by the shepherd. Then, she told the parable about the ninety-nine sheep and how God loved His people so much that He left the ninety-nine and went in search of the one that was lost until He found it. The children were all eyes and smiles when the sheep was securely brought home.

She used some of her own money to buy presents for injured pilots and even a radio so they could listen to the big band music they enjoyed. Daily, she saw the beds steadily fill with new patients even as familiar faces were missing, having died in the night. The most heartrending cases were the pilots who weren't able to bail out quickly and suffered terrible burns. It was on a Friday afternoon going into her third week in London when Mrs. Warnstead approached her at the hospital with a smile. "It's arranged, at last. Kylie and Andy have leave tonight. Francis is taking time off as well. We're having dinner at eight."

Vanessa returned with Mrs. Warnstead to help prepare for the dinner gathering. Afterward she bathed and changed into her favorite silky party dress of apple green and wore her hair down her back. Francis was late as usual and rushed to her room to change. "They're coming now," she called. "I saw the taxi just behind my car."

Vanessa ran to the window and looked out. The taxi pulled into the drive and two pilots in RAF blue got out. "They're here," she told Mrs. Warnstead, who smiled indulgently.

"The first few minutes are yours, my dear. I'll come in when the stars have settled."

Vanessa laughed and hurried to the front door.

Kylie was the first up the porch steps. Her first reaction was one of surprise. He had changed. She was first struck by how tired his face looked, and then how his once-electric blue eyes appeared to be so serious. He seemed to have lost a little weight too. Yet his energetic mood was the same, as though he were surviving on adrenaline.

"Vanessa!"

He hugged her but already his eyes were looking for Francis.

"She'll be down in a minute," Vanessa whispered, with a sparkle of mischief in her eyes.

And then there was Andy, pushing Kylie aside. Before Vanessa knew what he was doing, he pulled her into his arms and kissed her enthusiastically. Her eyes were still open in surprise as she looked over his shoulder at Colonel Warnstead coming up the steps, and just behind him, Kerc.

"Don't let us interrupt," the colonel said with a dry hint of humor in his voice.

"Huh?" Andy said, glancing over his shoulder. "Oh, hullo, Dad. Don't worry, I won't." He bent to kiss her again, but Vanessa already had her palms against his chest and was looking at Kerc.

"Later," Andy said to her, steering her into the front parlor where Kylie had already found Francis on the bottom stair and was complimenting her pink dress. Francis looked excited and a little flushed as she laughed gaily at whatever Kylie was saying.

"Darling," cried Mrs. Warnstead, and she came forward with her hands extended.

"Oh," said the colonel wryly, "for a moment I thought you meant *me*."

Mrs. Warnstead hugged her son and kissed his cheek. "But naturally I mean you too, darling," she said and smiled sweetly as she offered another hug and kiss to the colonel. There was laughter and a general exchange of greetings, but Vanessa felt strangely uncomfortable in front of Kerc. He was exceedingly well dressed, and just as handsome as the last time she saw him. Somehow she hadn't wanted him to witness the ardent welcome by Andy. The colonel introduced Kerc to the others.

"Kerc is here to see about his fishing boat," the colonel was explaining. "And he's representing Mr. Miles."

Vanessa saw Kylie's expression harden at the name. He gave Kerc a measuring glance as though he were suddenly on guard.

"Now I remember you, Kerc," Francis said smiling. "You're the captain who picked up the Norwegian refugees and got your boat shot-up as a thank-you from the Luftwaffe."

"It was worth it," he said amiably, with a smile. "How is the little deaf girl?"

"She's doing well. We call her Lara. Mum's thinking of adopting her."

Vanessa turned quickly to Mrs. Warnstead, smiling. "How wonderful! And why am I just finding out?"

"Well, it wasn't certain until this afternoon," Julia said, looking warmly at her husband. He smiled at her happiness and slipped an arm around her, showing he was in agreement with the decision. "There's so much red tape to go through. Someone could still claim her, though it's not likely."

"She's a blessed little girl," Kerc said.

"Thank you. I wish all of them could be placed into families that wanted them. Unfortunately, it doesn't work out that way."

They took refreshments in the other room, and after the usual pleasantries the talk inevitably turned to the war in general and the bombing in particular. The colonel thought the worst was yet to come. Kerc and Andy had little to say to one another, and Vanessa sensed a tension she didn't like. Andy was too possessive, obviously trying to scare off the intruder. She began to think he'd known that Kerc was coming behind him on the walk when he'd kissed her that way.

Kerc behaved the perfect gentlemen, and acted as though he hardly knew her. He spent most of his time talking to Mrs. Warnstead and the colonel. As soon as dinner was over he made his polite excuses to the Warnsteads while Andy was turning on the radio and moving furniture for dancing.

"Must you leave us so early?" Mrs. Warnstead said, the perfect hostess. "Do stay for ice cream. I'm sure there are many things you could share with us about Scotland. Vanessa has told us how beautiful it was there."

"Thank you, Mrs. Warnstead, but I've some very early appointments in the morning. I enjoyed your dinner, thanks for having me. Good night everyone. The best to you, Kylie—Andy."

Andy merely nodded, but Kylie, glancing at his sister and seeing her eyes narrow at him, suddenly smiled at Kerc and followed him into the hall to the door, as did Vanessa. Kylie put out his hand. "Thanks. And I appreciate you looking after my sister while she was in Mull."

"How do you like flying the Hurricane?" Kerc asked him.

"She's a breeze. A little slower than I'd like, slower than the German 109, but more maneuverable."

"Are the reports true about how many German planes are being shot down, or is that for the public?"

"A little of both. We're holding our own while we're making them feel it, but we need more planes and pilots."

"I suppose the bombers are fat cats up there."

Kylie grinned. "You said it. Fat and slow. It's a walk in the park to blow them to bits."

"How's morale?"

"Not bad. Not as high as the papers say, but good enough. There's not enough of us, is the problem. We've lost half the pilots we started out with—" He stopped quickly and looked at Vanessa.

"Don't mind me," she said. "You should know by now I go in for the truth, unpleasant or not."

"I'll let you get back to better things," Kerc told him, gesturing his head toward the gathering. "I've got to be going."

"Sure. I hope you get your fishing boat fixed up."

"Thanks. Happy hunting," Kerc said, and opening the door, he went out into the night without another word to Vanessa.

She just stood there, looking not at the closed door, but at the glimmering green peridots in the ring on her finger.

Kylie's voice startled her. She realized he'd been speaking to her and turned. "What did you say?" she murmured.

"You're making Andy nervous, bringing him here like that tonight. Kind of rough on old Andy, wasn't it?"

"I didn't have anything to do with his being here," she said in a low voice. "I wouldn't have wanted him to see Andy behaving the way he did tonight."

He tilted his head. "So it matters then, what he thinks."

"Of course it matters—" She stopped and folded her arms, meeting his eyes evenly. "Not you too. Both you and Andy treated him terribly. You reminded me of two collegians freezing out the newcomer. It was awful."

"Sorry. I made up for it, didn't I? Just as soon as I could see you had a crush on him."

She sucked in her breath. "Crush on him. I do not. It's pure civility, that's all."

He grinned. "Sure. That's all. Poor Andy."

"Look, stop it. I've got to talk to you seriously about Scotland."

"No dice. I'm not interested in knowing Robert Miles. I made that clear before you left. C'mon, let's get back to the others. I like that song and want to dance it with Francis."

She looked at him wearily. "Go on, then. Give me a minute."

He squeezed her shoulder affectionately and went into the drawing room.

Vanessa heard the romantic music and then quickly opened the front door and went out, closing it quietly behind her. She went down the steps and ran lightly across the lawn toward the gate. She looked down the quiet street, but Kerc was nowhere in sight. It was too late; he had already left.

As the evening wore on, Vanessa looked for the right opportunity to speak to Kylie again about Scotland, but he was so taken up with Francis that the moment didn't present itself.

Morning arrived, and he and Andy had to be back at their squadron at Biggin Hill. She and Francis drove them to the aerodrome in southeast London.

Biggin Hill was right in the path of incoming German bombers from the airfields across the Channel. It was under persistent attack by the Luftwaffe, who were trying to put it out of operation.

"The Germans won't succeed," Kylie said. "Bulldozers are constantly at work patching the runways."

Vanessa saw smashed runways, wrecked planes, and charred roofless hangars. She watched two planes land as they neared the gate.

Andy opened the car door and stepped out and Vanessa followed, hoping for a word with Kylie as soon as he and Francis ended their long kiss goodbye.

"Their relationship seems to have flourished since I went to Scotland," she whispered, amused.

"There's a marriage in the making."

"I wish he'd listen about Robert."

"Stop worrying about him, Vanessa." Andy turned her away from watching them. "He knows about the leave Dad has authorized. I've encouraged him to go see his father, and so has *my* father, and so has the chaplain. Give him time."

"I suppose you're right. I just hate calling Robert and telling him of the delay."

"Wait another day. Kylie may eventually see it your way."

Kylie came around the side of the car. "I'll call you when I get a chance, sis. What's that?" He was looking at the thick envelope Lucy had entrusted to her.

"It's from Lucy, your half sister. She asked me to give it to you."

"What is it?" he asked cautiously.

She smiled. "Suspicious? Just some photographs and a letter inviting you to Scotland."

"Thanks." He shoved it inside his jacket pocket. "I'll think about it, all right?"

Her smile brightened.

"That doesn't mean I've changed my mind," he protested with a mock scowl, "but I'll look at the letter."

Her smile deepened. She kissed his cheek. "Thanks, Kylie. Once you think about it, and pray about it, I know you'll decide to do the kind thing. God be with you. You too, Andy." She held out her hand.

Andy smiled ruefully at Kylie. "When a girl shakes the hand of her boyfriend goodbye, it means it's all over. I ought to punch Kerc in the nose."

"Don't be silly," Vanessa said, blushing. "He left early last night, didn't he? He wanted to get away."

"Don't sound so depressed."

"I'm not. Goodbye, Andy. Take care."

Francis stood on the car's running board waving frantically at Kylie as the two ran toward the airfield check-in gate.

"Goodbye, darling," Francis called again, waving urgently and blowing kisses. "I love you!"

Vanessa smiled. She would soon have a sister-in-law, one she could love as much as Lucy. The three of them should get along well together. And Kylie had even said he would consider seeing his father. Things were coming together after all.

28

Crumbled bricks and shattered cement caused the fresh dawn sky to become hazy with dust. Londoners took refuge behind what remained of blown up chunks of buildings or in pulverized gardens. Dazed, they stared in unbelief at the smoky shrouds where houses had once stood. Flames spurted up like erupting volcanoes from wooden structures.

The bombing raid the morning of August 15 awakened Vanessa from an uneasy sleep in which she was running through the heather toward the lighthouse near Devil's Cliff. She sat up, startled, to find her bedroom in the Warnstead house as bright as though the full moon were shining through the windows. Her first reaction was thinking how Mrs. Warnstead would scold her for not placing the blackout boards against the windowpanes last night.

Then she realized the brightness was not moonglow but flames from across the street. The roar of dreaded warplanes above London filled the dawn sky. Shadows from the fires danced wickedly across the bedroom wall.

They were under attack again! She threw the bedding aside, grabbed her robe, and rushed to the window to look out.

There were smoke and flames up and down the once-peaceful street. An angry staccato rattle came from a rooftop somewhere farther away. *An antiaircraft gun*, she thought. The terror of airplane engines overhead roared closer with their payloads of devastation. She couldn't see them; all she could do was listen to their growling engines. She placed her palms over her ears as bombs started falling. There was a vicious blast as the room shook. Ceramics and lamps rattled and shifted positions.

Outside, shattered window glass covered the pavement. Another blast reverberated. She covered her face, turning away. The shriek of engines somewhere above grew louder. The house rattled feebly, as though its knees quaked. A screeching bird flew past her window in terror-stricken fright.

Francis came rushing into the room, pale, but looking in control. "Get away from the window!" She grabbed Vanessa, and they landed hard on the floor as another deafening blast exploded nearby.

A moment later Mrs. Warnstead stood silhouetted in the doorway, tense and shaken. "Come help, quick! There's fire in the back of the house!"

They ran from the room and down the stairs into the hall. A window was shattered and glass littered the floor.

"Watch your feet," Mrs. Warnstead said.

Intense heat came from the kitchen followed by a gray pall of smoke.

"It's too late," Vanessa cried. "Don't go in there!"

"The fire brigade is already coming," Francis said, peering out a window toward the front walk.

Neighbors were running with buckets of water and sand. Someone had a hose. "The pipes aren't broken. Thank God."

The fire brigades worked only for small blazes that were caught in time, usually on the roof. Vanessa heard ladders being thrown against the wall and footsteps thumping over the ceiling. The chandelier swayed. From down the street fire bells were clanging.

There were shouts. Bewildered, frightened dogs were barking and howling. The fire engine arrived and men scattered to the task.

Vanessa drew Mrs. Warnstead away from the kitchen entry into the front hall, and out onto the lawn. Francis put her arms around her mother's shoulders as they watched. Vanessa saw smoke and rubble and small fires farther down the street, and people were rushing to get away, wetting blankets and wrapping their babies and children inside. Vanessa went to aid a grandmother trying to carry a small child to the lawn. Francis disappeared to use her nursing skills. Vanessa saw pink roses wilt, droop, smolder, and hiss.

The planes had gone again. But they would be back tomorrow, or that evening, or perhaps that very afternoon. The antiaircraft guns became silent after their vain attempts to shoot down the Germans.

A small crowd gathered, dazed. Who was unaccounted for? Had anyone seen the elderly widow, Miss Markham? Where was Toby the cat? The friendly spaniel who used to sleep under the porch? The porch was demolished. A canary was dead.

Vanessa sat, dazed. She brushed a tear away and smeared the soot on her face.

"Worst raid so far. It just came over the wireless. They're saying seventy-six German planes shot down to our thirty-four."

"Two to one," someone said proudly.

"We're jolly well giving it back to them, all right."

"We ought to be bombing Berlin! See how the ruddy Jerries like it!"

"Yes, but are the numbers correct?" someone asked suspiciously. "I say we're losing as many planes as the Germans."

The crowd turned and looked at him menacingly. "Whose side are you on, chap?"

"Stop it. Everyone knows Charlie, here. Let's form a search party. See if everyone's accounted for down the next houses."

Vanessa was shivering, her bare feet chilled from the damp grass, even though the heat-saturated air felt like an August afternoon in New York.

Vanessa lost all count of time. The fire was doused and the lower rooms all smelled of charred wood when they finally re-entered. Water was everywhere.

"Granny's crocheted pillows are wet," Francis said, holding one as though it might be her teddy bear from years earlier. Her tangled dark hair framed a pale, tense face. "Thirty-four of our pilots shot down," she said in the next breath, showing where her mind really was. "Thirty-four men like Kylie—like Andy—*thirty-four!*"

Vanessa's heart gave a lurch, then pounded erratically. Her teeth chattered from nerves and fear. Kylie—Andy—

The front door stood open and bleak sunshine filtered through a pearl gray pallor.

"I'll get some water going for tea," Mrs. Warnstead said. "We'll all feel better."

"Mum," Francis said quietly, "the kitchen appliances won't be working."

"Oh, that's right!" Her palm went to her forehead. "Nothing works in the kitchen," she said, coming out of her stupor. She suddenly looked more angry than she had over the bombing. "No tea," she said fiercely. "Nazis!"

"I'm calling Dad," Francis said moving toward the telephone. "I wonder if the line is working. He'll tell us what the radio announcer won't."

Francis picked up the receiver and held it to her ear. She groaned. "It's dead."

Vanessa, by some inner motivation, moved to the open front door and stepped out onto the porch. Someone was coming up the walkway. It was an air force chaplain. He saw her and removed his hat. His face was grave. Vanessa knew at once.

"Miss Miles?"

"Yes..."

She was aware that Mrs. Warnstead had come to the door. She stepped up beside Vanessa, an arm going around her protectively. "What is it, Captain? Have you bad news?"

"Not all bad, Mrs. Warnstead. Your husband sent me."

Kylie's Hurricane had been shot down, but he'd managed to bail out. He was in serious condition at the hospital, but alive.

Alive. Vanessa's hand went to her eyes in relief that left her weak.

"And Andy?" Mrs. Warnstead asked slowly.

"He's reported in at Biggin Hill, ma'am." He smiled. "He landed safely."

Mrs. Warnstead's eyes shut and a sigh escaped her lips. She turned to Vanessa and embraced her.

A wire was sent to her father at Gowrie House.

> KYLIE SHOT DOWN. STOP. ALIVE AND IN THE HOSPITAL. STOP. DON'T KNOW HOW BADLY INJURED HE IS. STOP. WILL LET YOU KNOW. STOP. LOVE, VANESSA.

Vanessa wasn't allowed to see Kylie for forty-eight hours, but Francis' nursing credentials allowed her to be admitted to the room he shared with three other wounded pilots. She didn't leave the hospital for the next two days, but called Vanessa when she went down to the lobby for tea.

"He's going to make it, Vanessa. I was so afraid he might lapse into a coma, but he didn't. He's awake. He remembers everything. He sends his love to you."

A few days later, when Mrs. Warnstead was working with Dr. Elsdon at the orphanage and the house was quiet, Vanessa changed to go to the hospital for the first time to see Kylie. The telephone, which had been repaired, rang just as she was headed out the door.

"Hello?"

"Vanessa? This is Kerc."

Incredible relief and something else swept through her at the sound of his voice. She gripped the receiver tightly. "Oh, Kerc! Where are you calling from?"

"London. About five minutes from the Warnstead house. Your father is with me."

"He is? Here?" she cried. "Is he all right?" She was thinking of the long train journey.

"He insists he's fine. What's wrong? Has Kylie taken a turn for the worst?"

"No, he's awake. Francis believes he'll make a full recovery."

"Then what else is wrong? You sound unhappy and tense." He hesitated. "Andy's doing fine, isn't he?"

She didn't want to say that it wasn't only Andy that was worrying her. She was unhappy because Kerc had left the dinner party without saying goodbye and she hadn't known if he would ever contact her again.

"Yes. Andy's all right."

He waited as though expecting further explanation, but when she said nothing, he said calmly, "I'll bring your father over to the house, if it's all right. I wanted to call first."

"Yes, of course it is. I was just on my way to the hospital to see Kylie. I'll wait. But, Kerc, do you think it's wise for Robert to walk into his room now? It might upset Kylie terribly."

"I don't know. I thought about that. We'll talk about it. Your father understands. We'll see what the doctor says."

He hung up, and Vanessa went out on the porch to wait for them.

They arrived within a short time, and she went to meet her father. He put his arm around her, patting her back. "We can give thanks in all things. Kylie is still with us."

"I hope this isn't too much for you, Dad." She noted the weary lines on his face. He smiled. "It feels good to be back home in dear old London. I'm feeling well enough to entertain the hospital convalescents. How about *Richard II?*"

She smiled. "You'd be smashing. But it's a little involved for a short performance, isn't it?"

"Yes. I'd better stick to a few readings from *Macbeth*."

She wondered if he were serious or just lightening the moment. "I'm afraid I can't offer either of you tea. We've been hit by a bomb, or whatever it was. We had a fire. The kitchen is ruined."

Kerc scowled. "Anyone hurt?"

"No. But it was the worst attack by the Luftwaffe yet. That's when Kylie's plane was shot down. He bailed out over a cow pasture just outside the city."

Kerc drove them straight to the hospital, saying very little and allowing her father to do most of the talking.

"Lucy wanted to come, but Scott thought it best if I came alone with Kerc. It might be too much for Kylie to handle with two of us at his bedside."

If Lucy were listening to Scott's advice, it meant they were in tune with each other once again. Vanessa was happy for both of them.

Her father told her Theo was improving, but mourning over Jodrell. Dr. MacGregor was very attentive to her. "I think James has cared for Theo for years," Robert said. "If anyone can pull her out of her grief, it's MacGregor."

"And Jodrell?" she asked.

Her father looked at Kerc.

"He'll stand trial for murder," Kerc said. "He's confessed. It would be best if Doc MacGregor could get Theo strong enough for a trip to America and keep her there until it's over."

Robert nodded.

Vanessa had telephoned Francis before her father arrived to let her know they were coming. She met them, looking more relaxed than Vanessa had seen her in weeks. After being introduced to Robert, Francis told them she'd just received a call from her mother that she was desperately needed at the orphanage. The girl who had taken Francis' place the last few days was down with stomach cramp.

"Mum has all the kids in her charge, except for the cook who's helping her this morning. Even Dr. Elsdon had a sudden attack of gout and had to stay home. So I'm on my way."

"The orphanage is a wonderful investment in young lives," Robert told her. "I'd like to have a tour while I'm here, if you wouldn't mind."

"Not at all," echoed both Francis and Vanessa at the same time. "You can come today if you like," Francis told him. "We have tea at four o'clock."

"I'd enjoy that tremendously. If Kerc, here, and Vanessa will bring me down."

It was settled on, and Francis left to catch a taxi.

"Nice girl," Robert was saying.

"Kylie's in love with her," Vanessa told him. "A marriage is in the making." She also told him about Lara, the deaf child, and how either Mrs. Warnstead or Francis intended to adopt her if they could.

"That would be good for Kylie."

A military doctor walked up and shook hands with Robert.

"Your son is doing quite well, Mr. Miles. He was lucky."

Son. Vanessa looked at her father and saw him blink back a tear. *What an astounding difference Jesus makes in a person's life,* she thought, awed. *All this care and remorse could only be traced to the work of God's Spirit in my father's heart. And if He is the One making the good changes, isn't it right to believe He intends to bring about reconciliation? Maybe my prayers are going to be answered after all!*

She felt Kerc watching her, and she turned to meet the steady look that seemed to read her mind.

The doctor was saying, "Kylie knows you're here. He asked to see you."

Vanessa drew in a breath. Her eyes rushed to her father's and she smiled, taking hold of his arm. It trembled. "Dad, he *wants* to see you."

He nodded, unable to speak. "Give me a minute to steady myself. This is more frightening than a stage performance before an audience of hundreds of critics."

"Just be yourself, the way you were with me," she encouraged. "Just open up your heart. If you do, I think he will too."

"Coming so close to death the way he did," Kerc told him quietly, "was sure to get his attention. If he's asked the doc to see you—and he knows you made the first move to come here—then it's a sure sign to me he's ready to reach out."

Robert closed his eyes and drew in a deep breath, steadying himself. His face was pale, and she could see his heart throbbing in his neck. She squeezed his arm. He nodded that he was all right. She and Kerc watched him walk to the door of the hospital room and after hesitating a brief moment, he opened the door and walked in...

Vanessa looked at Kerc and smiled. "Thank you for bringing him to London."

"Let's get some fresh air. They're likely to be in there a while. Or would you rather have tea? That's right. You like coffee." His disarming smile did something strange to her heart.

"Either one will be fine."

"There's a little place on the corner. I'll tell the desk nurse to inform Mr. Miles where we went. He might want to join us later."

They walked down the hall to the front exit. She came out as he held the door open. The gray mucky weather was even a little humid.

"Your father seems interested in seeing Lara," he said.

They walked down the sidewalk in the direction of the café where many of the military medical staff congregated.

"I think you're curious too," she said, smiling.

"How did you know?"

"You've been feeling sorry for her ever since that night on the wharf when you picked her up from the sea."

"Aye, you're right. She was such a desperate little thing. All alone, just clinging to a piece of wood. She was the first one I got into my boat. Scarron was with me and another fishing friend. They helped get the others aboard. Then that ruddy Me 109 came along. There was nothing to do except take it. I'd have given anything to have had an antiaircraft gun in my hand. I'd have blown him clean out of the sky. He was shooting women and children like a duck hunt."

"Yes. Look at London," she said angrily. "And it's just the beginning."

"Aye, it is. In my cabin I gave Lara a little book."

She looked at him, astonished. "You did? Where did you get it?"

"I bought it to give to a cousin's little boy."

"Which cousin is that?"

"Effie." He opened the door of the café. She entered. "I didn't know Effie was married."

"Sure. She has three kids and another on the way."

"Effie?" she repeated, dumbfounded. "I didn't notice she was expecting."

"You don't notice a lot of things."

She looked at him. He smiled and sat down. "Ready for lunch?"

"I'm not hungry. Coffee will do me fine. But you go ahead. You're probably used to eating at this time."

After he ordered, she asked: "And your fishing boat?"

"Better than it was."

The girl brought their order and Vanessa added milk and sugar to her coffee while Kerc ate a roast beef sandwich with Yorkshire pudding.

They lingered over the meal, discussing one small thing after another until the café was nearly empty.

"Are you coming back with your father to Scotland?"

"I hadn't planned on it. The Warnsteads used to urge me to return to America, but no one's said anything about that recently. Everyone is too taken up with what's happening, I suppose."

"Why did you come in the first place? Because of Andy?"

As usual, the casual conversation made its customary way back around to Andy. Vanessa found that she had put her left hand with the green peridot ring on her lap.

"Yes, partly," she said evasively. "I wanted to visit Kylie too. And I knew my father was nearby. I thought he was in London when I arrived. It was only later I learned about Scotland."

Adeptly, he brought the conversation back to Andy.

"He was mad as a wet hen about me being at the house for dinner the other night."

When she said nothing, he went on: "Can't say I blame him. He had leave for an evening and was with his girl. I wouldn't have wanted a third party hanging around either."

Vanessa set her cup down. "Are you merely curious about me and Andy, or are you trying to find out how serious our plans are?"

"Since you're being direct about it, I'll be the same. You're wearing that ring he gave you, you're staying in his parents' house, and his sister is going to marry your brother. That's all pretty close and cozy. Add to it that long kiss he gave you on the porch, and I'd guess you were close to sealing your engagement. But somehow you don't act like a girl in love."

Thinking of that kiss, she flushed and picked up her cup again. It was empty, and he took the carafe of coffee sitting on the table and filled it for her. His hand, unlike hers, was quite steady.

"He surprised me on the porch. He must have known you were coming and wanted to make sure you knew that I was 'his girl,' as you put it."

"Are you?" he asked quietly.

She found she couldn't meet his eyes and looked down at her cup, stirring too long. She had come to London to discover if she loved Andy. A few weeks stay had turned into several months, and still her heart was unsettled.

She looked out the window. Outside the sky was clearing, and the breeze wafted among the lone larkspurs growing thinly in the window box.

"I don't know," she murmured, shaking her head.

He pushed his plate aside and put his arms on the table, watching her. "Is it because you feel sorry for him that you can't make up your mind?"

That snapped her out of it. "Feel sorry?" she challenged.

"Sure. It happens all the time."

"It does not."

"Yes, it does. You're so tenderhearted you feel sorry for him because he's in love with you. It's wartime. He's a dashing and daring RAF pilot risking his life every day fighting the Germans for the heart of London. You can't bring yourself to hurt him. So you're delaying."

She stared into his face, intense and handsome, and felt the same rush of confusion, embarrassment, and something else she couldn't understand.

"In the long run you're not really helping him," he said.

She looked at the ring and covered the stones protectively. "I know I'm not," she said with a sudden rush, "but I think so well of Andy—"

"That you feel sorry for him."

"I can't bear the thought of—"

"Hurting him. You're allowing yourself to be governed by feelings instead of logic, Vanessa. There's nothing like bursting bombs and death lurking at every turn to bring out a girl's loyalty to her soldier. Maybe I ought to join the RAF," he said with a slightly irritating tone. "Maybe then you'd feel sorry for me too."

He reached for her hand, and his touch sent her heart racing. "I wish you'd take that ring off."

She pulled her hand away, flustered.

He stood abruptly, looking at his watch. "We'd better get back and pick up Mr. Miles."

He's angry, she thought. "Kerc, please. I need a little more time to know how I feel."

He gave her an encouraging smile, one she hadn't expected. "Let's bring your father to the orphanage."

29

Vanessa watched her father with concern. It was plain to see that his first meeting with Kylie had left him exhausted. They were seated in the backseat of the car, with Kerc driving them to the orphanage run by a private Christian charity sponsored by Dr. Elsdon and Mrs. Warnstead's church.

Her father didn't explain all the details of the sensitive exchange between himself and Kylie, because anything so personal and heartrending would naturally belong to them alone. One long look at her father, however, convinced her that the first meeting had gone better than expected. Although he was tired and pale, she knew that some of this was explained by his health and the exertion he'd been through in coming to London. She was satisfied that his eyes reflected an inner peace, as though the last mile of his pilgrimage had nearly been completed.

"We've agreed to see each other again," was all he told her, squeezing her hand with reassurance. "When he is able to leave the hospital, he's coming to Scotland to complete his recovery. That is, if Kerc agrees."

Kerc smiled into the rearview mirror, the wind tossing the dark hair on his forehead. "The front door is wide open, Mr. Miles. Maybe Vanessa will come too."

Subtly, and sometimes not so subtly, Kerc had been letting her know of his interest in her. Her heart began fluttering again.

"What was it you mentioned coming down on the train?" he asked Robert.

"Ah, yes. It was an idea that's been on my mind for more than a month, ever since Vanessa told me about the Displaced Persons hostel. I was thinking that a convalescent retreat for RAF pilots in Scotland would be a blessed thing. Gowrie House would be perfect."

Vanessa's breath caught with enthusiasm. She turned to him. "Dad, you mean that? Why, it's the most wonderful idea I've heard yet. A retreat for pilots like Kylie! It's just the place to get them back on their feet."

"Of course, the estate will soon officially belong to Kerc," Robert said. "Any decision is now out of my hands."

"Um…yes, naturally you're right. I'd forgotten that." It really was unfair to expect such a sacrifice of Kerc after all he'd put up with since childhood, and all he'd gone through to gain his rights of inheritance. Therefore, it surprised her when he said, "That sounds like the best idea yet, considering the war and the need for hospitals. You might think about asking Dr. Elsdon to become its visiting chaplain."

"Are you serious, Kerc?" she asked, trying to hold her excitement in check.

He looked at her through the rearview mirror where she sat next to her father. "It's needed. Why not? Anyway, I won't be around there myself much longer. It's a good use of the property while the war is on."

She remembered what he had said about joining some branch of the military. She hadn't taken him seriously about the RAF. The idea of him joining the army was depressing, and she pushed it aside for now. Before long, one would need to look far and wide to find any young healthy men out of uniform.

"Kerc, what a smashing idea. It's terribly generous of you, considering, but…well, you can't be serious."

"Sure I'm serious."

"Then if you're certain you'd like to do it, I'll be happy to talk to Dr. Elsdon. I know he'd like to expand the work he's doing now with the hostel to include servicemen. Mrs. Warnstead said he's already doing visitation work at the hospitals. He'll be thrilled about using Gowrie House. And so will I, and Francis."

She was aware that her father was watching her and Kerc with a gleam in his eyes. Naturally it would also mean that Vanessa would not be leaving for New York.

They neared the wharf where the white rambling house used for the Norwegian refugees and a host of young people and children was encircled with a fence. It was easy to spot by its red-painted steeple and the big white cross. Francis was out in the front yard with a dozen of the younger children, keeping watch as they played. Mrs. Warnstead saw their car and came out the front door and down the steps to welcome Robert. She opened the white gate in the picket fence, smiling. Lara followed her, grasping Mrs. Warnstead's skirt.

Vanessa smiled to herself. Lara was definitely a "mama's girl," and the new mama was Mrs. Warnstead.

"Is that the little deaf girl you told me about?" her father was asking.

"Yes, that's Lara. Kerc rescued her from the Channel."

"Kylie told me about her too, and he mentioned Francis. He's much in love with that girl."

"Of course he told you all about them," Vanessa laughed. "He can talk of nothing else."

"He told me, indeed. Said if Mrs. Warnstead doesn't take Lara, he and Francis will. Wonderful idea. I want him to be happy." He reached over and patted her hand. His eyes said, *and you too.*

"Mr. Miles?" called Julia Warnstead. "You're just in time for tea with the children. They've helped bake apple cakes to honor your coming."

"Ho!" he cried. "My favorite." He turned toward Vanessa and Kerc. "You two joining us?"

"One luncheon was enough for me," Vanessa said, laughing. "I need to watch my weight."

"What do you mean?" Kerc said. "All you had was coffee. Poor eating habits, Miss Miles. You could afford to gain a few pounds."

Her brows lifted. Indeed! So he thought she was skinny! She glanced at her image reflected in a nearby window cryptically and then saw a look of satisfied amusement in his dark eyes. She had showed she cared what he thought. She turned away.

Kerc also declined, making mention of a boat he noticed for sale a little farther down the wharf. "Thought I'd walk there and have a look at it. Just as soon as I give this to Lara."

Her father went in with Mrs. Warnstead, and Lara ran over to Francis. Vanessa watched as Kerc picked the child up in his arms and gave her something from his pocket. He spoke to her a minute and then left for the wharf.

Vanessa joined Francis over where the children were playing. Lara was now sitting on a painted white rock gazing in ecstasy at a small stuffed white lamb with blue button eyes. It was Kerc doing things like this that turned her to jelly.

There was a swing, and Vanessa pushed some of the smaller children as she talked to Francis about Kerc's offer of Gowrie House.

Francis became as excited with the prospect as Vanessa.

"Mum's going to be awfully bedazzled over this. Where is he?"

"He went to see a boat that's for sale." Vanessa could see it from the yard. "That blue one, with the cabin."

"Daddy knew he was bringing Mr. Miles to the hospital to see Kylie this morning. He told me to give this to Kerc, but I had so much on my mind with Kylie I forgot. Would you see that he gets this envelope?"

"From the colonel?"

"Yes. Daddy's joining Air Chief Marshal Dowding in a meeting with the prime minister today. Mum's having a spell over it. She's afraid he'll be transferred from London to head up the air defense in the western desert."

Vanessa couldn't blame Mrs. Warnstead much. Egypt seemed a million miles away. And it was hot, dusty, and unfriendly toward British jurisdiction.

"Mum insists she won't leave the work here in London. Daddy's upset. If the transfer is decided upon, there's little he can do about it."

"They'll work it out," Vanessa encouraged her. "They have a strong marriage."

"It's the kind I want with Kylie," she agreed.

One of the smaller children running toward the wooden rocking horse tripped and fell on her hands and knees. A heartbreaking sob rent the sunny afternoon. "Pamela," Francis called, hurrying toward her. "How many times have I asked you to not run? Oh dear, let's see your knee. It's skinned." She picked the crying child up into her arms and carried her toward the steps. "I'll need to take care of this, Vanessa."

An older girl, Jennifer, came to watch the children. After a minute or two Vanessa wandered toward the gate and looked down the incline toward the harbor. She could see the blue boat and Kerc climbing the ladder to the top deck. She held the official-looking envelope in one hand and opened the gate with the other. It could be important. Besides, it gave her an opportunity to walk down to the boat where Kerc was. Why would Francis' father be sending him a letter?

Kerc saw her before she reached the walkway and waited for her at the top rail. "Can you make it up?" he called.

"Aye," she said cheerfully.

He smiled.

Vanessa climbed gracefully over the side of the boat and then ascended the few short steps up to the top deck. The wind tossed her hair and tugged at her skirt. She looked at him. *He fits the sea well*, she thought, trying to reject the jumble of competing emotions he stirred within her. Now that the suspicion and misunderstanding which had set them at odds was no longer a factor, the vacuum was filling fast with even stronger emotions of attraction. Perhaps it had been there all along, but the conflict had concealed it. Whatever it was, Vanessa felt the pull growing like the waves, bringing her farther and farther out to sea.

She walked up to him. "Francis asked me to give this to you. She forgot at the hospital." She held out the envelope. "It's from Colonel Warnstead."

He took the envelope and opened it, turning his back against the wind to read the single sheet of paper. Curious, Vanessa watched his face. It told her nothing.

After a minute he folded the sheet, placed it in the envelope, and put it inside his pocket. He looked at her. "You're as curious as a cat."

"I am not!" she laughed.

"Sure you are. When you get curious, your eyes turn a darker green."

She leaned against the rail. "All right. I'm curious."

He grinned. "That's better. Always confess, Miss Miles. It makes me more compliant."

"When are you going to stop calling me Miss Miles?"

"What would you like me to call you?"

She flushed. "Vanessa, of course."

He tapped his pocket. "Colonel Warnstead is answering a letter I wrote him. There's someone in CID he knows well. He's arranged for me to meet him. There are openings in that line of military service if I'm interested, he says. All I need do is join the BEF."

"I see." Her lighter mood grew heavy once more. All he need do was join the BEF. Sign his life away. Face Nazis. Nothing to it.

"Are you going to do it?"

"After that bombing raid you told us about this morning?" His dark eyes flashed. "It's every man's duty to fight the enemy in whatever way he can. The more rubble from bombs I see in London, the more angry I become with Berlin. Kylie and Andy have their way of fighting. I have mine."

Espionage. In some ways it was even more dangerous because it was more subtle, more secretive. The stakes were deadly high.

"Were you and your secret friends able to discover who was smuggling agents from the island to England?" she asked in a low voice, though no one could hear them.

"We did. You wouldn't know the man. He was a fisherman. His boat made it a wee bit too handy to pick the infiltrator up and bring him to a lonely location."

She was quiet a moment and turned toward the harbor waters to look out. He watched her, a frown forming. He picked up her hand and looked at the ring.

"You're using this to hide behind. It's your protective armor. As long as you wear it, you feel you don't need to make a decision about how you really feel. You can keep delaying, pretending. But I'm not going to let you hide behind it anymore."

Her eyes came to his. She started to say *I don't know what you mean,* but the denial died on her lips.

"Andy or no Andy, I'm not waiting any longer. You're going to know how I feel about you. I didn't plan to say this, but I've fallen in love with you."

"Oh, Kerc," she said feebly, "I—"

"And I think you feel the same, but you're afraid to admit it."

"I'm not afraid of anything," she said in a shaky voice.

His eyes contradicted her.

"Then let's be honest with each other."

"You told me to leave and go back to America. You told me I didn't belong to Scotland. You said—"

"I said too many things I shouldn't have." In a moment he had taken hold of her and brought her close into his arms. The moment they touched her heart burst into song.

"Vanessa," he whispered, "you not only belong in Scotland, you should belong to me. Even when I didn't trust you, even when I thought you were working with Scott, I wanted you. I thought you were about the prettiest girl I'd ever seen. Now I'm sure of your heart, and it's filled with loving and giving. Had I never gotten hold of the estate, and Robert left it to you, I believe you would have used it for God's purposes. It may be mine now, but without you it means little. Everything I have is yours, including my heart."

She couldn't resist him. Their arms entwined in an embrace, and as he began to kiss her lips, she was sure the low roaring in her ears was her thudding heart, and that the deck beneath her feet was falling away. "Oh, Kerc," she breathed, "I'm falling in love with you too. Don't leave me. Don't ever go away—"

"Never, not now. Not for long, anyway. You're everything I've ever wanted, sweet Vanessa, everything I've ever longed for. And to think you love me too—"

"Yes," she kissed him again and again, "yes, forever—that sound—Kerc, what—?"

She felt his body tense. In a moment he drew her aside and looked out across the water. He groaned. "We've got unwanted company. A whole lot of company."

Planes. Swarms of them.

"The stinking Luftwaffe," he gritted.

The threatening drone of the engines left a sick feeling in her stomach. By now the RAF would be scrambling. Her heart pounded with breathless little jerks that made her legs go suddenly weak. The warning sirens were blaring their high-pitched sound that turned her blood cold.

The long dull roar gathered in intensity. "We need to take cover," he ordered. "Let's get below or some Nazi will have fun splattering us all over the deck."

Her gaze swerved across the wharf and up toward the hostel with its red steeple and white cross. Her father was in there—Francis, Mrs. Warnstead—the children—

She tugged at his arm. "We've got to get back to them, Kerc," she cried.

"There's no time, Vanessa. Below!"

Fear squeezed the life from her heart. She was suddenly afraid, not for herself, but for those she loved. Bombs were dropping. "I've got to reach them, Kerc."

He swung her around to face him as if she'd turned hysterical. The first explosions rocked the wharf with an earsplitting roar. Suddenly he pushed her down to the deck, holding her flat as a plane's roar swooped contemptuously low as it hammered a hail of machine gun fire into the boat. The wood splintered and the Union Jack on the pole crashed with a thud, barely missing them. It was over even before she had grasped the coming danger.

"C'mon," he shouted above the noise, getting up and helping her to her feet. He pulled her down the steps, to the lower deck. She tried to shake herself free from the terror she felt, as if she were stumbling through a nightmare while half-awake.

The thunder of antiaircraft fire filled the air, adding its own noise to that of the shrieking whistles of dropping bombs. Explosions of buildings bursting into flying bits sounded like angry thunder. Then suddenly—there came an empty silence, as terrifying as the previous barrage of noise. A short lull followed, a matter of mere moments, then the reign of terror began all over again.

The black smoke above the buildings was now lined with orange. Kerc took her elbow as she stood hesitating, staring at the awful scene, and forced her into the cabin. He held her tightly, attempting to soothe her as the explosions rumbled and the waves splashed the sides of the boat. Then, as mad as it was, he was kissing her as though nothing else existed.

He held her away from him, pushing her into a seat. "Stay here. I'll be back."

"Kerc!"

Vanessa dropped her head into her hands and tried to pray. There came a shattering explosion near at hand. The boat rocked and bounced, and she was tipped to the floor. She scrambled dizzily to her feet and groped her way to the small door. "Kerc—"

She leaned there until at last she heard his footsteps again. The door opened. He looked at her with compassion.

The look broke her heart. "What is it?" she choked, grabbing his arms. "Tell me."

"The orphanage took a direct hit," he said softly.

She gasped and turned her head away, sickened as the full impact of his words hit as hard as a bullet. She nearly collapsed. "No!"

He enfolded her in his arms, petting her hair in soothing gestures one might use for a child crying in pain.

Suddenly she pushed past him out onto the deck.

Smoke and fire were spreading along the wharf, and the wooden buildings were aflame. "Father! Francis!" She started blindly in the direction of where the white house had stood with its red steeple and white cross. Kerc gripped her arm and pulled her back. "No!"

But then he looked into her face. Something must have made him relent. His hand tightened on her arm.

"Keep beside me," he said above the noise. "One step at a time. When I say down, hit the pavement."

And then they were out onto the wharf, running.

The buildings were destroyed, only a few jagged stone walls remained untouched. The few green trees were down. She remembered seeing feathers blowing and nothing else. All the shops and warehouses were gutted, the names of owners obliterated in a moment. No matter that he was an aristocrat or lower class, no one had escaped the wrath of the German bombers and low-flying Luftwaffe.

"Don't look," he told her. But she did. She couldn't help it. On the street there were body parts of people and animals, and a few twisted motorcars and a red tramcar. Slabs of concrete were broken and twisted as if a giant earthquake had cracked them open and left smashed cement.

The attack was going on in another section of the city; she could still hear the deep guttural booming like angry thunder. The inevitable smoke and fire soon followed.

The only people out on the street now were Londoners with urgent, painstaking business. They ran or walked in a daze. People were getting up from the ground where they had flung themselves. Others were crying or praying, still others walked grimly on. One man shook his fist at the sky as if he could see a German pilot. Many people lay dead or wounded, but there were too many to stop and help. She had only one thing on her heart: the orphanage.

They approached the spot. Vanessa stared blankly. The low-hanging smoke made it impossible to see what really remained. Flames shot up, dancing higher than the dust cloud.

Growing flames sprang up all around the area. The smoke clouds were turning crimson. She shrank away, holding to Kerc's arm.

"Incendiary bombs," he said. "After the water supply was deliberately targeted."

"The children—," she cried.

They broke into a run toward the once-happy building.

They were close enough to realize now that there was no hope.

Vanessa stood staring, transfixed, her emotions too stunned to feel any pain.

"Wait," Kerc told her quickly, "over there—on that square of pavement."

She followed his glance and saw a small group of people huddled together, sitting on the cement. There were children there.

"Isn't that Francis?" he asked.

Vanessa broke into a smile. Tears filled her eyes.

"Francis!" Kerc called.

Francis' dark hair was blowing in the wind and the white blouse she wore, smudged now with blackened smoke, gleamed still in the darkening air.

Francis must have heard him, for she turned her head and looked straight at Vanessa. She raised a hand.

Vanessa ran toward her. Ambulances were already arriving to take away the injured.

"Vanessa—" Francis was crying, trembling, as they held to each other. "Mum's…Mum's dead…and your father…"

Vanessa saw Kerc take Lara into his arms and try to soothe her silent weeping. Some of the other children clung to his legs, then to Vanessa's skirt and to Francis.

Vanessa and Francis turned their attention to the children, hugging them as best they could.

"Your father was a hero, Vanessa," Francis said through her tears. "He came back for me and Lara—I was trapped under a beam, and a fire had started. But he struggled and freed us, and then helped us to this spot. He went back for more children…and got some out, but—then it burst into flames—and the roof caved in…" Her hoarse voice went silent. She closed her eyes even as tears quietly rolled down her face.

Kerc came to Vanessa, and setting Lara down, pulled her into his arms. "Robert gave his life to save what he knew would matter most to Kylie," he whispered. "Francis and Lara. We'll remember him for that. We'll turn Gowrie House into a retreat for both British pilots and the refugee children. That would make him happy. His real life began when he came to Christ a few months ago. He didn't live it in vain."

She cried against his shirt, but not just for the loss of her father so recently gained. Her tears were for all those suffering that afternoon: for the loss of Mrs. Warnstead, who worked so hard for her country, the RAF pilots, young and brave, and for the children bewildered and confused over the evil heaped upon them. She cried even for the sinless animals whose songs and wagging tails were silenced.

Kerc said nothing. He simply held her.

Epilogue

The following day Kerc brought word to Vanessa that Flight Lieutenant Andy Warnstead had given his life to halt the German advance. The RAF had risen to the fight and the Luftwaffe had lost more trained pilots in one day than they had in all attacks so far.

"Does Francis know?"

"No, not yet. Her father is going to tell her. She's at the hospital with Kylie. She brought Lara with her this time. She wants Kylie to know the story of what Robert did. Kylie's going to be very proud of his father."

She smiled through her tears. She nodded. Her father had finished his course. He'd even rescued the woman and child Kylie loved so much, hoping his son's future would hold the things he wanted most.

"All because you cared enough to reach out in forgiveness," Kerc told her. "You sacrificed and were misunderstood in order to love and to give what God placed in your heart." He kissed her tenderly. "Speaking of loving and giving, Gowrie House is going to be known as a place of love and healing, but it won't mean anything, Vanessa, unless you're a part of it, unless you're there to share it with me."

"Oh, Kerc, I'll always be there. I love you and need you desperately."

"Then let's bring Robert home to be buried in Scotland beside Norah. Lucy is going to need you. I wired Scott, and he'll break the news to her, but she hasn't the faith and strength you have. She'll need support. I've also talked to Dr. Elsdon. He'll be moving his mission to Gowrie House as soon as he can arrange it with the right authorities. You won't be alone. Francis will come too with Lara, just as soon as Kylie is well enough to be transferred there. For the rest of the war, your work will proceed on the estate."

She held him, her eyes searching his. "And what about you?"

He looked down at her hand. The ring with the green peridots was no longer on her finger. She had removed it yesterday after she knew where her heart belonged. He held her fingers to his lips and kissed them. His dark eyes were warm with a small flame.

"I'll never be so far away that you'll be out of my heart. Will you marry me before I join the BEF?"

Then, the dreaded moment of separation would come, but she didn't want to ruin this moment with tears. She smiled. "Oh, Kerc...yes."

They stood on the Warnstead porch in the purple twilight, and instead of charred wood and broken glass, Vanessa could almost believe she was smelling the spicy, heartbreaking sweetness of the old rose garden in Scotland, where she would always see Kerc in her memory and hold him in her heart.

Now, for a little while longer they had each other, and their hearts would blend, their lips too.

"It may be a long time, Vanessa, before I return. You understand that?"

She nodded. "Yes, Kerc, I know."

"But for us it will never be too long to wait," he said.

"Never. Not for us," she agreed.

She faced him again, and she was smiling with hope and courage, because she knew that's what he wanted her to do.

They kissed warmly, tenderly, pledging tomorrow and the many that would follow until, at last, they could be together forever. Tomorrow was just the beginning.

They looked up at the darkening sky and the stars of God, as they held one another, and Vanessa was certain she heard the song of a nightingale that had returned to the neighborhood. Her hand reached for Kerc's and found it waiting for hers.